EMPIRE OF NIGHT

EMPIRE OF NIGHT

KELLEY ARMSTRONG

HARPER

An Imprint of HarperCollins*Publishers*

Library of Congress Cataloging-in-Publication Data

Armstrong, Kelley.

  Empire of night / Kelley Armstrong. — First edition.

    pages cm — (Age of legends trilogy)

  Summary: "Separated while trying to save the children of their village, twin sisters Ashyn and Moria must draw on all their power and influence to defeat enemies of legend and avert war in the empire"— Provided by publisher.

  ISBN 978-0-06-207127-9 (hardback)

  [1. Adventure and adventurers—Fiction. 2. Twins—Fiction. 3. Sisters—Fiction. 4. Spirits—Fiction. 5. Supernatural—Fiction. 6. Fantasy.] I. Title.

PZ7.A7336Emp 2015   2014027407

[Fic]—dc23   CIP

                                                                      AC

Typography by Anna Christian

15 16 17 18 19   PC/RRDH   10 9 8 7 6 5 4 3 2 1

❖

First Edition

To Julia

ONE

I n retrospect, Moria should not have pulled her dagger
when she was attempting to pass through the imperial
city unnoticed. In truth, the pulling of the dagger was
not so much a mistake as the throwing of it. Even the
throwing of it wouldn't have been as grievous if her blade had
missed its target. But if Moria pulled her dagger, she would
throw it, and if she threw it, she would not miss, so the problem, she reasoned, could be traced back to the man responsible
for the throwing of the blade.

Of course, there was a reasonable chance she'd have been
recognized even without the incident. All the city knew that
the Keeper and Seeker of Edgewood were at the palace.
Northerners weren't exceedingly rare, but when people were
watching for a pale-skinned girl with red-gold hair, it was difficult to affect a sufficient disguise. And then there was the
matter of Daigo . . .

"I need to go into the city," she'd told him earlier as she'd fastened her cloak.

He'd walked to the door and waited.

"No, I need to go by myself. Quickly. Before Ashyn gets back."

Daigo had planted himself in the doorway and fixed her with a baleful stare. The huge black Wildcat of the Immortals was her bond-beast, as much a part of her as her shadow. A very large, very conspicuous shadow. Luckily, unlike her sister's hound, Daigo didn't feel the need to stick to Moria's side like a starving leech. He'd kept pace with her along the rooftops.

Moria was to meet Ronan in the third market, where merchants traded among themselves and with the casteless. He'd said to meet by the perfume stall. Presumably her nose would lead the way . . . except the crush of people meant she could smell only the stink of overheated bodies. The din of shouted barters didn't help. For sixteen summers, she'd lived in a village where "market day" meant four carts along an open roadway. This was enough to make her head ache.

Taking a moment's break, she spotted a man following a girl of no more than twelve summers. He made her think of the children of Edgewood, held hostage by the former marshal. Orphaned and terrified, children who trusted her—and she was forced to trust the emperor to save them . . . while he entertained dignitaries from some kingdom she'd never heard of.

As frustration flared, Moria watched the child. A merchant's daughter, her simple dress adorned with mismatched beads and crooked embroidery. The girl went from booth to booth, picking out the cheapest baubles and bargaining with the merchants.

The man following her had leathery skin and the squint and rolling gait of a fisherman. Eyeing pretty young girls two castes below him and thinking them unlikely to complain, perhaps even welcoming his attention.

Moria drew closer, her hand under her cloak, fingers wrapping around her dagger. She would let the man see that she was watching, in hopes that would frighten him off. If it did not, she would allow him to see the blade. A plan so devoid of her usual recklessness that even her sister would approve.

Then a large woman—her arms loaded with goods— waddled into Moria's path. Moria swung around her, and by the time she did, the fisherman was right beside the girl, whose attention was fixed on some trinket.

As the man's hand snaked into the folds of the girl's dress, Moria launched her blade. Her second blade followed so fast they seemed to fly as one. The daggers pinned the man's cloak to the stall behind him. There was a near-comic moment as he ran in place, pinned by his cloak. When he realized what bound him, he slipped free of his cloak.

Before he could get more than two paces, a shadow landed in front of him and let out a snarl that reverberated through the square. People screamed. People fled.

It was not, Moria mused, an inconspicuous entrance.

Daigo pounced. The fisherman let out a scream and dropped to his knees, hands shielding his head. The wildcat plucked one dagger from the wooden stall, took it to Moria, and returned for the second.

"He touched you?" Moria asked the girl.

"Yes, my lady." The girl flushed. "Inappropriately."

"I saw." Moria waved to two men standing nearby. "Deal with him."

She turned to walk away, as if she could make such a spectacle and then slip into the crowd. It didn't help that there was no longer a crowd to slip into, most having fled the huge wildcat. Those who remained closed in as they realized who she was.

"My lady . . ."

"Keeper of Spirits."

"Moria of Edgewood."

"A blessing, my lady?"

Moria reached into her pocket for a handful of coppers, blessed and threw them, hoping to slide away in the scramble that followed.

A woman caught her cloak. "My thanks to you, Keeper. He has bothered girls before."

"He won't anymore. I truly must—" She looked over her shoulder, but people pressed in, blocking her escape.

"I heard your wildcat has a name," a little boy said as he squeezed through. "The court Keeper's cat has no name, but they say yours does."

"Daigo."

The boy reached out to pat the wildcat. Someone yelped a warning, but Daigo sat there, ears back, bracing himself to suffer the attention. Soon a half dozen children were patting and poking him.

"We must go," Moria said. *Before someone tells the guards*

I've left the palace court. She was not a prisoner, but she'd been ordered to stay within its walls for her own safety.

"Did you truly throw those daggers?" one of the girls asked.

"Like bolts of lightning," an old woman in the crowd said.

"Spirit-blessed," someone said. "My uncle saw her when she entered the city. She threw her blades at a man who insulted Marshal Kitsune's son. He brought them here. Gavril Kitsune, returned to the city. Fortune shines on us."

Fortune? Oh, no. That is not what shines. It is death and destruction, and Marshal Kitsune is at the center of it. Your hero is a monster. His son no better.

"I—I must go."

"Yes, you must," whispered a voice at her ear. Fingers wrapped around her forearm and a firm hand tugged her through the crowd. A young man held her. Seventeen summers of age. Light brown skin. Dark curls hanging in his face.

"Ronan," she murmured.

"Hmm. Daigo? Help me get her out of here."

TWO

Daigo cleared a path through the crowd, bumping people and growling when they didn't move fast enough. Ronan nudged gawkers aside from the rear. Moria allowed herself to be led, well aware of the scene she'd caused and the trouble she was in. More important, she was aware of the trouble Ashyn could catch for not realizing her twin had left. If there was one thing that could melt the steel from Moria's spine, it was the prospect of causing her sister grief.

Only once they were out of the square did she regain her stride. Ronan took the lead, and they wound down two alleyways before finding a dark corner behind a bakery, the sweet scent of honey cakes wafting out.

Moria asked about his young brother and sister. After four moons of exile in the Forest of the Dead, he'd been anxious to return to his orphaned siblings, left in the care of an aunt he feared would have them picking pockets for their keep. But now he answered with a quick, "They're well," before saying, "You don't know the meaning of inconspicuous, do you? All I had to do was follow the commotion and there you were, in the midst of it."

"I have no training in stealth and disguise," she said. "Nor any reason to learn. I'm the Keeper of Edgewood. I should walk where I wish."

His look said she knew full well why she couldn't do that, but she only settled onto a crate. Daigo took a seat beside her, leaving Ronan standing.

"How is your sister?" he asked.

"As fine as can be expected, being held a virtual prisoner and worrying about the people of Fairview and the children of Edgewood."

Ronan sighed. "You have no gift for the art of conversation, Moria. All right. I take it Ashyn is well. Please tell her . . ." He struggled long enough for words that Moria sighed with impatience.

"I'll tell her you send your undying love and cannot wait to see her gentle face again."

From the look on Ronan's face, you'd think she'd suggested telling Ashyn he wished her a slow and tortured death.

"Fine," she said. "I'll tell her you asked after her and that it would be pleasant to speak with her, once she is permitted to do so."

"Yes, thank you. I have great regard for your sister, but she is a Seeker, and I have good reason for not . . ."

Moria peered at him. "Not what?"

"I . . . have great regard for your sister."

"Yes, yes, you said that. I didn't come to play matchmaker. I asked you to meet me—"

"Summoned would be a better word." He crouched against the wall. "Is it about Gavril? I heard that he has left the city."

"Yes, but that is not—"

"I wouldn't have thought him quick to leave your side. He seemed to have appointed himself as much your loyal guard and companion as Daigo."

Daigo growled, as if understanding enough to not appreciate the comparison. Bond-beasts were said to be the reincarnations of great warriors, and the wildcat comprehended more than might be expected of an animal.

"I did not come to speak of—" she began.

"What happened?"

She'd truly rather not speak of it, but he'd need to know if he agreed to help with her plan.

"You'll recall the message we bore from Fairview?" she said. "For the emperor, from those who held the children and villagers captive. It bore a seal. One that Gavril claimed not to recognize."

Ronan nodded.

"It was the Kitsune seal."

Ronan pulled back. "Gavril must not have known—"

"He did. It was a secondary seal used by his father. The former marshal did not perish in the Forest of the Dead. He is alive, and he is responsible for raising the shadow stalkers that destroyed Edgewood. He's also responsible for the death worms and the thunder hawk. The rumors are correct. The

Kitsune family knows sorcery. Gavril confirmed it in the Wastes. I forced him to, having caught him at it."

"But Gavril—"

"—betrayed us. After Edgewood was massacred, his task was to escort Ashyn and me to the emperor with a firsthand account of his father's power."

Ronan shook his head. "I cannot believe that. Gavril might be one of the least companionable people I've ever met, but I would want him at my side in any battle. He's steadfast and loyal—"

"—to his *father*. That's the warrior way. Filial piety above all else. Even integrity and conscience, it seems. Now you know why he's gone, and I would like to leave the subject alone."

"But—"

"I insist. I came to speak of Fairview."

Ronan studied her expression and then nodded. "You don't believe the emperor is taking the threat seriously?"

"I have no idea if he is or is not. I only know that the children are still gone and there is no army marching from the imperial city to rescue them. Which is why I need to return."

"To Fairview? Did Gavril not say they would be moved elsewhere?" He paused. "Oh."

"Yes, *oh*. Given that Gavril was lying from the start, the emperor believes the children are indeed at Fairview, and I agree, which is why I'm going there."

His lips twitched. "To rescue them yourself?"

"If I must. But I hold no illusion that I can swoop in and set them free like birds from a cage. I merely wish to assess the situation. Confirm that the children are there."

"You don't think the emperor has already done that?"

"He deems it too dangerous."

"Too dangerous for trained warriors and spies, yet you plan to do it? That's madness, Moria. Brave and bold and utterly mad."

"I agree," said a voice.

A young man walked into their alley. Like Moria, he wore a disguise. His was more elaborate—and less obvious—than a cloak with the hood pulled up. He'd dressed in a rough tunic and trousers, with a loose jacket to hide his dual blades. On his feet he wore a peasant's simple thonged sandals. His long, black hair was plaited and he wore the rice straw hat common to farmers, oversized to shade one's eyes from the sun.

Yet even with the hat shadowing his face, his disguise was as poor as her cloak and hood. It wasn't his coloring or his features. He was empire-born—the golden skin, high cheekbones, and dark eyes that were the most common look even in this cosmopolitan city. He was well-formed and strikingly handsome. What made him stand out was something no hood or hat could hide. The face of an emperor. Or, at least, an emperor's son.

Ronan's mouth dropped open in a very unattractive gape.

Moria narrowed her eyes at the newcomer. "You followed me."

"I tried. I'm not very good at it, though. I left too large a gap, and I lost you. Luckily, it's not easy to lose you for long. Just follow the sounds of chaos."

He grinned and tugged off his jacket. Ronan's stare dropped to the matched dagger and sword hanging from the young man's waist, the silver handles inlaid with flawless rubies. Then Ronan's gaze lifted to the red-and-black tattooed bands on the young man's forearms—the intricate dragon design of the Tatsu clan.

"Your highness," Ronan said, bowing so deep Moria expected him to fall over.

The young man made a face and waved him up. "That's for my brothers. One need not be so formal with a bastard prince."

Which was not exactly true. An emperor's bastard sons were treated little different from those born to his wives. They could not ascend to the throne, and they had tattooed cuffs rather than the full sleeves of highborn warriors, but otherwise Tyrus was as much a prince as his brothers. He just didn't like to act the part.

Tyrus picked up a crate and plunked it down closer to Moria's.

"Take off that cloak before you melt," he said. "It wasn't disguising you."

"Nor is that"—she waved at his peasant outfit—"disguising you."

"It isn't supposed to. It merely conveys the message that I'm attempting to pass incognito."

"That makes absolutely no sense."

Ronan cleared his throat. "Actually it does. His highness—"

"Tyrus."

"Um, yes. If people see him dressed like that, they know he wishes not to be recognized, so they grant him the courtesy."

"I'll teach you how to do it," Tyrus said to her. "For the

next time you sneak off, because expecting you to stay in one place is like trying to cage that wildcat of yours." He lounged back on his crate. "So, we're discussing the issue of Fairview."

"No, we are not. This is a private conversation."

Ronan sputtered and shot her looks of alarm. She ignored him. She'd spent enough time with Tyrus to take liberties— and to know he'd allow them, even enjoyed the informality.

"How can the meeting be private," Tyrus said. "If you're holding it in a public place?"

"Because I don't have a private place. Not even my suite. I was bathing yesterday and a maidservant brought in fresh towels."

"They're very attentive."

"Which is fine. Just not while I'm bathing."

Tyrus grinned. "I don't mind them."

She rolled her eyes.

He turned to Ronan. "Since Moria refused to extend proper courtesies, I'll presume you're Ronan?"

Ronan nodded mutely.

"I apologize for dragging you into this, but if Moria had asked me what my father was doing, I'd have said he has sent spies to survey the situation in Fairview. He must determine an appropriate course of action since he cannot meet Alvar's demands for their release."

The former marshal had demanded nothing short of the throne. As Emperor Tatsu said, Alvar Kitsune didn't expect him even to consider such a thing. It was not a negotiation but a declaration of war.

Tyrus continued. "If Moria had asked me, I would have

happily answered her questions. But she refuses to speak of the matter."

"Because you shouldn't be pulled into it," Moria said. "Your brothers have spies watching to see if you're paying attention to me because I'm a young woman or because I'm part of a situation that could further your position in court. The latter would suggest an interest in politics, which would suggest a *lack* of interest in a long life."

Two of the emperor's bastard sons had already died from paying an unhealthy amount of attention to matters of court. Tyrus aspired to be a warrior—a great one. Nothing less and nothing more.

"Yes," Tyrus said. "But I suggested finding a place where we could speak privately. Which you refused."

"Because I won't involve you."

"I said I wish to be involved."

"And I said I would not allow it."

They locked gazes, but she would not back down. If he wanted to give her sword lessons, she would not object to that. If he wanted to befriend her, she would not object to that. If he wanted to be more than a friend . . . well, that was open to consideration. Her sister deemed such matters affairs of the heart, to be approached with great care and forethought. To Moria, the heart did not enter into it. If Tyrus fancied her and she fancied him, she could use lessons in more than fighting techniques.

There was only one role she would not allow Tyrus to play: her champion. In court, everyone wanted something from you. She would not be part of that. She enjoyed Tyrus's company because his company was worth enjoying, not because he was a prince. She would do nothing to suggest otherwise.

"My father has sent spies," Tyrus said. "Two, to take separate routes, in case one is captured. He expects word from them at any moment. You may have noticed he is entertaining guests?"

Moria said nothing.

"I'm sure you're fuming at the emperor for throwing lavish parties while the children of your village suffer. He does no such thing, Moria. He entertains the Sultan of Nemeth and the King of Etaria. Minor principalities near the Katakana Mountains, where the Kitsunes once ruled. Both men were close friends of Alvar Kitsune. Someone has been sheltering him since his escape from the Forest of the Dead."

"Your father thinks it's one of them," Ronan said. "That's why they're here. So he can decide which is guilty."

Tyrus nodded and watched Moria, waiting for her to ask questions. She had a hundred of them. And to protect Tyrus, she'd ask not a one.

"He's doing what he can," Tyrus said. "He's not a perfect ruler, but he is a very good one. I know you think I'm only saying that because he's my father. But did he seem incompetent when you spoke to him? Did he seem uncaring? Did he seem to underestimate the threat?"

She shifted on the crate.

"I know you are frustrated," he said. "But there is no reason for you to go to Fairview. If it would help you to speak to my father, I can arrange an audience."

"No."

"I would be discreet about it. Allow me to—"

"No," she said, getting to her feet. She turned to Ronan. "I'll convey your regards to my sister. Please convey mine to your family. Thank you for meeting with me."

She glanced for Daigo, but he was already at her side. She walked off, stiffly, leaving the two young men behind.

THREE

When Tyrus did not come after her, Moria thought he was leaving her to whatever trouble would befall her for sneaking away from court. That was her ill mood speaking. It seemed he'd only stayed behind to speak to Ronan, and Moria had barely reached the market square before he fell in at her side.

Tyrus didn't pursue the conversation again. Instead he played city guide, pointing out landmarks and explaining the history. No dry, architectural lectures. Moria doubted he knew any. Like her, he favored tales of danger and daring and told her those—a duel fought here, a notorious bandit hideout there.

Nearly everyone they passed seemed to recognize him. Yet there were no bows or murmurs of respect. No cries for alms or favors. They saw Tyrus and quickly looked away. Moria kept Daigo at her side and left her hood down, and no one said a word to her.

She was certain her appearance with Tyrus would be commented on, in whispers and rumors. While the Keeper could not marry, she could take lovers. The prince would marry as his father wished, but he was not expected to eschew female company until then. The court already whispered of how much time the two spent together. Now the city would. And Moria and Tyrus would not discourage it because it meant his brothers would soon call off their spies, realizing there was no political angle here, simply a young man and young woman courting.

When they reached the palace, Tyrus didn't ask how she'd slipped past the guards. He went straight to her point of escape—the servants' gate.

"A word of advice," he said as they approached it. "While I'd prefer you to ask me along on your next unauthorized excursion, if you do go alone, you will find it much harder to return through this gate unnoticed. In fact, I'd say it's impossible."

The guards at the small gate were already moving forward. Then they saw Daigo and got a closer look at Tyrus, and they dipped their chins and gazes, welcoming the prince as he passed through.

"They hardly need to worry about spies and assassins *exiting* court," Tyrus continued after greeting the guards. "But you will not get back in without revealing yourself."

"So what are the other routes?"

His lips curved. "Did I say there were any?"

"You implied it."

"Perhaps. And the next time you wish to leave, you have only to tell me, and I will show you . . . and go with you."

"I'm quite safe in the city."

"But is the city safe when you are in it? That's the question."

He glanced up at the sound of harsh footsteps clacking over the stone path. "I will handle this."

She was about to say "Handle what?" when five figures rounded a building, bearing down on them. In the lead was a stout, gray-haired man—the minister of the imperial household. Two of his stewards flanked him. All three walked quickly, their faces set in expressions so grim one would expect they were headed to a public flogging. Yet no face was as grim as the fourth. A young woman dressed in a simple but elegant silk dress, her red-gold hair flowing almost to her waist, her blue eyes so chill Moria decided that if it *was* a public flogging, the girl would ask to wield the strap herself.

"I think I'm in trouble," Moria murmured.

Daigo grunted beside her, and when he did, the fifth figure—a huge yellow hound walking beside the girl—gave an answering growl.

"My lady Keeper," the minister said in his soft, steel-laced voice. "We had heard—"

"—that she escaped into the city and was raising untold havoc in the market?" Tyrus said. "I fear it is true."

The minister stopped short, his sandals squeaking. He'd apparently been too intent on his target to take a closer look at the person accompanying her.

"Prince Tyrus," he said.

"Yes, I'm the one causing trouble today. Or, at least, causing the trouble that caused the trouble. I wanted to show Moria the marketplace. She insisted on looking at books. I failed to see the attraction so I fear I wandered off. That is when the incident occurred. A man was harassing a young girl, and Moria stopped him." He paused. "You may wish to have the minister of justice send someone to investigate. It seems it's not the first time the man has done such a thing. He'll need some sort of disciplinary action, and it may be best if the merchants aren't allowed to administer it themselves. They were quite angry. And quite grateful to Moria."

"I'm sure they were." The minister turned stiffly to Moria. "Thank you for your intervention, my lady. The people will appreciate it."

Moria snuck a look at her sister. Ashyn's face was still stern, but her eyes had lost their chill. She mouthed something to Moria.

"And I, um, apologize for causing a disturbance," Moria said with a slow bow.

"It was for a good cause," Tyrus said. "As for taking the Keeper out of the court, that falls entirely on me. She was bored, and I wished to impress her." A disarming grin. "One can't blame me for that." He walked to Ashyn. "I apologize for stealing your sister away, my lady."

Ashyn's look said she knew full well what had happened. "No apology needed, your highness."

"I offer it anyway," he said with a half bow. Then he turned to the men. "Does that clear up the matter, minister?"

"It does."

"I'll understand if you wish to report it to my father. I did act impetuously and did spirit the Keeper out against his orders."

"Young men are impetuous," the minister said. "Particularly when it comes to young women. I see no reason to tell your imperial father."

"I will remember that. Thank you." He turned to Ashyn.

"I leave your sister in your care. Be gentle with her. We have a sparring appointment later this afternoon, and I'll be hard enough on her then."

He took his leave. The minister and his stewards followed without a word to Moria.

Once they were gone, Moria pulled a book from her cloak pocket and handed it to her sister. "I got this for you."

Ashyn gave her a withering look as her hound, Tova, grumbled under his breath as if to say that was a poor try, a very poor try.

"And I saw Ronan."

Ashyn went still. "You saw . . ."

"Ronan. That's where I was going. To meet him, because he deserved an update, and you refused to provide one."

"Because we're not supposed to leave the court. You didn't tell him— Did you say I wouldn't meet with him? If you—"

"Of course not." Moria waved for them to start back to their suite. "I told him you were busy, and it may have had something to do with that handsome courtier I saw you speaking to the other day."

Ashyn's eyes flashed with outrage. "I did not speak to any—" She caught her sister's smile. "You're not funny, Rya. Not at all."

"Oh, but you are. Tell me again how you think of Ronan only as a friend. A dear, kind friend . . . who just happened to kiss you good-bye the last time you saw him."

"I should never have told you that."

"You'd have burst otherwise. So tell me again how you are not thinking of him, not pining for him."

"You make me sound like the fainting heroine in one of your ridiculous bard tales."

"The lovely fair maiden, bound by destiny to a life of spiritual service, pining for the dashing thief, who escaped his fate, only to be torn from her side—"

"He hasn't escaped his fate," Ashyn muttered. "He's out there, hiding like a criminal, when all he has to do is let us speak to the emperor on his behalf, and he'd be a hero."

"Which would make a very happy end to the story. Unless the emperor *doesn't* pardon him, but throws him into the dungeons as an escaped criminal. Given the choice, I can see why Ronan's not eager to take the chance."

"He would be spared. He's being stubborn."

Ashyn opened the door to their quarters.

"I suppose you don't want to hear what he said about you?" Moria said. "What message he wished me to convey?"

"Message?"

Moria laughed and continued into their rooms, with Ashyn trailing after her.

FOUR

M oria hated court life. By the second day, she'd been eyeing the gates, plotting her escape. Admittedly, her attitude had been different when they first arrived. After they'd spent nearly ten days on the road, the imperial court—with its gardens and lake and forest and hushed tranquility—had been welcome sanctuary. That had changed once they were told that the emperor wished them to stay within the court walls until this matter was resolved . . . and Moria learned that the word "wished" meant something entirely different when it came from an emperor.

The court had quickly become a cage. It didn't matter if it was nearly as big as Edgewood. In their village, they'd been allowed to venture beyond the gates. That made all the difference.

The minister had tried to entertain them, in all the ways he expected young women would like to be entertained. He sent dressmakers and hairdressers and arranged teas and puppeteers. Moria had no interest in dresses or hair or tea or puppets. Ashyn was more inclined to enjoy them, but even she could not while the children of Edgewood were held captive. They'd spent their days in the library and the gardens, in the temple and the training grounds, and they'd listened to whispers that the Keeper and Seeker of Edgewood were very odd girls, uncultured, perhaps slow-witted, which was not surprising, given that they were Northerners.

That afternoon, Moria sparred with Tyrus. The court Seeker—Ellyn—had tried to stop the lessons, because Moria wasn't allowed to carry a sword until her eighteenth summer. Others seemed more concerned about Tyrus, who was learning dagger throwing from Moria in return. Warrior daggers were considered more tools than weapons. To Tyrus, though, any battlefield skill was useful.

As for the swords, someone—she hated to name him—had told Moria that she would never be able to wield one as well as a male warrior. She was determined to prove him wrong. At first, that task had seemed more daunting than she expected. The typical warrior's sword was a long, slightly curved, single-edged blade. But there were other types, and Tyrus had called in the imperial swordsmith to help. They had decided Moria would be best served with a side sword. It was a shorter blade, sometimes worn instead of the dagger, generally used as an auxiliary sword for close-quarter fighting. It was also used for beheading an enemy, which meant that the blade was as sharp and as strong as any other.

That day, Moria did not practice battle decapitation, Tyrus having drawn the line at offering himself up for that. They sparred while Daigo lounged, dozing. For Moria it was a full workout, leaving her drenched in sweat and gasping for breath. Tyrus didn't even get warm enough to remove his tunic, which was a shame, though the lack of visual distraction did help her accuracy with the blade.

"You need to work on your stamina," Tyrus said when they finished. "Are you running twice a day?"

She nodded, struggling for breath. "You said twice around the court wall, but I've been doing it thrice. I think I need more."

"Three times around, thrice a day. We're going to skip lessons for a few days and work on continuous practice bouts to build your stamina and your spirit and improve your attention. You need more of that. Much more."

Tyrus went on to list everything she'd done wrong. He offered no praise. Once, when Ashyn came to watch, she'd been appalled and shocked that the affable young prince could be so harsh a teacher. Ashyn had been quick to tell Moria she was doing very well. "Yes, she is," Tyrus had said. "For an untrained girl. But she wants to do well for a warrior." Ashyn had stayed away after that, and Moria was glad of it. Tyrus had promised to teach her as a warrior, not as a girl trying to play at being a warrior. She did not need her sister defending her from the sidelines.

Once the lesson ended, Tyrus shed that taskmaster guise as he shed his practice tunic. Moria watched. It was a very pleasant sight. He was lean-muscled, sweat making his golden skin shimmer. He wore an amulet band intricately tied around his left biceps. It was red silk, with tasseled ends, the band embroidered with his name and sewn with a tiny protection scroll inside. An old custom, amulet bands had largely fallen out of favor, but his mother had given it to him and he wore it for her.

Tyrus pulled on a clean shirt, caught her hand, and whispered, "Come. I've something to show you."

His dark eyes danced, and the smile on his lips promised a passionate tryst in some shadowy corner. Moria knew what that meant—they were being watched. Sure enough, two serving girls were strolling past, feigning no interest in the young prince, which was as good a sign as any that they were spies from one of his brothers.

Despite the attention Tyrus paid her, he showed no interest in more than platonic companionship. She'd wondered at first if he preferred men, but she'd heard enough stories to know that wasn't the case. It seemed that many foreign princesses and diplomats' daughters received real invitations to shadowy corners.

The disappointing truth was that Tyrus did not fancy her. Some men found Northern looks unattractive. More likely, though, given his taste for highborn ladies, it was Moria herself that didn't ignite those fires. As a companion, she was ideal. As a bedmate, he'd likely prefer a more feminine representative of her sex. She could not blame him. One's taste was one's taste, and it was merely unfortunate that hers ran to handsome warriors when she was surrounded by pretty courtier boys whose gazes said they'd happily keep her from growing bored in her confinement.

"Come?" he said, his brows arching, grin growing. He took

her hand and tugged it. "I've someplace to show you."

"I bet you do," she said. "Is it dark?"

"Possibly."

"Private?"

"Probably."

She laughed. "I think you've taken me there before."

"No, not this one. Come."

"But . . ." Moria motioned toward the two serving girls, now on a bench, one subtly watching.

He leaned in and whispered loudly. "They aren't looking. Now come. Quickly."

They scampered off, whispering and laughing, as the spies headed back to the palace with their report. Tyrus took her past the Chancery for Medicines, and then into the Grove of Pines. He led her through to the palace wall at the far side.

"Can you climb?" he asked, pointing to a generously branched pine.

She nodded.

While she easily scaled the tree, he had a little more trouble. There were situations in which having a long blade hanging at your side was problematic. She remembered in the Wastes, when she'd broken into a run upon seeing Fairview ahead, and she'd laughed at—

Moria banished the memory. She'd not recall any that included him. The point was that a warrior's blade could hinder running or climbing, yet as long as a warrior remained upright, his weapons stayed at his side or in his hand. There were no other choices.

Once up the tree, Tyrus pointed to the wall and said, "Can you jump?"

"Into the palace yard?"

He nodded.

"I can but—"

"Then follow me. Tell Daigo to wait."

He jumped onto the wall and then swung down. By the time she'd spoken to her wildcat, Tyrus had disappeared. She jumped to the base of the wall and looked about.

"Over here," he whispered, peeking from behind a building. When she caught up, he said, "Keep following. Quietly. Don't sneak, though. There's no reason I can't bring you to my quarters, but I'd prefer not to take the ruse that far, for the sake of your reputation. Just follow quietly and take note of the route. You'll want to use it again. Soon."

Like the court, the palace itself was a complex of buildings. The emperor's residence was in the middle—or so she'd heard, having not been here before. His first and second wives also had homes in the compound, as did his concubines, including Tyrus's mother. Tyrus himself lived here, like all the emperor's children, except the daughters who'd married and left.

When Moria once asked how many children the emperor had, Tyrus estimated fourteen—four legitimate sons, two legitimate daughters, and the rest by his official concubines, though he allowed he may have forgotten one or two. The legitimate offspring were all older than Tyrus. Two of the bastard daughters were older and married, living elsewhere. The remainder were at least three summers younger, meaning Tyrus was the only one who posed a threat, and thus garnered all his brothers' interest.

Given the size of the imperial family, the palace compound was not small. It may even have been larger than the court. Besides the residences, it included a number of other buildings, for guests and entertainment. Those were along the wall adjoining the court, and that's where Tyrus led her. They stopped outside a window shuttered against the late-day heat. Inside, she caught the bustle of serving staff preparing for a meal.

"Can you hear what they're saying?" Tyrus whispered, leaning in so close his breath warmed her ear.

She could pick up nothing of import. Just someone asking a steward about the menu, someone else being chastised for poorly arranging flowers. When she said as much to Tyrus, he nodded.

"I only wanted to know if you could hear them. The window ought to be open tonight, but if there's a sharp breeze, they'll close it."

"Why would I—?"

He waved for her to follow. When she caught up, he whispered, "You'll need to return to the court a different way. I'll show you."

He took her almost to the rear corner. One of the palace buildings came close enough to the wall that they could climb onto it. They emerged in a quiet pocket behind the armory. There was a bench there, with a small koi pond. They'd barely sat when Daigo appeared and settled silently at Moria's feet.

"When I was growing up, my father loved to tell me tales of dragons," Tyrus said. "I swear he didn't know a story that didn't have at least one." He rubbed his thumb over the red dragon on his forearm. "They were as important to him as our actual ancestors. One of his favorite tales was of a sand dragon.

I presume I'd be wasting breath if I asked whether you know your types."

"Sand, snow, rock, timber. Corresponding to the four major parts of the empire—the southern desert, the frozen north, the western mountains, and the eastern forest. There are also corpse dragons, but they aren't the same."

"This story is about a sand dragon, which lives alone, for very good reason."

"Because they guard treasure."

"Exactly. The problem with having treasure is that everyone wants it. No matter how far away the dragon hides, eventually men will come. Being in the desert, though, the dragon can see approaching armies from afar. So this one waited, and when the men arrived, he did not meet them with fire and death, but with kind words and hospitality. He was very pleased to see them, having been alone for so long, and if they would share his company for a time, he would happily share his fortune in return. Of course, the men suspected a trick. The first dinner they attended with hidden blades and anxious hearts, but the dragon was as pleasant a host as one could wish. The second night, some left their blades behind, but most were still mistrusting and prepared for battle. Yet the dragon was even more hospitable, the banquet bigger, the entertainment grander, and at the end, he gave them all a bag. Those who left their blades behind had received gold coins, enough to feed a family for many seasons. Those who'd brought their weapons found their bags filled with sand. They knew their host had detected their duplicity, and they were shamed. So on the third night, no one carried a blade to the banquet, and the dragon was in his best mood ever, the food and the entertainment beyond anything imaginable. At the end, he invited them into his treasure room, to take all they could carry, and once they were there, he barred the door and left them to die."

"As he should," Moria said.

Tyrus smiled and nodded. "As he should, because they came to his home with treachery in their hearts. They accepted his hospitality while plotting his demise. Now, like the men of the story, there is an invited guest on the palace grounds who came with treachery in his heart, and plots with Alvar Kitsune to bring about my father's demise."

"Either the Sultan of Nemeth or the King of Etaria."

"My father has entertained them sumptuously for two nights. This is the third night."

"Meaning whoever betrayed him will die."

Tyrus laughed. "No, that's where the story diverges, because it would hardly be in my father's best interests to murder a valuable source of enemy intelligence. Each night, while the food has grown richer and the entertainments more exotic, the number of invited guests has dwindled, allowing a more intimate affair . . . and allowing my father more time with his guests. Tonight it will be a very small gathering, with much wine and diversion, and he will determine who is betraying him."

"And the dinner will take place in that room."

"Yes."

"Where I can listen in."

"Yes." He moved so close their legs rubbed. "This will not help you get the children back, Moria, but it may help you see that progress is being made. We are all frustrated, but if we swoop into Fairview with an army, they will see us coming and slaughter the children and villagers. Alvar Kitsune is playing a game. A terrible and cruel game, but a game nonetheless. We cannot break the rules. We must find a way to subvert them. That's what my father is doing."

She nodded.

He leaned in further, taking her hand in his. "I can see how much this is hurting you. I just want . . . I want to make it stop hurting, and I know it won't until you have some resolution, not just with the children, but with Gavril—"

She pulled back so fast she nearly fell off the bench. "Don't—"

"Yes, I know." He straightened, anger spiking his voice. "We cannot say that name. We cannot discuss what he did. But you need to speak of it, Moria. It's like swallowing a dagger— it's ripping you apart from the inside. You can talk to me. He was my friend, too."

"If that's what you think, then you were as deluded as I. He told me you were simply someone he grew up with and trained with."

"Which for Gavril is as close to a 'friend' as one gets, as you well know."

"I don't know anything about him. That is obvious."

"No, you do. You know what kind of man he is, and for all his faults, lack of honor is not one of them. Nor is cruelty. Whatever is happening here, it is not what it seems. The Gavril I know would never have condoned the massacre of a village. When he realized what had happened, how did he react?"

31

I told him and he wouldn't believe it. He said I was mistaken. A foolish child. Then I took him back and he saw the bodies and . . .

She sucked in a breath at the memory, the look on Gavril's face.

"It doesn't matter," she said. "He was playing a role. He told me he was guilty. That whatever I thought he'd done, he had done. Those were his exact words."

"To protect you. Because . . ." Tyrus sighed as she rose. "All right, I'll stop. Deep down, you *want* to believe he didn't do this, which is exactly why you *refuse* to believe it. You will not be made a fool. Back to tonight—if you choose to listen in, wait until late. It will be a very long meal."

FIVE

oria told Ashyn she was meeting Tyrus that night. Her sister didn't question the lateness of the visit. She'd made it clear that she thought the young prince was the perfect remedy for what ailed Moria, and a nighttime meeting seemed to prove the situation was progressing as hoped.

Before leaving, Moria had casually asked Ashyn about the king and sultan. Ashyn said both were minor players. Royalty whose land hadn't been taken during imperial expansion primarily because of their friendships with Marshal Kitsune. In return, both paid homage to Emperor Tatsu, as did most of the border rulers. The emperor had risen to power not by lineage but because of the vital role he'd played in the empire's expansion push. Since then, there'd been only minor skirmishes. An era of peace and prosperity. Which meant, as Moria knew Tyrus worried, that the army was ill-prepared for war.

By the time Moria arrived at the dinner party building, they were clearing the fruit course inside, and she wondered if she was too late. But it turned out the meal was only the opening act. Then came the entertainment. Eventually the troupe of performers left, replaced by courtesans.

There were many women in the palace, most of whom seemed to exist purely to serve the whims and pleasures of the emperor. Two wives, four concubines, and six or seven master courtesans. Moria was somewhat confused about the function of the courtesans. There were also houses of them in the city. The bards' songs made it clear they were not prostitutes, and yet sex certainly seemed to be part of the "entertainment" they provided. When she'd asked Ashyn for a more detailed description of their function, her sister had turned bright red and stammered meaningless nonsense.

While the palace courtesans were for the emperor's bed, it also seemed they could be lent to guests who had not come with their wives. Rather like fresh clothing, if they forgot theirs at home. At dinner that night, the courtesans sang and played the lute and recited poetry—and flirted. Moria wondered if they were doing more than flirting, but it did not sound like it. Which was rather disappointing. How was one to learn such things, if one had no exposure to them?

As for learning anything more critical, that was a bigger disappointment. While she did not expect the emperor to outright ask who had harbored the former marshal, she thought the subject of Alvar Kitsune would at least come up. Some offhand comment, allowing Emperor Tatsu to study the inebriated and unguarded reactions of his guests. When it did not, she had to accept that Tyrus was mistaken. Love could blind one to a father's faults, and in Tyrus's case, filial piety was more than a duty. Sometimes one's father truly was one of the most important people in one's world. She knew that as well as anyone.

Finally, the dinner came to a close, and the emperor invited his two guests to select a flower to brighten their quarters. That seemed a strange offer . . . until she realized that by "flower," he meant "courtesan." He chose his own companion first and left the two men still deciding. Once outside, he told his courtiers to leave him for the evening and headed to his quarters with his night's companion.

Moria peered along the wall, making sure the way was clear before beginning the journey to her own quarters. She made it past two buildings. Then she heard someone speaking.

"I need you to go back to your quarters," the man's voice said, and she looked about, as if he were speaking to her, but the voice came from at least ten paces away.

She peeked around the corner to see a broad-shouldered man in his fifth decade. Emperor Tatsu, who'd tugged the courtesan into a dark gap between buildings. He released her and pressed a box into her hand.

"A gift for your trouble," he whispered. "Go and enjoy your evening."

The courtesan stared at the emperor, a plaintive note in her voice as she said, "Your imperial highness. I thought . . ."

"No, child. Now go—"

"Have I offended you?" she blurted, then stumbled over herself apologizing for interrupting him.

"You have not offended me," he said. "I had no intention of taking anyone to my quarters tonight. I have business to attend to, and it was merely an excuse to end my dinner engagement. Take your gift and go. Quickly now."

The courtesan didn't linger, but it was clear she would have preferred a night in his bed over any gift he might offer. Which piqued Moria's curiosity. Clearly, given the number of women in the palace, the emperor was experienced in such matters. Was that the cause of the courtesan's disappointment? That she'd miss out on a pleasurable evening? Or was it more a matter of position and favor—that by sharing his bed she'd gain status in the court? It was a fascinating subject, but not one she was likely to better understand anytime soon.

The courtesan hurried off as best she could in platform sandals a hand's-length tall. Voices drifted over from the dining house. One of the guests was leaving, having made his choice from the courtesans. Silk whispered, and Moria glanced down the gap to see the emperor poised at the corner, watching his guest.

A moment later, the King of Etaria appeared, so tightly entwined with his courtesan that it seemed they'd begun the evening's activities without waiting for the privacy of a bedchamber. As they staggered, giggling, past where the emperor waited in the shadows, Moria realized they weren't so much entwined by lust as by necessity. The king was too inebriated to walk alone.

"Your highness," Emperor Tatsu said, slipping from his dark post.

The king stumbled and the courtesan staggered under him.

"Allow me," Emperor Tatsu said, sliding his arm under the man's shoulder.

"Your imperial highness," the king slurred. "I appreciate the assistance, but I'm sure you have some young steward better suited—"

"Is that a hint that I've grown too old to hold your weight?" the emperor said with a laugh.

"No, of course not. I—"

"It's true." Emperor Tatsu gave an easy grin that mirrored his son's. "We do grow old, don't we? But I'm still strong enough to support my friends. We are friends, I trust?"

"Y-yes, of c-course, your imperial—"

"Enough with the courtesies. You're among friends. Now, let's send this lovely flower off, so we may speak."

The king sputtered at that. He certainly could not say he'd rather spend time with a courtesan. But he was drunk enough to let his disappointment show. Emperor Tatsu only smiled and joked about old men and young girls, and sent the courtesan off with a gift. For her part, she seemed only too happy to take it, and disappeared before the king suggested she wait in his quarters. Moria could not blame her. Despite his age, Emperor Tatsu was a handsome and well-formed man. The King of Etaria . . . was not.

When the girl was gone, the emperor turned to the king.

"So, friend," he said. "Admittedly, it is a stretch to call you friend. We have not always seen eye to eye on matters of trade and politics. But I still consider you such because I believe that the friends of my friends ought to be mine as well. Do you agree?"

"Yes. Absolutely, your imperial—"

"It's Jiro. Formal titles are so tedious."

The king hesitated. "Jiro, then. Thank you. I have always said that I wished my little kingdom could be of more service to the empire. We have a great deal to offer."

"Oh, you do. You absolutely do. But when I say you are the friend of a friend, you do not ask who I mean?"

Silence. The king's mottled face strained with the effort of clear thought, as if he were passing a kidney stone.

"Why Alvar, of course," Emperor Tatsu said. "There was a time—most of my life, in fact—when no man was closer to me than Alvar Kitsune. So, tell me, how is my old friend?"

Moria realized her mistake. A warrior must know tactics beyond the obvious. While Emperor Tatsu might not lead an army these days, the bards still sang tales of his victories as a warrior, fighting alongside the friend who would one day be his marshal. He understood the art of strategy . . . whatever the battlefield.

The king blinked and blustered and then finally found his voice. "Alvar Kitsune? He's long dead, and well he should be, for betraying your imperial—"

The king was cut off by a *whoomph*, air rushing from his chest as he landed hard on the cobbled path, flat on his back. The emperor had snagged the king's knee with his foot and yanked his leg from under him, and now the king lay there, gaping, mouth open as he heaved for breath.

"My—my—"

Emperor Tatsu leaned over the supine man, bending until his face was only a hand's breadth from the king's face.

"You accepted my invitation, knowing you had harbored a man intent on my destruction."

"I—"

"You came without hesitation. You sat at my table. You drank my wine. You ate my food. And all the while, your ally has unleashed an unspeakable evil on my empire, on *his* empire, massacring his own people."

"I—"

"Oh, I know why you came. In hopes of gaining intelligence you can feed back to Alvar. My stewards and my maids tell me you've asked many questions since you arrived."

"Curiosity, your majesty. You are the most powerful man in the world. Naturally, I would have questions—"

"And you received no answers. But I will. Whatever it takes to get them."

The king sputtered. "I am not some common courtier. I am—"

"I know who you are. The king of a country so insignificant I wouldn't risk the lives of ten warriors conquering it. Have no fear. I recognize your station. I will not throw you in the dungeon. You'll stay on, as my guest, while I question you. If you escape, I will send my fastest messenger to Alvar, to be sure he knows you were here, answering my questions."

The king bleated some excuse, some denial, but Emperor Tatsu only turned and called, "Lysias?"

A man appeared, seeming to materialize like a spirit. He was almost a head taller than the emperor, his clothing and skin as dark as the surrounding night, his braids swinging as he slid from the shadows. Moria flinched, momentarily imagining

39

another face, just as stone-hardened and grim as this man's, but younger, with green eyes instead of dark. The green eyes of a sorcerer.

She squeezed her eyes shut, mentally spitting curses for her foolishness. Lysias was clearly from the mountains, like the Kitsunes, but resembled Gavril only in his height, coloring, and braids. He was at least ten summers older and wore the five-pointed star that marked him a member of the emperor's private guard.

"His highness has drunk too much," the emperor said. "He stumbled and fell, and I fear I'm too old to carry him myself."

Lysias twitched his lips, as if he'd been watching and knew full well how the king had fallen—and that Emperor Tatsu could indeed carry him if he so wished. But he only dipped his chin and said, "Yes, your imperial highness."

"Place two guards at his door, please," Emperor Tatsu said. "I've heard rumors that cause me concern for his safety. He ought to remain in his quarters until I come to visit him."

"Of course."

Lysias lifted the king and took him away without another word. Emperor Tatsu watched them go and stayed there, unmoving, his back to Moria as she hid around the corner.

"Come out of the shadows, child," he said.

Moria jumped, but he could not be speaking to her. He hadn't even glanced her way.

"I know you're there." He looked straight at her hiding place. "The young Keeper, I take it?"

Moria took a careful step backward.

"If you run, I'll have to send someone to fetch you," he said.

40

"You need to work on your spying skills, child."

Moria stepped into the moonlight.

"Where's your wildcat, Keeper? You ought not to be out alone—"

She'd left Daigo on the other side of the wall, but as soon as the emperor said that, the wildcat slunk around the corner, as if he'd been there the whole time.

"Moria?" a loud whisper cut through the night, followed by running footsteps. "Where have you—?"

Tyrus appeared behind the emperor and skidded to a stop. "Father?" Under his breath, he pretended to curse, then said, louder, as he gave a slight bow, "I'm sorry. This is my fault. Moria wished to see the palace gardens . . ."

"And you brought her this late in the evening?"

Tyrus's gaze dipped lower. "I had . . . other intentions. Moria realized that, and she fled. I came after her, to make sure she got to her quarters safely."

"I see."

Tyrus glanced over at her. "I'm sorry, Moria. I behaved dishonorably, and I am shamed. I'll call a guard to escort you back."

"She is the Keeper," Emperor Tatsu said. "Have you forgotten that?"

Tyrus kept his gaze on his father's sandals. "No. I—"

The emperor's voice rose, the edge cutting through the silent palace grounds. "This is not a pretty serving girl to dally with. She is the gift of our ancestors, sent to protect their spirits and protect us from evil. She is sacred."

There were many lies Tyrus could tell if he wanted her to

41

follow his lead. But to suggest he'd been dishonorable? Moria could not allow this.

"Your imperial highness," she said, stumbling over the honorific. "Tyrus didn't—"

"I was speaking to my son." The emperor gave her a look that stoppered the words in her throat. He turned back to Tyrus. "I've allowed you to charm her and flirt with her. I see no danger in a few stolen kisses. But I trusted that you knew better than to take it further. Bringing her here, at night, a stone's throw from your quarters?"

"No, your imperial highness," Moria said. "He did not. He would not. It was a misunderstand—"

"Enough. To my quarters. Both of you. Now."

SIX

The emperor motioned for them to walk in front of him. Daigo followed Moria, as if buffering her from the emperor's fury. Tyrus walked silently at her side until the emperor slowed to speak to a courtier.

"It's all right," Tyrus whispered. "I suggested this. I'll fix it."

He shot a look back at his father, part anxiety, part bewilderment. Nothing was more important to a warrior than honor, and Tyrus ought not to have impugned his to protect her. Ironically, in claiming dishonor, he was acting with honor—taking her punishment because he'd suggested that she eavesdrop.

Her true anger was directed at the emperor. The Keeper was allowed a lover. If she had rebuffed Tyrus and he'd persisted, that would be cause for his father's disapproval. Yet if he'd merely tested her willingness . . . well, was that not what young men did? She took no offense unless they failed to understand the meaning of "no."

Moria was too caught up in her own thoughts for more than a vague impression of the emperor's residence, which was smaller and less conspicuous than she would have expected for a man who ruled most of the known land.

As they removed their shoes, Emperor Tatsu ordered out the servants with a brusque, "I wish to speak to my son." They scattered as if he'd wielded a blade. Once they were gone, the emperor walked farther inside. They followed him into a room with a desk inlaid with ivory. Woodblock prints of dragons adorned the walls.

"Sit," he said, his back to them as he looked at a print of the goddess riding a golden dragon into battle.

Tyrus lowered himself onto the nearest cushion. When Moria didn't move, he tugged at her leg. She stepped away.

"Your son did nothing wrong," she said. "He did not do as he claims, and I'll not have him suffer for—"

The emperor turned. "So you're saying he lied to me?"

Moria's mouth closed fast.

"Moria?" Tyrus whispered. "Sit. Please." His tone added *before you get me in worse trouble.*

"I was spying on your dinner party," she said. "I offer myself for punishment and ask that you pardon Tyrus. Whatever he did, it was my fault. I . . . I seduced him."

The emperor burst out laughing, startling Moria. "As pretty as you are, child, I cannot imagine you seducing any man. Threatening him at the point of a blade, perhaps."

"Father," Tyrus began, rising. "I apologize for her outburst. She's unaccustomed—"

"—to matters and manners of court." Emperor Tatsu waved

Tyrus down. "I'm well aware of that. She has spirit and honor. You choose your companions well, Tyrus. Though, if I truly thought you had brought her to the palace grounds to seduce her by moonlight, I would be as angry as I pretended. Now sit." He turned to Daigo. "You, too. While some would wish me to add comportment lessons to your sword fighting, the truth of the world, child, is that some of us are above such niceties. You are a Keeper. Position comes with privilege, and none greater than the ability to speak your mind. The sword lessons will serve you better. Now, I understand you are frustrated by the situation in Fairview. You don't believe enough is being done."

"No," Tyrus said. "If anyone said—"

"I do not need tattling tongues to tell me what anyone can plainly see. The Keeper is angry and frustrated. She throws herself into sparring and eschews the comforts and entertainments of the court. Her sister is equally frustrated, in her quiet way, losing herself in her studies instead. If you had sent Moria to eavesdrop on treaty negotiations, the punishment for both of you would be severe. But you sent her to prove that I was indeed making progress on the matter of Alvar Kitsune."

When neither said a word, the emperor pulled the low chair from his desk and sat on it.

"Yet that doesn't truly help, does it?" he continued. "What concerns her immediately is not the fate of the former marshal but the fate of the children. And on that, the news is less heartening." He turned to Moria. "I have sent spies to assess the situation. One on the very night I learned of the events in Fairview, another two days following. Neither has returned. Presumably they are dead or captured. Alvar expected them.

That is the problem with fighting a man who knows me so well."

"So what now?" Moria asked.

Tyrus cleared his throat.

"I mean, so what now, your imperial highness?"

Tyrus sighed. His father chuckled, then sobered.

"That is the question, child. What now? Am I to rally the army? March on Fairview? Free the captives? Slaughter the rebels? I suspect that is the answer you'd like."

"Tyrus already explained why you can't do that. They'd see an army approaching and kill the hostages."

"My son knows his battle tactics well and his politics better than he'll admit. Yes, that's why I cannot march on Fairview. But there is more to it. I do not prepare the army for war because I hope to avoid war. I allow the citizens of the empire to continue on their daily business because, again, I hope to avoid war. I will avoid war in any way I can, short of handing over the imperial throne. That includes the sacrifice of Edgewood's children and the citizens of Fairview."

Moria's head shot up. "Did you say . . . ?"

"Yes, I did. War would kill thousands. It would ruin the lives and destroy the homes of tens of thousands. Would I allow a few hundred to die to avoid that?" He met her gaze. "Yes, I would. Make no mistake, child. I will do what I can to save those children and that village, but my eye is on the rest of my empire. On stopping Alvar Kitsune and whatever sorcery he works before he captures more villages."

He paused, then continued, "You've no doubt heard Tyrus say he does not aspire to any high office. Part of that

46

is self-preservation, but part is this, too—emperors and marshals must make decisions that Tyrus could not. He has a good heart, a pure heart. He takes after his mother in that. He will make a great warrior someday. A great commander. But not an emperor. Not a marshal."

Moria snuck another look at Tyrus, but he kept his face averted. Anger flared in her as she looked back at the emperor.

"You think I ought not to speak of him like that in front of him," he said.

"Yes, I do."

Again, Tyrus cleared his throat. Again, his father only chuckled.

"You mean well, son, but she'll speak her mind as long as she has a tongue to do it with, and if she didn't, she'd still speak it with her eyes. She objects because she feels I insult you. You may even feel insulted. But you will do great things, and you will live to do them, which matters more to me than that you should be suited to a throne you would never see. The empire is built on great warriors. It can always use more of those, and fewer men vying to be emperor or marshal." He paused. "Speaking of uses for warriors, I have a task for you, Tyrus. Your first military assignment."

Tyrus shot to attention, his dual swords rattling. "Yes, my lord father?"

"I will dispatch no more spies to Fairview. It is time to send an envoy. One they will see coming, but one that is small enough to be of no threat. One that bears royal blood."

"You wish me to accompany it?"

"Sending your older brothers would insult Alvar, implying

47

that they are speaking for me. Sending you says I take the threat seriously and wish to open direct negotiations between myself and Alvar, and send you to arrange for them."

"You said he would not negotiate," Moria said.

"He won't. But it is only right for me to attempt it. I will send a convoy with my son and with the Keeper of Edgewood, presuming she wishes to go."

Now Moria straightened. "Yes, I do."

"Your sister, too, if she wishes. You brought Alvar's message, so you will return it. He sent you here accompanied by his son. I will send you back accompanied by mine. It is an honorable move. When you reach Fairview, you and Tyrus can accomplish what my spies could not."

"Assess the situation," Tyrus murmured. "Confirm that the children and villagers live, determine where they are being held and how one might free them."

His father smiled. "Precisely."

Emperor Tatsu had asked Tyrus to walk Moria and Daigo back to their quarters. As they crossed the palace grounds, she began to wonder if Tyrus had agreed only because he could not refuse. He'd been silent since they left the emperor's quarters.

When they reached the gate between the court and palace grounds, she said, "I can find my way from here."

He brushed off her words with a distracted wave, following beside her but still not speaking. Daigo bumped her hand, as if in sympathy.

Once they were out of the guards' earshot, she said, "I'm sorry."

He glanced over then, and it took a moment for his eyes to focus, as if he'd been lost in some other realm.

She continued, "I broke every rule of decorum, speaking to the emperor like that. But you were the one I hurt by digging us both into a hole. I don't blame you for being angry."

A faint smile touched his lips. "I think you've spent too much time with—" He bit off the sentence before saying Gavril's name. "If hearing you speak your mind upset me, I'd hardly have lasted a day in your company. I expect no less. I'm not angry, Moria. If I was, you'd know it. You don't need to search for nuances with me. If it seems as if I'm thinking, that's truly all I'm doing. Thinking about what my father said about the children and the villagers. And thinking of the trip to come, and whether he may be underestimating his enemy."

"You fear it's not safe."

He hesitated, then said, with obvious reluctance, "I do."

"Your father wouldn't put you at risk."

"It's not me I'm thinking of, Moria. Yes, you can take care of yourself. But you are a Keeper and unnecessary risk is still unnecessary."

"You think that sending me is unnecessary."

"Yes, I do. I've been quiet because you'll not appreciate my saying so, and because going along is what you'll want."

"I must go. Your father insists."

"That doesn't make it easier," he said softly.

She nodded. "You ought to go back to your quarters and prepare." A wry smile. "You'll be stuck with me soon enough."

His gaze met hers. "There is no one I'd rather be stuck with."

Moria tried to drop her eyes. She knew that's what she ought to do. Shyly look away. But it was all she could do not to move toward him, to take that first step herself, see if he'd reciprocate, if he'd reach out and—

"It grows late," Tyrus said, backing up. "You'll need to speak to Ashyn quickly. We depart at dawn, and my father brooks no delays."

ASHYN

SEVEN

Moria was gone. She'd mumbled something about possibly spending the evening with Tyrus but had said nothing more on the matter. Then, Ashyn had returned from the library to find their quarters empty and dark. There'd been a note.

I went out. Don't wait up.

That was it. Six words. Ashyn did not expect more. These days, even when Moria was in the room with her, she seemed not truly there—at least not as the brash, boisterous sister Ashyn knew. If their father were with them, he'd scarcely recognize Moria. Of course, if their father had been there, Moria would have less cause to be so unrecognizable.

They were orphans now. More than orphans—young women without a home or family, having only each other and an uncertain future. Life was not kind to those without kin.

Ashyn knew better than to broach these fears with her sister. If Moria hadn't realized their predicament, Ashyn wouldn't add to her burden by telling her.

That burden was already great. Whatever Ashyn had gone through, it was a pale shadow of her sister's travails. Both had walked through their village after the massacre, but Ronan had protected Ashyn from catching more than glimpses of the horrors. Gavril had not shielded Moria—he'd known better than to try. Both girls had lost their father, but it was Moria who'd found him, possessed by a shadow stalker, and been forced to kill him to escape. Both girls had journeyed across the Wastes, separated from each other. Moria had faced down a thunder hawk—*twice*. Ashyn? She'd gotten a smattering of death worm venom on her skin, leaving burns so minor they'd all but vanished by the next day.

The worst of it, of course, was Gavril himself. Ashyn remembered seeing them fighting mercenaries together, back to back, and where before she'd always failed to comprehend beauty in battle, she'd seen it then, in her sister and Gavril. He was a true match for her matchless sister. Even if Moria refused to entertain thoughts of more than friendship, when Ashyn watched them together, it was like looking through a scrying glass and seeing the summers fly past, the two of them together, happily bickering and battling into old age.

Then came the revelation. The betrayal so incredible Ashyn's breath stopped even thinking of it. As difficult as it was for her, it was devastating for Moria. She had trusted Gavril. Defended him. It was as if he'd turned in battle and sunk his blade into her back.

Moria was broken, and as desperately as Ashyn wanted to be the one who put her back together, the only person whose company Moria accepted these days was Tyrus. A young man she'd met six days ago. Moria didn't discuss with him her father's death or the village slaughter or Gavril's betrayal, so there was no cause for jealousy. Yet Ashyn still felt those pangs.

She heard footfalls on the cobbled path outside. Tova rose first, going to the door. Ashyn slipped to the window. It was Moria and Daigo. With Tyrus. In the beginning, to her shame, she'd searched for darkness in him, almost hoping to see it—the devious bastard prince masking his ambitions under amicable smiles, manipulating the vulnerable young Keeper to his advantage. In a bard's tale, that was exactly what he'd be. In life, though? There was nothing dark in Tyrus. Nothing false.

She watched them, Tyrus whispering to Moria, his head bowed over hers as she pulled her cloak hood down to listen. He said something that made Moria smile and that dagger of jealousy dug deeper.

She only smiles for him.

Ashyn balled her fists. *Stop that.*

Moria said her good nights and headed inside. Tyrus watched her go. Even after she'd passed into her quarters, he stared after her before wrenching his gaze away and plodding off into the dark, none of the usual jaunt in his step.

"Good, you're still up," Moria said.

Ashyn watched as her sister swept in, kicking off her boots, sloughing her cloak, Daigo grumbling as it landed on him before sliding to the floor. And it was like being back in Edgewood, the old Moria sauntering in after an adventure.

"I have news," she said, and for perhaps the first time since Gavril's betrayal, she smiled at her sister.

Once Ashyn recovered from her heart palpitations—she couldn't believe Moria had been caught spying on the *emperor*—she calmed and listened. With every word Moria said, Ashyn felt like she was exhaling after holding her breath. While she'd never doubted that the emperor was doing something, she'd quietly shared her sister's opinion that it seemed too little. This news came as a relief. Until Moria told her who'd be the envoys.

"You and Tyrus?" Ashyn said. "While I logically follow his reasoning, it seems . . ."

Coldly logical. Like admitting he would sacrifice the children and the villagers to protect the empire. She understood it, but could not fathom making such a choice herself.

She'd seen Emperor Tatsu's warmth and affection for his son. Now to send him as an envoy after two spies had presumably perished? While she agreed the risk was much smaller, it was still a risk.

"Do you have a choice?" As soon as Ashyn said the words and saw her sister's face, she knew it didn't matter.

"I must go," Moria said. "But you don't need to."

Ashyn went still.

Moria rose from where she'd collapsed, sprawled over cushions with Daigo, and she moved to sit beside Ashyn on the sleeping mat. Her voice softened. "You've been through enough. Tyrus and I can handle it."

Of every unintended slight Ashyn had suffered over the last six days, this one cut the deepest. Before the massacre, they'd never been separated for more than a half day.

Tyrus and I can handle it.

"I'd like to go," Ashyn said.

Moria grinned. "All right, then. If you're sure you want to give up all this"—her hand swept across the luxurious room—"for a horse and a hard pallet."

"I'm sure."

"Then start packing. We leave at dawn."

And that was it. Her sister didn't wish her to stay behind, but simply hadn't presumed she would join them. Life had changed. They were no longer children, tumbling on each other's heels. They'd not been for many summers. This was but another step down a path they couldn't avoid.

Moria rose. "We'll need to get a message to Ronan."

"Why?"

"Because he should know. I'm also hoping he'll offer to come along. He can't actually join us, of course—"

"No, he cannot. Because he has not been pardoned. He will not be until he allows us to ask for it."

"He hoped to see you today. With me. In the market."

Ashyn struggled to keep her face neutral. "The fact remains that he is a thief condemned to the Forest of the Dead, and until he seeks pardon, he is safest where he is. I'll ask you to humor me in this. Please. Until the sentence is lifted, I'd not have him in any danger, and sending him that message implies we need his help."

Moria hesitated, then nodded. "All right. I'll take that extra time to bathe. It'll be days before we have another chance."

"Fetch the water. I'll stoke the fire."

When her sister was gone, Ashyn heard a grumble and looked down at Tova, lying by her feet.

"Ronan should not be told," she said.

Tova fixed his dark eyes on her, and she squirmed under his stare. While she'd not have Ronan endangered, the truth was a little less selfless, a lot less honorable. But to admit her own troubles seemed to cheapen Moria's, as if by saying, "He hurt me," she put Ronan's betrayal on the same level as Gavril's.

When she'd first met Ronan, he'd seemed infatuated with Moria, which was no surprise. Yet as they'd traveled together, his attention had turned Ashyn's way. Before they reached the imperial city, Ronan had told her how to contact him. Then, as they parted, he'd kissed her. She was not as experienced in romantic matters as Moria, but there seemed no other way to interpret his actions. There truly did not.

After two days, she'd done as he'd said—tossed a missive over the courtyard wall, to land between it and a neighboring building.

It was a simple *I'd like to see you.* His reply came a day later: *I don't think that's wise.*

No explanation. No apology. A cool refusal, as if she were some starry-eyed village girl asking him to the Fire Festival.

While that had stung, she'd told herself she was overreacting. He merely meant what he said—that it was not wise at the time.

But then he'd agreed to see Moria, and Ashyn realized there was no excuse other than the obvious. His kiss had not been a beginning but the ending. A good-bye.

In bard songs, love was love, and when you found it, it was

forever. In life, romantic entanglements came and went, and sometimes they were not entanglements at all, but merely two people, brushing against each other before moving on.

That was what had happened here, and she ought to be mature about it. Savor the memory. Chalk it up to experience. That was certainly what Moria would do. Except, she was not Moria, and perhaps she was not all that mature, and so it hurt, and it did not seem likely to stop hurting soon.

EIGHT

The spirits bade Ashyn farewell as she left the imperial city. She heard their whispers, sometimes coming clear enough for her to catch a word or two, but often no more than circling murmurs, as much a part of her world as the wind sighing through the trees. A Seeker and Keeper did not converse directly with the ancestral spirits, as the spirit talkers could. Nor did they see them, if indeed they had form that could be seen, which Ashyn doubted.

The spirits did not serve the Seeker and Keeper. The Seeker and Keeper served the spirits. Ashyn was responsible for rituals and ceremonies to put them at peace. Moria protected the ancestors—and the living—from evil spirits, possessing the power to fight and banish them. Occasionally, the ancestors would demand something, like when they told Moria to give Ronan her dagger before he went into the Forest of the Dead. Why? Well, that was where the communications ended. Demands and vague warnings only. Or greetings and farewells.

"Pointless," Moria muttered as they left the city. "How about some actual words of wisdom?"

Take care, Keeper. Be well, Seeker.

"Helpful. Very helpful." Moria looked at her. "Is it just me, or do they seem a little too happy to see us leave?"

"Thea and Ellyn are their Keeper and Seeker. We're intruders."

Moria grumbled. Ashyn had read stories of wise old women eager to impart their wisdom to the younger generation. Thea and Ellyn imparted each bit of their wisdom as if it were a tooth and soon they'd have none left. With everything that had happened, Ashyn would have loved to seek counsel with the elderly Keeper and Seeker, but they hadn't even seen the two women since the day they arrived. Were they busy preparing for Alvar's war, preparing to fight shadow stalkers? If so, shouldn't all four have been doing it together?

Ashyn sighed to herself and then looked across the convoy. She and Moria were the only women. The caravan drivers would double as staff. Six warriors rode with them, half in front and half in rear, their sword sheaths clicking in the dawn quiet. There were two counselors, bound up in their cloaks, the morning's damp still on them.

"All is well, Ashyn?" Tyrus said as he caught her gazing about.

She smiled for him. "It is," she said, and they rode from the city.

* * *

By the second day, Moria seemed ready to jump out of her skin with frustration. Their pace was slow, the days were long, and the children of Edgewood waited. When Moria snuck off with Daigo—for the third time—Tyrus stepped up his efforts to keep her entertained, calling on one warrior or another to chat with them. After the midday meal, they stopped in a village where two men were to join their group. Tyrus, Ashyn, and Moria explored while the rest of the group awaited the new arrivals.

When the caravan stopped for the night, the three of them assisted with the pitching of the tents and then rode off so Ashyn could practice at daggers without providing amusement for the warriors. The lessons alleviated Moria's frustration and, if she was being honest, Ashyn would admit the physical work-out helped hers, too. She was as eager to reach Fairview as her sister. She simply hid it better. When they returned to camp, Ashyn went on ahead, leaving Tyrus distracting Moria with a heated debate on the tactics used in the Battle of Asteth.

Ashyn reached the tents. They were tall enough for a man to walk upright inside, with dividers splitting the space for multiple sleepers. Ashyn shared one with Moria and Tyrus— the prince taking the "front room," which was considered more appropriate than allowing the girls to sleep unguarded.

When Ashyn opened the flap on what she thought was their tent, she saw the younger of the two men who'd joined them that afternoon. He sat on a cushion as he wrote on a low table.

"Oh, I'm sorry," she said. "Wrong tent."

"Actually, your timing is excellent. I'll take tea, please. And

I believe there were some honey cakes? I'll have one of those."

She let out a soft laugh. "We haven't been formally introduced. I'm—"

"It doesn't matter."

"What?"

He waved his hand. "I don't mean to be rude, but I'll never remember your name, so there's no point in giving it."

Living in Edgewood, she'd seen people from all corners of the empire—exiled convicts and traders and travelers. It was impossible to say, from appearance, where someone hailed from. There were no restrictions on movement and there was much mingling of blood, so to presume someone with pale skin lived in the North was to mark yourself an ignorant peasant. The one true indicator was accent, which she was proficient at deciphering. This young man surely hailed from the steppes. He looked like it as well, with skin only slightly darker than hers, light brown hair, and ruddy cheeks, as if they'd been permanently burned by the steppe's legendary winds. As for whether he was handsome, it mattered little. He was rude—that canceled out any physical attractions.

"I am not a serving girl. I am Ashyn, Seeker of Edgewood."

A sharp look her way. "You ought not to play that game, girl. It might be mistaken for blasphemy."

"Game? I am—"

"And that is your Hound of the Immortals?" He waved to her empty side; Tova waited outside the tent. "I did not realize they could cloak themselves in invisibility. Is your sister invisible as well? I believe I'd have noticed twin Northern girls in camp. As someone who knows many from your home region,

61

I would suggest that you do them a disservice in concocting so preposterous a story. You will only further the stereotype of their intelligence—or lack of it. Now, my tea. Quickly or I'll report you to the wagon master." His gray eyes met hers. "I ought to do so anyway."

He turned back to his work. Ashyn withdrew from the tent. Tova was nudging the flap, as if trying to figure out how to open the ties and come to her rescue.

"I'm fine," she whispered as they walked away. "But someone is going to wait a very long time for his blasted tea and cake."

Tova looked shocked by her language. She smiled and patted his head.

"I know, but he deserved it."

"Who deserved what?" Moria asked behind her.

Ashyn turned as Moria and Tyrus caught up. Sweat streaked through the road dust on their faces and both were in desperate need of fresh tunics, but the jaunty gleam in Moria's eye kept Ashyn from moving farther downwind.

There was an extra bounce in Tyrus's step, too, and a light in his face when he looked Moria's way. She was happy, so he was happy.

He cares for her. He truly does.

"Who deserved what?" Moria repeated as they continued through the camp.

"Oh, just . . ." Ashyn fluttered her hand. "That young man who joined the caravan mistook me for a serving girl."

Moria snorted. "Idiot. You corrected him, of course."

"I tried. First, he told me not to give my name, because it's inconsequential. Then he lectured me on not furthering the intellectual stereotypes of Northerners with dim-witted tricks. I am to bring his tea and honey cakes at once. He may be waiting a while."

Tyrus laughed. Moria turned on her heel, her glare sweeping across the camp.

"That tent over there? The one we saw you exiting?"

"Yes, but—"

"Tea and honey cakes, you said?"

"Yes, but—"

Moria started toward the rations wagon. "We wouldn't want the poor boy to go hungry."

"Moria, don't—"

Tyrus caught her arm. "Let her." He leaned to her ear and whispered. "You know you want her to. And if a prince insists, you have no choice."

Ashyn and Tyrus caught up as Moria strode into the young man's tent, tea in hand.

"Finally," they heard him say. "You can put that right—"

"Here, my lord?"

The gurgle of rushing water. A shriek. Ashyn raced into the tent, thinking Moria had poured it on him. Of course, she had not. The water was boiling. She *had* poured it, though . . . onto the paper he'd been writing on.

"You stupid, clumsy—!"

"Oh, I'm sorry." She picked up a soaked page. "This wasn't important, was it?"

"You foolish girl," the young man said. "I ought to—"

"Teach me a lesson?" Moria opened her cloak, hand falling to one of her daggers. "Shall we take this outside? I'd rather a fair fight, dagger to dagger, but if you prefer a sword, I suppose that would . . ." Her gaze moved to his empty sash. "You've removed your blades? A warrior must never . . ." Her eyes widened in mock surprise. "Are you not a warrior?"

As Ashyn moved closer, Daigo reached Moria and settled in beside her. The young man looked at the wildcat.

"That is . . . You are . . ." He struggled for words, then said, "You claimed you were a Seeker," as if that erased the issue.

"I claimed nothing." Moria waved at Ashyn. "She said she was a Seeker."

He turned and saw Ashyn and gaped. Then his gaze went to the third person in the tent and he fell forward into the deepest bow one could manage without toppling.

"My lord prince. I—I had not realized—"

Tyrus cut him off. "Then I would suggest you spend less time staring at your books and more at your surroundings. It is quite impossible to miss a Wildcat of the Immortals or a Hound of the Immortals. Not to mention the fact that the only two women in our caravan are twins."

"Y-yes, your highness. I do apologize. My thoughts were elsewhere." He stepped forward. "My name is—"

"Oh, there's no need to tell me. I'll not bother to remember it."

The young man's face mottled as his gaze dropped.

"You are Simeon of Mistvale," Tyrus said. "Assistant to Katsumoto. I know who I travel with."

That rebuke seemed to cut even deeper than the first, and

Simeon stuttered an apology. Meanwhile, Moria wandered to his writing desk, peering down at the undamaged papers.

"You are a teller of stories?" she said.

Before Simeon could answer, Tyrus cut in. "Of a sort, one could say. I'm certain he'd be more than happy to entertain you with a tale tonight."

"I—" Simeon began.

"*More* than happy," Tyrus said.

Ashyn knew Katsumoto's name—he was a great scholar, not a bard. But Tyrus gave Simeon a look that forbade argument. This was the prince's lesson in making presumptions of identity.

"You'll sing our Keeper a song tonight, at the fire," he said. "I'd choose a rare one. She has quite the knowledge of tales, and you'll find she's easily bored. And when she's bored . . . you noted the daggers, I take it?"

Moria made a face at Tyrus. He smiled and waved for the girls to come out with him, leaving Simeon looking as if he'd just been ordered to commit ritual suicide.

NINE

Tyrus didn't actually make Simeon play bard. Shortly before the evening fire, he told Moria Simeon's true occupation, likely more to save her from embarrassment than Simeon. For the night's entertainment, someone played a flute, then someone sang a tale. Neither performance was expertly done, but there was no place for bards and musicians on such a journey. Moria grumbled that there was no place for frivolity at all—they should get to sleep and rise sooner. Tyrus had compromised by allowing the men this brief entertainment before declaring they'd rise at dawn and must retire sooner than usual.

Ashyn had settled her own anxieties with a tumbler of honey wine. A small tumbler, but the alcohol was enough to have her up in the night, needing to rid herself of the added liquid. She sighed and tossed and turned, hoping to rouse Moria. Moria and Daigo both slept as if dead. When she could not hold out any longer, she "accidentally" stumbled over Tyrus's legs making her way past him. He didn't stir.

It was not that she feared walking from camp after dark. It was simply . . . well, she seemed to have bad luck with it. First, on the Wastes, she'd encountered a giant scorpion. Then, between Fairview and the imperial city, she'd been taken captive by a merchant who'd hoped to sell her to a distant king.

At least she had Tova with her. When they crested a small hillock, the hound lifted his head, growling softly. There was no sign of anyone about at first, but he continued to growl until a figure slipped along the thin line of trees.

Ashyn ducked and took out her dagger. Tova hunkered with Ashyn as she flattened onto her stomach. In the distance she heard . . .

No. She tilted her head, frowning. She did not hear anything. She felt . . . It was an odd sensation, beyond description, as if she *sensed* someone calling to her.

Whatever she felt, it didn't come from the approaching figure, which had stopped twenty paces from the hillock. Tova lifted his muzzle and sniffed the air. Then he let out an annoyed chuff.

"Seeker?" a voice whispered. "Ashyn?"

It was Simeon. Ashyn barely stifled a growl of her own. She rose and made her way back down the hillock.

"You *are* there," he whispered loudly. "I thought I saw the hound leaving camp."

Tova grunted, as if apologizing to Ashyn.

"And you followed me?" she said. "You may not know court manners, but in what part of the empire is that appropriate?"

67

"I . . . I know I ought not to approach a young woman alone, but I thought with your hound in attendance, it was acceptable."

"I mean following me at night, away from the camp."

He blushed. "Yes, of course. I had not considered . . ."

That seemed to be the honest excuse in every facet of the young scholar's life. A basic ignorance of acceptable behavior. When he thought a thing, he did it. Not an uncommon failing with scholars. Brilliant at their work; lost when it came to social graces.

"Approaching an unaccompanied young woman might be frowned upon in some villages," she said, her voice softening. "It is not an issue in the city or in a group such as this. However, when you approach her at *night*, your motives could appear less than seemly."

She meant it kindly, but his blush deepened, and he stammered that he had not intended any such thing.

"I wish to apologize for my earlier behavior," he said. "There was no excuse."

"Accepted," she said.

He continued—still apologizing, it seemed—but her attention was only half on him, the rest tugged again by her surroundings.

It's a spirit, she thought. *That's what I feel, though it's unlike any I've encountered.*

In the distance, she detected a faint light, suggesting another camp.

"Ashyn?"

"I'm sorry," she said. "I thought I heard something."

She immediately regretted the lie. He stiffened and reached for . . . Well, he reached for nothing. He was not warrior caste. He could not carry a blade. Instead his hands clenched, and he straightened awkwardly, his gaze sweeping across the land.

"It's just some small creature," she said. "Tova would warn me if—"

The hound sniffed the air and growled.

Ashyn adjusted her dagger. "We ought to get back."

Tova seconded that with a louder growl. Simeon stared into the night. When she nudged him, he jumped so high one would think she'd pulled him in for a kiss.

"Go," she whispered. "I'm behind you."

He nodded. "Yes, I ought to lead the way."

She did not correct him, but she was taking the rear because she was the one with a dagger, and the danger was *behind* them.

The moment they began walking, a cry rang out. A cry of alarm, followed by running footsteps. Ashyn wheeled, her dagger raised, Tova crouched to spring.

She saw a figure, shadowy in the moonlight, arms and legs akimbo. A second figure chased it, fast and silent, tackling the first like a wildcat taking down a deer. The sounds of struggle ensued, the besieged figure yelping in terror as the attacker pinned him to the ground.

Ashyn ran toward them, ignoring Simeon's cries of "No!" and "Stay here!" While it was possible that both figures had been chasing her, it seemed far more likely that she'd just been rescued, presumably by a warrior guard.

As she drew near, she slowed. Even from a distance, she

could see her rescuer was not a warrior. Despite holding a sword, he wore a peasant's garb: a simple tunic, trousers, and sandals. He was young and wiry, with black curls falling around his face as he bent over the prone man.

He glanced up, and she recognized the shadow-shrouded shape of his features.

"Ronan?" she said. "What are you doing here?"

"Keeping the world safe for you to piss in," he said. "Apparently, it's a full-time job."

She couldn't tell if he was teasing or grumbling. Probably a little of both.

"At least this time you had the sense to bring a guard with you," he continued, waving at the approaching figure of Simeon. Then Ronan's eyes narrowed. "That's not a warrior. Who is he and what is he doing out here with you, in the middle of the night?"

Simeon strode over. "The question, boy, is who are you? And why are you wielding a blade when you are obviously no warrior yourself?"

"Boy?"

"Actually," Ashyn cut in, "I think the more pressing question is: who is *he*?"

She pointed to the man beneath Ronan. He was rotund and at least in his fifth decade. She could not judge caste by his attire—it wasn't fine enough to be a merchant's, rough enough to be a farmer's, or elegant enough to be an artisan's, and he lacked a warrior's blades. His feet were bare, which was odd, given the chilly night, but more than that, the bottoms of his feet were blackened, the flesh burned and healed over.

"A penitent," Simeon murmured. "A fire walker."

Ashyn struggled against letting her distaste show. It was not the empire's practice to impose its faith on its people. Most religions, though, including this one, were still offshoots of their core beliefs.

It was commonly accepted that all living things had a spirit. The essence of life flowed endlessly around them. All spirits deserved their respect. Ancestral spirits deserved their devotion and in return, would protect and bless them. If negative spirits meant them harm, it was not through ill will but a misalignment of balance. They had been wronged—or felt themselves wronged—and lashed out in retaliation. Every effort should be made to correct the imbalance before resorting to banishment. The spirits needed care and kindness and respect. They did not, however, need fear or groveling or debasement.

Yet some religions felt that the spirits' anger was more terrible, their forgiveness more reserved. Enlightenment required suffering. That was certainly the view of the penitents. Some walked on hot coals. Others used flagellation, starvation, or isolation. While Ashyn had been raised to accept religious beliefs beyond her own, she struggled with the penitents. Even after all she'd seen, she did not believe the spirit world demanded human suffering. If anything, suffering seemed to dishonor them—rejecting the fullness of the world the spirits had created.

"Why did you come after us?" she asked.

"I came for you, my lady Ashyn, Seeker of Edgewood."

The man could not bow lying prone, so he pressed his face into the ground, hard enough to make her wince.

"Let him rise, please, Ronan."

Ronan did but kept his blade on the man, warning him not to approach the Seeker. Ashyn doubted the warning was necessary. The man fairly shook with servitude, his eyes pointed straight down, as if even gazing on her feet would be unseemly.

"You know me," she said.

"Of course, my lady. We know of all the Seekers and Keepers. By name and by description. To serve the world of the spirits? We can only dream of such glory. The emperor himself ought to bow—"

She cleared her throat in alarm. "We serve the empire, and the emperor is the physical embodiment of it."

"Well-spoken for one so young."

"It's past midnight," Ronan said. "We are a half day's walk from the nearest town. Perhaps you could save the flattery, and tell us why you're stalking the Seeker."

"I was not stalking her. We passed a caravan that spoke of your expedition. It was as if the ancestors themselves had answered our pleas. We rode back to search for the camp. The spirits guided me here, where I saw her." He lifted his gaze as far as Ashyn's knees. "We need your help, my lady. We have somehow angered the spirits. I suspect one of our order has been negligent in his penance."

"I very much doubt—"

"It is something, my lady," he said, lurching with the emphasis. "Something terrible. An omen. A portent. We do not know. But it is the work of evil spirits. Our caravan is just over that ridge. If you could please come and speak—"

"No, she cannot," Ronan said. "I don't know what trickery—"

"Trickery?" the man sputtered. "I am with the Order of Kushin."

He shot his arm out from his sleeve. It was covered with circular scars, so thick and ugly that Ashyn couldn't imagine what had made them . . . and would prefer not to try.

"Kushin are the most respected order of penitent monks," Simeon said. "We ought to aid them if we can."

"I don't care who they are," Ronan said. "I don't trust anyone who asks Ashyn to follow him into the night. Only a fool would suggest she obey."

"Fool?" Simeon bristled. "I am a scholar under Master—"

"A scholar? Well, that explains it." Ronan turned to Ashyn. "We'll let the scholar investigate. You need to get back to camp."

The monk pleaded. Something was wrong, dreadfully wrong. As for exactly what, he wouldn't say, only growing agitated and telling them he'd explain as they walked.

"I'll crest the ridge," she said. "If I see no caravan, this young man will escort you back to the prince to explain yourself."

TEN

"How much do you know of penitents, my lady?" the monk asked as they walked.

More than I want, she thought, but said only, "Some."

Simeon explained, "Penitents believe that the path to enlightenment lies through suffering—"

"We don't need a religion lesson," Ronan cut in. "We need to know what's over the ridge."

"Have you been to the shrine near Westerfox, my lady?" the monk asked.

"Until a fortnight ago, I had not left Edgewood since arriving before my first summer."

"Of course, because it guards the Forest of the Dead," the monk said. "There are many shrines, my lady. For pilgrims and those seeking spiritual guidance. The one near Westerfox is particularly sacred to penitents. That is where one might see our deepest, most holy form of penance. The mummies."

Simeon sucked in breath. "Yes, of course. The Order of Kushin—"

"Let the old man tell his story," Ronan said.

"Have you heard of our mummies, my lady?" the monk asked.

"No, but I understand the basic concept, as it is practiced in the desert regions. On death, the body is exposed, and the heat dries it."

"True, that is their custom. With us, as monks near the end of life, if they do not feel they are close enough to enlightenment, they begin refusing food. Then they start drinking a special tea, which slowly poisons them and preserves their body as it withers from lack of nourishment."

"They mummify themselves?" Ronan said. "While they're still alive?"

"When they are nearing the end, they are placed in a special box, dry and heated to create a desert-like environment. Inside is a bell that they ring several times a day. When the bell no longer rings, the box is sealed and transported to the shrine. If the spirits have shown favor, when the box is opened, the monk is mummified. He is then dressed in fine clothing and placed on display, so that pilgrims may reflect on his sacrifice."

"That is the stupidest—" Ronan began, but he was silenced by Ashyn stepping on his foot.

"That is the purpose of your journey, then?" she said. "You are transporting these . . . potential mummies?"

"To Westerfox, yes. It is a long and slow procession, but we do it each spring. This time, we bring four boxes."

His voice lifted, as if this were some great accomplishment, and Ashyn dutifully murmured her congratulations, while secretly agreeing with Ronan. To mummify oneself while still alive? Surely that could not honor the spirits.

The group crested the ridge. Below were two wagons—basic, open affairs, each bearing two coffin-like boxes. Two men huddled around a fire. Both were dressed like the monk—in simple clothing and no shoes. Their camp lay on open ground, with no trees or rocks nearby large enough to conceal attackers.

Ashyn started down the hill. Ronan prompted the monk again to explain the situation.

"It is . . . difficult," the monk said.

"Try."

"I do not mean that I am loath to do so, but that I know what I have to say will be difficult to believe. It would appear . . . that is to say . . ." He turned to Ashyn as they walked. "The bells have rung again."

"The bells . . . ?"

"Inside the boxes. The boxes were sealed and yet the bells ring. Even when the horses are at rest."

Dread crept into Ashyn's gut, but she forced it from her voice. "You say, then, that you believe the men within the boxes live."

"Yes, as impossible as that is."

"It's not impossible at all," Simeon said. "There are ailments that make the victim appear dead, unconscious sometimes for days. Coupled with the mediocre diagnostic skills of the average village healer, it is not surprising that many cultures have incorporated certain checks and balances in their funerary customs, such as laying out the corpse for three nights or—"

"Just say it's possible," Ronan said. "I'd like to get this over with before dawn."

"The young scholar is correct," the monk said. "That is why we do not seal the box as soon as the bell stops ringing. These are not men who perished a few days ago. The newest stopped ringing his bell a moon past. And the oldest stopped last summer."

"It is not possible that they live," Simeon said. "There is a malfunction of the bells. Perhaps earth tremors."

"It is . . . more than the bells," the monk said carefully.

His gaze flitted toward the camp. Beside Ashyn, Tova growled. When she strained to listen, she could catch the sound . . .

Scratching. She heard a dry, rustling scratching. Then a thump.

She glanced at Ronan and saw his face pale. Simeon continued to insist that what the monk feared was, quite simply, impossible. The dead did not wake. At least, not the long dead.

Simeon knew nothing of what had transpired in Edgewood. To those in the convoy, it had been explained that Ashyn's village had been beset by a fatal outbreak of illness, which may have spread to Fairview and may not have been a natural occurrence.

Ashyn turned to Simeon. "I must investigate these claims. However, I fear they arise from duplicity. Not the monks, of course. But someone may be tricking them for nefarious purposes, and this ought to be brought to the attention of Prince

Tyrus. I need you to go to him now and tell him what has happened."

"You wish me to wake the prince?"

"You have nothing to fear from Tyrus. Tell him and my sister what has happened and have them come back here with you."

"Should I not ask a warrior to rouse him?"

"Are you questioning the Seeker?" Ronan snapped.

"The young man is correct," the monk said. "To question her will is to question the will of the spirits themselves. It is akin to blasphemy."

"Please," Ashyn said.

That plea worked. He left after she enjoined him to speak to no one else of this. "There are many superstitious folks in the empire," she said. "I'd not wish to start outrageous rumors of resurrected mummies."

Once he was gone, they continued down the hill. Soon it was impossible not to hear the sounds from the boxes—the scrapes and scratches and thuds and bumps.

"I fear their bodies have been possessed by evil spirits," the monk said. "Though I've not heard of such a thing outside of nannies' tales."

As they reached camp, the men at the fire rose, and their monk hurried forward to explain, leaving Ashyn and Ronan staring at the boxes.

"They're moving," Ashyn whispered.

"Hmm." Ronan moved closer and lowered his lips to her ear. "Shadow stalkers?"

"I . . . I don't think so. Shadow stalkers take the form of

that dark smoke to enter bodies, and they can leave it the same way. Why stay in those boxes?"

"Hoping someone will open them?"

"But no one has."

"And we'll not do it either," he said.

"I believe we must look—"

"I said we'll not."

She glanced at him. "Were you not just chastising Simeon for questioning my decisions?"

"Simeon? Is that his name?" A derisive snort. Then his dark eyes narrowed. "I don't believe you ever explained why you were with him in the first place."

"No, I did not." She stepped toward the monks as they approached. The one who'd brought them performed introductions. His own name was Ivo. The other two monks barely stayed long enough for Ashyn to greet them properly before they slipped back to the fire. They'd spoken not a word. Silence was part of their penance, Ivo explained, as he led Ashyn to the boxes.

"Can they be opened?" she asked.

Ivo stared as if she'd asked him to crawl into one. "I do not believe that's necessary, my lady. If you were simply to placate the spirits, they would leave the bodies, without any need to look within."

"But if I do that, how do we understand what has happened?"

Ivo's expression said he could live the remainder of his days quite happily without ever knowing.

Ashyn continued, "Do you not think we ought to bear

witness? Otherwise, if we are to tell someone, they will think we were duped."

"Is there any need to tell someone?" Ivo said.

"Yes. An occurrence such as this must be documented."

"The Seeker wants a box opened," Ronan said. "Stop arguing and open one."

"They are sealed and—"

"You said you open them at the shrine. It's easily done then. Just pry off a lid."

ELEVEN

At first, Ivo claimed they had no tools. But after some arguing, one of the other monks came over with a strong shovel. Apparently, withdrawing into silence did not prevent one from eavesdropping.

As Ronan worked at the lid, Ashyn asked Ivo the route they'd taken from their monastery. It was as she feared—they'd passed so close to Fairview that they'd seen the shimmering white town beyond the wall. They'd not entered nor even drawn close, having been warned of an illness there.

When Moria arrived with Tyrus, she said to Ronan, "You? What are you doing here?" proving she had not secretly sent him a message.

"It's good to see you, too, Moria."

She turned to Ashyn. "We left Simeon behind, but he said something about mummies. Penitent monks who mistakenly believe their dead are about to rise—"

A fresh scratching sounded from the box.

"That is, apparently, the mummy," Ashyn said. "I've asked Ronan to open the box to confirm it."

The thing within began to thump on the lid.

Moria glanced at her sister. "Unless they've accidentally interred giant rats, I think we can safely say it's the mummy."

"I would agree." Tyrus moved toward the box, paying no attention to the monks dropping into the dirt at his approach. "But Ashyn is right. We must confirm it." He glanced at Ashyn. "Are there any preparations we should make before it opens?"

"Yes, of course," she said. "I ought to begin the rituals of soothing."

Ashyn whispered ancient words to acknowledge and soothe the spirits. Beside her, Moria stood at alert, ready to use her own power of banishment, should something evil arise from that box. Ronan prepared to open the lid while Tyrus moved in on the other side, taking hold.

When it seemed as if whatever lay in the box was calming— the scratches and thumps fewer and weaker—Moria nodded and Ashyn said, "Now. Open the box."

The young men heaved on the stone lid. It rose half a hand, and Ashyn peered in.

"We need a lantern," Moria said.

As Ivo scuttled off, Moria told the young men to hold the lid until a light could be brought.

"We'll try," Tyrus grunted. "This isn't exactly as light as silk."

"Set it back down then. We just need to get a glimpse inside before the opening's big enough for the thing to spring out."

"It's a bag of dried bones," Ronan said. "I don't think it'll be doing much—"

The lid flew off. A gust hit Ashyn with the force of a blow, dust and dirt blinding her, and she reeled back, hands going to her face as she coughed. She heard a curse. An oath. Then a thud and a yowl. She forced her eyes open and saw Tyrus and Ronan on the ground, the stone lid atop Ronan's leg. She raced over to pull it off. Tyrus sprang up to do the same. The first in motion, though, was Moria, sprinting to . . . look in the box.

"Your help is vastly appreciated," Ronan grunted to Moria.

"If your leg's broken, moving the lid faster will hardly help."

Tyrus heaved it off, with Ashyn doing what she could. As they helped Ronan to his feet, Moria said, "Blast it!"

Ashyn glanced over.

"That wind was the spirit escaping," Moria said.

Tyrus got Ronan upright, then walked over beside Moria. "Huh. Well, the good news is that the mummification process was successful. The bad news is that I doubt the monks will want to display this fellow at the shrine."

"That's what they do?" Moria said. "Display them?"

"Yes. Mummified monks posed on cushions and at writing desks and taking tea. It's quite macabre. I'll have to take you there sometime. But the better ones are the shrines near Violetmere, with mummified demons."

"Demons?"

Before Tyrus could explain, Ashyn and Ronan approached the box. In the bottom lay the monk. While Ashyn had read about mummification, that did not prepare her to see it. *This* looked like a demon, a profane mockery of human form.

The thing was wizened into what could best be described—though the analogy upset her stomach—as dried meat. The limbs were twisted and deformed. The head was a discolored skull with bulging yellow teeth and matted hair.

The worst, though, was the proof that the monk had indeed been alive moments ago. The dried lips were peeled back in a soundless scream. The eyes—sunken and withered—were wide. Both arms were outstretched, the hands like claws, the fingertips broken off from scratching at the stone lid.

A spirit had possessed this body. Been thrust into it as a side effect of whatever magics Alvar Kitsune was using at Fairview. Someone had died—perhaps at the hands of Alvar's men—and the spirit, roaming, not yet ready to cross into the second world, had been thrust into the nearest vessel: this interred horror.

"The other boxes," Ashyn said quickly. "We must open the others and free—"

The mummy twitched. Ashyn stopped. They all stared as the thing went still and silent again.

"Did it just—?" Tyrus began.

The mummy hurled itself at him. Even as her eyes saw it happen, Ashyn's mind could not comprehend it. For that "bag of bones" to sit up would seem an impossibility. But to fly from the box, leaping on Tyrus, arms and legs scrabbling . . .

Ronan fumbled with his blade as the thing knocked Tyrus off his feet and fell on him like a dervish, clawing and kicking.

Moria did not hesitate. She grabbed the mummy by the back of its tattered tunic, shouting "Begone, spirit!" But the thing clung to Tyrus, now scrambling to its feet as it beat at him. Tyrus pulled his blade but there was nothing he could do with it—the mummy had one arm wrapped around his neck as it hung off him. He sheathed his sword and grabbed that arm instead, heaving at it as Moria continued to pull on the tunic and command the spirit to leave.

Tyrus could not unclench the mummy's grip, and when Moria grew frustrated and yanked harder, the fabric tore in her hands, sending her staggering back. Ronan had his blade out then and rushed for the thing, but the beasts were there first. Tova grabbed a leg. Daigo made the mistake of doing what wildcats do with prey—leaping onto its back and going for the neck. The jolt of Daigo's landing knocked Tyrus down again.

Ashyn had recovered from the shock and was speaking to the spirit within the mummy. She promised they meant it no harm and apologized for what had happened. Neither assurance was particularly convincing—not when two very large beasts bit at the mummy and one very angry Keeper shouted at it. It was also admittedly difficult to apologize when the mummy was the one causing the trouble. But Ashyn thought of that poor, twisted thing in the box, of the horror the spirit must have experienced, and she focused on that, telling it that freedom was close, the second world was close, its suffering was almost at an end.

She'd like to think her words loosened its resolve and calmed its fevered panic. But she acknowledged that Moria— snarling at it to be gone and pummeling it with spiritual energy—probably played a greater role in its eventual decision to depart. There was, again, a rush of wind. Then the mummified remains fell still.

Tyrus pushed the mummy off him and rose, whisking sloughed bits of dried flesh from his tunic.

"Well, that wasn't at all humiliating," he said. "Please tell me I didn't shriek. And if I did? Remember I am of imperial lineage. Lie to me."

"You didn't shriek," Moria said. "Still, it is a shame Simeon wasn't here to record the encounter for posterity. Prince Tyrus, attacked by a mummified monk. Truly, though, it looked more like a monkey. A crazed monkey, clinging to you—"

"Enough," he said with a feigned scowl. "Speaking of monks, did they see . . . ?"

He looked around. Ivo had sidled off as they opened the box. Now he huddled with the other two a hundred paces away.

"Well, at least they didn't bear *close* witness," Tyrus muttered.

"You needn't worry," Ashyn said. "Two of them have taken vows of silence."

"Though they might have been tempted to break them," Moria said. "To relay that particular story."

"But I did not shriek, correct?"

She smiled. "You did not shriek." Her gaze swept over him. "That thing didn't bite you, did it?"

Her tone had Tyrus touching his face, eyes widening in alarm. "I don't think so. A bite doesn't turn one into a shadow stalker, does it?"

"That would be ridiculous," Moria said. "I meant that being bitten by any dead thing cannot be healthy. But I don't think we're dealing with shadow stalkers either. Not the sort we've seen."

She glanced at Ashyn, who nodded and said, "I suspect it's a . . ." She looked at the distant monks and lowered her voice. "A related incident. If Alvar is using such strong spirit-based magics, side effects could be expected."

Moria nodded. "Alvar raises shadow stalkers and disturbs the natural process of death and passage to the second world, trapping spirits in this realm and forcing them to seek other habitation."

"I'm not sure they seek it." Ashyn looked at the broken mummy and shuddered. "I cannot imagine voluntarily trapping oneself in that."

"Which begs the question," Tyrus said. "Why return when it had been freed? We felt the spirit leave. It fled the moment it could. And then returned?"

"I don't think it actually—"

The mummy twitched. This time, both Ronan and Tyrus leaped on it, blades slashing. Ronan severed an arm. Tyrus cleaved the corpse clean in half, the legs falling free. Yet the thing was already in flight, hurtling itself at Moria . . . who skewered it on the end of her outthrust dagger. She held it there, casually, as the mummy gnashed its teeth and clawed with its remaining arm.

"Need some help with that?" Tyrus asked.

"No, it's remarkably light. That must be a result of the drying process."

"And the fact it's missing three limbs."

"True."

Ashyn cast a nervous glance at the huddled monks, now shifting and looking their way. "We ought to lower our voices. Or be more respectful. It is a monk, after all."

"Mmm, not truly," Moria said. "It's only part of a monk." She caught Ashyn's look. "Yes, I know. Give me a hand getting it free."

Ashyn looked aghast at the mummy, and Moria sputtered a laugh.

"I mean the spirit," she said.

Ashyn started her entreaties, while Moria ordered the spirit gone. It didn't take long before the wind came, signaling the spirit's departure.

"Now let's hope it stays gone this time," Ronan said.

Ashyn cleared her throat. "Actually, as I was trying to say, I don't think the spirit returned." She pointed at the sealed box next to the open one. "That one's been quiet since the first attack. And now I'll wager one of those two"—she pointed at the boxes on the other wagon—"is quiet."

Tyrus nodded. "Because those spirits hopped into this fellow."

"They can apparently jump bodies on their own, but cannot move to the second world without help. I think the attacks were more panic than anything. Realizing they'd leaped, only to still not be free."

"So let's help the last one," Moria said. "Ronan? Pry open that fourth box. I'll guard this"—she indicated the hacked-up mummy—"in case he makes the jump. Ashyn? Can you go with Ronan and perform the rituals? If we can do this without me bullying the spirit, that's best."

"And my task?" Tyrus asked.

"I would not presume to give you one, your highness."

Tyrus laughed. "Which means you don't have anything for me to do. I'll help Ronan. Shout if that comes back to life."

"I think I can handle it."

He grinned. "I've no doubt."

They laid the last spirit to rest without incident. Then Tyrus spoke to the monks. He told them that he had no idea what had happened, but it was resolved now and they ought not to speak of it to anyone until he'd related the events to his imperial father.

Moria went with Tyrus, leaving Ronan and Ashyn alone.

"I suppose you'll be scuttling off into the shadows again," she said.

He tensed as if he didn't like her choice of words. Then he motioned for her and Tova to follow him farther away so they could speak.

"What *are* you doing here?" she asked when they neared the ridge base.

"Tyrus hired me to accompany you."

"Oh." That was, of course, not what she'd hoped to hear.

"You ought to have told me you were leaving the city," he said.

"Then you ought to have accepted my request for an audience, so I could have explained the situation."

He paused. "Was that what you wished to see me about? I thought . . ." He inhaled. "When I left. That kiss. I . . . I feared how you might have interpreted it."

She said nothing. She couldn't. It was hard enough to stand

there, listening to her fears made real.

"We had been together for days," he continued. "I came to care for you, but . . . it was not the sort of caring that my kiss implied. I apologize for that."

Ashyn clenched her hands at her sides. *Stop talking. Please stop talking.*

"You're a wonderful girl, Ashyn. You're brilliant and you're beautiful and you're . . ." He trailed off, as if he could find no more adjectives to flatter her with.

Stop talking now. Please.

He continued. "I *do* care for you. But I feared that after my kiss, you may have expected more."

She gathered all her strength and lifted her gaze to his. "Truly? Do you think I've never been kissed before? I'm past my sixteenth summer. I took it as nothing more than a farewell. Perhaps foolishly over-affectionate, which did make me fear *you* might have meant more, but I'm glad to hear you did not. I am the Seeker of Edgewood. You are . . ."

As hurt as she was, she couldn't bring herself to say the rest. *You're a thief. A criminal.* Ronan still recoiled, his gaze lowering, but not before she caught a glimpse of pain.

I may have no experience with kisses, but he lies if he says that was a simple farewell. He changed his mind, and he does not have the integrity to be honest with me. He makes me feel the fool. So I'll not retract my words.

He didn't look at her as he said, "Whatever you were about to say, I am that. And more. Or, perhaps, less. I . . ." He closed his mouth, paused, and then said, "Do you wish me to return to the city? Or continue along to Fairview?"

"Why do you ask me?" she snapped. "You came for money not—" She bit off the words, but it was too late. His gaze swung to her eyes and she knew he'd caught the anger in them, the hurt.

"Ashyn . . ." he said.

"Do as you will," she said and walked away with Tova.

TWELVE

They'd stopped for their midday meal. While Moria hated the pause, the horses needed the break, and she would never argue to overwork the horses.

Tyrus and Moria sat away from the others, ostensibly giving Daigo a chance to prowl the nearby woods, though in truth Moria had suggested it because she suspected Tyrus needed a break from playing the amicable prince. He always took time to ride with the others, out of both imperial responsibility and natural camaraderie, but that morning, it had seemed more of the first. Now, as they ate, he lapsed into silence, idly fingering the dangling ends of his amulet band.

"Thinking of your mother?" Moria asked between mouthfuls of cold rice.

He glanced up, as if startled.

She nodded at the band, then said, "You've been quiet since the monks, and I noticed you watching when we passed the

road to Seven Oaks. That's where she's gone on h[...]
isn't it?"

A faint smile. "Excellent deduction. Yes, I w[...]
she'll be home soon, and she will not be pleased with[...]
He's been talking about sending me on a mission [...] the
winter. She asked him to wait until I passed my next summer."

"And you've wanted to go sooner."

"I have, which makes me glad she wasn't there. Not that
she could have stopped my father from sending me but . . . It's
awkward."

"You're her only child, and you're constantly in danger.
She fears adding to that. And you fear having to tell her you're
ready."

"Hmm." He stretched out his legs and squinted toward the
forest until he caught sight of Daigo. Then he looked back at
Moria. "I don't like causing friction between her and my father.
It's a difficult enough relationship as it is."

"Because she's a concubine, not a wife. Yet she's also the
mother of an imperial prince."

"It isn't an easy life, and there are times . . ." He rubbed
the back of his neck. "To solidify his position, an emperor must
make choices that I personally disagree with. The taking of
concubines is one. Fathering sons by them is another. Yet the
concubines allow political alliances that the empire requires
and the children provide additional heirs and bolster his reputation for virility, which is important. For a warrior to be
unable to have children, preferably sons . . ."

Moria remembered Gavril saying he was his father's only
child, despite three successive marriages. That had reflected

93

ᴾoorly on Alvar Kitsune, particularly compared to the emperor's brood. It excused nothing, but it might help explain the resentment that had grown between the two friends.

"It would be difficult," she said carefully, "to see your mother suffer for choices your father had to make."

"It is. There's a reason I'm her only child. She has . . . avoided having others."

"By avoiding your father's sleeping pallet?" Moria paused. "Or is that an indiscreet question? I think Ashyn would say it is."

Tyrus laughed softly, relaxing as he leaned back, his ponytail brushing the ground. "With an emperor, such matters are as open as his daily schedule. If you listen to court gossip, you will hear that he has indeed not visited my mother's quarters in seventeen summers. Which, I suspect, is true. They don't meet at her quarters. Or at his."

"Ah."

"Yes, if you recall when you first arrived, my mother was on her pilgrimage and my father was taking a couple of days away from court business. My mother is a very devout woman, but"—he winked—"not as devout as all her pilgrimages would suggest."

"But by avoiding each other's quarters, your mother does not incur the jealousy of the other wives and concubines. She focuses on her life of faith, and is not seen as a threat. Just as you focus on your martial training rather than politics."

"Her example has taught me the best path for those who have no interest in a high position. It is still a . . . confining life. My mother is an artist. You've seen her work in my father's quarters, although no one knows it's hers. She is cautious with her appearance as well, never wearing the latest styles or fixing her hair in the latest fashion. She loves my father, though, and he returns her affection. More than that, they are comfortable with each other, which is no small thing in an imperial family."

"She wants nothing from him. As you want nothing from him." Moria moved closer, their legs brushing. "While this mission of yours may upset things between them, it is a storm that must be weathered eventually. You will finish this mission, and return victorious. Your father will be pleased, your mother placated, and you will officially be a man, a true warrior."

"You make it sound easy."

She squeezed his hand. "It is easy. You're ready for this, and they will both see that very soon."

Moria was watching Ashyn. Her sister rode to the side, far enough from the others that it was clear she wasn't in the mood for conversation, but close enough to Moria that Simeon wouldn't pounce. The young scholar had taken a fancy to Ashyn, one which her sister did not reciprocate. Moria wanted to warn him off.

"He's lonely," Ashyn had said. "He's not blessed with social graces, so he's having difficulty fitting in. I don't mind talking to him sometimes. Just not . . ."

"All the time?"

"I can handle it."

As for her sister's distant mood, Moria knew the causes. The situation with the monks was one. Ronan was another. He was still with them—secretly guarding them—and that upset Ashyn. He'd behaved poorly, leading her on and then pretending he hadn't. Disingenuous and dishonorable. But what did one expect from a thief?

Moria had not objected to a romance between them. If Ashyn wanted an illicit dalliance with a rogue, she could have done worse than Ronan. Moria would mourn the loss with her, but if this was how he treated Ashyn, he did not deserve her.

"And there it is," Tyrus said, snapping Moria's thoughts back. "Fairview."

She looked up to see the white-plastered town shimmering in the distance, and her heart beat faster.

Tyrus rode to the front of the convoy, saying, "That's close enough. Light the fires."

There was no need of campfires on a warm spring day. They were for the smoke, which would be seen from Fairview, alerting the guards inside to the envoy's presence.

"Are you ready?" Tyrus said as he rode back to her.

Moria lowered her voice. "If I ask you again to allow me to go without you—"

"No."

"But—"

"No." He brought his horse closer. "This isn't a matter of what is expected of me, but what I expect of myself. You worry that, by going with you, I present a target Alvar may be unable to resist. But if he kills me without cause, my father will kill Gavril. My father has other sons. Alvar does not."

"I still don't like it."

"I know." He took her hand and laced her fingers with his.

96

"You are thinking of me not of politics, and I . . ." He released her hand and backed his horse away. "I do appreciate it. Now, if you're ready . . ."

She was.

THIRTEEN

Two of the warriors ordered to stand watch were mounted archers. Traditionally, warriors had fought only with blades and considered other weapons the province of hunters and farmers, which left imperial forces at a disadvantage facing armies with ranged weapons. Even once the mounted archer troop began, the stigma had remained until the mounted archers had begun performing at festivals. Then it became an exalted position, with boys training from the time they could hold a bow.

The task of these two archers, then, was to guard Tyrus from afar, ready to loose their arrows on any attackers. Only the counselors accompanied the prince and the girls, though at twenty paces to act in an auxiliary capacity.

As they rode, Moria kept her gaze fixed on that distant town. The beasts did, too—Tova sniffing the air, Daigo's ears forward. It stayed silent and still. A town held captive.

"Do you truly think the children are there?" Ashyn whispered.

Tyrus's shoulders twitched, and Moria knew he'd been as focused on Fairview, the question an unwelcome interruption. But he found his civility before answering.

"I believe the chance is good," Tyrus said. "If not in the town, then close to it."

"We ought to be quiet," Moria said. "Silence will help us hear preparations within."

"Of course," Tyrus said. "My apologies."

He'd know she was not rebuking him. He took the blame to deflect it from Ashyn. Always honorable. Always considerate.

I could lose my heart to him.

The thought startled her. As she watched him, though, she wasn't merely admiring a handsome young warrior. She wanted to be with him. And she wanted more from him.

Yet he was satisfied with friendship. It was a new experience for Moria—not simply to have found someone who might capture her heart, but to have her interest not reciprocated. It was a lesson she supposed every girl had to learn. One may fall for a boy, and he may not fall in return.

She turned her attention back to Fairview. A wall encircled it, twice as tall as a man. Guard towers squatted on either side of the main gate, but unlike the simple platforms at Edgewood, these were boxed shelters. She squinted, trying to see guards within. Tyrus pointed at the tower on the left, motioning for her to look on the far right side. She could just make out the pale fabric of a tunic within. As they drew closer, she noted a figure in the second tower as well. Both sentinels watched from deep in the shadows of their shelters. The gate itself was closed, with no one standing guard.

"They've gone in," Tyrus murmured. "Saw us coming, retreated, and shut tight the gate."

Moria understood the strategy, but Ashyn asked, "Why?"

"It forces us to draw nearer," Tyrus said. "If they come to meet us, our archers can cover us. If we are forced to knock at the gates, with their guards posted above . . ."

"The gates are shrouded in shadow from the afternoon sun," Ashyn said. "So the archers will have a difficult time reacting swiftly and accurately."

"We ought to have come when the sun moved," Moria said.

Tyrus nodded. There was naught that could be done now, though, without retreating. So they continued until they were less than ten paces from the gate. Tyrus pulled his horse forward and shifted position, displaying his forearm tattoos should anyone watching have failed to notice them as he rode.

"I am Tyrus Tatsu," he called. "Son of the emperor and his first concubine, Maiko. I bring the Seeker and Keeper of Edgewood. We wish to speak to Alvar Kitsune, if he is here. If he is not, then his son, Gavril, or his commander, Barthol."

Moria stiffened. She knew Gavril might be here. What would she do if those gates opened and he walked out? How would she stay her daggers? Worse, what if she did not even reach for her daggers, but stood like a wounded child, hoping for an explanation.

It's not what you think, Keeper. I'd never hurt you, never betray you.

She squeezed her eyes shut.

"Moria?"

She looked to see Tyrus, worry darkening his eyes.

"I'm fine," she said.

A half nod, acknowledging without believing. Then he straightened and turned forward again. There was no sign of movement at the gates. The shadowy figures of the tower guards stayed where they were.

"I am Tyrus Tatsu!" he said again, louder this time. "I come as an envoy to discuss the situation, and I expect the courtesy of a reply!"

When no response came, the minor counselor eased his horse forward. "My lord—"

Tyrus raised a hand to cut him short. His dark eyes blazed with rising fury. He might be more modest than one would expect of a prince, but he was still the emperor's son.

"We'll ride forward," he said to Moria. "Ashyn? Retreat with the counselors."

He glanced back at the two men, as if making sure they'd heard, but more seeking their approval of the plan. He was no seasoned diplomat, and he knew it.

The major counselor gave the barest nod. "Ancestors watch you, my lord."

"Ride back and compel the archers forward," Tyrus said. "Have them stop midway between the camp and here."

Tyrus rode to Moria as Ashyn retreated with Tova.

"Watch the towers," Tyrus said as they continued forward. "I'll keep my eyes on the gate."

The figures in the towers remained exactly where they'd

been since Moria first spotted them, and she began to suspect they'd miscalculated the darkness of their shelter and thought themselves hidden.

As they rode into the shadow cast by the wall, cool air rushed past on a strong breeze. Moria picked up traces of an unfamiliar scent and heard a slow *thump-thump-thump* from inside the wall. Not footsteps—the thumps were too regular.

Moria realized the sound was the gate itself, opening a little and then closing in the wind. As they drew closer, she could see something under the gate. Feet? It was hard to tell.

"You there!" she called. "In the tower. Acknowledge us."

Silence.

"Do you think I cannot see you both?" she snapped. "On the left, you wear a light tunic and your hair is long and loose. On the right, your tunic is brown and I see no hair, so I presume it is short. The shadows may hide your faces, but that is all."

When still neither moved, her hand went to her dagger.

"Moria," Tyrus murmured.

"I would not," she said.

"I know." His voice dropped more. "I mean watch your temper. They're hoping you cannot."

His own eyes simmered with outrage, but he controlled it. The guards were mocking them, and if Moria and Tyrus seethed they'd say, "You may think you are a Keeper and an imperial prince, but we see only two children playing at being warriors."

"Remember these are bandits," Tyrus said. "I may give Barthol the honorific of commander, but he is no warrior." *And thus they could not expect them to act with honor.* "Remember who you are."

She backed up her horse to look again at the unmoving guards. When she noticed Tyrus dismounting, she stopped him.

"Remember who *you* are," she said.

Few people in the empire outranked a Keeper, but an imperial prince was one of them. So it fell to her to open the gate. When she tried, though, she discovered why it was banging in the wind. It was barricaded from within.

"They toy with us," she muttered.

"As is to be expected. Here, I'll—"

"Remain on your steed, your highness. If those guards will not respond, perhaps they are hard of hearing. I'll take my message to them."

Moria shimmied up the posts as deftly as a cat, if not quite as gracefully. Tyrus's gaze swung from one guard tower to the other, ready to alert her to trouble. Daigo climbed the other post and they both drew up to the window openings—

"Moria!"

She looked to see Tyrus swinging off his horse, his face taut with alarm. "Down! Now!"

She went still, trying to hear or see what had caught his attention.

"It's a trap!" he hissed. "They're fake."

She'd planned to drop down as he asked, but at that she paused. "Fake?"

"The guards still have not moved. Get down!"

She boosted herself up the last handspan to peek into the tower. This guard was no fake. His arms were bare, as she'd noted from below. They were held oddly, though, at his sides, as if in a gesture of surrender, palms out . . .

His palms were darker than his brown skin. And there was something in the center of them.

Spikes. There were spikes through his hands, nailing them to—

Her gaze shot up. She saw the hair first, the loose hair she'd noticed before and—

It was not a guard. Not even a man. It was a woman, nailed to the back of the guard box by her feet and hands, her head lolling, her eyes dead and staring.

"Moria!"

She tore her gaze from the corpse.

"It's a woman. She's dead. They've nailed her up to look like a guard."

"A woman?" He frowned. "Why would they use—?"

He stopped short as Moria squeezed through the window.

"Where are you going?" he said, but she was already in the tower. With a clatter of blades, Tyrus followed.

FOURTEEN

Moria climbed down the tower ladder. At the base was a door leading into town. When she reached it, Tyrus called, "Stop." His tone was not that of a friend giving advice, but a prince issuing an order. He jumped down the rest of the way, knocking into Daigo, who snapped and glowered.

"Don't shove me aside next time, then," Tyrus said to him.

When Moria reached again for the door, Tyrus caught her arm. He held fast, his free arm going around her waist, pulling her against him, his mouth at her ear, whispering, "Steady," as he held her still. She could feel herself shaking against him. She tried to pull away, embarrassed, but he only tightened his grip, his body against hers.

"I know . . ." She swallowed. "I know why they used a woman. I know what's out there." *It is like Edgewood.*

"You don't know that."

Her chin shot up. "I do. I—"

"You *suspect* it. You cannot know. It could be a trap, and if you rush in, you'll . . ." He trailed off, and when he spoke again, steel threaded his voice. "I feared a trap with the guards, and I wanted you to come down."

"I—"

"I may outrank you, Moria, but no one commands you. I understand that. I will ask, though, that you pay me the courtesy of at least listening when I speak."

"I—"

"I had cause to be concerned. You ignored me. We are partners, Moria. I'm watching out for you, as you are watching out for me. I would like you to remember that."

Shame washed over her. "I'm sor—"

"Don't be. Just heed me a little, now and then." A half smile. "If only to make me feel like an equal partner."

"You are," she said. "And I do apologize."

He let her go and leaned against the door, listening. Moria could hear only the thump of the gate. Tyrus motioned her behind him, unlatched the door, and swung it open. She could see the gate now, barricaded by cloth-covered heaps along the bottom. Corpses lining . . .

They weren't corpses. They were bags. Of sand or something similar. Tyrus eased closer to the open door for a better look around. From where Moria stood, she could see exactly what she had seen the first time she'd been brought through these gates: a silent town. People had stayed in their shuttered homes then, waiting for their ordeal to end. Yet there had been bandits and mercenaries milling about, keeping the town under control. Now there was no one.

"I want you to watch the nearest homes," Tyrus said. "Particularly the windows to see if anyone peers out and tries to warn us."

She nodded. He withdrew his sword and moved through the doorway. Daigo slipped past, and Moria swung out at his side, both daggers drawn.

The gate thumped. The wind whistled past, whirling sand. When Moria heard that wind, she realized she didn't hear something else.

Spirits? Where are you?

Not even the faintest murmur answered. After four days on the road, she'd grown accustomed to the silence. Now, it chilled her. There ought to be spirits here.

A thump, like the gate only softer, came from the house on her right. She whipped around to face it, but only a window shutter moved. Blame her dark imagination, always seeing the worst.

She motioned to the window. Tyrus hoped the towns-people would warn them, but that had not been her experience on her first visit. They'd been too terrified.

"I am Tyrus Tatsu!" he shouted, startling both her and Daigo. "My father, the emperor, sends me with the Keeper of Edgewood, who bore your master's message. I come in my father's name, without guards, to meet with you honorably. The former marshal would not wish his men to hide behind civilians. Come and speak to me."

No answer.

"All right, then," he muttered. "I'll find someone who *will* speak to me."

They approached the house where the shutter had moved.

It had gone still now, but inside, Moria could hear scuffling, as if the inhabitants sought hiding places. Tyrus rapped at the door and waited only a heartbeat. As he opened it, noise erupted on the other side. A scrabbling. He adjusted his grip on his sword. The door swung open and—

A shape sprang at them with a bloodcurdling yowl. Tyrus's blade flew up just as Moria caught a glimpse of orange fur and shouted, "No!" It may have been her cry that stopped him. Or he may simply have realized he was about to cleave something much too small to be a human attacker. He caught the creature with the side of his blade, knocking it away. A blur of orange fur as the beast hit the floor, then shot off, hissing, brush-like tail behind it.

"A cat." Tyrus looked at Daigo as they walked inside. "You could have warned us."

Daigo stood there, stiff-legged, his yellow eyes fixed on the doorway the cat had run through. His growl reverberated through the room.

"He doesn't like house cats," Moria said.

"All the more reason for him to warn us." He started to lower his blade, then went still. "Do you smell that?"

"Yes. Someone has not provided that cat with a proper box. No wonder Daigo is annoyed."

Moria pointed at two piles of feces. Then she paused and glanced around the room. It was the cooking area, situated close to the front door to allow ventilation in warm weather. Besides the cat's mess, the room was tidy and clean. This was no squalid hovel, where cat feces might go unnoticed, and Moria doubted even the most slovenly housekeeper would allow it so close to food.

Then she saw the marks on the floor. Long scratches in the rough wood. Blood-smeared scratches, as if someone had been dragged, nails raking the floor, splinters digging in, blood filling the creases—

The scratches led to an interior doorway.

She raced for it, but Tyrus caught her arm.

"No," he said.

"But—"

"I'll not have you run onto a blade, Moria. Nor into something worse. I'll not allow it. Is that clear?"

Fury whipped through her, and she glanced at Daigo for help, but the wildcat sat on his haunches, watching. Telling Moria he agreed.

"Steady," Tyrus murmured.

"I am steady," she snarled.

"No, you are not, and we both know why you are not." He met her gaze, then he released her arm. "Be steady and stay at my back. Guard me."

She still bristled. Tyrus walked into the next room with Daigo at his side, and she bristled at that, too, but paused only a moment before duty compelled her to follow.

The next room was the living area. Two doors presumably opened to bedchambers—one for the homeowners, one for their children. The left was partly open, and bloodstained streaks led into the room beyond. They were not gouges now, only trails of blood. There were gaps, though, oddly spaced, and when Daigo bent to sniff the trail, Moria had an image of the orange cat lapping at the blood. She shuddered and turned away.

"I think it was the cat," Tyrus said.

"Yes," Moria said. "Judging by the feces, it's been locked in here a while. I suppose it had to eat something."

He frowned. "I meant the window shutter."

He pointed, and she saw a table beneath the window, everything on it now scattered across the floor. It had been the cat moving the closed shutter upon hearing someone outside. Which meant . . . She swallowed and looked from the blood to the piles of feces. Was she truly questioning what it meant? No. She knew.

She followed the blood to the bedroom door. She put her fingers against it. Across the room, Tyrus tensed, but she was being cautious, and he didn't try to stop her. She pushed open the door and saw . . .

Nothing. There was blood on the floor, but otherwise, nothing except—

"By the ancestors," Tyrus breathed, his eyes widening as his hands shot to his nose.

It was the scent she'd noticed on the breeze earlier, but magnified now, a thousand times over, hitting her like an anvil to the chest, her gorge rising.

Daigo pushed past. He snorted, as if clearing his nose, but continued padding forward, his head lowered as he walked around the sleeping pallet. There, on the floor—

Tyrus retched. It happened so fast that Moria barely had time to glance at him before he was doubled over, the contents of his stomach spewing out, the horror in his eyes . . . She knew it was horror partly for what they were seeing, but perhaps, even more, for his reaction. He clapped a hand over his mouth and staggered backward.

"You need air," she said. "It's the smell."

He shook his head and squeezed his eyes shut, then loosened his grip on his mouth and inhaled deep breaths, sucking air through his fingers. Finally, he let his hand fall away and straightened, and she saw the shame in his eyes.

"It's the smell," she said. "And the pickled eggs you had this morning."

Again, he shook his head, rejecting the excuse.

"If you want to step out, there's no one here but me."

"And me," he said. "There's still me."

She opened her mouth, but he said, "I'm fine. We ought to . . . make an accounting. We'll need to tell what we've seen." He paused. "Unless you'd prefer not to."

"Yes," she said. "I would very much prefer not to take a closer look." She met his gaze and he nodded, acknowledging her admission. "But you're right. We need to. So I will."

Daigo waited at the side of the pallet, fastidiously perched beyond the reach of the vomit. And the blood. As ashamed as Tyrus was, it had been a spontaneous reaction to the smell and the sight. If she'd eaten more today, she might have done the same.

The woman was dead. Of that there was no doubt. Yet the stench was not so much rot as infection. Moria recognized that from being with Ashyn when she'd assisted the healer. This woman hadn't been killed by her attacker. She'd been battered and beaten, her legs both broken, one bone poking through. She'd been clawed and bitten, her flesh torn and gouged. Some of the damage, though . . . There were cat prints through the blood. Many prints, as if the cat had visited and revisited, and

111

Moria wanted to tell herself the beast had come in, distressed and worried about its mistress. And yet, some of those bites . . .

Her stomach lurched. Best not to think of that. No need to think of that. The point was *what* had attacked the woman, and judging by those deeper gouges and bigger bites, it was no cat. Moria suspected the culprit, yet she feared if she spoke the words too soon, it would seem as if she was fixated on that one answer, on the creature that haunted her nightmares.

"Moria?"

Tyrus had bent beside her, and she was about to say she was fine. Then she noticed he was lifting the blanket on the pallet. At first she saw nothing. Then she bent to peer underneath and . . .

There was an arm. Yet not an arm. A twisted thing, muscles and tendons bulging and contorted, fingers elongated and wizened, the nails thickened to claws. The same claws that had gouged tracks in the dead woman. She'd seen that arm before . . . or one like it. On her father, on the twisted thing that he'd become.

"Shadow stalker," she whispered. "That is . . . My father . . ." She swallowed. "I have seen such a thing."

Daigo bumped her arm, ignoring the pool of blood now as he rubbed against her. She put her arm around him. Tyrus squeezed her shoulder.

"You should step out," he said.

She shook her head. "You're right. It needs to be documented. We ought to . . . take the thing. If we can. When we're ready to leave the town. Take it so the court physician can examine it."

Tyrus nodded. "That's a good idea. I'm not sure I'd have thought of it."

He would have. Making plans, though, steadied her better than any deep breathing. Tyrus took hold of the thing under the blanket, tugging it by its clothing while Daigo and Moria stood at the ready, in case it was not truly an empty shell. It was. She knew it as soon as she saw that terrible, twisted face. The demented spirit within had fled.

Moria looked at the dead woman. She had fought. Fought hard, even without a weapon. The body the shadow stalker had inhabited wore a tunic cut of the same coarse hemp cloth as this woman's dress. Her husband. What had that been like? Seeing your husband turn into that thing, having it drag you through the house, attacking you, breaking you, biting you? Worse than it had been with her father? Perhaps. But the woman had fought hard enough to send the thing crawling under that blanket, injured, the spirit within fleeing. And then the woman . . .

That was the worst of it. Moria looked at the woman and swallowed. The bites and gouges oozed yellow pus—the flesh had been rotting while the woman still lived. She'd survived the attack, only to be trapped here by her broken body, the infection spreading as the days passed and no one came . . .

Why did no one come?

Moria knew the answer to that even if she dared not speak it.

"We need to check the village," she said. "Look into more homes. The children—"

She stopped herself. That was what she'd come for. The

113

children. Yet now she hoped they were not here, because if they were, she'd find them like this woman—

"They are not here," Tyrus said, as if reading her mind. "Alvar Kitsune had them brought all the way from Edgewood. He's using them as hostages. He'd not do all that only to unleash this upon them."

"I hope not."

He walked over and squeezed her shoulder again, leaning in to whisper, "I am certain of it, Moria. He's keeping them alive. We'll find them."

As they headed into the sitting room, the orange blur zoomed past again, as if the cat had just realized the front door was open. Daigo growled.

"We have more things to worry about than a house cat," she murmured, and Daigo grunted, as if acknowledging that.

They moved to the next house, then to the next and the next, and within every house they found the dead. Another wife. An elderly couple. A wife and a girl. The girl was no more than fourteen summers. She'd barricaded herself in her parents' room. Red smears covered the door, as if the creature—her father?—had beaten himself bloody trying to get inside. Finally, he had, breaking a hole in the door, the splintered edges red with blood as he'd reached through. And the girl within? She'd taken his shaving blade and slit her wrists.

Moria stared down at the girl, her body rotting in a pool of blood so deep it was still tacky. Moria looked at the thin blade, fallen at the girl's side.

"Why did she not use it to protect herself?" she said.

"Perhaps she never thought of it," Tyrus said. "She looks

114

like a merchant's daughter. It may not have occurred to her."

Moria shook her head. "I cannot believe that. If any girl saw that thing reaching through the door, and she had a shaving blade, she would use it, even if she'd never been trained to defend herself."

A moment's pause. Then his voice lowered. "Perhaps she did not see the point. She could hear what was happening elsewhere in the village. She'd seen what had happened to her mother. Perhaps she thought there would be no sense fighting. That she would not—could not—escape."

And perhaps she was right. No. She *was* right. The girl could have fought off this one shadow stalker, but there were more beyond the door. All the men of the town had turned to monsters, hunting and slaughtering.

There'd been no escape except this: a quick death where she did not need to look into her father's eyes and see the horror he'd become.

Moria spun on Tyrus. "Why was the emperor not quicker? If he'd been quicker—"

"The bodies are rotted, Moria," he said, his voice still soft. "These people did not pass yesterday or even a few nights ago. I believe this happened almost as soon as you left."

"And what would be the point in that?" she snapped. "Alvar was holding the village hostage, threatening to do exactly this. Why do it before your father has a chance to respond?"

"Because he knew my father could not respond. Could not give him what he asked for. So there was no reason to keep the townspeople alive. Better to slaughter them quickly, before they revolted. Harvest the menfolk for shadow stalkers. Leave

115

the corpses as a message to my father, one that says 'you are responsible.' He knows my father too well, and he knows exactly how he'll play his hand—"

"This is not a game!" she roared, so loud the words scraped her throat raw. "Everyone here is *dead*. Everyone in Edgewood is *dead*. Every person I have known since I was a babe has been slaughtered or turned into a monster, and I'm not sure which is worse, but I know one thing—this is not a game!"

He reached out for her. She backed away and slid in the blood, and he caught her, arms going around her, gathering her in. When she struggled, his grip tightened. She pounded her fist against his back and he only said, "Go ahead. Let it out." But she couldn't vent her rage on him, and she froze there, torn between anger and grief until her chest heaved. Then the tears came—great, gasping sobs, hot tears flowing down her cheeks, her body shaking, Tyrus holding her against him, whispering in her ear, telling her it was all right, no one was here, just him.

She'd cried twice after the massacre at Edgewood. Once when she found her father's Fire Festival gift. Again when she finally broke down with Ashyn, sharing their grief. But those were nothing like this, her whole body consumed, the sobs so deep they hurt, the tears like acid, stinging her eyes and her cheeks. This hurt. Everything hurt. Everything was wrong, so horribly wrong.

"I couldn't stop it," she whispered, finally pulling back. "Not at Edgewood. Not here."

"I know." Tyrus held her face in his hands, fingers against her burning cheeks. He kissed her forehead. "I know."

"I'm the Keeper. I'm supposed to be able to stop it."

"I know," he whispered again. And kissed her again, on her forehead, on her cheeks.

"I don't know what to do. I don't know how to stop it."

"I know." More kisses, his lips blessedly soft and cool. "Neither do I, Moria. Neither do I."

She looked up at him. His face moved over hers, mouth lowering toward hers. Then he stopped. He hovered there, then pulled her against him in a fierce hug. When she finally moved away, he rubbed his hand over his face and looked around, as if momentarily forgetting where they were.

"Thank you," she said.

A wan smile. "No need. You keep my secret about what happened in the other house, and I'll keep yours about this." He said the words lightly, but the haunted look crept into his eyes, fear and shame returning.

"It was the smell," she said.

"No, it was a weak stomach. I've always had one, and I suppose I never realized the impediment it might cause on a battlefield. I . . ." His gaze shifted away. "I've never been on one. A battlefield."

"The empire isn't at war." *It hasn't been since before your birth.* She didn't say that. While it might allay his guilt, it would only remind him of that deeper fear, the one that said, after so long at peace, Tyrus wasn't the only one unprepared for war.

"There are still skirmishes at the borders," he said. "I should have insisted on going. Sparring in the court isn't nearly enough. I see that now. This . . ." He motioned at the girl on the floor, then waved out toward the town beyond. "I've heard the stories, Moria, but they do not prepare one . . ."

"Nothing can," she murmured.

"I worry now whether I—" A sharp shake of his head. "And now is not the time to think of that. We must tell the others what we've found. The town needs to be thoroughly searched for survivors. And then we'll search for the children of Edgewood. For now, remember them. They are still alive. I am certain of that."

FIFTEEN

I t did not take long to retrieve the others. There were already four warriors at the gate—the counselors having become concerned by their prince's vanishing inside— and Ashyn, who'd been threatening to go in herself.

On Tyrus's instructions, the warriors were to search the homes for survivors. The counselors, along with the scholars, were to follow, taking notes to convey to the emperor—the number of dead, the manner of death, anything they could glean from the bodies. Simeon did not make it past the first house, where he vomited so quickly that no one noticed someone had left a similar mess before him. Katsumoto and the counselors did not take to the task any more easily, requiring frequent breaks for air. Even the warriors often found excuses to step outside.

Ashyn wanted to aid the scholars and counselors. Moria forbade it. Ashyn was not trained in such reporting, so there was no need to add to her nightmares. Finally, Ashyn relented and took Simeon to find the town hall, where they could retrieve records. Moria and Tyrus joined the search for survivors.

There were almost a hundred houses in the town. The task was as long as it was unpleasant. With each home, they would open every door and check every room. There were no cellars in Fairview, with the volcanic rock of the Wastes not far below the soil. That made the task swifter. It also, however, had robbed the townspeople of the best place to hide and survive. When the shadow stalkers had struck Edgewood, that's where Moria, Ashyn, and Ronan had been—underground, in the cells.

People here had fled to the community hall. The main doors were open. Inside, bodies carpeted the floor. Two lay at the foot of a closed interior door smeared with blood. The hands of the corpses were battered and swollen, as if these two had—like the woman in the first house—survived the first wave and died of their injuries, pounding on that door to be let inside.

"It's the storeroom," Moria said. "When they brought us here to speak to Barthol, I saw inside. It was communal food storage, for charity and festivals and such."

"That is where the townspeople went," Tyrus said. "Where they could barricade themselves in and survive."

Moria looked down at the two bodies by the foot of the door. Townspeople had fled into that room and dared not open it even for their neighbors.

Tyrus banged on the wooden door and announced himself.

Sounds came from within, but no one answered. After being in there a fortnight, any survivors would be much weakened. Tyrus tried again, and Moria did the same, telling them who she was, that she'd been here with her sister, that they'd come back to rescue them.

"We'll need an axe," Tyrus said, stepping over the strewn bodies.

Moria pushed on the door. It moved a crack before banging shut again.

"Something's against it," she said. "But it's not properly barricaded. Help me push."

He did. Daigo came closer, but only to supervise. As soon as they got the door open a couple of handspans, he leaped through.

"Daigo!" Moria cried. "Don't—"

A hiss. A scrabbling. A shriek. Moria shoved the door wide and burst through, ready to calm the frightened—

The smell. *By the ancestors, the smell.* It sent her back out that door, propelling Tyrus with her. She pulled her tunic up over her nose. He did the same as he heaved breaths through his mouth to calm his stomach. Inside, Daigo hissed and spit. Enraged shrieks answered, so shrill that Moria's first thought was *Children! It's the children!* Then she caught the smell again and thought, *No, please don't let it be the children.*

Stepping back through the door, Moria saw what Daigo was chasing. Rats. That's what had been making the squeals and the skittering. The only people in there . . . Moria saw what had been stopping the door. Bodies.

When the killing had started, townspeople had fled in

here. And then they had died, not because they'd run out of food or drink, but because there were men with them, and the shadow stalkers had sought out and possessed them. Then those who'd barricaded themselves inside had found they were trapped here.

Moria thought of those dead outside the door. Had they known what was happening within? Had they heard the screams and been trying to help? She squeezed her eyes shut and wished she'd not been blessed with such a vivid imagination.

After she surveyed the carnage, she turned to Tyrus. "There are no children. It is like Edgewood. No one under twelve summers remains." Which was not entirely true. They'd seen babes in arms, as in Edgewood, but she'd not think of that.

"They've taken the children again," Tyrus said. "As hostages."

That, then, was all she could take from this. A spot of hope. The children lived.

"We should go," Tyrus said. "The others can make the accounting here. It does not help to linger."

She was about to call Daigo when he let out a snarl, and she spun to see him facing off with . . .

It was a rat. Yet it was not.

In the Forest of the Dead, they'd seen a twisted creature with quills. Gavril had said it must have adapted to the conditions of the forest. She looked at this rat, up against the wall, and she knew he'd lied. Whatever magics Alvar Kitsune had been working in that forest, preparing to raise the shadow stalkers, they had warped that beast.

This rat was nearly twice as big as the corpses of the others, swollen and bloated, with huge patches of angry pink skin showing through its coarse fur, as if it'd been stretched almost to the bursting point. Its eyes were lost in the lumpy, bloated mass that had become its head. Only the tips of its ears and nose protruded. And teeth. The swelling seemed to have pulled its lips back, its pin-sharp teeth exposed all the way around. A creature in transition, bloating and swelling as it metamorphosed into something else.

"It's sick or poisoned," Tyrus said. "Daigo! Away!" He turned to Moria. "Call him off."

Sick or poisoned. Yes, perhaps that was it. Her imagination was getting the best of her.

She did not command Daigo to leave his prey, though. It would be an insult to call him off. She threw her dagger instead. It caught the rat-thing in the side and there was a grotesquely wet popping noise as the beast shrieked its last.

"Or you could just kill it yourself," Tyrus said.

"That is the advantage to thrown daggers," she said. "No need to get close enough to be attacked."

"Just wash the blade well. Please."

Daigo was looking around, as if for more enemies to fight. Tyrus bent and pulled out Moria's dagger. When he did, it seemed half the rat's insides bubbled out of the hole, like an overstuffed sausage roll.

"Well, that's disgusting," said a voice behind them.

Moria turned to see Ronan. He stood in the doorway, and his gaze was no longer on the rat-thing, but sweeping the room, and as it did, any glimmer of humor fell from his face.

"It's all disgusting," Moria said. "Unspeakably disgusting."

Ronan nodded soberly. Moria reached for her dagger, but Tyrus was cleaning it and ignored her.

"You think that beast was infected?" Ronan asked Tyrus as he scrubbed the dagger with a cloth and wine from an open skin.

"Either that or it ate far too much."

Ronan exchanged a look with Moria. He was thinking what she had been, and while she wanted to see that as proof that her imagination wasn't taking liberties with her common sense, she knew that, like her, he was probably overly quick to blame sorcery. They'd seen too much of it, in too short a time.

"We should take the corpse," she said. "For study. Ronan can do that."

"No, Ronan cannot," Ronan said. "Because he isn't under your command, my lady. That thing will not walk away. Leave it for the warriors to collect. I have found something more interesting. A survivor."

Tyrus and Moria hurried through Fairview, with only Daigo accompanying them. Ronan had given them directions and then slipped off.

He'd said he'd spotted a woman darting across a road, while Ashyn was still in the town hall. Had Ronan been keeping an eye on her? Moria hoped he wasn't playing with her sister's heart, as he determined his own feelings. She'd let it happen once with no repercussions. It would not happen again.

When they neared the house the woman had entered, Moria noted movement beyond a half-closed shutter. Across the road, a pair of guards searched. They all made enough noise that any able-bodied survivors should be dashing from their homes.

"But how would they know we're rescuers?" Tyrus said. "She may have heard me identify myself. She may have seen me and recognized my armbands. Yet even if she knows who I am . . . ?" He shrugged. "Would you come out so quickly?"

After being beset by bandits and shadow stalkers, one might not trust the emperor himself if he appeared and offered sanctuary. And given what Moria had seen, if someone had been trapped in this town for almost a fortnight, it was entirely possible she was not in her proper mind.

"In here," she said, motioning to a house across the road.

From inside, they watched the house where the woman hid. Finally, the front door opened. A woman peeked out. She was younger than Moria expected, no older than Tyrus. She looked one direction and then the other, and, once convinced the way was clear, the young woman darted out and slipped into another house farther down.

"Avoiding the search," Tyrus said. "She does not want to be found."

"Well, she will be," Ronan said, appearing as if he'd come in through a window. "Do we have a plan?"

SIXTEEN

Tyrus's plan was neither complicated nor contentious. There truly was only one solution—confront the young woman while blocking her escape routes. Moria went through the front door, presuming a young woman around the girl's age would be less intimidating. She even concealed her daggers. At the door, she turned to Daigo.

"Will you stay here? In case she runs past me. And so you don't spook her."

He grumbled but planted himself in front of the entrance. Moria went inside.

"I saw you come in here," she called. "My name is Moria, Keeper . . ." She trailed off as the hairs on her neck rose. The shutters were drawn, the room dim and cool, and she peered about it. Something was not right here. It plucked at her memory, telling her she'd sensed this before. Similar yet different.

After a slow look around, she began again. "I'm Moria, Keeper of Edgewood. I come from the emperor, with his son, Prince Tyrus. I was here a fortnight ago. Perhaps you saw me with my sister, the Seeker."

Silence.

"We were held captive here, before being sent to the imperial city with a message. I was supposed to negotiate the terms of your release—you and the other townspeople. I suspect we did not make it far before—"

"The shadow stalkers came."

The voice sounded so suddenly that Moria started. She turned to see the young woman in the doorway of a bedchamber. She was empire-born, somewhere between plain and pretty, a thin girl wearing a simple dress. She had long, dark hair and dark eyes. "It was the first night after you left. The shadow stalkers came."

"You knew what they were?"

The young woman laughed, the sound so jarring in light of the tragedy that the hairs on Moria's neck rose again. She looked at the girl, who stood in the doorway as if greeting an unexpected visitor.

She's not . . . right. Because of what she witnessed?

The girl continued, "I may never have seen a shadow stalker, but I'd certainly heard of them. It would've been difficult to mistake those creatures for anything else."

"What happened?"

Behind the girl, Ronan had slipped through a window into the bedchamber. Now he stopped, his forehead creasing, perhaps wondering why she'd ask such a question. This was hardly the time for an interrogation.

The girl didn't seem to think the question odd, though. She said, "They came as black smoke and possessed the men, who turned on the women. During the slaughter, the mercenaries took the children. The shadow stalkers did not seem to bother them—the mercenaries or the children."

"And your family?"

"My father was possessed like the other men. He killed my mother and my older sister."

"I am sorry for your loss."

A pause. Then panic lit the girl's eyes as she must have realized how dispassionate her account sounded. Her town had been massacred. Her mother and sister were murdered by her father. Yet she recited the events as if they were facts in a history book.

"The shock," the girl murmured, gaze dropping. "It has been great."

"I'm sure it has. But we'll need you to help us identify the dead. You can do that, I presume?"

"Yes, my lady, I will—"

She broke off midsentence and ran for the front door. Daigo lunged through. She didn't shriek or fall back but only cursed and started to veer. Ronan was already in flight, grabbing her by the shoulders and taking her down. He pinned her to the floor.

"Possessed," he said to Moria. "Like Wenda."

"Hmm."

Wenda had been a girl from Edgewood, one of the survivors who'd accompanied Ronan and Ashyn across the Wastes.

In Fairview, Ashyn had learned that the girl they knew as Wenda was long gone, her body possessed by a spirit tasked with bringing the Seeker.

This could be the same situation. And yet . . . Moria finally recognized the sensation she'd felt earlier. It was similar to the one she'd noted near the resurrected mummies. A sense of disturbance, which Ashyn had not noticed with Wenda.

Tyrus stepped into the room, having caught enough of the conversation to know the girl was possessed. He studied her briefly before walking to Moria.

"Can you trap the spirit in there?" he whispered. "I know you can command it out . . ."

If she could trap the spirit, they could question the girl. But that was not something she'd ever covered in her studies, there being no scenario where one should need to do so.

The world is changing. My role in it is changing, and I hadn't even mastered the old one.

"I don't know," she whispered back. Then she turned to Ronan. "Can you fetch Ashyn?"

He nodded, and Tyrus took his place, standing at the girl's back with his sword tip on her neck.

"Do you know who I am, spirit?" he asked.

"Tyrus, son of Emperor Tatsu and his first concubine. I am well versed in the affairs of the empire, your highness. I have a name, too. It is Guin."

Moria crouched in front of the girl as Daigo took his place beside her.

"You stole a body *and* a name?" Moria said.

She had expected the girl to put on a performance when

Ronan jumped her. To cry and sniffle that they were making a dreadful mistake. To babble and protest when they spoke of possession. Now, as Moria asked the question, the girl merely raised her dark eyes to hers.

"I stole neither. Guin is my name, and I found this body spirit-abandoned."

"Spirit-abandoned?" Moria said. "Is that like finding an empty wagon by the roadside?"

Tyrus snorted a laugh, but Guin only held Moria's gaze. "You mock, but that is exactly what it is like. I found it without an owner, with no owner likely to return, and so, being in need of conveyance, I took it. You won't need magics to keep me in here. I've no intention of leaving."

"And the spirit who owns that body?"

"Gone."

"Dead?"

Guin wrinkled her nose. "I'd not take over a corpse. That would be like stealing a wagon with two broken wheels and the others about to shatter. When the shadow stalkers possessed the villagers, there was confusion. Some spirits were taken out of the wrong vessels. Like this one."

"And you were one of those spirits?" Moria asked. "Taken from your body?"

Guin laughed. "I have been without a form for a very long time, child."

"What are you?"

Guin smiled up at her. "You are a Keeper, are you not? Tell me what I am."

"A marine ghost, an honorable spirit, a ruined spirit, or the vengeful dead," said Ashyn, appearing behind Moria.

"Ah," Guin said. "The Seeker. They are known to be brighter than their sisters."

"Oh?" Moria said. "Forgive me. I thought I was the one who saw through your ruse and knew you for a possessing spirit."

"True. I'll give you that, then. You are clever. Your sister, however, possesses more conventional intelligence. She is the book-learned one." Guin looked at Ashyn. "Which type am I?"

"You can get free, yet you choose not to," Ashyn said. "Despite the fact you may suffer imprisonment or even torture. You are desperate enough to keep a body that you'd risk that."

"She uses a human name," Moria said. "Guin."

"There are four primary types of human spirits that remain in the first world. First, marine ghosts, those who died at sea and attempt to drown others."

"No sea nearby," Moria said.

"See how clever she is?" Guin said.

Moria ignored her. "There are also honorable spirits, great men who were terribly wronged and cannot control their wrath."

"And ruined spirits," Ashyn said. "Those unable to pass over to the second world. However, if she'd merely failed to pass over, she would appeal to me for help. That leaves . . ."

"The vengeful dead," Moria said. "Which is the same as honorable spirits, only the vengeful are women. It is an insult to our sex. The name ought to be the same."

"I agree," Guin said. "And now that you have solved the mystery, as I said, I will remain in this body, on the understanding you will hold it captive and question me. I only ask that when you have what you need, you will free this body."

"We must speak to the court Seeker," Ashyn said. "If the spirit that belongs in that body can be returned to it—"

"It cannot. But I am confident enough in that to agree. If you can reunite this girl's spirit and her body, you may do so."

"Where are the children?" Moria asked.

Guin blinked up at her.

"We will agree to your terms," Tyrus said. "If you answer the Keeper's question, and we find your response to be truthful."

"I can tell you what I saw, but it does not include where the children were taken. By that time, I was in this body and far more concerned with keeping it alive."

Moria got the sense that even if the situation were not so dire, Guin wouldn't have taken much notice of the children's predicament.

"Prince Tyrus?" It was the minor counselor, calling from the street. "Your highness? We've finished our accounting."

"Then we're done here," Tyrus said. He turned to Guin. "You'll be taken into custody with minimal explanation to the others. You'll provide no more information unless asked by one of us four here. Understood?"

"Yes, your highness."

There was much still to be done, and the responsibility for organizing it fell to Tyrus. He could have abdicated it to the major counselor. The emperor would not expect his young son to handle a disaster of this magnitude. Yet Tyrus expected it of himself.

First, two warriors had to be dispatched to tell the emperor what had happened. Then Tyrus needed to interrogate Guin before planning their next move. While Moria assisted him with that, Ashyn went back into Fairview, to cast the proper rituals to put the spirits at rest.

Tyrus and Moria briefly asked Guin about her past, but she refused to speak of it, and it wasn't important. Whatever had happened to her in life, it had turned her into a spirit bent on revenge, wandering the world lost and confused, and likely causing trouble among the living. Now that she had a form, though, she was mortal again, and she understood that whoever had wronged her was no longer alive. She was no more danger to the group than any stranger.

About the children of Fairview, all Guin could say was that they'd been gathered and taken. As for the children of Edgewood, she'd seen their camp before the shadow stalkers came, while she was still wandering as a spirit. They would have moved by now, but the site might yield clues.

More important was what Guin had overheard as she'd flitted about. Alvar Kitsune planned to strike more border towns, amassing a larger army of the dead.

SEVENTEEN

W as it possible to grow accustomed to the sight of death? Ashyn thought it must be. If you were a healer or a midwife or a warrior, you would see so many lives pass that you would steel yourself against it, remind yourself that they'd gone to join the ancestors and were happy. That's what Ashyn tried to do as she put Fairview's spirits to rest. It didn't help. With each body, she saw a life lost, horribly and tragically, and the weight grew, like stones tied to her cloak.

"Is there anything I can do?" Simeon asked. He'd accompanied her, along with two guards. The warriors stayed back to give her room. Simeon hovered. While she could be annoyed with that, she took comfort in it, too.

"Turn the lantern up a little, please," she said. "The night grows dark."

He hesitated. "I thought perhaps, as long as you can see the way, there is no need to see more."

She smiled over at him. He was kind. Awkward and lacking in social graces, but kind and thoughtful. He had a blazing intelligence—that was a given, or he'd not have been apprenticed to the famed scholar Katsumoto—but he also had a way of understanding more beyond his books than she'd expected from their first encounter. She'd come to appreciate that and, perhaps, at times, to regret that there was no spark between them.

"I should bear witness," she said. "It is only respectful."

He turned up the lantern.

"But I appreciate the thought," she added.

He flushed and lowered his gaze. There might be no spark for her. But for him? Ashyn tried not to think of that. To presume a young man's feelings seemed like conceit. And if he did have such feelings and she did not? That felt unkind. Better to think she was misinterpreting. She'd certainly done it before.

She continued saying the ritual words, soothing the spirits. They deserved her full attention.

"Ashyn?"

Her sister's voice, accompanied by running footfalls. She smiled. Moria was here. That reassured and soothed her better than Simeon's anxious hovering or Ronan's silent vigil.

"Are you almost done?" Moria asked.

"Almost."

"They'll be starting the meeting soon," her sister said to Simeon. "You should join them. Give me the lantern, and I'll stay with Ashyn."

* * *

By the time they joined the meeting, it was rancorous enough that Ashyn found herself giving thanks they weren't all armed warriors, or there might have been more spirits for her to soothe. The counselors thought the next move was clear. They brought in their map, laid it out, pointed to the nearest border town, and said, "There."

"That's exactly where Alvar Kitsune would expect us to go," Tyrus said. "Which is why he will not be there. He will go there." Tyrus pointed to the next border town.

"While I mean no offense to the young prince," the major counselor said, "may I point out that I worked closely with the former marshal for many summers?"

"You may," Tyrus said. "But my father knew him best, and it is my father's insights I am relying on."

"The young prince is correct," the scholar Katsumoto said. "My study of the marshal's tactics suggests he would not choose the most obvious target. However, as well as the emperor knew the marshal, so, too, the marshal knew the emperor. He could foresee that we would know he'd not choose that town . . . and target it because we will not go there."

Tyrus groaned. "Or he could foresee that, too . . . and so target it anyway. We'll tie ourselves in knots if we follow this logic. What of the towns themselves? The geography, the defensibility, the number of guards . . ."

A fine idea, except neither town seemed the obvious choice. As they argued, Ashyn could see Tyrus growing more frustrated, Moria with him.

"There is no clear answer," Moria said finally. She paused,

catching Ashyn's eye and dipping her gaze. "I mean no disrespect, your highness."

Tyrus passed her sister a tired but affectionate smile. "If I didn't want you speaking your mind, I'd have asked you to stay outside. Go on, my lady."

"There is no clear answer," she repeated. "But the longer we argue, the more likely we are to ride out to find another Fairview. Either we choose one at random or we split up and ride to both."

"I'll not split our force in two," Tyrus said. "Nor will I let mere chance decide our course. The decision—and the blame—must be mine. I choose Riverside. I believe Alvar will quickly tire of playing in the safety of shadows, and the bolder strike is Riverside. We ride there now."

By the time their party was to leave, the moon was past its zenith. They headed out immediately.

The warriors found a camp farther along the edge of the Wastes, but the fires were cold and scattered, the refuse rotted. No tracks led from it, suggesting the bandits had taken the children and retreated into the rocky plain of the Wastes. Tyrus could not spare men to look further. The Wastes were too vast; their party too small.

As they traveled they used the wagons to catch brief moments of sleep. When dawn came, Tyrus was asleep in the wagon, having practically needed Moria's blade at his throat to convince him to rest.

"The emperor was wrong," Moria said.

Ashyn hushed her, but they were scouting off the road with

their beasts, and Moria clearly saw no need to hold her tongue.

"As happy as I am to have Tyrus here, it should have been the crown prince."

"I think Tyrus is doing a fine job."

"Of course he is," Moria said. Then she steered her horse around a rabbit hole. "The point is that he should not have to make these decisions. If anything goes wrong . . ."

Moria sucked in breath, as if she did not wish to contemplate that. Nor did Ashyn. If Tyrus had chosen wrong and another town perished, the blame would fall at his feet. Would Emperor Tatsu let that happen? Worse, had he considered that and sent the son he could most afford to lose?

"The emperor killed our mother," Moria said, as if sensing her fears.

"No, Moria. Our mother took her own life—"

"—so that she and our father wouldn't be exiled to the Forest of the Dead. That is *his* law. The emperor's."

"It's the law of the empire. A very old law."

"He could change it."

Ashyn said nothing, just twisted the ring on her finger—her mother's ring. She understood the weight of tradition and the difficulties of reforming it. Moria would not. She blamed Emperor Tatsu for their mother's death. It was difficult to remember that in the presence of the man himself. But out here, when Moria had other cause to think poorly of him?

"What if Tyrus succeeds?" Moria said. "What if he saves Riverside, finds the children, and rousts Alvar Kitsune? How would his brothers react then?"

He would be a hero, and that was as dangerous for Tyrus as failure.

"Ashyn?" called a voice. The horses started. The girls got them under control just as Ashyn saw Ronan loping over.

"Blast it," Moria muttered. "We survive shadow stalkers and death worms and thunder hawks, and you're trying to make our horses unseat us and dash out our brains."

"If your beasts were better guardians, they'd have warned you."

"You can't expect horses—"

"I meant them." He waved at Tova and Daigo, who joined forces in a simultaneous growl.

"They are not—"

"Mere beasts, I know. They are the spirits of great warriors. Sometimes, though, I think if they were the spirits of great beasts, they'd be more useful."

"You're in an ill temper," Ashyn said as she climbed off her horse. "I'm sure this is longer than you planned to be away from your brother and sister. If you wish to go back, I'll make sure you have supplies. Tyrus would understand. We know you need to look after your siblings."

"They looked after themselves for four moons without me. Yes, I've been gone longer than anticipated and I'd like to return soon, but they need the prince's money more than they need me home. It would make my job easier, though, if you two weren't always wandering off."

"I thought your job was scouting," Moria said.

"Precisely. *My* job is scouting. Not *yours*."

"We are permitted to wander," Ashyn said evenly. "We're both armed with blades, and we have our bond-beasts. However, we take your meaning, and we'll return to the convoy now."

"Wait," he said. "I've spotted a camp. It's . . . not right."

"How?"

"Is the prince still resting?" he asked.

"Moria can ride back for him," Ashyn said. "I'll wait with you and—"

"You can both ride back for Tyrus. I'll go on ahead. You'll see the camp to the east of the road."

EIGHTEEN

Tyrus found them before they made it back to the others. Ronan had been right that they'd see the camp without further instructions. When Ashyn spotted smoke, she picked up her speed, but as soon as they crested a small rise in the road, she could see it was simply a campfire.

"Why is it smoking so much?" she said.

"I suspect that's what Ronan meant by something seeming wrong," Tyrus said. "They might as well send smoke signals to bandits."

He spurred his horse, and they galloped the rest of the distance, with Tova and Daigo running alongside. Ronan waited ten paces from the camp. The tents were silent and still. There were three of them, just large enough to sleep in. No horses, carts, or other belongings in sight.

"Hello?" Tyrus called as they dismounted.

When no answer came, he waved Ronan in closer. Then he threw open one of the tent flaps. Moria was at his side, her daggers raised, Daigo alongside her. Ashyn stayed back with Tova.

"Empty," Tyrus said.

He checked the other two with the same results. Ashyn moved in for a closer look. Ronan crouched to enter the nearest tent, then announced, "It wasn't bandits."

"How——?" Ashyn began.

Ronan tossed out a full and fastened pack as he emerged from the tent.

"There are packs in these two as well," Tyrus said. "Untouched."

"And no sign of blood means it wasn't wild beasts," Moria said, stalking around the exterior.

Each tent had a single set of sleeping blankets, laid out as if for the night. Each also had a pack with a man's clothing in it. While the clothing was not fine—no one would travel in their festival best—it was well made of quality fabrics. They found money in the bags, too. Enough to travel on for many moons. Ashyn suspected the men had been merchants. Her father used to say that after selling his goods, he'd travel as inauspiciously as possible, presenting what seemed like a poor target for bandits.

Tova and Daigo went into the tents next. Tova snuffled about while Daigo gave dainty sniffs, as if both had understood Ronan's earlier complaint and now were trying to do their part. When neither looked alarmed, Ashyn knew they'd detected no traces of blood.

As the beasts came out of the tents, Tova stopped and lifted his head. He looked toward the woods and whined.

"Split up," Tyrus said. "Moria, approach from the north, Ronan, the south. I'll take it straight on. Ashyn? Ride toward the road and call a warning if our wagon draws near."

Ashyn stifled a sigh. While she didn't wish to be her sister, there were times when she'd rather be where the action was.

She mounted her horse and moved toward the road. The wagon and guards were still only dots along the horizon. She glanced back at the others as they approached the forest from different angles. When Tova grumbled, Ashyn said, "You can go with them if you like."

He grunted and lay down, and they both sat by the road-side, casting longing looks at the forest and dutiful ones at the slow-approaching convoy.

A cry sounded from inside the forest. Then the boom of Tyrus's voice, ordering someone to stay where he was. Running footfalls. The whistle of a thrown dagger. Daigo's snarl. A shriek. A crashing through the woods. A thump.

Tyrus appeared, his fingers wrapped in an old man's tunic, propelling him forward. Moria and Ronan followed. Daigo leaped into the lead and spun in front of Tyrus and his captive, as if ready to attack. As Tyrus threw the man down, Ashyn saw he was not as old as she'd supposed. Gray-haired, yes, but perhaps prematurely. He was dressed in a long tunic, as if he'd been roused from sleep and fled, his legs and feet bare and scored with scratches from the forest.

"Enough," Moria said, loud enough to be heard over the man's blubbering. "Do you know who holds you captive?"

The man twisted to look up at Tyrus. When he saw the lacquered wood cuirass, he hesitated, likely recognizing it as the armor of a warrior. He took in Tyrus's clean-shaven face and gleaming, tied hair. Moria cleared her throat and directed the man's gaze to the bare forearms holding the blade. The man stared. Blinked. Stared some more. Then—

"You are . . . Those are . . ."

"Tatsu inkings," Moria said. "Imperial Prince Tyrus, son of Emperor Tatsu and First Concubine Maiko, commander of an expedition escorting the Seeker and Keeper of Edgewood. We came across your camp, and we were concerned by what we found."

"In other words, we're here to help you," Ronan said.

"Unless you're responsible for the disappearance of your traveling mates," Moria said. "In which case members of the imperial family are invested with the ability to mete out justice—"

"N-no. I did nothing. I was hiding in the forest. We were set on last night."

"By whom?" Tyrus said.

"I—I don't know. It seemed . . . No, I do not know."

"Explain."

The man said he'd woken in the night at a cry and he'd gone out to see his younger brothers leaving their tents, still in nightshirts and bare feet. They'd been walking toward the road. He'd called after them. One had turned and—

"His face. There was something wrong . . ." He swallowed. "I apologize, your highness. I know it sounds like the words of a madman and perhaps my mind tricked me, in the darkness and the confusion of waking so abruptly."

"Describe what you saw."

"It was my brother, yet it was not. His face was wrong, twisted. Ghastly. Like something from a nightmare."

"Then what happened?"

"I fell back in horror while he turned away and they both kept walking. There were figures on the road. Distant figures, walking. Fearing for my life, I fled into the forest. From the road, I heard marching footsteps. They did not stop. I don't know where my brothers went."

To join them, Ashyn thought. *They went to join them.*

At the tramp of feet, she jumped, turning so fast she forgot she was mounted and nearly slid off. It was only the rest of their group.

"Which way?" Moria asked the merchant. "Tell us which way they went."

Ashyn watched as the man lifted his finger and pointed in the direction they'd been traveling.

The road to Riverside.

Tyrus released the man. When the merchant saw where they were going, he decided to head out on his own—in the opposite direction. Ashyn didn't blame him.

Ashyn waited with Simeon while Tyrus and Moria told the counselors about the man. After the conference, Tyrus looked as if a lead-lined cloak had been lifted from his back.

"The counselors agree," Moria said as she rode to Ashyn. "Given what that merchant saw, we've made the proper choice in going to Riverside."

Ashyn exhaled in relief. The counselors openly supported Tyrus's decision. Which meant if anything went wrong, the blame would be shared, as he'd been acting with their counsel.

Tyrus allowed Ronan out of hiding, explaining that he was a scout Tyrus had brought along to help with exactly these situations. Ronan would need to keep his swords hidden, but otherwise, he could freely join them as they continued toward Riverside, and whatever awaited them there.

NINETEEN

It was nearly night again. They kept at the wagons' pace, knowing they didn't dare whip the horses into a lather, but it seemed frustratingly slow to all.

Ronan was scouting ahead. Ashyn hadn't seen him since they'd taken a brief break for a midday meal, stopping mostly to water and rest the horses. Moria was with Tyrus, not so much for camaraderie now as support. Simeon rode with Ashyn.

"Do you mind companionship, my lady?" Simeon asked.

Ashyn managed a weary smile for him. "We sometimes had scholars stop by Edgewood, wishing to see the Wastes and the Forest of the Dead. My father always found a chance for me to speak to them, but it was never enough. Truth be told, I don't think they took my interest seriously. There aren't many girls apprenticed to scholars, I presume?"

It took a moment for him to say, "No, not many," and even then the words came hesitantly, as if she'd not answered the question he asked. Which she had not.

"Ah," she said. "That explains it, then. Well, I do appreciate the chance to converse."

His cheeks colored, and she wondered if she'd misspoken. It was such a difficult line to tread—not wanting to encourage romantic attentions but not wanting to refuse his friendship either.

Relations between young men and women were so complicated. In this instance, also so ill-timed. There ought to be a universal law that if dire circumstances arose, they happened only to those past the age of romantic entanglements, so as not to interfere with the more pressing issues at hand.

"I must ask you a question, Ashyn," Simeon said as she craned her neck to look for Moria and Tyrus. "I fear you'll think it impudent."

"Hmm?" she said distractedly.

"It's about the scout. Ronan. What is his caste?"

She tensed. "Yes, that is indeed impud—"

"I know he carries a blade, though he hides it around the warriors. Does the prince know?"

When she didn't reply, Simeon continued, "I am aware that there are men who break the laws in such matters. Mercenaries and bandits. I can see how the imperial family might find use for such men, so I am not questioning—"

"Ronan comes from an old warrior family. Common warriors of low ranking."

It was true, though she did not say Ronan *himself* was a warrior. She was not certain when his family had lost their caste, only that it had been several generations past.

Simeon's face fell, as if in disappointment, and she felt a prickle of annoyance. Was he hoping to discover Ronan was indeed a bandit or mercenary? He'd never seemed the sort to indulge in scandalous gossip.

"Then I must ask another question," he said after a few moments of riding. "As much as I'd hoped that, in your answer to the first, I could avoid this one." He gripped the reins tighter. "Are you courting?"

"What?"

"I've seen the attention he pays you, and I had hoped he was lowborn, so I might be certain that attention was only the reverence due a Seeker."

She opened her mouth to say that since she could not marry, there was no need to worry what caste her suitors were. But that would imply the answer to the question was yes—they were courting.

"We are friends," she said. "He accompanied me across the Wastes."

"Oh, he is from Edgewood? I did not know that." A slow smile touched his lips. "Well, then, that makes perfect sense. I am glad to hear you are not otherwise involved. He seems somewhat . . . disreputable."

Ashyn stiffened. "He has had a difficult life, and he is not wealthy."

"Yes, of course. I meant no offense. He is your friend, as you said."

They rode a few paces more, and Ashyn checked again for Moria, wondering if she could politely leave Simeon and ride with her sister.

"Is there anyone else?" Simeon asked. "If not Ronan?"

"Hmmm?"

"Are you unattached?"

"Yes," she said. "However, given the current circumstances, I'm not looking to change that—"

"Of course not," he said quickly. "But when this is over, and we are back in the imperial city, I . . . I wish to know you better, Ashyn."

"I—"

He hurried on. "I'm very fond of you. You have a quick mind and a pleasing face. I mean, a *pretty* face. You are both attractive and accomplished. And kind. You are very kind. I am certain there are many young men vying for your attention, but you seem to enjoy mine, so I'm hoping I'm not being too forward when I ask . . ." His gaze didn't quite meet hers. "If you'll permit me to court you."

She wanted to say yes. Which was a ridiculous answer because she most assuredly did not want that. She wished to agree, because his speech was so sweet and so earnest, and she felt monstrous saying she wouldn't even let him try. Perhaps she expected too much of romance, but she did not want to be with someone when there was no spark.

She took a deep breath. "It's very sweet of you to ask, Simeon, but I have so much upheaval in my life that I am not looking for romance."

"You prefer warriors? I know young women do, and you are surrounded by them."

"No, actually, artisans and scholars are more my—" She stopped, realizing that this would not soften the rejection.

"I have no preferences, Simeon, because I have no interest in romantic relationships at this time."

"Is it Tyrus, then?"

"*Prince* Tyrus," she said, annoyance clipping her words. "No, I do not have designs—"

"You must. There's hardly a girl in the empire who doesn't dream of the handsome young prince turning his gaze her way. His attention is for your sister, yet you imagine a day when he tires of her ill manners and boyish ways. Or, perhaps, when he discovers that rough-mannered young women who embrace the warrior life do not fancy young men at all."

Ashyn stared at him as his lip curled and his gaze hardened.

You rejected him. He has an ego, despite his awkward ways. And it doesn't matter how gentle your refusal, it was still rejection.

"My sister likes young men very much," she said. "Though if you hoped to insult her by suggesting otherwise, it's a poorly aimed dart because I would care not whether she liked women or men, so long as she was happy. I understand that you are displeased with my words, but they are truly spoken. If you wish to upset me, you have only to insult my friends. If you wish to divest yourself of my company completely, you have only to insult my sister. I see her riding back. I'll take my leave."

They did not reach Riverside by sundown, and it was not the fault of the horses. They stopped short because Ronan spotted the bandit camp. The minor counselor, Tyrus, and the girls left their exhausted horses and followed Ronan across the wooded

151

fields. Now they lay on a hillock, peering at the camp below.

"It's them," Moria said. "See the huge, bald man? That's Barthol. The smaller man with him is Fyren."

"I count ten tents," Tyrus said. "Presuming two men to a tent, that's twenty. Less than I would have expected. It could be enough to capture a town, though."

"It is," the minor counselor said. "Riverside has only a few hundred people, and perhaps ten warriors. Warlord Jorojumo's compound is to the east. They can call on him for aid, so they do not require more."

"We'll dispatch one of our men to ride to the warlord then. I will request his assistance."

"It is better to demand it, your highness."

"You're right. I'll do that," Tyrus said. "I see no sign of shadow stalkers, but I suppose they'd not keep them with the camp. I don't know how easily they are controlled."

"According to legend, they are under the command of the sorcerer who raised them," Moria said. "The fact that they seemed able to kill women and old men—while leaving the children—supports that they can be restrained. Either way, I'd not want them in my camp."

"I suspect these bandits would agree. So the shadow stalkers will be held elsewhere, under guard."

"Meaning they have more bandits or warriors nearby," Moria said. "Guarding the shadow stalkers."

Tyrus nodded. "And more still with the children. We'll send those in our party who are not warriors on scouting missions, searching for the shadow stalker camp and the one holding the children. One warrior will go to speak to the warlord. When he returns—hopefully with others—we will attack, in hopes of catching them off guard."

He glanced at the counselor.

"A sound plan, your highness," the man said.

"Then let's return to the others and prepare."

TWENTY

While one rode to speak to the warlord, the other warriors suited up. They did not have full battle armor. The emperor had not dared send them with it, even hidden in the wagons, in case Alvar's men insisted on searching and found Emperor Tatsu's warriors prepared for more than simple negotiations. They had worn breastplates and helmets when they approached Fairview, but they did have gauntlets and leg guards in the wagons, and they were putting them on now.

The process was not simple, and Tyrus and Moria took their leave of the group to help each other. They started with the undergarments—a short robe and breeches. Before Tyrus put on his robe, he glanced at Moria several times, until she asked, "Do you need help?"

"No, I was just . . . I was wondering if you'd do something for me."

"That's what I'm here for."

"It's not the armor. It's . . ." Spots of color rose in his cheeks and he fingered the dangling ends of his amulet band. "Would you bless this before I cover it? I know it's an old custom, and no longer—"

"I have done it before," she cut in. "Simply because a custom is old does not mean it is meaningless. Some of Edgewood's warriors wore them and would ask Ashyn and me to bless them before they went into the forest."

Faith was a strange thing, Moria reflected as she walked over to Tyrus. No one would argue that the ancestors did not watch over them and could not influence the living world, but customs changed, and openly calling on spirits for support and guidance these days was often seen as a sign of weakness. Which was foolish, in her opinion. Whether an amulet band worked or not, it couldn't hurt. As their father would say, what often counted was whether one *believed* such protective rituals worked. Confidence in battle guarded one more than any spirit could.

So she blessed Tyrus's amulet band, asking the spirits to watch over him in battle and make his heart strong and true. Not that he needed help with his heart. She did, however, add a silent plea for his stomach, which *might* need steadying.

They continued with the armor. At first, seeing the pile of it, Moria had been satisfied. Surely with all that, Tyrus would be safe. Yet as she helped him with his gauntlets, she thought, *But he should have thigh armor, too*, and as he put on his helmet, she snuck a worried look, thinking he needed a neck ring as well.

He ought to have full armor. It's his first battle. This isn't right. It isn't safe.

It didn't matter. Even full armor only protected against a glancing blow. A sound strike from a well-made sword would slice through it like a blade through butter.

And that thought did not make her feel better at all.

She wished she'd blessed his amulet band more. That her supplications had been longer, more ornate and detailed.

What if I've done it wrong? What if it's not enough. What if—

"Moria?" Tyrus looked over as he fussed with his head-gear. He wore a dragon helmet, like those worn by all Emperor Tatsu's men, but his was dark red, the color of his tattoos, forbidden to all but the imperial family.

A true imperial helmet for a true Tatsu—a true dragon warrior. That was what Tyrus was, and he did not need armor or blessings to keep him safe. His skill would do that. And so would she, fighting at his side.

"Let me help with that," she said.

The plan was in place. The warriors were prepared for battle. And . . .

And nothing. As the moon approached its zenith, the bandits headed into their tents. Tyrus had yet to hear word from the warrior who'd ridden off to speak to the warlord. So they were waiting.

Ashyn had gone with Ronan and the others to search for the camps holding the children and shadow stalkers. The remaining warriors had spread out, surrounding the bandit camp. Moria was alone with Daigo and Tyrus, lying on her

156

stomach on the same hillock where they'd watched the camp earlier. The wind sighed through the long grass, and she pushed a stalk aside impatiently as it tickled her cheek.

"I can see the warlord's compound," Moria hissed, scowling at the distant hill, now faintly lit. "Why does he not come?"

"It's farther than it looks," Tyrus said. "The night is dark, and the light carries."

"I don't mean to grumble. You have quite enough to worry about."

He smiled over at her. "But I'm not allowed to grumble. You can do it for me, and we'll both feel better."

She shivered.

He shifted closer. "Cold?"

"No, just . . ."

"Anxious?"

She shrugged. "Perhaps. If the warlord doesn't send his men . . ."

"Then we'll find a place to camp and wait until morning. We may have the strength to fight, but not to fight well enough. Not without sleep."

With so little rest, they should hold off until morning anyway, but the longer they waited, the more chance they'd be spotted. Or that Alvar's reinforcements would arrive.

Blast Jorojumo. Why was he not moving more quickly?

Tyrus eased closer and stretched his cloak over her. "Even if you aren't chilled . . ."

"Thank you."

"You could rest." A wry smile. "I'll not start the battle without telling you. I'd never hear the end of it if I tried."

157

"I'm fine."

A moment's silence. She could feel him watching her as she kept her gaze on the camp.

"Your first battle," he said finally.

"Yours, too."

He nodded, and she could see the fear in his eyes. Not for the battle itself, but for the weight of it, the responsibility of it. And perhaps, yes, just a little for the battle itself. Now she was the one moving closer, tugging his cloak over them. He reached out, his arm going around her waist, pulling her against him, and when she turned to look at him, his face was right there, so close that with the slightest movement, she could—

She kissed him. There was no forethought. No moment of indecision or even of decision. She saw that haunted look in his eyes, and she wanted to make it go away. So she kissed him.

He hesitated only a moment, not even long enough for her to register that he was hesitating, and by the time she did, he was kissing her back, a deep, incredible kiss that banished every awkward, behind-the-village-hall buss from her mind, as if they could not even be called by the same name. This was what she'd been looking for in those fumbling embraces that had left her feeling as if someone had dangled the sweetest honey wine just out of reach, and she could see it, smell it, but could not grasp it, could not taste it. This was what she'd been aching for. A kiss, just like this. A young man, just like this.

When it stopped, she hung there, eyes still closed, feeling drunk, her mind buzzing. And then—

Tyrus's voice. Rough, low. His words, a mumbled, "I'm sorry." His hands tugging his cloak from over them. Her eyes, flying open, seeing his gaze averted. His voice again. "I didn't mean to do that."

Then the shame. The humiliation and the cold wave of anguish, as if in pulling that cloak back, he'd shoved her into an icy pool.

He looked over then. He saw her face, and he reached for her.

"Moria, I—"

She scrambled back. "I'm sorry. I—I didn't mean—"

"It's all right."

No, it wasn't. She'd shamed herself. Dishonored their friendship. Worse, she could barely even consider that. All she thought of was that kiss, and how it felt, and that it was over, and she wasn't ever going to feel it again.

She pushed up on all fours. Tyrus caught her cloak.

"Moria—"

"There was no excuse. I . . . I'm tired and I'm frightened and I wanted . . . I should go."

He held her fast. "No."

When she pulled, as if to slip out of the cloak and escape, he took hold of the front, gripping the sides together, his hand right under her chin.

"No," he said, his voice soft and gentle despite the iron grip. "You did nothing wrong."

"Yes. I . . . I behaved dishonorably. I did something you did not want. Something you'd made clear you did not want and—"

He kissed her. She was still talking, and he pulled her down and kissed her. It was not the same as before. No deep, delicious kiss, but still so sweet, so achingly perfect.

This time, when he pulled away, he held her close.

"You gave me *nothing* I do not want, Moria," he said, enunciating each word. "You gave me something I cannot have. You aren't mine. You cannot be mine. Not until I am sure . . ." He loosened his grip. "Gavril is my friend."

Moria yanked so hard she would have tumbled onto her back if he'd let go. He didn't.

"Yes, you do not wish to have this conversation," he said. "We've been avoiding it since we met, because I've known if I pressed the matter, you'd walk away. You cannot walk away here, Moria." He waved at the camp. "So settle in, because we are having this discussion, one-sided though it may be."

She seethed and glowered, but she'd do nothing to give them away.

"Gavril is my friend," he said. "And you will notice I do not use the past tense. I do not believe he's done what he seems to have done. That may make me a fool. But in my heart, I don't believe him capable of this, and I don't think you do either."

"Of course I do. He—"

"That was a statement, not a question. Perhaps, again, I'm wrong. Yet I cannot help but wonder what would happen if he were to appear here now and explain everything to your satisfaction. If he could convince you he'd not betrayed his empire. That he'd not betrayed you."

"Any betrayal of me is trivial and unimportant—"

"No, it isn't." He met her gaze. "Not to you."

"If you are implying that Gavril and I—"

"—were lovers? No, I am quite certain there was not so

much as an affectionate exchange between you, let alone a kiss. If Gavril knew all along what he had to do for his father, then he'd not have allowed that. But he wanted to. He'd fallen for you and—"

"No."

"Yes. I know him, and as much as you don't want to believe that I know him well, I do, and I could tell his feelings for you—"

"No." She struggled against a stronger objection. She wanted to snarl the word, to yank from his grip and stride away into the night, slough off this conversation and cleanse her mind of it. But all she could safely say was a harshly whispered, "It was not like that. Not at all."

"Perhaps. I hope it's not. But if I believe he had feelings for you, which could be returned should the circumstances change, then I cannot let anything happen between us. It would be dishonorable."

"Your sense of honor is misplaced."

A quirked smile. "Perhaps. But it's still mine to misplace." He settled her cloak around her. "If my reaction felt like rejection, then you have very little experience of kissing. Quite clearly, it was reciprocated. I . . ." His gaze lifted to hers. "What I feel for you . . . It's not anything . . ." He swallowed. "If you were mine and then he came back with an explanation, and you realized that you loved him—"

"I do not."

"I believe you cannot know that until the option is there. Or until it is clear there is no option forthcoming."

"What if I said it didn't matter? That I want to be with you, and even if he came back, explained everything, and declared himself, I would still want to be with you."

That twist of a smile again, this time with a flash of longing and pain in his eyes. "Perhaps I am a coward for not taking a chance, but I don't want my heart broken. If you do believe me a coward, and if that changes your opinion of me, then I regret that more than anything."

"I think you're wrong." She leaned forward and kissed him, a quick press of the lips. "But I respect you for it. And when you realize you are wrong, if you still feel that way about me . . ."

"I will. I'm certain of that. Until then . . ." He kissed her nose. "Are we still friends?"

"We are." She turned her attention to the warlord's compound, lit on the hilltop. "If I return to complaining about *that*, will you return to listening to me complain?"

He smiled. "I will."

Soon after, the warlord's men silently appeared from the rear, escorted by the warrior who'd been sent to retrieve them. The warlord—from the Jorojumo clan, with fierce spiders inked on his arms—was a man long into his fifth decade, though age would not keep him off the battlefield. Warlords were hard men, often not achieving their position until near the end of their careers. Even then they'd never rest on the sidelines in a battle. If they did, their men would abandon them.

If Jorojumo had any qualms about working with a prince who'd barely reached manhood, he gave no sign of it. In truth, after decades of peace, there were warriors twice Tyrus's age whose experience was confined to sparring and mock battles.

Together, Tyrus and Jorojumo quickly determined a course of action—split the troops, encircle the camp, and ambush the bandits while they slept. It would not be a battle filled with honor, but under the circumstances, they could not worry about that.

And those circumstances, as conveyed to the warlord? Simply that the bandits had, with a larger troop, invaded both Edgewood and Fairview, decimating the towns for reasons not yet known.

Next Tyrus assigned positions to the warriors. When he did not include Moria, she presumed it was because her position was clear. At his side. She said as much as they walked away from the others afterward.

"No," he said. "You'll be here."

She stopped walking. "Where?"

"Here."

He pointed to the hillock where they'd spent most of the night. He didn't look at her. Nor did he stop walking, and she had to run to catch up.

"You're keeping me out of battle?" she said.

"Yes."

"Was it something the warlord said when you conferred with him? I know he cannot have an issue with women wielding blades. One of his warriors is a woman. I saw her."

"He has no issue with you on a battlefield. I do." He stopped her protest with a raised hand. "I did not tell you sooner because if I had, I'd never have heard the end of it. You've no time to argue now."

She opened her mouth to speak, but couldn't force words past the boiling rage. Beside her, Daigo snarled, his tail lashing.

"Watch over her," Tyrus said to the wildcat.

"And who'll watch over you?" she said. "That is what I planned to do, Tyrus. Not pretend I am a warrior. Not get in anyone's way. I am no trained fighter. But I can fight—for you. That's all I wanted."

"And that is exactly what you'll do. From here. With your throwing daggers and your wildcat."

"Then why am I wearing . . ." She plucked angrily at her armor.

"Because I want you to be safe."

He pulled her closer, leaning in to kiss her forehead, but she squirmed away. He sighed and released her.

"If you think I'm doing it because you're a girl, and you hate me for it, then that is your prerogative. But it has nothing to do with your sex, and I'd hope by now you'd realize that has no import with me. You have no experience on a battlefield. And yes, neither have I, but I have trained for it my whole life. Also you are a Keeper. If I was to allow you out there, fodder for a bandit's blade . . . ?" He shook his head. "I'd not be fit to lead battle hounds. I'd like you to keep an eye out for your sister, in case she returns early with Ronan. If you can also watch over me, I would appreciate that." A wry smile. "I fear I'll need the help."

He leaned in again, as if to kiss her cheek, but again she would not let him. With another soft sigh, he squeezed her shoulder and went to join the others.

As she watched him go, her stomach twisted. Daigo's tail whipped against her.

*He's right. You know that. If you expected anything else, you do
not know him very well. Call him back. Give him a kiss. Wish him
luck. Tell him you'll watch over him.*

"Tyrus?" she whispered as loud as she dared.

He didn't hear her. She took a few running steps. "Tyrus?"

Jorojumo strode over to greet him, and Moria knew she'd
lost her chance. She hovered there, waiting for Tyrus to turn,
to look her way, so she could mouth an apology, smile, and tell
him all was fine. He spoke to the warlord. Then they took their
men and walked their separate ways, and Tyrus never looked
back.

TWENTY-ONE

When Tyrus claimed she had no experience, it had taken all Moria's self-restraint not to snarl back. Had *he* fought shadow stalkers? Thunder hawks? She'd even battled a slaver's mercenaries. How dare he say she'd no experience.

But as the battle unfolded, she realized he was right. She had envisioned herself fighting alongside Tyrus as she had with Gavril. That showed how little she knew of a true battlefield. Even watching Tyrus's back from a distance was a challenge. If she'd been immersed in that chaos . . .

And it *was* chaos. There was no other word for it. Perhaps that shocked her most of all. When bards told tales of clashing armies, she envisioned rows of warriors, fighting as if they were in a festival demonstration, paired off and maintaining position.

This was madness. Bloody, thunderous, stinking madness.

The clang of swords and the grunts and screams of hits. Blood arcing through the air. Blood spattering over the tents and the grass. Clouds of dust and dirt obscuring the fighters. The warriors themselves were blurs of armor and steel, fighting this bandit only to be hit from behind by that one.

With the warlord's men, they'd expected to outnumber the mercenaries. Not by enough to make it a quick and bloodless routing, but enough to make it an easy battle. Except another twenty bandits had arrived almost immediately. They fought with blades and whips and cudgels, ignoring the warrior code.

It was a treacherous, filthy, backstabbing brawl. And Tyrus was caught in the middle of it.

He may have never fought on a battlefield either, but Moria would wager anyone seeing him would not believe it. She had worried about how he would do, after his response to the deaths in Fairview proved that battle training did not equate with battle readiness.

He was magnificent. More skilled with a blade than any warrior on the field. The first mercenary who rushed him was nearly cleaved in two before he could even swing, and that early victory seemed to add fuel to Tyrus's flame. He cut down one opponent after another. As he did, though, he was drawn deeper into battle. Farther out of range of her daggers.

"We need to get closer," she whispered to Daigo as two fighters blocked Tyrus from view.

Daigo grunted but did not move.

"I know he's handling himself well, but he told me to watch over him. I can't do that from here."

She could feel Daigo's gaze on her, and in that moment, she had no doubt there was a warrior's spirit inside him, and that it was considering, assessing. She might have a duty to watch over Tyrus, but Daigo's was to watch over her.

"I won't join the battle," she said. "I'm not ready. I see that now. I just want to be ready for *him*—in case he needs me."

Daigo chuffed and rose. He peered out at the field. Then he snorted, his yellow eyes narrowing. Moria turned to look and—

"Tyrus?" She scrambled up. "*Tyrus.*"

He was gone. She started forward. Daigo caught her trouser leg and growled, telling her to pause and consider. Tyrus had not vanished from the field but simply from her sight. The battlefield was an amorphous thing, always contracting and expanding, and it had constricted again. Where Tyrus had stood, there was a knot of flashing swords, so dense Moria could not tell who was fighting whom, let alone pick out one warrior in the seething mass. She looked for his helmet. Surely she'd see that red dragon helmet. Yet she could not.

Tyrus was there. He had to be.

She crept through the long grass and around the sparse trees. She had her cloak on, hood pulled tight to cover her light hair. It did not, however, mask her face, and she'd gone about half the distance when one of the warlord's men—a young warrior—looked her way. As he did, his opponent lifted his sword, taking advantage of the momentary distraction. Without thinking, Moria flung her dagger square at the man's chest, as she'd been taught, and it was only as the dagger left her hand that she realized what she'd done.

The dagger hit its target. It pierced the simple leather tunic the bandit wore and drove squarely into his heart. His eyes widened. She saw the realization in those eyes. The horror and the fear. And she saw him fall.

She stumbled to a halt, staring at the downed bandit. He lay ten paces away, his mouth working, his fingers fumbling blindly for the dagger. He pulled it free, and the blood gushed, soaking his tunic, running off him in torrents. His life blood. Spilling on the ground, unstoppered by that dagger.

No, by *her* dagger.

I've killed a man.

She had fought her father's corpse and banished the shadow stalker within. She'd helped bring down the thunder hawk. With the slavers they'd fought on the road, while she'd injured two, the only man who'd died had not been by her hand. The scene flashed in her mind, Gavril's blade cleaving through a man, his look of shock as he realized he'd killed him. Shock and, yes, horror, and now that's what she felt, watching this bandit die.

I've killed a man.

Moria looked out over the battlefield. At the men on the ground. Dead and dying. Some bandits. Some the warlord's men. A couple of their own—warriors she'd traveled with for days now. There lay Kinuye, who'd recently married and carried a lock of his new wife's hair. There lay Reynard, whose young son just won his first riding tournament.

"My lady."

It was the young man she'd saved. He was rushing to her side, awkwardly bowing as he hurried over.

"Thank you, my lady."

She looked at him, her gaze struggling to focus. Then she

glanced at the bandit, lying still on the ground, her dagger at his side.

I regret that I had to do it. But I do not regret what I've done. I cannot.

Her gaze swept the battlefield. Her ears rang with the clang of swords, but they did not miss the softer sounds—the gasps and the grunts and the cries of pain.

I regret that all of this had to happen. But it did. They die and a town is saved. That is the warrior's duty. To die so that others may live.

She took a deep breath and clutched her remaining dagger. Daigo sprinted off to retrieve her other blade.

Moria turned to the warlord's man. "I apologize for distracting you in battle. I'm watching over Prince Tyrus, and I lost sight of him, so I was getting closer." She peered into the melee. "I still do not see him."

"He was beset, my lady."

"What?"

"Three men went after him at once. On a signal, I think. I was going to his aid—"

She lunged toward the battlefield. The young warrior caught her arm.

"They did not cut him down, my lady. They surrounded him, and they were driving him off in that direction—" He pointed. "They mean to take him hostage. I'm certain of it."

"Then we'll make sure they do not succeed."

The young warrior led Moria around the battlefield. Some of the men noticed her, but only a few and thankfully none of them was distracted.

As they hurried around the camp, Moria searched the

fighters for Tyrus, in case the young warrior was mistaken. But there was no sign of him.

"They led him behind these tents," the warlord's man said. "But it seems quiet now."

They've taken him.

If someone had suggested before the battle began that a prince could be kidnapped in front of his own men, she'd have laughed. Surely someone would see. Surely *she* would see. But each warrior was locked in his own fight for survival and could ill afford a moment's distraction.

The warlord's man led her to the largest tent. All was quiet and still behind it.

"Blast it," the young warrior said. "We're too late. Can your wildcat follow a trail?"

"He's no hound, but he—"

She caught a blur on the battlefield. A plait of long, black hair whipping as a warrior spun.

"Tyrus," she breathed.

If it had been difficult to pick out men on the field from afar, it was even harder now that she was right beside it. They truly were a seething mass of flashing swords and whirling bodies. But she knew that hair—and the dragon helmet atop it. He was in the thick of the fight, with Jorojumo at his side. Tyrus said something, grinning, and the warlord replied with a smile.

"He's there," Moria said. "The prince is there."

The young warrior exhaled. "Thank the ancestors. Lord Jorojumo must have helped him drive off his attackers. Let us get you to safety, my lady. This is no place for you."

While she followed him around the large tent, she kept

glancing back at Tyrus, assuring herself he was fine. He had blood on one arm and cuts in his breastplate, but none seemed to have penetrated.

The battle had slowed enough that the remaining bandits seemed in no hurry to take on both the young prince and the warlord at once. The two had a moment to catch their breath on the sidelines. Then Lord Jorojumo pointed at someone in the fray. Tyrus started forward, attention fixed on his target. Behind him, the warlord raised his sword.

Why? There is no one close enough to strike except—

Daigo let out a snarl and ran. Moria stood frozen, certain she was mistaken, that the warlord was only hefting his blade.

Lord Jorojumo swung. At Tyrus. At his back.

"Tyrus!" Moria screamed, lunging forward as Daigo flew from the long grass beside him and—

Something hit Moria's head. Pain flashed. Then darkness.

TWENTY-TWO

Moria awoke to darkness. Complete black, as if she hadn't opened her eyes. It was bitterly cold, too, like stumbling from the house on a winter's night, forgetting to pull on her cloak, that first step a shock that sent sleep scattering. She leaped up, only to fall face-first to the dirt as something around her leg stopped her short.

I'm bound. I'm in the dark, and I'm bound. Why—?

She remembered and lunged again with Tyrus's name on her lips. Then she realized she was alone. Completely alone, that chill coming not only from the air, but from deep inside her.

"Daigo?"

She scrambled onto all fours and frantically patted the ground.

"Daigo!"

Even as she felt about wildly, she knew in her gut he wasn't there.

"Is anyone . . . ?" She choked on the word, on her panic, and had to restart. "Is anyone here?"

Her voice echoed in the silence. She squeezed her eyes shut and remembered the warlord swinging his sword at Tyrus, Daigo leaping in, and the last thing she saw . . .

That was the last thing she saw. Not a moment more. She lay there, straining and searching her memory, as if by concentrating harder she could catch a glimpse of what happened next. When her memory failed, her imagination filled in the hole, sending images of the sword cutting through Tyrus or deflecting at the last moment to cut down Daigo instead. Of the warlord's men turning on them both, Daigo and Tyrus dead on a blood-soaked field and—

Bile filled her mouth, and she spat. The movement made her head pound as if it were about to crack open, and she fell to the dirt floor, heaving breath.

Tyrus. Daigo.

And Ashyn. Where was Ashyn? Safe. Moria had to trust in that. Whatever she thought of Ronan, he was clever and he was cautious. He would not have let Ashyn come to danger.

Ashyn would be safe.

And Tyrus? Daigo?

Her stomach lurched again as her fingers dug into the cold dirt.

She closed her eyes and tried to speak to the spirits. Any spirits. She tried and she tried and she tried. Not so much as a whisper answered.

She gave up then, shivering and instinctively reaching to pull her cloak tighter. Like her armor, it was gone, and at that, her throat tightened. After everything she'd lost, the cloak should seem inconsequential. It was not. Her father's last gifts to the girls were Ashyn's ring and Moria's cloak. Now it was gone forever, and in her despair, it felt like losing him again.

When the cold ground beneath her vibrated, she prayed it was a sign from the spirits. But as she pressed her hands against the floor, she heard footsteps. She scrambled up and raked her fingers through her hair and wiped her sleeve over her mouth. She'd not be found lying in the dirt, broken and crying. She would not.

She heard the clang of a bolt being swung free. Then the creak of a wooden door. Light rushed in and the suddenness of it made her head throb. She lifted a hand to shield her eyes.

A man walked in, temporarily blocking the light, so that all she saw was a figure. Tall. Dark-skinned. His hair cut so short the light reflected off his scalp. She could make out nothing more, as hard as she blinked. Then he moved aside, and the light hit again, blinding her.

"I do not see what purpose it serves to show me wretches in the dungeon," a voice said. "I know they're here. I do not enjoy their plight. Nor am I particularly unnerved by it, if that's what you fear. I am supposed to be meeting an ambassador from Umeweil, and I do not think keeping him waiting is wise."

That voice. I know that . . .

The second man appeared. She saw his braids, his bright green eyes, the black-inked sleeves tattooed on his dark

175

forearms, and suddenly she was lying by a campfire, studying those tattoos.

"It's beautiful work."

"I'll remember that when they're doing the inking, and I'm trying very hard not to cry out."

She laughed. "If you fell from a thunder hawk without so much as a gasp, I think you can handle inked needles."

She rolled onto her back, staring up at the dark sky. He reached over and moved her hair away from the fire.

"Before it catches alight," he said.

She'd told herself that if she ever saw Gavril Kitsune again, she'd kill him. Without hesitation. She'd leap up and strangle him with her bare hands if need be. But here he was, standing close enough that she might indeed be able to grab him, yet she did nothing.

Tyrus was right. She remembered the boy who'd fought by her side, the boy who'd confided in her, the boy who'd lain by the fire with her, and no matter what he seemed to have done since, she could not truly believe it.

As she moved, the chain on her leg whispered across the dirt, and Gavril looked her way for the first time. He stopped mid-step and stared, and in his eyes, she saw . . . She couldn't name what she saw. She was afraid to.

"Moria?"

The other man chuckled. "You don't even consider for a moment that it might be her sister? You do know her well."

Moria looked at the man. He was wide-shouldered, shorter and broader than Gavril. His skin tone was lighter. His features were rougher, coarser. But there was no doubt who he was.

Alvar Kitsune. Gavril's father.

The man who killed my father.

Just the other day, she had told Ashyn that she blamed the emperor for their mother's death. That conviction paled against this one. Emperor Tatsu had failed to amend old traditions that had caused their mother to take her life. Yet Alvar Kitsune had murdered their father as surely as if he'd wielded the blade himself. No, worse than that, because he hadn't wielded any blade. He'd hidden in the shadows and let monsters do it for him.

Rage boiled up in Moria, and if she'd been close enough to spring, she would have. For Alvar Kitsune, she would have.

"I lived in Edgewood for nearly two summers," Gavril said. "Of course I can tell them apart."

His tone was clipped and cool, as it'd been when he'd objected to this excursion into the dungeons. An odd tone for a son to use with his father, but that was Gavril. Blunt-spoken. Ill-tempered. Coldly polite to everyone except those he honored with the sharp side of his tongue. Good humor with Gavril was a droll comment, a quick-witted exchange, a teasing insult, a half smile. He was as mercurial and unpredictable as a summer storm. And as invigorating. To weather the storm and catch the flashes of sunlight no one else saw had made her feel . . .

She inhaled softly, air hissing through her teeth.

"What's she doing here?" Gavril said.

"A gift," his father said. "For you."

Confusion crinkled Gavril's forehead. Then something flitted through his gaze. A moment of unguarded expression, as when he'd first seen her. He hid it just as quickly.

"I don't understand," he said, his words brittle. "Why would I want—?"

"I'm asking myself the same thing," his father cut in. "It's not as if there are a lack of women here. Beautiful women, eager to catch the eye of my son. But you pay them no heed."

"Because I have no time for such frivolities. We are preparing for war."

"All the more reason to indulge in pretty distractions. Yet you snap and you snarl and you send the poor girls scattering. That's hardly the behavior of a healthy young man."

Gavril's eyes flashed. "Whatever you are implying—"

"I'm implying that they do not distract you because you are already distracted. By thoughts of a girl you left behind."

"Moria?" Gavril looked at her as one might gaze on a pile of offal. "I ignore the women in camp because I am focused on my goal—on *our* goal. To decide I'm mooning over some mewling chit of a Keeper? Believe me, Father, after our five days in the Wastes together, I'd be quite happy if I never saw her again."

"Is that right?" His father's voice was deceptively soft.

Gavril looked his father in the eye. "Yes. Now, if you'll excuse me. I have an appointment with—"

"You reject my gift?"

Gavril went still then. When he spoke, a veneer of courtesy coated his words. "I apologize if you thought I wished such a gift, though I am at a loss to understand why you would. However, I concede that you no longer know me as well as we'd both like. Perhaps you presume that, after my many days alone with the Keeper, something transpired between us. I can assure you, it did not. I have little patience for such *distractions*, but even if I made an exception, my tastes would run . . ." A curl of his lip as he looked at Moria. "Elsewhere. She's uncultured and headstrong. Not terribly bright either. The empire should exempt Northerners from holding such high positions."

His father laughed. "Agreed. But a lack of intelligence isn't a bad thing in a bedmate, my son. Your mother may be one of the loveliest women in the empire, but she's as empty-headed as her dolls."

Gavril stiffened.

His father patted him on the back. "Don't take offense, boy. You may have gotten your handsome face from her, but the mind behind it comes from me, ancestors be praised. As for the girl, she's your responsibility now. Take her to your bedchamber. You cannot have spent all those nights in her company and never wondered what it would be like to have her."

"No," Gavril said sharply. "Perhaps we do not share the same opinions on such matters, but I'll not soil myself in such a way."

"Oh-ho." His father laughed and turned to Moria. "Did you hear that, child? Are you not offended?"

She was too shocked to take offense. Not shocked by the insults, but by Alvar's words. She wasn't Ashyn, blushing at any mention of relations between men and women. That was a natural part of life. But telling Gavril to bed her as if . . . Well, as if to say, "You're hungry; here's food." She'd grown up in a garrisoned village where girls were raised to understand that no man should lay a hand on you without your permission and the penalties for transgressions were severe.

As a captive, she lost her rights and privileges. She understood that. But to treat her as spoils of war . . . ? Was that something men did?

But Alvar Kitsune was no mere man. He had set shadow stalkers on two villages to slaughter every woman and enslave every man. He was a monster. Did she truly need more proof of that?

She'd still hoped . . . She did not know what she'd hoped. To learn that Alvar Kitsune had been . . . duped? Enslaved? Betrayed by someone he trusted and forced to raise shadow stalkers against his will?

Moria and Ashyn had thought they'd been spared because whoever raised those shadow stalkers was a pious man who didn't dare harm a Seeker and Keeper. She saw their mistake now. They'd been spared because they'd been useful.

You are a child and a fool, Keeper.

As she looked at Gavril's face, she swore she could hear those words. She turned her face away so he wouldn't catch the pain and the grief there.

"What shall I do with your gift, then?" Alvar asked his son. "Kill her?"

Gavril's face remained blank, his eyes empty. "You could, but I can't see how that would help our cause. She's a Keeper and little more than a child. The people would be outraged."

"True. But since I brought her here for you, she is your responsibility. If you don't take her, then she stays here. In the dungeon."

"All right."

A moment of silence. Then, Alvar said, "You'll leave her

here, in the dark and the cold?"

"Certainly." Gavril turned to go.

"Daigo?" Moria said. The name came unbidden, and she hated herself for her weakness. Yet that did not stop her from following with, "My wildcat. Is he . . . ?"

Gavril did not turn. He kept his back to her, stiff and still.

"Well?" Alvar said. "The girl asks after her bond-beast."

"Then tell her," Gavril said.

"She's your responsibility. Any question she asks is for you."

"I don't have time to chase down answers, so she'll have to do without."

Gavril walked out without a backward glance. His father paused there, watching him go, studying him with that hawk-ish stare Moria knew well from his son. Then he turned it on Moria.

"You don't look surprised, girl."

"I'm not. If you were expecting anything different from your son, then I'd suggest that you do not know him very well."

"Oh, we'll see about that."

He gave a humorless smile and the door clanged shut behind him, pitching her into darkness.

TWENTY-THREE

Moria lay in the dark for at least half a day. Or half a night. She had no idea which it was, no way to tell. Darkness. Silence. Cold. That's all she had.

A few times, she rose and tried to pace, but she couldn't see the leg iron and kept tripping against it, and with each stumble, the metal bit into her leg, which was already tender from rubbing against the iron. When she felt blood dripping down her ankle, she stopped and curled into a ball on the floor.

Daigo. Tyrus.

Was Daigo alive? If not, she should feel it. Same with Ashyn.

But Tyrus . . . ?

They'd parted in anger. When he hadn't heard her, she should have gone after him, but at the time, she'd only thought, *I'll do that later.* What if there was no later?

And Gavril . . .

Given what may have befallen Tyrus, she ought not to spend a moment thinking of Gavril. He had betrayed her nearly a fortnight ago.

So why did it still hurt so much?

And what of Edgewood's and Fairview's children? Did they still live? Had Ronan and Ashyn found them? Or could they be here, wherever *here* was?

When the door clanged open, she scrambled up. In walked an elderly woman, her face so lined it seemed lost in its nut-brown folds. A guard followed at her heels. From his bearing she could tell he was not a mercenary, but a warrior of the empire. Sworn to protect the emperor. Now he'd sworn loyalty to a traitor who murdered innocents.

Rage filled Moria, like a flash fire that ignited all her tamped-down anger. She dug her fingers into the dirt floor to keep from launching herself at the traitor.

"This is the healer," the guard said. "She does not speak the common language, so there is no sense attempting to converse with her. She has been sent by Lord Gavril to tend to your wounds. If you raise a hand against her, she will be taken away and will not return, and your injuries will be left to fester."

"I'd not raise a hand against an old woman," Moria said. "You've been too long in the company of the Kitsunes if you expect that."

"I would suggest, Keeper, that you remember where you are and refrain from insulting your hosts. It will not help your situation."

"Alvar Kitsune raised shadow stalkers to massacre my village."

To her surprise, the guard laughed. "Is that what the emperor would have you believe?"

"No, it's what I saw."

"Is it?" All humor left his eyes as they hardened. "Perhaps then you are not a gullible child, but an instrument of the tyrant on the imperial throne. Is that the tale he told you to spread? Shadow stalkers? It would be funny if it weren't so heinous an accusation. The marshal warned us that the emperor would resurrect the old accusations of sorcery."

"Because he *is* a sorcerer." Moria got to her feet. "As is his son. I saw Gavril—"

His hand hit her across the mouth and she fell back, tasting blood. The old woman tensed but did nothing.

"I would beg the ancestors' forgiveness for striking a Keeper, if I did not believe you have already lost their favor. What has that imperial snake promised for your lies?" The guard stepped closer, eyes narrowing. "Or perhaps the rumor is true. They say his young Seeker and Keeper have not been sleeping in their own quarters. Twin girls sharing his sleeping pallet? The old lecher may be guilty of every possible perversion, but that would not be one he's sampled before."

Moria laughed. She couldn't help it.

"You find that amusing, girl?"

"No, I find it ridiculous. First, I can hardly imagine the emperor ignoring a declaration of war to amuse himself with young women. Second, if I'm supposedly his new plaything, why was I captured several days walk from the imperial city, fighting alongside his son? I would hope if he did bed me, he'd not tire of me quite so quickly."

Did she imagine it or did the old woman's lips quirk?

"You think highly of yourself, don't you, girl?" the guard said. "And you don't know when to keep your mouth shut."

"I won't sit by and listen to lies in silence. I should not be surprised, though. How could the Kitsunes expect to woo honorable men to their side if they admitted to sorcery? To raising the dead? To unleashing monsters and massacring—"

"Enough!" He sprang at her, hand raised, but she knocked it aside and glowered at him.

He headed for the door and waved for the old woman to leave with him. She shook her head and teetered over to Moria as she said something in a language Moria didn't recognize. From the guard's expression, he didn't know it either. But he caught the tone and the name Gavril and her meaning was clear enough. Gavril had ordered her to tend to Moria's wounds, and she was doing as she was told.

"You want to stay?" the guard said. "Stay alone, then, and hope she does not snap your old neck."

The guard stormed out. The old healer motioned again for Moria to sit and examined her head to toe with crow-sharp black eyes. She muttered under her breath and toddled off.

"No!" Moria called after her as she scrambled up. "My leg is hurt. The skin's broken, and I fear infection. If you have something clean, I'll wrap it myself—"

The woman walked out and shut the door behind her.

Moria struggled against panic.

I must warn the emperor about Alvar's lies. I must get back . . .

She shifted and heard the chain scrape over the rock-strewn

185

floor. How was she going to escape? Gavril seemed prepared to let her rot in here.

I would not kill you, Keeper. Not kill you. Not harm you. Not ever.

That's what he'd said. But there were so many ways to hurt. Not all of them required fists and blades.

Yes, I have done whatever you believe. I have deceived you. I have betrayed you. Remember that. Whatever happens, remember that.

When the door clanked, she sat up quickly. The old woman had returned, this time with a maidservant bearing a basin of steaming water and a torch. The girl set down the basin and lit the torch, then went, leaving the door open. Moria tried to peer out, to get some sense of where she was, but she saw only a hall with more thick doors.

The old woman said something in her own language. When Moria looked over, the healer motioned for her to undress, waving toward the door as if to assure her no one would come and see her naked. Moria could have laughed. That was truly the last thing she was worried about.

She stripped out of her filthy clothes and began to bathe as the old woman tended to her injuries.

When Moria was done bathing and her ankle had been cleaned and bound, the old woman gave her fresh clothing. As Moria pulled on a shift, the woman passed the bundled tunic and trousers. Moria motioned that she was still getting herself into the shift—the silk stuck on her damp skin—but the woman took Moria's hand and pressed it against the fabric. There was something hidden in the folds. Something small and hard.

Moria reached in and felt a knobby thing small enough to close her fist around. She pulled out her hand, then carefully opened it.

In her palm lay a black figurine. Obsidian carved in the form of a wildcat. Moria raised her gaze to the old woman.

"Does this mean . . . ?" she whispered, unable to finish.

The healer's words came thickly accented and awkward, like a magpie repeating a phrase it had heard.

"He lives."

Moria squeezed the stone figure tightly as tears filled her eyes. The old woman laid a hand on her arm and said something, again in her own language, the words incomprehensible, but the intent clear. Words of comfort and reassurance.

Then, the old woman said, "Keeper."

Moria looked into the woman's black-bead eyes and understood. She was showing her this kindness—the wildcat and the comfort—because Moria was a Keeper. Did the old woman follow their ways? Or perhaps someone else here did, some pious warrior, who'd given her the figurine and the message.

"Tyrus," Moria said. "Prince Tyrus. Does he . . . live?"

Moria could see a glimmer of comprehension in the old woman's eyes.

"I was with Prince Tyrus when I was captured," Moria said, speaking slowly. "He is a friend. A very good friend. He was in danger, and I fear . . . Is Prince Tyrus all right?"

The old woman seemed to search her face then. Searching for what?

After a moment, the healer shook her head.

"No? You mean . . ." Moria could barely force the words out. "He's dead? Tyrus is dead?"

The woman shook her head more vehemently this time. Then she shrugged and shook it again before patting Moria's arm. She didn't know if Tyrus lived or not. That was all she'd been saying.

"What about the children?" Moria asked.

The old woman's face wrinkled in confusion.

"Children?" Moria said. "The little ones? From my village and from Fairview?"

The healer continued to look confused. It did not seem a problem of language comprehension but of context. She knew nothing of captive children. Like the guard, she'd been fed lies. That meant the little ones were not being held here.

Moria finished dressing while the healer brought stew. It was hardly palace-worthy cuisine, but it was hot.

The old woman departed as Moria ate. When the door opened again moments later, it was the guard from earlier, bearing a bucket and a thick wool blanket.

"You'll need this to piss in," he said, throwing the bucket across the cell. "Mind that you do. As for this—" He threw the blanket on the floor beside the bucket. "The old witch thought you might be cold."

He started to leave, then stopped and turned. "I know you Northerners aren't too bright, so let me show you how to use that bucket."

He walked over to it and reached into his trousers. Moria looked away and waited for the sound of him relieving himself in the bucket. When she heard nothing, she glanced over to see him urinating on her blanket. She lunged to grab it, but it was too late.

"Huh," he said. "It seems I missed. It's so dark in here. An easy mistake."

He hitched his trousers up, grinned at her, and sauntered out the door. Moria lifted the blanket, in hopes that perhaps he'd only soiled a corner. Of course he hadn't. The middle was soaked through, rendering the blanket unusable. Worse, the smell . . .

She threw the wet blanket into the corner, curled up on the floor, clutched her wildcat figurine, and shivered against the cold.

TWENTY-FOUR

"He's going to die," Guin said as she gazed down at Tyrus's still form.

"No." Ashyn wiped a cool cloth over Tyrus's sweat-soaked forehead. "He is not."

"He will. It was a powerful poison." The girl glanced at the dark form lying beside Tyrus. "The wildcat may pass, too. He seems to have gotten less of the poison, but there's still a chance."

Ashyn gritted her teeth and kept cooling Tyrus's brow. They'd laid blankets on the floor of the abandoned hut and put Tyrus and Daigo on them. Ronan had undressed Tyrus to help with the fever, but had draped an extra blanket from his midriff to his thighs, for modesty. When Ashyn had returned from refilling the water bucket, she'd caught Guin peeking under the blanket. The girl hadn't been the least bit ashamed of her actions—instead making observations that

Ashyn was still trying very hard to forget.

She'd like to forget Guin herself, as well, but that was more difficult. She couldn't even send her off in good conscience—there was no one to take her. The expedition was lost.

Lost. That was one way of putting it. The expedition was dead—that was another.

Everyone who'd accompanied them from the imperial city had been slaughtered by the bandits and Lord Jorojumo's men.

Ronan and Ashyn had returned shortly after the warlord's treachery to find only one remaining warrior. Tyrus was with him. He'd been fighting like a whirlwind. Before Ronan could join the fray, Tyrus had fallen.

He'd not been attacked—he'd simply fallen. Poisoned by a blade or a dart, as they later realized. Aided by Daigo and Tova, Ronan had managed to fend off all attackers and drag Tyrus from the battlefield. That's when Daigo had fallen, too. The remaining warrior only survived long enough to cover their retreat before being cut down.

Later, Tyrus had roused and managed to tell them what had happened. How the warlord had betrayed them. How Moria had vanished. Tyrus had spotted her on the edge of the battlefield with one of the warlord's men. Then she was shouting his name, and he'd turned just in time to avoid a fatal blow from the warlord.

By the time he managed to get off the field, Moria was gone. Presumably taken by the young warrior. Now held captive by the warlord? Perhaps. More likely by Alvar Kitsune himself.

If Moria was with Alvar, Ashyn hoped Gavril was there.

191

While Moria believed he'd betrayed them, Ashyn had seen them together on the road. Gavril cared for Moria. He'd not let her be harmed.

Please let her be with Gavril. Let her be safe. Let her return to me soon.

And let her return to Daigo. The wildcat lay unmoving by Tyrus's side. He was conscious. Ashyn suspected he wasn't even asleep, though he kept his eyes shut. His leg had suffered a sword slice, and as the poison took hold, the wound had festered until he couldn't walk. Which was just as well. When he'd still been able to hobble, he'd kept trying to go after Moria.

Ronan had followed Daigo a few times, in case he did in fact know where Moria was, but the wildcat was only searching blindly, so they'd confined him to the hut. Since then, he'd barely lifted his head to drink. He chose not to move. He chose not to eat.

After they'd found the hut, they'd gone searching for the rest of the convoy and found only two survivors.

When they'd seen the warlord's men coming for them, riding hard, the scholar Katsumoto had insisted Simeon take their scrolls and hide in the woods. Ashyn and Ronan had found him there, and he'd volunteered to take the only remaining horse and ride for help. Ashyn had suggested Ronan go instead—so he could get back to his brother and sister. Ronan refused, and she was, admittedly, glad of it. Simeon would have been useless out here, and while Ronan might not be a shoulder to cry on, he understood how much her sister's absence affected and worried her.

So Simeon had gone. By now, he should have reached the imperial city. The emperor would know what had happened and be sending troops.

Guin was the other survivor. Confined to the wagon, she'd kept silent during the attack. Ashyn had released her and occasionally regretted that. It seemed that once one became a spirit, one's capacity for human compassion evaporated. After two days, Guin had suggested they abandon Tyrus and Daigo, forget Moria, and let nature and fate run their course. Ronan had told her—repeatedly—that she was free to leave. He'd eventually offered her one of his blades and half their food. She'd still stayed.

Ronan came in and slung a bag on the broken table. "Apples, rice, dried fish . . . I even found some honey."

"Honey?" Guin perked up. "Do you know how long it's been since I've tasted honey?"

"It'll be longer still," Ronan said. "This is for Tyrus and Daigo."

"They need sustenance," Ashyn explained. "They can only take water and that's not enough. I'll mix in the honey." She smiled at Ronan. "Thank you."

She didn't ask where the food came from. He'd stolen it. There was no choice. They were still deep in Jorojumo's lands and didn't dare appeal to his farmers and peasants. Ashyn hoped Ronan stole only from those who could afford the loss, but she knew she was being foolish if she expected him to heed such concerns. They were in fear for their lives while nursing an imperial prince from the brink of death. Ronan would take supplies wherever he could find them.

Guin looked down at Tyrus. "I'm sure he wouldn't mind if I had a little of his honey . . ."

"He's a prince," Ashyn snapped, more harshly than she intended.

"A bastard prince. It's not quite the same thing. But I take your meaning. The emperor will reward us handsomely if we do manage to save his life."

"That is not why we're—"

"Go for a walk with Tova, Ash," Ronan said. "I can look after Tyrus."

"I ought to watch Tyrus."

"He's sound asleep."

As if on cue, Tyrus groaned. He writhed under the sheet, moaning. Ashyn quickly wet a cloth and pressed it to his forehead.

His eyes opened, and he smiled. "Moria . . ."

She'd corrected him the first few times he'd woken, fever-fuddled, mistaking her for her sister. He wouldn't listen. Daigo was at his side, and when she leaned over him, he saw Moria. The few times he'd woken while Ashyn was out, he'd flown into a delirious rage, attacking Ronan and Guin, as if they'd stolen Moria from him.

"Moria," he said again now, reaching for Ashyn's hand, fumbling to find it, as if his vision was as fuzzy as his mind.

"I'm here," she said, and clasped his fingers in hers.

She sat beside him and held his hand. He never noticed that she didn't act or sound like Moria. She looked like her, and that was enough. His eyes fluttered open and closed as he murmured things she couldn't make out, fevered mumblings, clasping her hand so hard it almost hurt. Then he drifted off again. She waited until his grip relaxed and slid free.

"He loves her, doesn't he," Guin said.

Ashyn looked at her.

"The prince," she said. "He loves your sister."

Now it was Ashyn mumbling something unintelligible. A few days ago, she'd have said only that Tyrus cared for Moria and she for him. Now . . . ? Was it love? Perhaps, but it seemed an invasion of Tyrus's privacy to speculate, especially with Guin.

"It's very romantic," Guin said. "I hope they don't die."

Ronan turned on Guin. "If you don't stop that, I swear I'll send you back to the spirit world. Moria is Ashyn's sister. Tyrus is our friend. We care about them. We do not want them to die." He turned to Ashyn and muttered, "I can't believe I needed to explain that."

"I don't want them to die either," Guin said. "That's what I said."

"How about you don't mention the possibility of their deaths at all."

"But it is a possibility. A very real one. I'm only—"

"Stop. No one needs the reminder."

Guin looked confused, and as much as Ashyn agreed with Ronan, she said, "I'm glad you don't want them to die, Guin. That's . . . kind of you."

"Thank you. I know people think romantic stories are better if the lovers die, but I can assure you, there is nothing romantic about death. I would rather see them live. The dashing bastard prince and the brave and beautiful Keeper." She

195

pursed her lips. "Perhaps not beautiful. Quite pretty, though, for a Northerner." She glanced at Ashyn and said, "And, of course, you're pretty, too," in a halfhearted way, as if she was not Moria's identical twin. Guin turned to Ronan. "Do you think I am?"

"What?"

"Do you think I'm pretty?"

"It's not a question I've spent a single moment contemplating."

Guin rolled her eyes. "I'm not asking if you're attracted to me. That would be very awkward. I'd need to remind you that you're a lowborn boy, and that I could never return your attentions."

"Goddess be praised," Ronan muttered.

Guin turned to Ashyn. "Do you find the body I'm inhabiting pleasing?"

Ashyn stared at her as Ronan choked on a laugh.

"I don't believe I understand the question," Ashyn said slowly.

"I'm asking if I've chosen an attractive form. I had to act quickly when the vessel was free, and I did not have time to properly assess it. I do not recall any obvious deformities, and from what I've seen when I disrobe—"

Ronan coughed. "We do not require details. If you're asking if the girl you inhabit was pretty, she's . . ." He glanced at Ashyn for help.

"Yes, she is pleasant in appearance," Ashyn said. "However, right now, it is more important that she is strong and healthy, so that she may survive this ordeal."

"Certainly, but I intend to survive, and after that, beauty will stand me in far greater stead than strength or health. I was twenty summers when I passed, and not yet wed. Nor had I any suitors. My mother blamed my face and form. I was not an attractive girl, and too thin by far. That was why no man had chosen me."

"Not necessarily," Ronan muttered again.

Guin settled on the floor and crossed her legs. "In my village, I saw many girls who were as dull as a hoe and as stupid as a cow, all wed by their fourteenth summer, so long as they were fair of face."

"Fourteenth summer?" Ashyn said. "When did you live?"

Guin shrugged. "It was a very long time ago. But I learned the value of beauty, and if I have been given a second chance at life, I'm relieved that I've overcome that obstacle. This time, I will wed, and wed well, and I will grow fat and old, surrounded by every luxury." She looked at Ashyn. "That's the advantage women have. To improve their station, they need only stay charming and beautiful long enough to catch a good husband. It's much harder for men. To better themselves, they must work at it their entire lives. I'm glad I'm a woman."

Ashyn looked at Ronan.

"Best not to comment," he said.

She turned to Guin. "I believe you may find times have changed somewhat."

"I still need to be beautiful to wed. That never changes."

"Well, if I may be so bold, I've always found that one of the keys to beauty is frequent bathing. The longer one goes between washings, the more the dirt and grime become engrained in one's skin, until it is quite impossible to remove. The best water of all is fresh from the source." She handed Guin the bucket. "Do you know where the spring is?"

"A goodly walk from here."

"Yes, but you need not hurry. I have enough water to last until sundown. And the longer your bath, the more your skin and hair will shine."

Guin thanked her for her advice, and left as Ashyn turned her attention back to Tyrus.

TWENTY-FIVE

Ronan and Ashyn were outside the hut now. She would stay close enough to hear Tyrus if he woke, but she needed the fresh air and the chance to stretch her legs. They walked along the path leading from the hut. A tree had fallen over it—a small one, easily moved, but they'd left it to discourage anyone from investigating the path.

The hut was only a single room. It had no amenities to speak of, not even a shelter out back for the toilet pit. Ashyn could not imagine living like that for long. Obviously, someone had. Someone who lived off the land. *Stole* off the land, to be more accurate. They were close enough to the warlord's compound that all this land would belong to him. Even growing crops on it would be considered theft. Which explained why the hut was so well hidden, a distance from both the road and the spring.

Ashyn didn't dare walk as far as the road, but they could see it from a curve in the path, and she peered along that seemingly endless stretch of road that would, ultimately, lead to the imperial city.

"Simeon ought to have reached the palace two days ago," she said. "He'd know he couldn't stop even for the night. The situation is too urgent. And the emperor would send a fast horse back, ahead of any troops. The rider ought to be here."

"You're worried about Simeon?"

She nodded. "He's no warrior. No great rider either, despite being from the steppes. I fear he didn't reach the imperial city."

"You've grown fond of him."

She shrugged and shaded her eyes to look down the road. "He was very knowledgeable and quite companionable."

"Were you courting?"

She turned sharply, her distraction vanishing. "What?"

Ronan cleared this throat. "I do not ask out of jealousy, of course."

"I would not presume you do, given that *you're* the one who rebuffed *me*."

He winced. "I did not rebuff—"

"Call it what you will. I was reacting to the absurdity of the question. I'd just seen Fairview massacred. We were on the trail of murderers, praying to find my village's children alive. Do you truly think I was batting my lashes at the nearest young man?"

"I didn't mean courting as in . . ." He struggled for words and then said, "I only asked if you were moving in that direction, so I could better commiserate with your concern for his well-being."

"I don't need you to commiserate with anything. Yes, I am

200

worried, as I would be if it was anyone I know. While Simeon did express an interest, I made it clear his feelings were not returned."

"Was he angry?"

"I suspect it is impossible to be anything but a little angry when one is romantically rejected."

Ronan glanced away. After a few moments, he said, "Are *you* angry? With me?"

"I was confused, Ronan. I did not initiate the kiss. I did not give any indication that I expected it. Yes, I reciprocated—I was returning what seemed to be obvious interest on your part. Later, you acted as if I'd thrown myself at you."

"I didn't—"

"That's how you made me feel. Like a foolish girl who's been kissed once and presumes a marriage proposal will follow. Perhaps I ought to laugh and say that I am relieved, because I did not truly care for you at all. But I have little experience at lovers' games, and so I am honest. You may not have intended to hurt me, but I was hurt. Clearly, I'm not wallowing in misery. I only wish you had handled it with more sensitivity."

"There is more to it than—"

"Hello!" a distant voice called, weak and crackling. "Is anyone there?"

"Tyrus," she said, and raced back to the hut.

When they reached the hut, Tyrus was sitting up, the blanket tangled around his waist. He looked at her and, without hesitation, he said, "Ashyn," and she knew his fever had broken.

He glanced at Daigo. The wildcat stretched, his claws extending.

"Where's . . . ?" he began. Then he stopped. "Moria. She's—"

He went to leap up. The blanket started to fall and he grabbed for it, the movement too sudden, sending him nearly falling flat on his face. He cursed as he struggled to get his balance. His face was so pale he could pass for a Northerner. Ashyn darted forward to help him as Ronan riffled through the pile of clothing.

"I'm fine," Tyrus said, brushing her off. "I just need . . ."

His legs wobbled, and before anyone could grab him, he collapsed back onto the blankets, the one around his waist falling free. Ashyn turned away quickly.

"I need my trousers apparently," he said with a strained laugh. "We'll put that at the top of the list. My apologies, Ashyn."

She murmured that no apology was needed, but her cheeks flamed nonetheless. Ronan passed Tyrus his trousers, which Guin had cleaned—if haphazardly.

"We needed to undress you because of the fever," Ashyn said.

"I wasn't about to ask for an explanation."

She heard the swish and shimmy of fabric as he pulled his clothing on behind her.

"Now, with trousers acquired, I'm fit to get outside this . . . whatever it is. The smell is enough to send me back onto that pallet."

Ashyn turned as he swayed. "You truly shouldn't strain yourself—"

"I'm fine. I just need—" He took one step and dropped to one knee, catching himself before he fell completely.

"You've been poisoned, your highness," Ashyn said. "And four days in a fever. You cannot expect to get up and walk out of here."

"You sound like your sister. Except she'd inject more snap and less civility in the sentiment. Now, speaking of Moria . . ."

Again, he trailed off. The fever may have broken, but he hadn't quite recovered his wits, and he kept forgetting himself.

"Is she still . . . ?" He looked up sharply. "She was captured. Did you find her?"

"We could not," Ronan said. "Daigo could not either. We believe she was delivered straight to Alvar Kitsune, as a prize of war."

Tyrus nodded slowly, and Ashyn could see his mind turning. "Yes, that would make sense. If she's with Alvar, then she's with Gavril, which means she is safe. Whatever he's done, it's not as if he'd allow her to rot in a dungeon."

"That was my thinking as well," Ashyn said.

"Good." A weak smile for her. "Then we can both rest easier until I recover her, which I intend to do as quickly as I can. I presume the counselors have been sent back to tell my father what's happened?"

Ronan looked at Ashyn.

"I fear the counselors are dead," Ashyn said. "They were waylaid after we searched for the children's camp. Which we did not find."

"Because the children were never here," Tyrus said.

She nodded. "It seems so. The man with the story about his brothers was likely a trap to convince you that you were heading the right way."

"While Alvar's men attacked Northpond instead."

"I don't know." She'd been trying hard not to think of that.

When she looked over, she knew that this was exactly what he was thinking. Of Northpond. Massacred because he'd made the wrong choice.

"The counselors supported your decision," she said.

"Which would be much more helpful if they'd survived to confirm that."

"*We'll* confirm it. And Simeon. He survived, and we've sent him back to the city to tell your father. A fast rider should be along any moment now."

Tyrus nodded, but his gaze was still distant.

"Simeon will tell him what happened," Ashyn continued. "You made the best possible choice, and you had the full support of both counselors. We all heard that. You will be fine."

"The people of Northpond will not be fine. Nor will the counselors. Or the warriors who rode with us." He fell quiet, then managed a wry twist of a smile. "Well, I always said I had no interest in politics or a high military position. Now I don't have to worry about it. And I've long wanted to see the desert. I've heard the outposts there aren't nearly as bad as they claim."

"No one is exiling you to a military outpost," Ashyn said. "You did nothing wrong."

"I'm joking." He paused. "I hope. But enough of that. When exactly did you send Simeon and what were his orders?"

"A rider should have come by now," Tyrus said when Ashyn finished explaining. "Something has happened to Simeon." He stood again and looked about. "You have my blades."

Ronan passed them over, along with Tyrus's belt and tunic.

204

"We'll start for the city," he said.

"Now?" Ashyn said. "You're not recovered enough for the journey."

"I have to be. The longer we delay, the longer my father doesn't know about Jorojumo's betrayal. And the longer before I can go after Moria."

"You truly aren't in any condition to travel. Ronan can go. Guin's here, though I'm not sure she's more help than hindrance."

"Guin . . . ? Ah, yes. The spirit-possessed girl." A half laugh. "I cannot believe I just said that quite so casually. We do make an unlikely group, don't we? The Seeker, the thief, the ghost, and the bastard prince." He shook his head. "We are leaving, though. All of us. If I can't manage it, Ronan will go on ahead, but I need to try. We leave before sundown."

TWENTY-SIX

Ronan stole horses for their journey. No, Ashyn corrected. *They* stole horses. Ronan only found the steeds and facilitated the theft. They needed mounts as much as they'd needed food.

Tyrus made a note of the homesteads they'd taken them from and vowed that he'd pay the owners back tenfold. But they were still on Jorojumo's land, so the chance that Tyrus *could* pay them back was slight, though it made them feel better. Or it made Ashyn and Tyrus feel better. Ronan and Guin seemed to consider the entire discussion a waste of time.

Having come from homesteads, the horses were not accustomed to galloping long distances. Neither, Ashyn would admit, was she. Not that she mentioned it, even when she could barely walk upon dismounting. To her surprise, Guin didn't complain either, though she seemed to be in as much discomfort as Ashyn.

The horses did their best, but by the time they were two days' hard ride from the imperial city, it became clear they could go no farther without resting. The group stopped at an inn to water and feed their mounts and themselves.

Tova and Daigo stayed in a patch of forest near the stables. Tyrus hid his tattoos and blades under a light cloak. In his present state, it was unlikely his face would be recognized even in the city. It was still wan from the poison and filthy from the road, with a yellowing bruise on one cheek and a healing cut on his chin.

"I'll be going home when we reach the city," Ronan said as they sat in the inn's dining room, pulling apart pork buns. "I've been away longer from my family than I expected, so I'd rather not linger."

"Go on ahead as soon as you're rested," Tyrus said. "I appreciate everything you've done for us, and your recompense will reflect that."

"Recompense?" Guin said. "You mean money?"

"It was a polite way of saying that," Tyrus said. "I hired Ronan to aid us, and he's gone well beyond what was expected of him."

"So I'll be paid, too, then. For helping out."

"Absolutely," Ronan said. "Just tell us what you actually did to help, and we'll pay you accordingly, once we've deducted your expenses. Which by my rough calculations, means you owe us about ten silver."

Guin glowered at him.

"You will receive a stipend from my father," Tyrus said. "After you've spoken to his advisors, and they've learned whatever else you might know that can help us."

Tyrus said more, but Ashyn didn't catch it. She was exhausted, and her mind retreated into simple quiet. The voices faded, as did the smells of the pork buns and the tea, and she drifted between the worlds, only faintly aware of the others.

Come, child.

The spirit's voice startled her out of her reverie. She looked around, blinking, as if it had come from a real person.

"Ash?" Ronan said.

Come now.

"Sorry. I'm drifting off. I'll go out and get some air, see to Tova and Daigo."

"I'll come with you," Ronan said, rising as she did.

She waved him down. "Rest. I'm only stepping outside."

This way.

Ashyn followed the spirit's voice. She checked outside the inn before stepping into the midday sun. A moon ago, she would have hurried after the spirit without hesitation, never needing to worry that it might be summoning her for anything but good.

The spirit continued whispering, just a word or two, drawing her along. She was rounding the stables when she heard a soft footfall behind her.

"Ronan?" she said. "I know you're there."

He stepped from beside the stable wall. "I didn't wish to startle you."

"And sneaking behind me is less likely to do so than simply walking up and saying hello?"

He walked toward her. "I was hoping to wait until you

were with Tova, so we could speak privately."

"About what?"

"I know what I said in there upset you."

She stared at him in confusion. "What did you say? My mind had drifted."

He stopped in front of her. "Don't, Ash. I handled it poorly. I should have told you I was leaving before I told the others."

"Leaving?"

"Yes, I said that when we reach the city—"

"You're going on ahead to reunite with your brother and sister. Is that what you think made me run outside?" She gave a soft laugh. "No, Ronan. I'm quite aware that you intend to return to them quickly. If you must know, I came out because a spirit summoned me."

Now it was his turn to laugh under his breath. "You don't need to make excuses—"

"You do think highly of yourself, don't you? I'm truly following a spirit. Which is getting impatient. Now, I need to find out what it wants. If you wish to follow, you may do so, though I'll warn you it may be disappointing when I don't break down sobbing behind the stables."

He had the grace to look abashed. "I didn't think you were coming out for that."

"No, just to wander about the stables, wallowing in my grief and the stink of horse dung." She continued on as the spirit summoned her, more urgently now. "I know you're eager to return to your siblings. I'd think less of you if you didn't hurry back to them. You're a good brother."

His gaze slid to the side, his eyes filling with a look she

couldn't quite catch. "Not always."

"Tyrus offered to pay you handsomely. You weighed the options and decided Jorn and Aidra were better served if you came with us."

"It's not a matter of option, Ash. I don't truly have . . . It's not as if I could simply . . ." He trailed off and rubbed his mouth.

She slowed, but the spirit urged her on.

"There's something I need to speak to you about," he said. "I tried, before we parted the last time. I should have. It would better explain the decision I made . . . not to be with you."

"Can we not discuss this again?"

They'd come around the stables now to a side yard, where a girl was currying a horse while two traders talked, both trying to impress her.

Stop, child. Hide yourself.

Ashyn backed around the side of the stable. Ronan did the same, without comment.

"Do you remember our meal in the inn?" he whispered. "The last one? Before we parted? We spoke of the girl you'd met. The casteless one."

Listen now, the spirit said.

"Yes, but I need to—"

"You know that my family was stripped of their warrior caste for backing the wrong imperial successor. Do you understand what that means?"

"Of course. Your family is no longer allowed to claim their caste. They're moved down the ranks, according to the severity of the crime. Can we discuss this later? I truly need to—"

"And I truly need to explain this, Ash. While it's usually a lowering of rank, sometimes—"

"—bastard prince?" one of the traders was saying.

Ashyn urgently waved Ronan to be silent, but he'd already stopped and moved closer to listen.

"That's what you expect, isn't it?" the man continued. "From a bastard? He was a clever one, though. Playing the fool."

"I didn't think him a fool," the servant girl said.

The second man snorted. "Because he's young and handsome. And he was no fool. He simply played one. That was the game. Smile for the crowds. Take no part in politics. Spend his days sparring and chasing pretty girls."

"As a prince should," the other man said. "I know that's what I'd do if I were an imperial bastard."

"Because you're a fool. Young Tyrus was not."

Ashyn stiffened. It had certainly seemed they'd meant Tyrus, but until they named him, she'd not been sure. As she tensed, Ronan laid his hand on her hip, squeezing it as he braced himself against her.

"No?" the other trader said. "I'd say that's exactly what he was. An overreaching fool who proved himself a coward. That's what I expect from a bastard. Weakness. When the emperor spreads his seed so far, it thins, and the result is always this. Weak sons. Cowards."

"So it's true then?" the girl said. "What they say Prince Tyrus did?"

"It is indeed. Ran from the battlefield and left his men to die. Which sounds very familiar, doesn't it?"

When the girl said nothing, one of the traders laughed. "She's too young to remember. He means Marshal Kitsune. That's the crime he was exiled for. Running from a losing battle and sacrificing his men. Which we all know was a lie. The emperor feared the marshal's power and had him framed and exiled. Now the goddess has exacted her punishment. His own son has done the same thing. Judgment has already been passed. When the bastard prince slinks back to the imperial court, his father plans to exact the same penalty. Death to the coward who bears his name. Fitting, don't you think?"

The spirit whispered something, but Ashyn was already racing back to the inn with Ronan right behind her.

TWENTY-SEVEN

"I t's a lie," Tyrus said when they had him outside, far enough from the inn to speak in private.

"Of course it is," Guin sniffed. "Even I saw enough of what happened at the battlefield not to believe such nonsense."

"I mean it's a lie that judgment has been passed. What you've heard is a rumor. An alarming one, to be sure, but I *did* lead a troop into an impossible battle. I was spirited away from that battle. I am the only warrior who survived. The charge is not untrue."

"Yes, it is," Ashyn said. "Because the circumstances are much more complicated than that."

"But to some, no matter how the facts are laid out, they will see exactly what those men do. As Moria would say, people like a good story."

He went silent for a moment, and Ashyn could tell he was

thinking of her sister. He'd been struggling with his decision not to search for her first. Duty and honor bound him to this path, but his heart pulled him in a very different direction.

"I wouldn't call that a good story," Guin said.

Tyrus gave his head a sharp shake, as if clearing it. "Moria would tell you a good story doesn't need to be true or happy. It merely needs to be satisfying. And for some, this would be supremely satisfying. They believe my father falsely exiled Alvar Kitsune. What better fate than to have his own son be guilty of the same charge?"

"This is Alvar's work, then," Ashyn murmured. "Starting this rumor."

"Perhaps. But the only impartial survivor was Simeon, who seems, poor soul, not to have survived the journey. My father won't defend me against these rumors—he does not dare, for fear of seeming indulgent. But he won't believe them either, until he has proof. The horses should be sufficiently rested. We'll ride to the city—"

"No," Ronan said.

"We—"

"No." Ronan stepped in front of Tyrus. "You are not riding to the city until I have gone ahead and investigated this rumor."

Tyrus's brows shot up. "Is that an order?"

"I'm being impudent, I know. But you are the one who's told us, repeatedly, not to treat you as a prince. Out here, you've said, you're simply a friend. So, I'm going to insist you stay here, while I investigate, as a friend."

"I appreciate that . . . I think. But I can't allow it. Every moment we delay is another moment in which my father is, presumably, unaware of what has happened—with Fairview, with Northpond, with Jorojumo. And it's another moment in which I am dealing with this while Moria is held captive. So I'm sorry if you disagree, but I'm returning to the city—"

As Tyrus stepped forward, Ronan pulled his blade.

"Ronan!" Ashyn said.

Tyrus only shook his head. "Obviously you feel strongly about this."

Ronan adjusted his grip on his blade. "I do, your highness."

"And I feel equally strongly that any risk I face is outweighed by duty. I must return to the city. Immediately. If you say I may not, we are at an impasse."

"We are."

Tyrus eyed the blade. "If you draw that against me, you ought to be prepared to use it."

"I am." Sweat beaded along Ronan's forehead, but he kept the sword steady.

"I would need to defend myself."

"You would."

"All right, then. I would prefer to avoid open combat, so let's handle this civilly. Do you know how to score a strike?"

Ronan nodded.

"If you can, I'll stay. If I can disarm you first, you'll let me leave."

Tyrus unsheathed his blade, and Ashyn realized they were going to spar, which was not her idea of "handling it civilly." Before she could say so, Ronan was lunging, sword swinging and—

A resounding clang, so loud that Ashyn jumped in spite

of herself. She saw the blades strike. She saw Ronan's sword fly up, knocked clear out of his hand. It hit the ground, and he stood there, gaping at it.

Tyrus shook his head and sheathed his blade. "You may have been trained to fight, but I believe you need a little more practice. Now, I'll ask one more favor of you, Ronan, before I leave. See to Ashyn, please. As there is some danger with me returning to the city, I'd rather she didn't accompany me there. Please escort her back with Guin. I'll speak to you both once this matter is cleared up."

Tyrus began walking away.

"Your high . . ." Ashyn began. "Tyrus!"

He glanced back.

Ashyn stepped forward. "Moria would try to stop you."

"I'm sure she would. More effectively, too. But she'd also understand that this is what I need to do. Now take care on the remainder of the journey. I'll see you in the city."

He continued toward the stables.

Ronan retrieved his sword, grumbling under his breath. "He might be more even-tempered than your sister, but he's just as stubborn."

Ronan was still sliding his blade into his belt when Tyrus rode from the stables.

"We can't let him go alone," Guin said.

Ashyn looked at her in surprise.

"We won't get a reward if we don't accompany him to the gates," Guin said, but in her eyes, Ashyn thought she detected a shadow of genuine worry.

Ashyn looked back toward Tyrus. As he rode onto the

lane, a dark shape shot from behind the stables. It was Daigo. The wildcat stopped by the roadside. He looked at Ashyn, then back at Tova, loping out from where he'd been hiding. Tova started for Ashyn. Daigo gave one last look from Ashyn to Tova to Tyrus, then raced after the prince.

"Daigo's right," Ashyn said. "We need to go with him."

"Didn't I say that?" Guin murmured.

"I agree," Ronan said to Ashyn. "But he'll not allow it."

"Then we'll follow him."

TWENTY-EIGHT

They said all roads led to the imperial city. Of course that was true—all roads linked up with other roads and would ultimately take you anyplace you wished to go. This road did in fact become the Imperial Way, though, and was busy enough that they could follow Tyrus unnoticed.

"Oh, he's noticed," Ronan said when Ashyn commented.

"But he hasn't looked back once."

"No, we haven't *seen* him look back. He's a prince and a warrior, Ash. He's not going to glance about like a nervous trader with a full purse. He acts as if no one would dare attack him, so they give him wide berth. But he's fully aware of his surroundings. He knows we're here. He's just not going to do anything about it unless we come closer."

"He's in danger, isn't he," Guin said. She'd been riding quietly until now.

Ronan took a moment to respond. He'd become accustomed

to ignoring her, and he seemed to have to struggle against that urge now. "Yes, he's in danger."

"Do you think the rumor's true? That the emperor has already condemned him?"

Ashyn considered carefully. "I do not know the emperor well enough to say with certainty, but I believe that the court of opinion may have condemned Tyrus, though his father has not. That is equally dangerous. It is, however, a matter easily resolved."

"Is it?" Guin asked.

Ashyn's reply was firm. "It is."

She glanced down at Tova. He walked at her side, making no effort to hide. Hounds of various types were common enough in the empire that, while his size garnered a few curious glances, he was dismissed as a rare or exotic breed. Daigo was the one who stood out, which meant that he did not walk beside Tyrus, but slunk along the buildings and long grass and any other obstacles he could find at the road's edge. With Moria gone, the wildcat acted in her stead, watching over Tyrus.

"I don't think we're the only ones following the prince," Ronan said after a moment.

At first, she thought he meant Daigo, but then she saw his tight face.

"Where?" she whispered.

"Guin? Fall back."

"Please," Ashyn added.

The girl did. She'd been pensive since the scene at the inn, as if finally realizing this was not some grand adventure. She wasn't stupid. Nor as unfeeling as she seemed. Simply unaccustomed to worrying about danger—or worrying about others. She'd been a spirit for so long. How long? If girls had wed by their fourteenth summer in her time, it could be several ages ago.

"They're on your side," Ronan said. "Near the edge of the road. Three warriors."

She counted to five under her breath and then swept her gaze over the other travelers. It was not difficult to spot the men. The dual swords hanging from their waists meant even on a crowded thoroughfare, no one got too close. While jostling a warrior's sword no longer carried a penalty of death, few cared to risk the insult.

Warriors served in many roles. This trio was clearly not in the army. While uniforms were worn only for tournaments, processions, and imperial events, there was a standard of dress required at all times. Simple, well-made, but generally somber garb. The outfits on these three were ornate, colorful, and not particularly well-made. Their clothing reminded her of the bandits, yet those men had clearly not been warrior caste—their bearing, their grooming, and their overall demeanor had given them away. These three were clean-shaven, with gleaming hair, white teeth, and no jewels. Men who understood the warrior way. Men who followed it, though?

She moved her horse closer to Ronan. "I don't think they're regular warriors. Their manner of dress is ostentatious."

He frowned at her, puzzled. He was literate and intelligent, but not quite as book-learned as she was. *No one is as book-learned as you, Ash*, Moria would say. Which wasn't true—Simeon had been her superior in that area.

Moria. Simeon.

Moria was fine. She didn't know about Simeon. She

220

prayed for his safety. But her sister was fine. Daigo would know otherwise.

"It's not proper warrior attire," she said. "Wealthy warriors may show it in their garb, but they would buy proper fabrics and hire proper tailors. These three look like . . ."

"Whores trying to dress as court ladies?" He caught her blush. "Sorry."

"Not the analogy I'd use, but yes. Perhaps they're mercenaries?"

"I'm more concerned with what they're doing."

What they were doing was watching Tyrus—not with the simple curiosity of men who think they've seen a face before, but with the hawkish stare of predators.

Ronan's hand went to his blade hilt. "You ride back here with Guin and Tova. I'm going to speak to them."

Ashyn reached to lay her hand on his. "I'll speak to them and distract their attention while you ride ahead and warn Tyrus."

"I'd rather—"

"Yes, I'm sure you would. But I have this."

Ashyn reined her horse toward the three men. She came up behind them, but they didn't notice her even when she said, "Excuse me." Or perhaps they were simply ignoring anyone impertinent enough to hail warriors.

"Excuse me," she said louder. "I'm very sorry to bother you but—"

The youngest glanced her way. His eyes widened. He reined his horse in so quickly that hers nearly bumped it. The other two stopped as well, and looked at her with varying expressions of surprise. They hadn't noticed Tova, who'd slipped into the crowd and now had come out on the other side of them, standing watch.

When the men turned, she noted that each wore his fore-lock in a braid with red, blue, and white beads. The beads likely signified membership in some criminal group, though that was hardly her area of expertise.

"My sincerest apologies for interrupting your travels," she said, her voice soft and her gaze lowered. "I . . . I fear I didn't know where else to turn. My father is Lord Vernay of Cold-wall, and I'm hoping that forgives some of my impudence in speaking to you."

The youngest of the three straightened in his saddle. "Of course, my lady." He looked over her shoulder. "Where is your escort?"

Ashyn's gaze dropped further. "That is the problem. I have not been long out of the North, and the sights of the empire are so new and exciting. My maidservant"—she waved to Guin, who had stopped on the other side of the road—"and I rode on ahead. We could clearly see my father's wagons, but then the road became more congested, and we rode farther still and . . . and I fear we rode quite far, perhaps past a branching road that my father may have taken. We've gone back and forth but there is no sign of him."

Out of the corner of her eye, she could see Ronan speaking to Tyrus. *Get him moving. Quickly. While their backs—*

The oldest warrior glanced over his shoulder, as if remembering their target. He saw Ronan, and Ashyn tensed, but only nodded as if relieved that some random traveler was slowing Tyrus's progress.

He turned back to Ashyn. "We would be happy to assist

you, my lady, but I fear our own lord expects us, and we are already late."

"Oh? Who is your warlord?"

The man hesitated. One of the others jumped in. "Asano Bakenko."

"Truly?" Ashyn leaned forward, her eyes wide. "My father knows Lord Bakenko. In fact, we're due to visit him next moon. This is quite fortuitous. Your lord and my father were boon companions in their youth. Their fathers fought at the Battle of Dahuran, alongside the emperor himself. But, of course, you know that."

They nodded, but their blank expressions said they had no idea what she was talking about. As they struggled to follow her blathering—and not give themselves away—none thought to check on their target, who was leaving the road quickly, Ronan guarding his rear.

"I'm so glad we've met," she continued. "Your lord will certainly understand if you are delayed on my account. My father will reward you most handsomely. Now, we're looking for a retinue of two wagons and—"

Ronan rode up behind Ashyn and exhaled loudly. "My lady. There you are. I've been looking for you and asking after you . . ." His gaze traveled to the three warriors. "Oh. Thank you, brothers, for finding her."

"These are Lord Asano Bakenko's men," she twittered excitedly. "What is the chance, to meet friends so far from both our homes?"

Ronan's gaze took in the three men's attire. "Lord Bakenko . . . I see . . ." He gave the men a hard look, as if to say he knew they lied. A wise move, which kept them from looking more closely at him—shabbily dressed for a warrior despite his blades.

"Well, I thank you, brothers, for your kindness," Ronan said with a half bow. "I'll take my lady to her father's retinue. Her maidservant, too." An equally hard look Guin's way. "The girl will be properly chastised for this."

"Me?" Ashyn said, eyes wide. "But I only—"

"I mean your maidservant, my lady, for allowing you to wander." He rolled his eyes at the warriors and mouthed *Northerners*, and they shared a small laugh at the silly, empty-headed girl before he ushered her off.

"You're a very good performer," Ronan said as they rode back to Guin.

"Who says I was performing?"

He chuckled, his dark eyes glittering conspiratorially, and she felt a rush of warmth, as if he'd paid her the highest compliment. She glanced away and waved for Guin to join them.

They headed back the way they'd come, as if returning to their retinue.

"Guin?" Ashyn whispered, moving closer to the girl. "Can you tell me what they're doing?"

Guin frowned.

"You're supposed to be my maidservant," Ashyn said gently. "Your curiosity will seem less suspicious than ours."

"They aren't looking in this direction," Guin said. "They're searching for the prince. Where is he?"

"Safe," Ronan said. "We'll keep him that way by not riding directly to him. Follow my lead."

* * *

"Blast him," Ronan hissed as they surveyed the empty space behind the roadside shop. "He may tell us not to treat him as a prince, but he cannot stop acting like one. He does as he pleases."

"Only when it's in my best interests," Tyrus said as he rounded the shop.

Ronan glowered. "Which is anytime you don't like what you're told to do."

Tyrus grinned. "True." He clapped Ronan on the back. "I was simply keeping an eye on those three, so we don't lose them."

"That would be the idea, your highness. To lose them. Which means *they* lose *you*."

"Testy, aren't you?"

"Because this could have been avoided if you'd heeded our warnings—"

"I did heed your warning. I hid back here, didn't I?"

Ronan's glower deepened. Of course Tyrus knew that wasn't what he meant. The prince might claim no head for politics and machinations, but he could be as conniving as any courtier. His trick was to smile and charm and, if needed, play the fool. And, ultimately, get his way because he was indeed as obstinate as her sister. If Moria was a lightning storm—meeting every obstacle with fire and thunder—Tyrus was a steady spring rain—calmly but steadily wearing away everything in his path.

"We need information," Tyrus continued, ignoring Ronan's scowl. "If those men hope to collect a bounty on me—"

"Bounty?" Ronan said.

225

"Of course. They're bounty hunters. Did you not see the beads on their forelocks?"

When Ronan looked at him blankly, Tyrus said, "It signifies that they are imperial bounty hunters. It's a secret society, but as with all such things, that secrecy is often more a hope than reality. If you've not heard of them, then I suppose they aren't quite as well-known as my father fears."

"Your father has set a bounty on you?" Guin said.

"My father has nothing to do with such matters. And I cannot imagine there is a bounty on my head at all. I think those men recognized me, and they were trying to decide what to do about it. The trick now is to confirm that, find out what they know, and enlist their aid in getting me safely back to the imperial city."

"And if I think that's a very poor idea?" Ronan said.

Tyrus smiled. "I'd be disappointed if you didn't. Your task is to watch over me, which includes exercising caution when I do not."

"But does not include you actually listening to me when I do?"

"I listened when you told me to get off the road, didn't I? I'm listening to your counsel now. I'm not planning to march out there and ask them to return me to the imperial city."

"Then what do you plan to do?" Ashyn asked.

Tyrus explained.

TWENTY-NINE

Ashyn and Guin stood by a tree, far enough from the road to hear only the murmur of voices and the clatter of wagons. Tova lay at Ashyn's feet. Daigo was, as always, with Tyrus, who was . . . elsewhere.

"I don't understand it," Guin was saying. "There's a freedom to dresses that trousers simply don't have. I don't care if women may wear trousers now; I cannot wait to be out of these."

"Trousers are certainly better for horseback riding. Nor would I want to walk any great distance in a dress. But I'll admit I'll be happy to put one on again. And the ones at court are certainly prettier than any pair of trousers. I've had fine dresses, but those were quite spectacular."

"Tell me about them," Guin said.

While Ashyn was playing a role, chattering with her "maid-servant," Guin clearly found the conversation to her liking.

227

Ashyn had to admit it was not particularly a chore to talk about pretty dresses. The ones she'd been given at court *had* been the stuff of dreams, though at the time, she'd been too worried about the children to enjoy them properly. Now, as she waxed eloquent on the fabrics and cuts—and Guin responded with increasing delight—she was so caught up in the conversation that she forgot it was staged.

When Ronan darted toward them, winding his way through the elm grove, she grinned at him . . . and then caught his expression of alarm, forgetting that this too was part of the act. Fortunately, by saying "What's wrong?" with genuine concern, she was playing her role.

"They're still hunting for the prince," Ronan said, not lowering his voice. "We need to get him out of here."

"Where will we take him?" Ashyn asked.

"I don't know. Just get on your mount and let's go."

He waved for them to ride away from the road. Ashyn fumbled getting onto her horse as Ronan helped her, urging her to hurry. Over his shoulder she caught a glimpse of a man sneaking through the trees. It was the youngest of the three bounty hunters. There was no sign of the other two. Tyrus had expected they'd split up to cover more ground.

As Ronan helped her, Ashyn "slipped" and "accidentally" kicked him in the face. Admittedly the script of their performance did not specify such an action, only that she delay getting onto her steed, but at least it meant his *oomph* of surprise and annoyance was genuine.

The young bounty hunter continued moving toward them, faster now, spurred on by the certainty they were too preoccupied with their escape to notice him. In turn, he was too preoccupied to notice the figure slipping up behind him.

"Stop there," Tyrus said as he pressed his blade to the back of the bounty hunter's neck.

When the man's hand fell to his sword, Tyrus said, "I'd rather you didn't do that."

"You'll not allow me to defend myself? You truly are a coward, aren't you, boy?"

There was no shock in Tyrus's face at that. Just quiet grief, as if, despite his words, this was exactly what he'd feared.

He allowed the man to withdraw his sword. Ronan rocked forward, his hand on his own blade.

"No," Tyrus said. "He's right. He's a warrior, and he's my father's man. I must allow him to defend himself."

Which was, of course, ridiculous. What was the point in ambushing someone if you were going to let him draw his sword?

The bounty hunter withdrew it slowly, as if considering whether he truly wished to fight an imperial prince. Then, the moment it was free, he wheeled and lunged, hoping to catch Tyrus off guard. Tyrus met his thrust, their swords clanging. Then Tyrus's blade circled back the other way, faster than the bounty hunter could recover from the clash, and when Tyrus's sword slashed his arm, he hissed, eyes rounding in surprise. The cut was deep enough to draw blood. He swung his blade, but Tyrus evaded easily.

"Are you quite certain you wish to do this?" Tyrus asked.

The man sneered. "You expect me to surrender because you landed a lucky blow? Yes, *your highness*, I wish to do this."

He lunged at Tyrus and the fight began in earnest. It ended with the bounty hunter on the ground, blood soaked through his tunic in three places and his trousers in two. Tyrus had a nick on his elbow.

"The prince is no coward, as you see," Guin said.

Tyrus quieted her with a look. When the man started to rise, Tyrus put his sword tip at his throat. "I gave you the chance to do this civilly. Now we'll do it like this."

The man looked over his head, taking in Ronan, Ashyn, and Guin. His gaze fell to Tova then to Daigo, as the wildcat slid to Tyrus's side.

"So the whore left you her beast?" he said.

Ashyn stiffened. Tyrus did, too, but hid his reaction faster.

"If you mean—" Tyrus began.

"You know who I mean, boy. The fact that you still care for her beast—and her sister—suggests you're too big a fool to even realize what she did to you."

"Perhaps. Enlighten me. Please."

"She betrayed you. Seduced you, then sold you out, all at her lover's command."

"Her lover?"

"The Kitsune boy."

"Ah, Gavril. I see."

Ashyn stood, tense, ready to leap to her sister's defense, but Tyrus's expression said that he was not entertaining the accusation for a moment. He knew Moria too well for that.

"Yes, Gavril Kitsune," the bounty hunter said. "He sent you his whore, and she played on your weakness for pretty girls. You've betrayed the empire, and you'll pay for that. Your father has promised it."

Now shock did flicker over Tyrus's face.

The man laughed. "Did you honestly think he'd defend you? After what you did to his men? There's a bounty on your head, boy. Every man has been dispatched to hunt you down, and the one who does receives twenty gold as long as you're returned alive so the empire can see you properly punished. I hear Edgewood is no more, having been laid to waste by Alvar Kitsune, with the help of his son and the Keeper whore. So you'll not be exiled to the Forest of the Dead. But I'm sure your father will find a suitable punishment. The empire may even demand blood for what you've done."

"He's done nothing," Guin said, stepping forward.

Ashyn tried to grab her back, but Guin wrenched from her grip and turned on her. "You'll stand here and listen to these lies? You'll not say a word to defend him? To defend your sister?"

"Because she knows it will do no good," Tyrus said, his voice low. "Listen and be still, Guin."

"I'll not be still. How does the emperor leap to such conclusions when he cannot even have questioned anyone who was there? Everyone is dead."

"Not everyone," Ronan murmured.

"Yes, you survived, as did Ashyn and I. We'll all tell the same story. That Tyrus was betrayed by Lord Jorojumo. That Moria was captured by their forces. That—"

"Enough, Guin," Tyrus said. "Please."

"Oh, but she tells such a pretty tale," the man said. "What have you promised these children in return for their lies?" He looked at Guin. "You are forgetting one other survivor, girl."

Ronan shifted beside Ashyn, and the moment he did, she

knew who the bounty hunter meant. Ronan glanced over at her, worry drawing his lips tight.

"Simeon," she whispered. "No, that's not . . . It isn't possible. He was there. He knows the truth. We sent him for help."

"If you mean the young scholar, oh yes, girl, he helped. Helped the empire unmask treachery. He promised the prince he'd spread his lies so the coward would not slay him. But he is a man of honor. When he reached the court, he told the truth."

"What story did he tell?" Tyrus said.

It was almost exactly as they'd heard, except for Moria's supposed role. The prince had been seduced and swayed by his false lover. She'd convinced him to march on Riverside, when the counselors and scholars had insisted Northpond was the proper target. In battle, Jorojumo had betrayed his emperor, working in league with Moria. Tyrus had realized what had happened and fled the battlefield while his men were slaughtered. Then Tyrus himself had murdered the counselors and scholar Katsumoto in hopes of hiding his cowardice. Finally, he'd commanded Simeon to court with a very different story.

"The prince would send a *scholar* to do that?" Guin said. "A man he barely knew? Not the Seeker or his scout here?"

Which proved, Ashyn admitted, that Guin was not as empty-headed as she seemed.

"The false prince didn't know that the scholar had witnessed him murdering the counselors," the bounty hunter said. "Clearly, his highness underestimated his choice of messenger."

Tyrus continued to interrogate the bounty hunter, but when Tova looked to the left, Ashyn's attention followed. The hound's jowls vibrated with a growl, but before the first note of it erupted, Daigo sprang. He landed on a second bounty hunter as the man lunged out from a stand of trees.

Ronan wheeled. Tova barked and Ashyn saw a third figure run from the other direction.

"Ronan!"

She pulled her dagger and said, "Tova! Go!" Not a command but a release. *Help Ronan. Don't worry about me.* Tova hesitated long enough to be sure she had her blade, then he let out a roar and charged. The bounty hunter under Tyrus's sword tried to take advantage of the commotion to leap up, but Tyrus pinned him and then shouted, "Ashyn!"

She saw the figure burst from the trees and thought Daigo had lost his prey. But it wasn't one of the bounty hunters. It was another warrior, his sword out, running straight at her. Tova broke off his charge, leaped on the man, and took him down, but that left his former target running at Tyrus. Ashyn shot toward them, but she was too far away. Tyrus kicked the man under him, foot connecting with jaw in a sickening crunch as he swung his sword at the running bounty hunter, cutting the man's charge short with a spray of blood.

A fourth figure appeared behind him. Yet another warrior.

"Ashyn!" Tyrus said. "Take Guin! Go!"

She hesitated, blade gripped in her hand. Then she looked at Guin, wide-eyed in shock. The warrior running for Tyrus saw Guin and veered off, heading straight for the girl. Tyrus swung at the man, but he was too far and couldn't reach without releasing the bounty hunter on the ground. His sword only grazed the man's arm.

Ashyn ran for him. Tyrus's eyes widened in horror as he mouthed something, likely *What in blazes are you doing?* Or possibly *Get your dagger up!* She was running straight at the warrior, her blade lowered. At the last moment, she reached out and shoved him. As he stumbled back, his blade nicked her arm. But the push did what it was meant to—landing him within Tyrus's reach. The first bounty hunter was rising again, blood streaming from his mouth. Again, Tyrus kicked him down, this time in the nose. His blade flashed as it cleaved into the warrior's arm, cutting clean through the bone and—

Ashyn staggered back as the warrior's arm flew through the air, sword still clenched in his hand. The warrior screamed and blood arced and all she could think was, *I need to bind it.* Bind the severed stump so he wouldn't bleed out and die.

But he must die. He dies or we die.

The shock of that hit her and she gasped for air, the warrior still gurgling with pain, stumbling toward his arm as if to retrieve the blade.

They were not playing with daggers. This was a sword fight. How did they test a warrior's sword? By making sure it was sharp enough to cleave through three corpses with a single blow.

"Ashyn!" It was Tyrus. That mighty swing had thrown him enough off balance for the bounty hunter to stagger to his feet, his ruined nose and jaw streaming blood, but his sword raised as he faced off with Tyrus.

Tyrus had his back to her and didn't turn, just said, "Take Guin and go! Now!"

She looked at Ronan. He'd dispatched his assailant and

was running to Tova's aid. Daigo had his target pinned and disarmed.

"Ashyn!" Tyrus's voice came harsh now as he circled with the bounty hunter, both looking for an opportunity. "Your sister!"

That's all he said: your sister. She knew what he meant. *Moria would want you to go. Moria would want me to make sure you go.*

He was right. Tyrus and Tova—and perhaps Daigo and Ronan—were keeping part of their attention on her, ready to run to her aid. Which meant the sum total of their attention was not on their opponents.

Ashyn grabbed Guin and yanked the girl out of her stupor. She took her by the hand and ran as swords clanged behind them.

THIRTY

There was no escape from this place. None.

One might say that after five days in the cell, Moria's situation had improved, but when one was locked alone in a cold, dark cell, any change had to be for the better.

Her leg iron was off. The healer had apparently insisted her ankle was infected and needed to be free to heal. With that treatment came sponge baths and clean clothing every other day. Moria was also now getting three meals of rice and soup, and if the guard Halmond didn't bring them, she could actually eat. She had a clean blanket. Halmond had chastised her for soiling the last one, then taken it and said she'd have none until she was ready to appreciate it. The old woman had come the next day, realized she didn't have a blanket, and ordered Halmond to bring a new one.

That was the pattern they'd settled into. Halmond would

punish her—for no misdeed greater than existing—then the old woman would undo the guard's punishment. If he spit in her food and she didn't eat it, the healer presumed it was not to her liking and brought something else. If he pissed in the corner of her room, the healer thought the bucket had overturned and ordered someone to scrub the floor. When he kept snuffing out her candle, the healer replaced it with a lantern.

Moria never complained about Halmond. She had no idea whether the woman was in any position to have him reassigned, and if she wasn't, tattling on him would only make things worse.

But by the end of those first five days, she had a lantern, an extra blanket, regular hot food, and sufficient clean water. Compared to the initial hell, it was relative extravagance. And now that she'd recovered from her exhaustion and shock and hunger, she'd begun trying to figure a way out of her situation. Unfortunately, there was none.

The cell had no windows. From the damp and the stink of dirt, she suspected she was underground. There was one door. Every time it opened, it revealed Halmond, a serving girl, or the healer. The women were always accompanied by a guard. Whenever Moria looked through the open doorway, she saw two more warriors outside as permanent guards.

Now, hearing the scraping of a key in the lock, she tensed. While she had no way to tell time in this dark place, her life had fallen into a reliable schedule. That door opened only for two things—her meals and the healer's visits, which came every second day. She'd had her breakfast not long ago, and the old woman had come yesterday. Meaning that door should not be opening.

Unless he's come. Gavril. Or his father. Come to tell me my fate. Come to kill me.

When she saw Halmond, she almost exhaled in relief. That lasted only a moment before she caught sight of the murderous glint in his eye.

Moria's fingers scraped against the dirt floor as she struggled not to creep away.

Something's happened. And I'm about to pay the price.

Halmond wedged in the door stopper with his foot. While the hall light shone in, he crossed to her lantern and lit it, filling the room with wavering light.

Without a word, he returned to the door and retrieved a bowl from the hall. A steaming bowl, like the one the healer brought. Moria tried not to smile. The old woman was coming early. That was the only surprise in this place she'd welcome. There was still no conversation between them—and no sign that one was possible—but the healer was kind. The hot sponge bath and clean clothes had become a luxury Moria dreamed of on the nights before the old woman's visits.

That's why Halmond was annoyed, then. Because Moria was getting a treat.

He brought the bowl and laid it beside her. Then he returned to the door, kicked out the stopper, and walked back toward her.

"Isn't the healer—" Moria began as she struggled to her feet.

"She can't come today. You'll bathe without her."

"But it's not my day to—"

"It is now." He shoved her shoulder. "Undress."

She glared up at him. She didn't say a word, though. She understood. Something had happened, quite possibly something that had nothing to do with her, and this was how he was handling it. Venting his frustration by finding fresh humiliations for his prisoner. Well, he'd chosen poorly, then. She was no timid maiden, clutching her tunic together for fear some man might glimpse her breasts. While she knew better than to flaunt herself, she saw no shame in nakedness. Compared to pissing on her blanket or spitting in her soup, this was a punishment she could bear.

She started unfastening her tunic.

"What did you tell her?" Halmond asked.

She looked up.

"What did you tell that old crone about me?" he said.

"Nothing."

"No? Then why has Lord Gavril summoned me to speak about you? And why did the messenger warn he was in a foul mood when he gave the order?"

She met his gaze. "I've said nothing. I know you'd retaliate if I did."

His eyes narrowed. "You think you're clever, don't you? So much more clever than me."

Moria bit her tongue against a retort. Even when she was civil and reasonable, he still found fault. Ashyn would say he was an angry man, an unhappy man. Perhaps so, but that wouldn't stop Moria from putting a dagger through him if she got the chance. Nothing excused humiliating and torturing a helpless captive.

"Are you still undressing?" he said. "Because if I need to

help you, you won't be able to wear that clothing again, and I'll not bring you anything new."

Moria yanked off her tunic and trousers. When she finished, she was wearing a thin silken shift that fell to the top of her thighs. She reached over to take the cloth from the bowl of hot water. As she did, she tensed, waiting for him to tell her to remove the shift. He said nothing, and she didn't look at him—just took the lump of soap, rubbed it on the wet cloth, and began to clean her arms.

When she glanced up, he was staring at her. She'd been ogled by men before, but she was beginning to realize this was far more dangerous than having him spit in her stew.

Her gaze fell to his blades. Could she distract him and grab his dagger? If she could distract him, *would* she distract him?

Yes, she would use his ogling, if that was the path to freedom. But it was not. Even if she pulled his blade, the hall was guarded.

She lowered her gaze and put the cloth back into the bowl. "I'm done. The water's cold, and I'm quite clean. Thank you for bringing me an extra—"

"Finish bathing." The growl in his voice warned her. *Tread carefully.*

"I have. Thank you for bringing the water. I appreciate—"

He rose from his crouch so fast that her fingers automatically dropped to her side, where her blade should be. He was on his feet now, standing beside the water bowl.

"You'll not do it yourself?" he said.

"I truly don't need—"

He plunged his hand into the water and took up the soap.

He squeezed it, suds and ooze running through his fingers. Then he dropped the soap and advanced on her, his jaw set. He grabbed her bare knee. And she grabbed his dagger.

It wasn't planned. Wasn't even intentional. He yanked her leg, and she went for his blade, as if there was no other option. Even as her fingers closed on the cool handle, she knew she'd made a mistake.

It wasn't too late. She could let go and pray to the ancestors that he hadn't noticed. But nothing in her would allow him to touch her, because if he did it once, he'd not stop doing it. So she grabbed the dagger, and she plunged it into his gut.

He let out a howl and fell back. She yanked it out. Blood gushed, and he howled again. She gripped the dagger, ready to stab him again if he reached for his sword. But he only let out a snarl, grabbed the front of her shift and yanked so hard the silk tore.

His eyes rolled in pain and fury, his hand still wrapped in her shift, blood soaking it now as his wound gushed. He wrenched, as if to pull her onto the floor. She stabbed him again. She didn't know where. It didn't matter, truly, only that she stabbed him as he yowled in fresh pain. Still, he grabbed for her, and she was raising the blade again, ready to deliver the final blow when the door swung open.

THIRTY-ONE

Someone gasped. Moria didn't turn to see who it was, didn't dare look away from Halmond as his hand swiped for her again. She caught it with the blade while footsteps pounded on the dirt floor. She saw another hand swinging down at them, and she thought, *I'm dead. They caught me attacking my guard, and now I'm dead.*

But the hand grabbed Halmond instead, catching him by the back of his tunic and throwing him aside.

"Get him out of here. Now!"

"He's hurt, my lord." Another guard's voice. "He needs a healer—"

"Then get him one someplace else. Preferably the next cell. Where he will remain if he survives."

Moria looked up to see Gavril, fairly shaking with rage. She saw that and perhaps, if it had been her first day here, she would have wept from relief. She'd have seen that rage and thought, *See? He does care for me. Things are not as they seem.*

But it was no longer that first day. She'd suffered Halmond's torments for five days. She'd been under Gavril's care for five days, and he'd not even looked in to see how she was faring.

If he was furious now, it meant nothing except that Halmond had betrayed his trust.

So now she looked up at him and thought of the dagger still in her hand. His gaze was fixed on the guards carrying Halmond out. He didn't see her, lying at his feet, close enough to leap up and . . .

Her fingers tightened around the handle.

"Don't," he said. He didn't even bother to glance down.

She rose slowly, tensed to spring, bloodied blade clutched in her hand.

"Moria . . ." He looked at her then. "You don't want to do that."

"Oh, yes." She met his gaze. "I do."

Something flickered in his eyes, and he turned away, his hand rising to rub at his face as he sighed. She threatened his life and he only sighed, as if she'd called him a foul name.

"Perhaps you do, but it won't help," he said. "If you raise that blade, I'll pull mine, and we both know how that turned out the last time."

"I'll do better."

He crouched in front of her. "Even if you manage to kill me, Keeper, what good will that do? You wouldn't leave here alive after that. You're no martyr. You want to punish me, and you want to live. You cannot do both. Not now."

He waited for her to respond. He expected her to respond. To make her case for killing him.

This was the Gavril she'd come to know, after getting past the snaps and the snarls. The young man who couldn't carry on a conversation without turning it into a debate.

Except he was right. She wanted to punish him. But if she did it now, she'd die for it.

She laid the dagger on the floor. He took it. As he rose, she did, too. She felt the prickle of cold air and looked down to see her shift torn down the middle and soaked in blood. When Gavril saw her, anger seeped back into his eyes. He tightened his grip on the dagger.

"What did he do?"

Moria reached for her clothing and started putting on her tunic.

"What did he do, Keeper?"

She pulled on her trousers.

"Moria?" A warning edged into his voice, that anger seeping through. "What did he do?"

She reached under her tunic, ripped her shift free, and tossed it aside. "I'll need another of those, if it's not too much trouble."

She started to turn away. He caught her by the wrist, gripping hard, only to let her go almost as quickly, backing up fast, as if she'd burned him.

"Moria."

"He brought me water to bathe. In front of him. Wasn't that kind?"

Gavril swallowed hard. "Did he touch you?"

She didn't answer.

"Moria, answer my question or I swear by the ancestors—"

"He did not succeed in whatever he intended to do."

His mouth opened. He hesitated. Then he snapped his mouth shut, and, teeth clicking, turned and marched from the cell.

Moria sat cross-legged on the floor of her cell. What else did she expect? At least she wouldn't need to worry about Halmond anymore. Unless whoever took his place decided to avenge him.

She sighed. Not quite the proper reaction, but there was no sense weeping and raging over her predicament. It would only waste energy she might need. She lowered herself to her blanket and clutched her wildcat figurine and was closing her eyes when the door opened again.

Gavril walked in, followed by two guards.

"Come," he said. "You'll have new quarters."

For a moment, she considered being contrary and saying that she liked these quarters just fine. But there would be self-pity in that, too. A sulking child, still smarting from his betrayal, crossing her arms and being stubborn.

At least she stood a chance of escape someplace else. So she rose and gathered her blanket.

"You'll not need that," he said.

She hesitated. She'd planned to secret the wildcat figurine under it. Thinking fast, she bent and lowered the blankets to the ground, using the opportunity to slip the figure into her pocket, before following Gavril out the door.

"You'll note there are no windows," Gavril said as he paced about the room. "There is one exit. It will be guarded by two warriors at all times. If you somehow managed to make it past them, you would find yourself in the middle of a military compound, home to sixty-three warriors. Your chances of escaping that are nil."

Moria tried not to gape about the room. Five days ago, if she'd been given this cell, she'd have looked at the straw pallet on the wooden floor and thought how thin and uncomfortable it would be. She'd have looked at the stiff sheets and plain cushions, and thought how scratchy the fabric would feel, how lumpy the padding looked. She'd have gazed around the otherwise empty room, lit by four wall sconces, and wondered how she'd survive without going mad from boredom. Now, it all seemed luxury beyond reckoning.

She did not, however, fail to miss the lack of windows. Or the way the candle sconces were high enough that she could not grab one and use it to light something on fire. Nor did she miss the thick wooden door.

"It's a cell," she said.

"What did you expect? You're a prisoner."

"I mean, this is for captives. Presumably prisoners of war. Prisoners who've committed no greater crime than choosing the wrong side. Is that correct?"

He barely seemed to pay attention, clearly impatient to finish this transfer and be off. He gave a curt nod and said, "Yes, yes. Now—"

"Then why was I not here before?"

246

He paused and turned slowly toward her.

"I am exactly the sort of prisoner this cell is intended for, am I not?"

He stood there, saying nothing.

"What have I done to you, Gavril?" she said. "Besides being foolish enough to fall for your tricks. Even then, one would think you'd feel some debt of gratitude that I was not clever enough to expose you for a traitor before you could escape."

He cleared his throat, as if to say something. But he didn't.

She stepped toward him. "What did I do to you to deserve being thrown into a dungeon cell? To be degraded and nearly defiled?"

"My father—"

"—put you in charge of my care. Which I'm sure was a dreadful bother, and perhaps you blame me for that, allowing myself to be captured. But there was no reason to leave me down there. Your father left my care to you. I could have been up here."

"I ought to go." He turned on his heel, heading for the door. "I have other obligations."

"Is that your answer, Kitsune? Truly? To run from the question? Do you remember in the Forest of the Dead? When you told me how much you hated letting Orbec drag you away when the shadow stalkers struck? That it felt like cowardice? I thought then that no one could ever accuse you of cowardice. Which goes to show, I suppose, how little I knew you."

He stood there, his back to her.

"Yes," he said gruffly. "You did not know me at all. Now, if you'll excuse me, Keeper . . ."

He reached for the door. It opened before he could pull it. His father stood there. Gavril tensed.

"Father," he said. "There was an incident in the lower cells. Moria—"

"I heard what our little Keeper did."

Alvar walked in, nudging Gavril back, as if to prevent his escape.

"I apologize for my oversight in her care," Gavril said. "Halmond seemed loyal, and it did not occur to me—"

"It did not occur to you that putting a young warrior in charge of a pretty captive might be unwise?" His father's brows shot up. "Sometimes, Gavril, I wonder how old you truly are. You are unbelievably naive when it comes to men and women. Your mother's influence, I suppose. It would be a perfectly fine quality in a daughter, but in a son?" He shook his head.

"Perhaps, Father, it was not naiveté, but the expectation that warriors will show honor."

"Ideally, yes, but those who join the army of the emperor's enemy cannot necessarily be expected to behave like warriors."

"Then, once again, I apologize for my mistake. Now, if you'll excuse me . . ."

Alvar looked at Moria. "He always seems to be rushing off, doesn't he? So many important things to do."

Gavril's jaw tightened. "I *do* have many things to do, as you know, because you have assigned them to me. Including . . ." A wave at Moria. Then he hesitated. "Actually, while I do have an engagement, this incident raises an issue that we need to discuss." He motioned to the door. "May we step outside?"

THIRTY-TWO

Gavril sent the guards away as his father moved to the common area just outside the cell. It was not easy to hear through the thick door, but Moria put her ear to it.

"We need to do something about Moria," Gavril said. "And no, she's not coming to my quarters. Forgive me if I do not see women as spoils of war. I suggest negotiating with Tatsu in exchange for her return. She's a valuable prisoner but a difficult one. Best to get some benefit from her and be done with the matter."

"You wish to see her free, then. Her captivity upsets you."

Gavril sighed. "No, Father. Your obsession with making me admit to some attachment grows tiresome. It makes good sense to use her for negotiation."

"Yes, it will, when Jiro has someone we want in return."

"Until then, we keep her as our captive? So the next guard

she pulls a blade on can turn it on her, and we'll be guilty of a Keeper's death?"

"Is that what you're worried about? That she'll be hurt?"

"Blast it! No! What do I need to do to convince you that I don't care for her?"

"Bed her."

Now Gavril's laugh was raw, frustrated, and angry. "How does that make any sense? Bed a girl to prove I *don't* care for her? Sometimes I wonder if you aren't as mad as—"

Moria heard the slap that cut him short. She heard Gavril gasp and stumble back, then a soft sound, almost like a growl, as he recovered.

"I apologize, Father," he said, his voice tight. "Still, I will respectfully ask that you consider returning Moria. She's nearly killed one man. If the opportunity arises, she'll do it again, and she'll be harder to control now that she's out of the lower cells. It's difficult to properly secure anyplace here with so few men."

"More are coming."

"That may take a fortnight, a moon even. Until then, we have vulnerabilities. If Moria was to escape to the north part of the compound, she'd hardly encounter a single guard."

"I think you overestimate your girl. In fact, I'd be willing to wager on it. How about we set her free right now? Tell her to attempt escape. See if she manages it."

"As entertaining as I'm sure such an exercise would prove, neither of us has time for amusements. I only ask that you reconsider trading her to Jiro Tatsu. In the meantime, I have an appointment to keep."

* * *

Gavril's father left with him. They hadn't been long gone before the old woman came to check Moria for injuries. Sure enough, she discovered several gouges and rising bruises where Halmond had grabbed her. As the healer tended to those, she muttered under her breath in her own language. When one of the guards dared stick his head in, she snapped at him as if he'd been the one to attack Moria. When he hesitated, she motioned lifting food to her mouth. He nodded and withdrew.

"I'm all right," Moria said.

The woman kept grumbling. She pointed emphatically at the gouges and then stalked to the fresh pile of clothing she'd brought. She held up a new shift and shook it at Moria.

"I'm fine," Moria said. "Truly, I'm—"

The woman jabbed a finger at the shift and gave Moria a look as if to say, *If you're fine, where's your old one?*

"I *will* be fine," Moria said. "Halmond didn't do anything." Except humiliate her. Make her feel helpless and powerless. Remind her that she wasn't the Keeper of Edgewood here. She was just a girl.

The door opened again, and the young guard carefully pushed in a food tray, as if he didn't dare set foot inside. When he tried to leave, the old woman barked something at him. He clearly didn't understand the words, but he caught the meaning well enough and paused.

The healer looked at the food. Then she made a few gestures to the guard. He seemed to take a moment to understand, then nodded as he withdrew.

The old woman set the tray in front of Moria and glowered

at her, as if she was going to stand there and watch her eat every bite. Moria looked down at the plate. Sticky rice, a steaming pork bun, and dried persimmons. A simple peasant's meal, but better than she'd had in five days. She set on the fruits first, devouring them as if they were honey cakes. When the guard entered again, he had a pot of tea, a pear, and an apple. The old woman grunted her approval and, this time, waved that he could come in and set them on Moria's tray.

He did, keeping his gaze down.

"Thank you," she said.

"Whatever you need, my lady," he said. "You only have to knock."

"I'd like my daggers back."

His lips twitched in a smile. "Except that, I fear."

She was about to let him leave when she caught sight of the ink on his arms. Stylized dogs.

"The Inugami clan," she said. "There was one of your family in Edgewood."

"Orbec. He is—was—my uncle."

"Gav . . . Lord Gavril has told you what happened to him then?"

"He has."

Moria wanted to ask exactly what Gavril had said. It was not, she suspected, the truth. But she heard her sister's voice, telling her to hold her tongue. To be cautious. She'd not win allies in this place by turning them against the Kitsunes.

The young man continued, "My uncle spoke of you, my lady, in his letters home. He said he taught you to throw a blade."

252

"He did."

A faint smile. "All the more reason why I'd not return yours. I know my uncle's skill."

"He was an excellent teacher and a warrior who died with honor. When I was brought here, I had two daggers. One was his. I took it to return to his family, but I haven't gotten the chance. If you want it, ask Lord Gavril. He'll see it's returned to you."

"Thank you, my lady."

The young man withdrew. When he was gone, the healer nodded, as if pleased that Moria had been so courteous. She motioned for Moria to eat while she examined her wounds.

The healer grumbled when she reached Moria's ankle, though it was in no worse shape than it had been down in the cell. Perhaps in the better light, it simply looked worse. The old woman bound it as Moria knelt, eating. Then she pointed toward Moria's foot.

"Walk."

Moria lifted her brows. The woman's accent was so thick it was sometimes hard to tell when she was attempting words in the common language.

"Walk," she said again. "Need walk."

Moria waved at the small cell and said, "No room." The woman motioned that Moria needed to go out, both for exercise and air.

Moria laughed at that. "I would truly love to, but I think I'm as likely to get that as I am to get my dagger returned."

The healer snorted, as if she got the gist of Moria's words. A few emphatic gestures followed. None of them made any sense to Moria. Then the old woman motioned for Moria to finish her food and tea as she gathered her things and departed.

Moria attempted to contact the spirits as soon as she was alone. One answered . . . and told her to be careful. Very unhelpful. Moria asked the spirit for assistance. When that failed to get an answer, she set aside all her dignity and begged. Finally, the spirit relented . . . and said she was safe enough. That was all. It did not know anything about Ashyn or Daigo or Tyrus or the children of Edgewood. Just a weak and random spirit, called forth by her pleas, unable even to act as her spy. Useless. Like 90 percent of the spirits out there. And the other ten never seemed to be around when she needed them, blast them.

It wasn't yet time for the evening meal when Moria's cell door opened again. Gavril walked in, followed by one of the guards that had accompanied him earlier.

"What's this you told Rametta about needing to walk?"

"Rametta?" Moria said. "I suppose you mean the healer. I don't know her name. Conversation is difficult when one doesn't speak the common language."

"Oh, you two seem to be communicating just fine." Gavril waved for his guard to come in and close the door. "Rametta is from my family's homeland. The old witch is too blasted stubborn to learn the common language, but as I'm sure you've noticed, she understands quite enough of it. About this walking nonsense—"

"It was her idea."

His glower deepened. "I'm sure it was. Just as I'm certain you only wish to walk to stretch your legs."

"What else would I do? I'm in an armed compound. There's no way for me to escape."

"That won't stop you from trying."

Moria sighed and lowered herself, cross-legged, to the floor. "Believe what you want. I would still welcome the exercise, even if it came with ten guards."

"Of course, Keeper. Whatever you wish. Shall I return your dagger, too?"

"That would be lovely."

She met his glare with a smile. He shook his head and turned to go.

"There will be no walks, Keeper. And I would suggest you not keep at Rametta about it or she'll go to my father. She was his nursemaid, and she has more sway over him than anyone ought. I don't need that kind of trouble."

THIRTY-THREE

It was almost exactly a day later when Gavril stormed into Moria's cell again.

"Did I warn you not to bother Rametta with this walk nonsense?" he said.

"I didn't say a word."

He skewered her with a look.

She straightened. "I know you won't believe me, but I did not, Lord Gavril."

His eyes narrowed. "Do not call me that."

"It's your new title, is it not? If I don't use it, I'm failing to pay the proper respect."

He stepped closer, lowering his voice so the guard couldn't hear. "Don't mock me, Keeper."

Moria sighed and, once again, lowered herself to the floor. "I cannot win, can I? If I called you Gavril or, worse, Kitsune, you would accuse me of showing disrespect—"

256

"Enough."

She looked up at him but didn't rise. She refused to give him the satisfaction of a fight, and that only made him fume all the more. He backed up and crossed his arms.

"I told you—" he began.

"—not to woo Rametta to my cause. I did not. In fact, I said I had changed my mind, and I no longer desired the walks, as the very request had angered you, and I could not afford to anger you. I'm out of that dungeon cell, and I'd not like to be thrown back in."

"I never threatened—"

"I told her that while a walk would be enjoyable, the cost of pursuing the matter was too high." She looked up at him. "I know my place now."

She swore she heard him grinding his teeth.

"Don't play the submissive, Keeper. You do it poorly."

"If you'd like me to apologize—"

"Ancestors forbid," he muttered.

She lifted her gaze to his. "I was going to say that I'll do that. Happily. I sincerely apologize for any misunderstanding with Rametta. If there is anything else you'd like me to apologize for, Lord Gavril, you need only to ask. If it would help to issue a blanket apology, for all past, present, and future grievances and insults, real or imagined—"

"By the ancestors, stop," he said through gritted teeth. "Just stop talking."

"I'm trying to figure out what I need to do"—she looked him in the eye again—"to make you leave my cell."

His cheek twitched, and his folded arms tightened. "I am

not here on a social visit, Keeper. I came to inform you that you'll have your walks. Twice daily. You'll be accompanied by two guards. I asked for four, but my father thinks it sends the wrong message to suggest a girl requires so many warriors. He seems to believe there is no danger of your escape."

"He is correct, because the compound is far too secure for such a thing. You needn't worry about me, Lord Gavril. I'll not even glance at the walls."

He snorted under his breath and muttered, "I've warned him. That's all I can do." With that, he turned on his heel and marched out.

And so, Moria got her walks. Twice a day she was escorted by Orbec's nephew, Brom, and a second guard. Brom was a pleasant companion, a not-quite-handsome young man who enjoyed the attentions of a young woman. Moria would do nothing to cause him trouble, but if he found their discussions pleasant and her attention flattering, she was hardly going to discourage him . . . or warn him when he spoke too openly of the compound. The other guard saw no harm in it, though admittedly, he did seem less than intellectually alert. So Brom and Moria walked and talked, and Moria soon knew the layout of the entire compound, where each sentry was posted, and the schedules and routes of the patrolling guards.

Gavril was right. The northern portion of the sprawling camp was indeed underutilized and under-guarded. The compound was as big as the village of Edgewood. Moria had no idea where it was located—she could not see far enough beyond the walls to identify the landscape and, truly, Ashyn was better suited to such things. Moria focused on what she could see and how to escape it.

During her walks, she also looked for any sign that the children were here, but found none, and discreet questions to her guards were met with confusion. Disappointing but not surprising—if Alvar was trying to convince his men that he was no monster, he'd hardly be holding children captive here.

For six days, Moria lived in her new cell and walked the grounds and gathered intelligence. She'd catch sight of Gavril on her walks, but he'd pretend not to notice her and she'd do the same, and they were both happier for it. Sadly, it was not an arrangement that could last forever. On her eleventh day of captivity, Gavril walked into her cell, holding a bundle of fabric at arm's length, as if it was plague-cursed. Rametta accompanied him.

Gavril held the bunched fabric out to Moria, not saying a word. When she only stared at him, he tossed it onto her sleeping pallet. Rametta *tut-tutted* and scurried over to lift it up, jabbering at him in her own language. Gavril replied in the same tongue. His words were harsh and abrupt, the language only making them more so. Moria expected the old woman to take affront. But she smiled, and when she looked at him, her smile was indulgent, pleased. No, not pleased. Proud.

Rametta may have been Alvar's nursemaid, but it was obvious she was fond of Gavril, and Moria was grateful that she'd not spoken against him.

Moria rose from her cushions and set her book aside. "Lord Gavril, to what do I owe . . ."

She trailed off as Rametta lifted the bundle of fabric,

straightening and smoothing. It was a dress. Not a simple dress, but the many layers of a formal gown.

When Moria saw it, ice trickled down the back of her neck. She found her voice and said, "That's a truly lovely dress, Lord Gavril, and while I cannot say that I appreciate gowns as much as I ought, I *do* appreciate the gesture. However, I'm not sure it goes with my cell. Perhaps something in a shade of blue?"

"There is a reception tonight," Gavril said. "My father is entertaining several warlords who are considering joining us. Two of them are particularly pious men, and I made the mistake of suggesting we not mention that we've taken a Keeper hostage. My father pointed out that they've likely heard the rumor. My strategy was to deny it. My father wishes to embrace it."

"Embrace . . . ?"

"To let them know that we have the Keeper of Edgewood, and that she has joined our cause."

Moria laughed—a long, sputtering laugh that nearly toppled her to the floor. "Lord Gavril, I did not realize you had a sense of humor. And such a sharp one. I am truly impressed by your many hidden qualities—"

"Enough." He stepped closer, lowering his voice, though Rametta and the guard could clearly hear. "We have a predicament here, Keeper, and mocking me is not going to solve it. My father's idea is preposterous. And dangerous. But he insists. You will join the reception as my guest."

She wanted to laugh again. It was indeed preposterous. And yet . . .

She was to be allowed out of her cell. At night, with Gavril, who would be preoccupied with his hosting duties. A reception meant music and feasting and drinking—in a word, chaos. Lots of happy, drunken chaos.

"If your father insists . . ." she said.

Gavril gave her a hard look. "If you do not behave, you'll be returned to the dungeon. Behaving includes 'not attempting to escape.' I should also warn you that the dungeon guards are comrades of Halmond. He is doing poorly. His friends are not pleased with you."

"I understand. I have no intention of attempting—"

He cut her short with a look. "If you are sent back there, I'll not help you, Keeper. I'll not."

Now her look was dead serious as she met his gaze. "I have no doubt of that, my lord."

"Good. Now, I will leave you to bathe and dress under Rametta's care. Then I will return to explain your role for the evening."

THIRTY-FOUR

Escorted by two guards, Rametta took Moria clear across to the next building, where she had a proper bath with a proper hair washing, followed by a thorough scrubbing, waxing, and plucking. Or . . . not completely thorough, at least not when it came to the waxing and plucking. Moria knew that was the custom in the imperial court, but even with the language barrier she was able to tell Rametta that there was no need for her body to be *completely* without hair.

While Alvar Kitsune was not empire-born, he was adhering to the customs and practices of the empire. Moria supposed that made sense. To do otherwise would only remind people that his heritage lay elsewhere. He intended to rule the empire, not conquer it.

The reception, then, would be court style, one that hearkened back a decade. A message that said that the empire's golden age had passed with Alvar Kitsune's exile.

While the current custom was for ornate, upswept hair styles, the previous one called for long, straight hair on women. The longer the better. In both cases, extensions were often employed, but Moria—who as Keeper was not permitted to do more than trim her nearly waist-length hair—needed none. Nor, she would argue, should she need to apply rice powder paste to whiten her face. Rametta agreed, after trying it and frowning at the effect, and settled for a dusting of powder instead.

Next came the makeup. Charcoal for her eyes and brows. Red dye to make a "rosebud" of her lips with honey glaze to add shine—a small pot of which was to be tucked into her dress to reapply after eating and drinking, though Rametta seemed wise enough to realize the chance of Moria actually doing this was about equal to the chance of the sun consuming the earth.

Finally the dress. First the under-robe. Then the split skirt, with a short train. Then silk, silk, and more silk. Ten layers in all, each brightly colored or brocaded. Finally the most ornate layer of all, in the finest silk, covered in gemstones and iron. A warrior's heaviest leather scale armor did not weigh nearly so much. Moria wondered why Gavril had bothered to warn her against escape—her outfit would hold her as fast as metal shackles.

At least there were a few beauty customs that had disappeared from fashion long enough ago that Alvar didn't see fit to resurrect them. Foot binding had gone out of style in the last age. More recently, but before Emperor Tatsu's reign, there'd been the custom of teeth-blackening. One problem with whitening women's faces was that it made their teeth appear yellow. The solution, back then, had been to black them out altogether, leaving a dark hole of a mouth, which Moria was sure had been a lovely sight.

Once Moria had the dress on, the serving girl returned heaving a large looking glass, which Rametta made her prop in the corner.

Moria walked over, glanced at her reflection, grunted, and stepped away. Rametta scolded Moria like a chattering squirrel. Moria sighed. She stood in front of the looking glass. Then she glanced through it at Rametta, beaming behind her.

"I know you put a lot of work into this," Moria said. "So I will refrain from pointing out that I look—and feel—like an overstuffed cushion."

She watched Rametta narrow her eyes. The woman understood far too much of the common language.

Moria sighed again. "All right. Given that this is the customary attire for such an occasion, I look perfectly serviceable in it."

"Serviceable?" The serving girl stared at Moria, her eyes round. "You are beautiful, my lady. Your hair shines like gold. Your eyes are like sapphires. And that gown? I have never even dreamed of something so . . ."

She couldn't finish, her face filled with such longing that Moria felt a stab of shame. For a girl like this, such a gown wouldn't be possible even on her wedding day. While Moria may have looked in the glass and seen an awkward girl stuffed into an equally awkward outfit, the girl saw a fantasy come to life.

"I'm sorry," Moria said. "I'm in an ill temper today. Thank you very much for the compliments. It is a lovely gown. I am blessed to wear it."

"But you *should* be blessed. You are the Keeper." The girl moved behind her and fingered the silk before Rametta's throat-clearing made her stop. "You look lovely, my lady. And on the arm of Lord Gavril . . ." She sighed. "He is so handsome. You are blessed to have him favor you."

"He doesn't favor me," Moria said as gently as she could. "He's escorting me because his father demands it."

"But he is still escorting you, and he will see you in this gown and . . ."

As much as Moria tried to hide any reaction, she must have failed, because the girl looked alarmed.

"You don't find him handsome, my lady?"

At one time, Moria would have readily admitted she'd not seen a young man more pleasing in face and form. But that young man had locked her in a dungeon. Deprived her of any comfort. Refused even to tell her if her bond-beast lived. There was no way she could look at Gavril now and find him handsome.

But when Moria said nothing, she felt the weight of not only the girl's stare but Rametta's. Refusing to flatter Gavril risked insulting the healer worse than refusing to enthuse over her new dress and makeup. She opened her mouth to lie, but nothing came out, and panic ignited in her gut.

Just say yes. It's one word.

She could not. She absolutely could not.

Rametta chittered at the girl, waving her hands, telling her to be silent. The girl apologized, but Rametta chased her out of the room.

Moria looked in the glass again. She no longer saw an awkward girl in an awkward dress. She saw half a girl. No wildcat at her side. No twin sister either. The loneliness rose up and washed over her, and she wanted to cry. Fall to the floor in her silly dress and sob.

When she felt a hand stroking her hair, she saw Rametta beside her. She tried to straighten, to suck back her loneliness and despair, but the blasted dress seemed to drag her down— shoulders slumped, chin lowered, even her gaze barely able to reach up to the looking glass. Rametta stroked her hair and then pressed something into Moria's hand. The figurine. Moria didn't even need to look down—she knew it by touch. She wrapped her fingers around it, and she thought of Ashyn and of Daigo, and she made her decision.

She would not merely look about for a chance to escape tonight. She would *make* that chance. If she failed and Gavril cast her back into the dungeon, then that would be the risk she took for trying. Because she would try. She had to.

"This isn't going to work," Gavril said, pacing Moria's cell. "It's a preposterous plan and it will fail, and when it does, we'll pay the price."

He'd come in a few moments ago. Rametta had heard him approaching and made Moria stand in the middle of the room, where she'd be the first thing he'd see when he walked in. Then the old woman had waited beside the door, beaming like she was presenting a bridegroom with his bride. Gavril had stalked in, cursing and snarling, his gaze passing over Moria as if she were a piece of furniture . . . much to her relief. Anything else would have been unbearably awkward.

Rametta had not been nearly so pleased. As Gavril paced and fumed, she kept trying to draw his attention to Moria until, finally, she planted her tiny body in front of him, jabbed a finger at Moria, and admonished him in her native tongue.

Gavril cast a quick glance Moria's way. "Yes, yes, I see. She's all ready for the reception, which is a relief, considering that's where I need to take her."

Rametta waved at Moria, talking fast, her words laced with annoyance.

"All right. All right." He turned to Moria. "I'm looking. I have no idea what I'm supposed to be looking at. All I see is the Keeper in face paint and a rather ridiculous dress."

Moria bit her tongue to keep from laughing. Rametta looked ready to smack him. From the doorway, Brom stepped forward quickly, his face lighting with alarm.

"I don't think it's ridiculous at all." Brom turned to Moria. "You look beautiful, my lady."

"I'm sure you think so," Gavril said dryly. "However, if you knew Moria, you'd know you did not need to jump in with compliments. She's hardly insulted by the lack of them. Now, if we failed to notice her prowess with a blade, that would be another story."

Brom cleared his throat. "It would still seem only polite, my lord. She does look beautiful."

"Then perhaps *you* ought to take her to the reception. That would solve all of our problems."

"You could take ill," Moria said.

Gavril looked at her as if the furniture had spoken.

"I believe you appear slightly queasy," she said. "Something you ate earlier might not have agreed with your stomach. You could, with deepest regrets, bow out of the reception, and Brom could escort me."

"And would you like me to drop my dagger as I leave?"

"Please." She plucked at the sides of her gown. "I could probably even hide your sword under here, if you chose to leave that behind as well."

"You could not wield my sword, Keeper."

"True. I should probably try it out to be sure. If you could give it to me and stand right there . . ."

A snort of a laugh, and he glanced at the other two. "You wonder why I don't shower her with compliments."

Rametta replied, her words still sharp, but with an overtone of sympathy. The latter was wasted on Gavril, who only snapped back something in her language, any trace of good humor falling away. The healer sighed and shook her head.

"What's wrong, Lord Gavril?" Moria asked.

His shoulders tensed at the title, but she wasn't mocking him now. That was what she would be expected to call him, out there at the reception, and she couldn't afford to make a mistake.

"You're upset about tonight," she said. "What's happened?"

"Nothing . . . except that I'm to escort you to a reception, without a guard, and expect you to neither attempt escape nor humiliate us in any way. The chances of you doing neither are nearly equal to the chances that Rametta will stop scolding me for every infelicity she imagines I make."

"True," Moria said. "But you knew all that earlier, which does not explain your current cursing and fuming. What else has happened?"

His cheek twitched, but he said nothing.

"Kitsune," she murmured, before she could stop herself.

He looked over and it was as if they were back in the Wastes. On the road, just the two of them, bickering and goading each other.

"My father has asked . . ." He inhaled sharply. "No, my father requires . . ."

"He requires . . . ?" she prompted.

Gavril wheeled on Rametta and spoke in her language, rapid-fire and furious, striking his palm for emphasis as he spoke. The healer shook her head and said something back, quiet, meant to soothe, but he only pointed at Moria and shook his head as he spoke. Rametta continued trying to calm him, but he resumed pacing.

"Gavril . . ." Moria said. "What's going on?"

Rametta said something else, pleading now, but he kept walking, briskly, as if growing only more agitated.

Moria stepped in front of him. "Gavril . . ."

Before he could answer—or refuse—the door opened. Alvar and his guards walked in.

"Ah, good, you're already here," Alvar said to his son. "You've told her the news, I presume."

"I—" Gavril began. "I was . . ."

"He was working up to it," Moria said. "Slowly." A pointed look at Gavril. "Very slowly."

"Well, we haven't time for that. As the guests of honor, you're expected to make your grand entrance before the attendants can open the rice wine. And our visitors will not want to wait a moment longer than necessary to drink it."

"Guests of honor?" Moria said.

"Of course." Alvar smiled at her, his teeth glinting. His eyes glinted, too, like Daigo's when he caught a particularly elusive bird. "It's your betrothal party. Tonight I announce that you'll be marrying my son."

THIRTY-FIVE

"**I**s that too tight?" Tyrus asked as he wound the strip of clean cloth around Ashyn's arm. The "nick" had turned out to be a gash, much deeper than she thought.

She shook her head. As Tyrus fastened it, Ronan paced, occasionally aiming glares Guin's way. The girl sat at the base of a tree, her knees drawn up, arms wrapped around them. They'd escaped the bounty hunters—the surviving ones, that is—and were now catching their breath and tending to injuries.

"Why did you stop him?" Guin asked Tyrus. "He was running at me. If you hadn't cut him, he wouldn't have turned on you and Ashyn wouldn't have been hurt."

"So it's Tyrus's fault Ashyn was injured?" Ronan snapped.

"No, it's my fault," she said softly. "I'm asking why the prince didn't let him cut me down. Why Ashyn didn't leave me there."

"That is the stupidest—" Ronan began.

Tyrus cut him short with a raised hand and said, his voice gentle, "I *could* stop him so I did. Ashyn *could* help so she did."

"I wouldn't have done the same for you. Either of you."

Ashyn looked at the girl, hugging her knees, her gaze fixed somewhere on the ground between them. She'd said the words not with defiance but quietly, as if she was still working through the scenario in her mind.

"Sometimes that doesn't matter," Tyrus said as he tied off the bandage and stood. "For some *people*, that doesn't matter."

"But in a group, it matters." Ronan strode over. "Guin's right. She wouldn't have done that for us, and she almost got us killed. We can't have someone like that. Not now. She's deadweight. She eats our food, drinks our water, slows our pace, and requires our protection."

"We can't just leave her—" Ashyn began.

"By the roadside? No. As tempting as that might be. When we near the next town, we ought to send her on her way with a few silver. She'll be fine. She's a healthy young woman of marriageable age. We'll give her a story, and the villagers will take her in."

"So she can tell them where we're headed?" Tyrus said.

Guin jumped to her feet at that. "I would never—"

"How does your arm feel?" Tyrus asked Ashyn. "Can you move it?"

She nodded. "How are *you*?"

He fingered a fresh gash on his chin, below the earlier one. "It stings, but I'll live." He tilted his head, still touching the cut. "Do you think it will scar? I could better intimidate my enemies if I had a scar."

"Tyrus . . ." Ashyn gave him a hard look.

He lowered his hand and sobered. "I've always said I aspired to nothing except to make a name for myself in battle. The goddess has granted my wish. At least now I don't ever have to worry about my brothers seeing me as a threat. They won't bother killing me. The rest of the empire, though . . ."

He caught Ashyn's eye. "Don't give me that look, Ash. I'm not being flippant. I'm dealing with this the best I can. I'm sure the shock will set in soon enough. Until then, I need to make plans."

"You must tell your father the truth," Guin said.

"Yes, and while I would love to think he does not truly believe me capable of what Simeon has claimed, I cannot rely on that. I'll worry about clearing my name later. For now, I'm going after Moria."

"Because you think she might have done as they say?" Guin said. "Betrayed you?"

"Not for a moment. But she's being held by Alvar Kitsune, as his prisoner, and if she gets any chance to escape, she will. She'll flee to the nearest village, where she'll discover—"

"—that she's been branded a traitor," Ashyn said, her breath catching. "She'll have no way of knowing it. If she escapes and identifies herself to anyone—"

"She won't," Tyrus said. "Because I'm going to get to her first."

Before they left, Tyrus insisted they rest and recover from the fight and flight. Not that he himself rested. He prowled about

273

the perimeter of their camp with Daigo, clearly anxious to be gone. Ashyn found them in a small gully. Tyrus was crouched, peering into a rabbit burrow.

"I'd smoke them out the other end if I could trust you to catch one," he was saying to Daigo.

The wildcat busied himself cleaning a paw.

"Or you could smoke them out," Tyrus said. "And I'll catch one."

Ashyn laughed as she walked over. "You're wasting your time."

"On the contrary," he said, straightening. "I'm wearing him down. Eventually, he will tire of not having fresh meat."

Tova walked over to sniff at the hole. Daigo hissed and batted him with a paw, as if to say, *That's mine.*

"See?" Tyrus said. "He's considering it. Soon he'll realize there's no sense resisting. I'm more patient—and persistent—than he is stubborn."

"I need to speak to you."

She climbed down the small gully and seated herself on the edge. Tyrus sat beside her. Tova settled in at her feet while Daigo set off prowling.

"You must let Ronan leave," she said.

"He's free to go at any time, Ash. If I haven't made that clear—"

"I'm sorry. I misspoke. I meant that you must *make* him leave. Send him onward to the city so he can be with his brother and sister. Otherwise he'll stay at your side until you've found Moria and cleared your names."

"Which is unlikely to be anytime soon," he murmured. "All right, then. I'll insist he continue on."

"I'm going, too."

Tyrus turned sharply. "What?"

"My priority is always my sister. But you can best search for her on your own, in disguise. I will go to the city to seek information that might help you."

"If you walk into the imperial city—"

"I'm not so foolish as to stroll in and announce myself." She gave him a look, which Tova seconded with a grunt. "But even if I were caught, there are no rumors about me." None at all, which was, admittedly, a little disheartening. She had once again faded into obscurity beside her sister's supposed wild deeds. "I could convince them I was not at the battlefield, that I know not what happened."

"And Simeon? He clearly started these stories to punish you."

"I'm not convinced of that. Part of his reason, it seems, was hurt over my rejection, but there must be more to it."

"Still . . ."

"If it came to it, I would convince him that he'd misinterpreted my rejection. As much as I might hate deception, there are times that warrant it. However, I'm not my sister, Tyrus. I have no wish to defy or tempt fate. I'll quietly gather what information I can, while Ronan tends to his siblings. I will also get word to your mother, tell her you are well."

"I cannot ask you to endanger yourself, for me or my mother—"

"I will if I can. I know you are worried about her. It's settled, then? We part?"

Tyrus gazed out as he considered it. "As much as I dislike the idea—and I suspect Moria would strangle me for agreeing to it—I trust your discretion and your judgment, Ash. There's only one thing I ask of you."

"What's that?"

"Take Guin."

When Ashyn laughed, Tyrus said, "I'm serious. I can hunt for Moria much better if it's only me and Daigo."

"I know," she said. "I will take her."

"I've done something wrong," Ronan grumbled as he shoved his spare tunic into his pack.

"You know you haven't." Ashyn handed him his sleeping blanket.

"See? Even you're trying to get rid of me. I've done something."

She sighed. "Yes, Ronan, you have. I'm sorry, but it must be said. You've committed a grave offense. You wouldn't go back to check on your brother and sister until Tyrus put his boot to your arse."

His brows lifted at her choice of words. Just because she rarely used strong language did not mean she did not know it. In fact, she'd wager her vocabulary for profanity exceeded his own. That's what came of extensive reading . . . and growing up around warriors and traders.

"You know Tyrus is right," she continued. "You ought to check on them, and you *want* to check on them. You just needed . . ."

"A kick in the arse?"

"Exactly." She rolled dried fruit and meat in a cloth.

"He's making a mistake," he said.

"Perhaps."

"There's no perhaps about it, Ash. How will you survive without me?"

Her brows shot up.

"Will you steal for your supper? Will he? I'm sure Guin would try, for a lark, but she'd be more likely to end up with twenty lashes than food."

"We have food. We have money, too, thanks to you."

"It's not enough."

"It will be." *When there's only one person who needs it.* She didn't say that, of course. As far as Ronan knew, he was leaving alone. He wouldn't readily agree to take her to the city and they'd no time to argue.

"What if you're attacked? I'm sorry, Ash, but as much as you've been practicing with your blade—"

"I'm not as good as my sister. I know that."

"I was going to say that you're not as good as me."

She smiled. "Of course."

"And Guin is less than useless."

"I can hear you," Guin called from the fire.

"Good. Perhaps it will spur you to remedy the situation," he called back. Then he said to Ashyn, "I'm concerned—"

"Yes, we know," Tyrus said, walking over with a cloth in hand. "You're still leaving. It's a two-day ride to the city. Take a day to check on your siblings. If you wish to return after that, you'll go here."

He held out the cloth. On it was a map drawn with burnt wood. "Once I have Moria, I'll need a place to stay, and a powerful ally to take my case to my father. If you'd asked me a fortnight ago who I could trust, I'd have listed name upon name. But it's not until your life and the lives of others are at stake that you reevaluate. Harshly reevaluate. My list has been reduced to one. When I reached my twelfth summer, I was sent to live with Goro Okami until my thirteenth. He knows me. His family knows me. While he is a loyal subject, he is not slavishly devoted to my father. He has a sharp mind, and a sharp mind questions before accepting. He'll listen to my side of the story."

"I *will* return," Ronan said. "So you want me to meet you there?"

"In the area. I'll want you to stay clear until I am absolutely certain it's safe. I've marked an inn on the map, just beyond Lord Okami's compound. Wait for me there."

THIRTY-SIX

Ashyn and Guin followed Ronan at a distance. It was easy enough. He didn't expect trouble now that he traveled alone. Ashyn just had to wait until they had enough distance from Tyrus that Ronan couldn't send her back to him.

"Do you love him?" Guin asked as they rode.

Ashyn started to say an abrupt no, then stopped herself and said instead, "That's a complicated question."

"No, it isn't. You do or you don't. It's that simple."

"Is it?" Ashyn looked at the young woman. "I used to think so. I'm not so sure anymore. It isn't like lighting a candle, which either catches or it doesn't. It's like trying to light a fire. Sometimes you get a spark and you aren't sure if it's enough. It might start the fire. Or it might just sputter out."

"Candles can be lit and then go out."

"True."

"Love can, too. Or perhaps it isn't love. You think it is, and then it goes wrong, and you realize it probably wasn't at all. It was just desperation."

Ashyn looked over sharply. Guin kept her face forward, expressionless.

"I imagine such a realization would be . . . difficult," Ashyn said carefully.

"It is, at the time. Later . . ." Guin shrugged. "Later you see your error. Unfortunately, it can come too late."

"There was someone, then?" Ashyn prodded. "For you?"

"No. There was no one for me." Another moment of silent riding, then she continued, "I simply thought there was. I have mentioned that my parents had difficulty finding me a husband. I became a burden, as unwed daughters do. I tried to fix the problem. I was too thin, so I ate as much as I could, but it went into the wrong places. I was plain of face, so I tried elixirs of every sort, but all they gave me was bad skin. I sought to be pleasing to men in other ways, to be accomplished and sweet-natured, and I discovered . . ." She shrugged. "I discovered I was a poor performer. I cannot be what I'm not."

"One shouldn't need to."

"One does, if one wishes a husband and has nothing else to entice him with. Finally, as I approached my twentieth summer, my parents sent me to a widowed shopkeeper, to cook and to clean for him. To replace his wife, as my mother said. I did not fully know what that meant. I soon learned."

Ashyn paused, trying to think what Guin *did* mean. Then she realized it and said, "Oh," her cheeks heating.

"Yes. I was to warm his pallet as well. It was not as unpleasant as I expected. He was quite unattractive, but there is pleasure to be had in a man's embrace, and if the lantern is off, it hardly matters what he looks like."

"I . . . see." Ashyn was sure her cheeks were bright red now, but Guin took no notice.

"He told me he loved me, and I began to believe I loved him in return. Then I became pregnant."

"You . . ." Ashyn stopped her horse. "You had a child?"

Guin continued riding, her gaze straight ahead. "No, I did not."

Ashyn caught up. "I'm sorry."

"As was I, at the time. In fact, when I first learned I was with child, I was delighted. I thought the shopkeeper would marry me. Instead, he sent me back to my parents and demanded the return of all consideration. That means he wanted back what he'd paid for me. Of course, it was not legal to sell a free citizen, even in that age, but there could be an exchange of goods for services. Which is the arrangement he'd had with my parents."

Ashyn tried not to stare in horror.

"My parents were displeased with me." Guin hesitated. "No, that is what I believe is called an understatement. I had dishonored them. Whored myself, they said."

"But—but—they . . . They expected you to share his pallet."

"Yes, but because they'd *said* no such thing, they claimed innocence. As they must. Selling one's daughter as a whore is as bad as selling her as a slave. Perhaps the tradesman misunderstood the deal, but I do not think he did. Either way, I had shamed them. Though, in truth, I do not know what they expected."

Guin rode a few paces in thoughtful silence before continuing, "I suppose they thought I would take measures to prevent pregnancy. However, to do such a thing requires knowing that it exists. I don't know if the situation has changed, but in my time, one certainly did not discuss those matters with girls." Another thoughtful pause. "Though it would seem, since they are most affected, they ought to know."

"Yes," Ashyn said. "They ought."

Her own father had asked a neighbor woman to explain the facts of "marital relations" to Ashyn and Moria. He'd had the foresight, however, to stay within earshot, and later he'd had to explain it properly, to his obvious embarrassment. As for avoiding pregnancy, he'd only mumbled something about speaking to a healer once they were older. *Much* older.

At the time, Ashyn had thought Moria might need that conversation a little sooner, but she'd never had the nerve to suggest it. Now, hearing Guin's story, she realized she ought to make sure Moria *did* speak to a healer about it. Soon.

"Did you . . . lose the child?" Ashyn said. "I do not mean to pry—"

"You do not pry. I broached the subject. As I said, my parents were displeased. My mother gave me the name of an old healer and told me not to come home until I'd visited her. The woman lived quite far from our village. I told her my situation and gave her the money my mother sent with me. The next thing I knew, I woke in a field, alone and bleeding. Apparently, she had ended the pregnancy, and something had gone wrong."

Ashyn gripped the horse's reins so tight her fingers ached. She waited, barely breathing. But Guin said no more.

"And then?" Ashyn prompted finally. "What happened then?"

"Nothing. That was the end."

"Th-the end? Y-you mean . . ." Ashyn stammered and stared, unable to get the words out, until finally they came and she blurted, "You died?"

"Yes."

"There? In that field? Alone?"

"Yes."

Nothing Guin had said was more horrifying than the *way* she said this. So calm. So matter-of-fact. As if this was all one could expect from life. To be sold to a man, impregnated, rejected by your family, and sent to a stranger—with no idea what she has in mind—and then to wake in a field, the baby gone, your own lifeblood seeping into the ground. Used, abused, abandoned, and left to die. Alone. Utterly alone.

"I . . . I'm sorry," Ashyn said. "I don't know what else to say but that."

Guin's lips curved in the smallest smile. "You say it and you mean it, and you know me hardly at all. That is more than I expect. I'm glad I told you."

"I'm glad you did, too."

She reached to squeeze Guin's hand, seeming to startle the girl. But Guin managed a smile in return, and they continued on in silence.

When Ronan paused to eat a quick meal by the roadside, Ashyn and Guin rode his way. He reached for his blade but stopped when he saw Tova. Ashyn braced, expecting him to scowl and march over to confront them, but he only smiled.

"Changed his mind, did he?" Ronan got to his feet and scoured the landscape. "Where is his highness? Off prowling as usual?"

"He headed west."

"There's nothing there. I just came from that way."

"So did we. I meant that he headed west after you left. We're going with you."

Now the scowl came. "I hope that's a joke, Ash."

"It is not. I'm going with you so I can get the news from the city. It's our best chance of hearing gossip on Moria. When you return to Tyrus, we'll ride back together."

He argued, but there was little he could do now with Tyrus long gone. Finally, he waved at Guin. "And her?"

"I asked Guin to come along," she lied for Guin's sake. "I thought that best. She can find a place in the city and—"

"I'm coming to care for your siblings," Guin cut in. "So you will have no cause for concern on their behalf."

Ronan sputtered, then settled for aiming an accusatory look at Ashyn.

"That was not what we discussed," she said slowly. "But perhaps it is not a bad idea . . ."

"Not a bad idea? She's been non-corporeal for an age. She's barely stopped walking into walls."

Guin glowered at him. "I have not walked into anything since my second day in this body. I can care for children. I had younger siblings when I was alive. They all survived the ordeal of my care."

Ashyn expected Ronan to snap back a retort, but he only glanced away and grumbled, "You'll not care for my siblings. Since the prince is long gone, though, I must accept Ashyn's companionship."

"You're too kind," she murmured.

He glared at her and said to Guin, "And since I accept hers, you—unfortunately—come as part of the deal. But if you impede our progress or endanger Ash at any turn—"

"I would never endanger Ashyn," Guin said hotly. "You, perhaps. But not her."

Ronan opened his mouth to reply, but Ashyn cut him off. "If I can find information on my sister, I'd like to do that *soon*. Can we stop arguing and start riding?"

THIRTY-SEVEN

At nightfall they stopped at an inn that had sprouted its own settlement, as inns sometimes did, with enterprising traders and artisans making their homes nearby to profit from travelers. The building itself was typical for the region—two stories, with an exterior walkway along the second floor.

Ronan and Guin went inside to get a room while Ashyn and Tova waited. Once a bedchamber had been acquired, they smuggled Ashyn up the outside steps to their room. It wasn't a given that she'd be recognized, but they took no chances.

Once inside she was expected to stay there until morning. Guin and Ronan would be more sociable, dining downstairs and wandering among the trading carts in hopes of hearing news.

Ronan managed to sneak Tova up when he brought Ashyn's evening meal.

"There's something going on out there," he said. "A rumor. I'm trying to track it down."

"What are they saying?"

"Not much. But when trouble is afoot, people get anxious. There's almost a . . ." He struggled for the word. "Something in the air. A sharpness. A tightness."

"Does Guin notice it?"

He made a face. "Hardly." He leaned against the wall. "There are things you learn growing up as a thief, and some of them aren't as obvious as others. You need to be able to tell when people are nervous so you can get out before it goes bad."

"Is that what you want? To get out of here?"

"Not yet. It feels like a mix of trouble and excitement. People know war is coming and it scares them, but it's exciting, too. A chance for change."

Ashyn paused. "Do *you* want change?"

"Not from a man who slaughters villages with shadow stalkers. My issues with the empire aren't from anything Emperor Tatsu has done. But dissatisfied people don't always see that. To them, revolution means rice wine and honey cakes for all. I've been getting that sense of tension and excitement every time we pass through a village. Here, it's multiplied tenfold."

"Perhaps there's news? Of actual war? Or another incursion?" She paused. "Or perhaps something about the children. Of Edgewood and Fairview . . ." She knew that was not their priority now. It couldn't be, with Moria captive and Tyrus wanted for treason. But she still thought of the children. Often.

"I must be discreet," Ronan said. "But I said that I'd heard something about children being taken, and no one knew anything of the sort. As for the war, everyone who has news is eager to share it, but the rumors are the same. The empire still is preparing."

"Perhaps those preparations are escalating, and it's having some effect here."

He considered it. "They will recruit for the army. Not for warriors, of course, but for cooks and blacksmiths and such. But I can't see how that would be any cause for anxiety or secrecy."

"What if it's not Emperor Tatsu who's recruiting?"

He nodded slowly. "Let me make another round, then, with more pointed questions."

After Ronan left, Ashyn paced. She could do nothing else. There wasn't even a window to peek out. She did open the door a crack. Though night had fallen, she could see torches. An inordinate number of them, it seemed, and lanterns, too, as if people were milling about waiting for something.

She was still looking when she heard the thump of footsteps on the stairs and glanced over just as Ronan crested them. He waved her back inside. She'd barely gotten the door closed before it opened again.

Ronan strode in, caught her by the shoulders, and kissed her cheek with a loud smack. "You are a genius. Have I mentioned that?"

"Not lately."

He grinned and squeezed her shoulders. Guin came in and shut the door as Ronan and Ashyn moved farther into the room.

"You were absolutely right," Ronan said. "A few of Alvar's mercenaries and bandits are here, recruiting. They're finding able-bodied young men and women and offering them positions. They're being very secretive about it, and of course no one wants to admit to being approached, but nor does anyone dare report them. Not that there's anyone here to report them to. They're choosing well, canvassing small settlements like this, without any regular guard."

"You're sure that's what's happening?"

"They approached me and asked my views on the current situation. When I said I hadn't made up my mind, the man started telling me why my life would be better under Alvar. He said the rebellion needs young men like me, and I could be raised to the warrior caste if I demonstrated an ability for battle. I told him I'd consider it."

"Wise," Ashyn murmured. "These aren't men you wish to cross."

"It's also the truth. I am considering it." He flashed a broad grin as she looked over, shocked, and when he spoke again, his voice strummed with excitement. "Think of it, Ash. Where better to get information on Moria? On the entire situation? I could be a spy."

"No, you could not."

He paused, his mouth open. When he shut it, his face darkened. "If you think I could not handle it—"

"I'm sure you could, but—"

"I have martial training. I *could* be a warrior." When she opened her mouth, he cut her short with a wave. "I don't mean truly ascend to warrior caste, Ash. I mean within their ranks.

289

That would get me more information than if I was working the stables."

"It could also get you killed."

Guin cleared her throat. "I'm going out. I saw a vendor selling sugared plums—"

"Yes, yes," Ronan said. "Go."

Once she'd left, he rolled his eyes. "We're discussing a serious situation, and she flits off to buy sweets."

"I don't want to talk about Guin. I want to talk about you. There are men on Alvar's side who've seen you. Who know you're with us. Barthol and his confederates—"

"He wouldn't recognize me. I look like a hundred other low-caste brats."

"And Gavril? Let's say they make you a warrior, and they present you to Alvar Kitsune. Do you not think Gavril would be at his side? That he'd not recognize you?"

"There would likely be many warriors present. Gavril wouldn't notice me."

He gave the argument weakly, and Ashyn could tell she was gaining ground.

"What about your brother and sister? How would you check on them?" She paused for a moment, thinking fast. "I'd have to do it for you."

"What?"

"Someone needs to stay with them. We can't trust Guin to do it. So I would."

"You, living in the city? The exact twin of the girl wanted for highest treason?"

She lifted her chin. "It's a risk, but if you're taking one, so will I. You'll infiltrate the ranks of Alvar's men, and I'll infiltrate the city. We must both do what—"

"Enough," he grumbled. "I may call you a genius, but I would prefer you used that genius to help me, not thwart me."

"I would never—"

"Don't give me that wide-eyed look, Ash. It worked well when we first met, but you've learned much since then."

"I have an excellent teacher."

His scowl deepened, but only for a moment before he shook his head and took her hands. He held them for a moment, fingers rubbing the backs of them.

"There are times when I think those teachings are for the best," he said. "And times when I regret them."

"Because I use them against you."

He looked up. "No, because I fear I am a bad influence."

She pulled her hands away. "I'm not a child, Ronan. I would have you teach me *more*. I ought to know how to steal, how to—"

"Absolutely not."

She looked him in the eye. "I'm not asking because I think it would be fun to take things that don't belong to me. I'm as much an exile as Tyrus and Moria, even if no one speaks my name with theirs. As long as I cannot walk into a town and ask for shelter and food, I am reliant on you."

That smile quirked the corners of his mouth. "I don't mind that so much. I ought to, I know, but—"

"That won't work. I'll not be distracted. I want to learn—"

Tova got to his feet and stared at the door. He looked toward Ashyn and whined.

"He hears something," Ashyn said.

She walked to the door and cracked it open. Lanterns and torches still lit the darkness, perhaps a few more than before, but the people carrying them only milled about, as if they weren't sure why they were out of doors and were looking for a cause.

Ronan brushed past onto the walkway. "I don't see any-thing . . ."

A man's voice sounded beside him. "If you're joining us, you'd best hurry. That was the signal."

The man passed the partly open door. Ashyn shrank back, but he didn't glance into the room. That would be rude. He wasn't much older than them, perhaps entering his second decade. A Northerner, with light hair and skin, dressed as a merchant. He bounced down the steps and into the night.

"The man I spoke to said they'd give a signal when they were ready to assemble and leave." Ronan glanced at Ashyn.

"I can't stop you," she said. "But I am serious. If you leave, I must stay with your siblings for you, so at least tell me where to find them so I'm not wandering the city."

He shook his head and reentered the room. "I'm not going. And not because you threatened—"

"It wasn't a threat."

His look said they both knew better. "I'm staying because you're correct that I could be recognized, and that won't help anyone." He closed the door. "I want to circulate some more, but I'll wait until after they leave. If Alvar's mercenaries don't get as many volunteers as they'd like, I'd not put it past them to impress young men into service." He crossed the tiny room and sat cross-legged on the sleeping pallet. "We'll be at the city tomorrow, and we need to discuss what we'll do once we're there. I know you wish to get word to Tyrus's mother and we'll figure out how to do that, but at first, you'll have to stay outside the city with Guin."

"So you won't leave her with your siblings?"

"I don't trust her not to simply flit off when the mood strikes. She's easily distracted."

"They aren't babies," she said carefully. "Aidra is six summers, is she not? And Jorn is ten? It's not as if Guin would turn her back and they'd wander—"

"No," he said sharply, getting to his feet. "All it takes is a moment, and I'll not entrust their lives to her care."

He walked to the door and opened it enough to peer through. Ashyn watched him, his shoulders tight, his gaze fixed outside.

She rose and walked over. "Guin would—"

"Shhh," he said. "Something's happening."

She caught the sound of raised voices. Ronan walked out, letting the door close behind him.

THIRTY-EIGHT

Ashyn pulled on her cloak and tightened the hood, making sure her hair was tucked in. Then she stepped out to find Ronan on the balcony walkway, his hands braced on the railing as he looked down at the collection of wagons below.

Beyond the wagons was an open area where people could take their food, sit, and talk. Now, the benches had been cleared aside. No one stood in the square, but people ringed it, as if something was coming and no one wished to miss the spectacle.

"A performer, most likely," Ashyn said. "An acrobat or a bard. I'd suspect they've been paid by Alvar's men to provide a distraction as the recruits make their getaway. Clever."

When someone finally entered the empty square, though, it wasn't a performer, but a warrior. Dressed in the colors of the imperial army.

Ronan swore under his breath. "Alvar's men picked the wrong settlement after all. There's going to be trouble, Ash. Get back in—"

He stopped. Then he cursed again. A second warrior had joined the first.

"That's the man who tried to recruit me," he said.

"The warrior?"

He nodded grimly. "Not one of Alvar's men, apparently. Back inside, Ash. *Now.* I don't know what's going on—"

Ashyn rose on tiptoes for a better view as the warriors herded a group of young men and women into the square. They were bound with hemp rope, like convicts. As the warriors propelled them—at blade point—one of the young men fell to his knees. Ashyn recognized him as the Northern merchant who'd hurried past them moments ago.

"This is a mistake!" the young man cried. "I never—"

One of the warriors raised his sword to the man's throat, but the first warrior—the apparent leader—waved the blade down. He unfastened the man from the rope, grabbed him by the hair, and dragged him to the center of the square. Protest rippled through those watching. An old man stepped forward, but one of the warriors stopped him with a wave of his sword.

The warrior in charge kicked the young man's feet out, forcing him to kneel while still holding him by the hair, suspended, his knees not quite reaching the ground. When the young man tried to rise, the warrior kicked him back down again.

"You were approached by a man recruiting for the traitor

Alvar Kitsune. Do you deny that?"

Ronan's curse hissed in Ashyn's ear as he shifted uneasily beside her.

"I do not deny I was approached," the young man said.

"Then do you deny that an offer of recruitment was made?"

"No, but—"

"Do you deny that you accepted the offer?"

"No, but—"

"Then you cannot deny you are a traitor yourself. That you were willing to join the enemy and betray your people, destroy your land."

"N-no. He offered money. Good money. My family needs—"

"You were joining the enemy cause. That is treason. High treason. Do you know the penalty for that?"

The old man who'd tried to move forward earlier did so again, saying, "My grandson meant no harm. Please. We are traders who have had a run of bad luck, and he made a foolish choice. Do not exile him—"

"Exile him? Where, old man, would we exile him? The Forest of the Dead? Have you not heard the news? Edgewood is gone. The people of Edgewood betrayed the empire, letting Alvar Kitsune live and then hiding him for these ten summers. The village has paid for its treason, executed by order of the emperor. Every man, woman, and child has been put to the sword—"

"No!" Ashyn cried before Ronan could slap a hand over her mouth. Her cry went unheard, as a similar one rose from the crowd assembled below, shock and disbelief and outrage. She twisted in his grip and peeled his fingers away. "They lie. Why would the emperor lie?"

"Look closer, Ash. Do they truly look like imperial warriors to you?"

Below, the crowd had erupted in chaos, held in check only by the men's blades. As she peered closer at the warriors, she remembered what Moria had said about when she'd first come to Fairview. How she'd known that the "warriors" standing guard were no warriors at all. Little things. A general slovenliness of appearance, such as stains on tunics, and signs they'd made hasty attempts to clean themselves up, like poorly braided hair and shaving nicks.

As Ashyn looked at these warriors, she saw the same signs. Yes, they wore the uniforms of the imperial army. They bore the twin blades. A few even had imperial army helmets—the distinctive horns and dragon crests at the temples that marked them men of Emperor Tatsu.

But faced with the panic and unrest of a growing mob, a warrior should not forget his caste. He did not shout at commoners or bicker with them or threaten them, and below, she could see "warriors" doing all three.

Why would Alvar's men recruit volunteers and then pose as imperial warriors? Why lead the recruits into fake exile?

No, the leader had said there was no exile. Not anymore.

"The old ways were soft," the leader said, his voice ringing out as the crowd came under the warriors' control. "Your emperor realizes that now."

There was a commotion in the audience, and he had to stop as his men subdued it. While they waited, Ashyn's gaze swept over the prisoners, six young men and two young women—she choked back a gasp.

"Guin," she whispered.

She raced along the walkway for the stairs. Ronan let out a stifled cry as he came after her. He caught her arm before she descended.

"Guin," she said. "She's among the captives. She volunteered."

His face screwed up. Then he shook his head. "You're mistaken. Guin looks like many empire-born girls. She's certainly not going to volunteer for something—"

"—that will *help* us?" She looked him in the eye. "After someone repeatedly reminded her that she's useless? That she never does anything?"

"She wouldn't—"

Ashyn wrenched from his grip and hurried down the steps. She set out at a run across the yard. Ronan raced after her, calling for her to come back as loudly as he dared.

Ahead, the leader was still talking. "Your emperor has realized he is too soft on criminals. None of this would have happened if he'd followed the ways of the great emperors past."

Ashyn tore around a cart and stopped on the other side, where she could see the crowd. *All* she could see, though, was that crowd—the backs of onlookers, with the warriors and captives lost in the middle.

The leader was now speaking of the great emperors, the first emperors.

She looked around wildly. Then she glanced at the cart beside her. A trader's, one big enough to be affixed to horses.

Behind it, the merchant had stacked barrels. Ashyn clambered onto them. Ronan was at her side, saying nothing now that she was hidden. From the barrels, she heaved herself onto the roof of the cart.

"Ashyn, no!" He grabbed at her leg. "They'll see—"

She kicked him off and flattened herself, pulling her cloak hood down farther. Ronan climbed up beside her.

"There!" she said, pointing at the last captive. "Are you to tell me that's not Guin?"

The young woman stood in the line of the prisoners, wearing shackles, looking confused as she listened to the leader.

"How did the great emperors of old deal with threats to their lands? To their people? Did they exile traitors to a forest? No." He kicked the young Northerner onto all fours and waved for another warrior to take his hold on the young man's hair. "The great emperors of old knew how to deal with serpents."

His blade flashed, so fast there wasn't even time for a gasp from the crowd. The Northern merchant fell, and the warrior holding his hair swung his head into the air.

"That is how one deals with a serpent!" the leader boomed. "You chop off its head."

The warrior flung the young man's head into the crowd. A cry went up, delayed shock, and then the onlookers surged forward, enraged. The warriors fell on the first few, knocking them to the ground, holding them there, blades at their necks.

"Are the rest of you traitors as well?" the leader said. "I've shown you how we deal with them now, and I would suggest you take a moment to decide whether you are one of them."

The crowd rumbled and shifted. The old Northern

merchant crouched by his grandson's body, weeping. The warriors kept their targets pinned, swords at their necks. Slowly, the mob backed off. Some on the edges began looking around, as if wishing to leave. Other false warriors appeared from behind buildings and carts, surrounding the crowd.

"If you are good citizens of the empire," the leader called out. "Then you will wish to bear witness. If you do not, we will know you are not good citizens." He turned to his men. "Let them decide for themselves if they have changed their minds."

Those pinned to the ground rose as soon as they were able and silently merged back into the throng. The leader strode to the next chained man. When a warrior went to grab him, the prisoner fought wildly, writhing and kicking, but three of the false warriors held him down. Others came forward to subdue the rest, and even as Ashyn saw the leader's sword rise, there was a part of her that did not make the logical assumption. That refused to make it.

He's bluffing. Threatening. Posturing. One death is enough. He does not need—

The blade fell. The young man heaved himself up at the last moment, in a final attempt to escape, and instead, lost the mercy of a quick death. The blade caught him too high, cutting but not slicing through bone. Blood sprayed like a fountain.

I'm not seeing this. I cannot be seeing this. The spirits. The ancestors. The goddess herself. None would allow—

Ronan clamped his hand on her collar and heaved her backward, dragging her off the roof of the cart. When she realized what he was doing, she stopped resisting and scrambled down herself, hitting the barrels hard, toppling one in her haste. She leaped to the ground, her ankle twisting, recovering fast as she lunged forward to race around the cart and—

Ronan hauled her back. She fumbled with her cloak's fastening, got free, and almost darted away again before he caught her by the tunic. He yanked her back and seized her arms instead.

"No," he said. "You cannot—"

"I must. Guin."

"You can't."

"I can try. I will try."

She gave a tremendous pull, but he only tightened his grip. When she began to struggle, he did the same as the false warriors in the square. He pushed her to the ground and pinned her there. Only he didn't pin her with a sword, but with his own body, holding her down, wincing as she kicked and fought. When she opened her mouth, he jammed his forearm against it, and she had to stop herself before she bit him.

"There's nothing you can do," he said. "Nothing."

She wriggled away from his forearm. "I can try—"

"How, Ash? It's a dozen men. Guin is chained. If you interfere at all, they will see who you are. You'll be captured, and Guin will still die."

"But I need to do something. Anything. Please."

"We can't. I'm sorry. I'm so sorry."

He touched her face, wiping away tears, and only then did she realize she was crying. He wrapped his hands around her face, fingers entwined in her hair, and he pressed his palms to her ears, shutting out the screams and struggles of the dying. She lay there, gasping for breath, trying not to think—

Not to think of what was coming? To ignore Guin's death? To leave her out there, surrounded by strangers as she died?

"I need to be where she can see me."

He shook his head. "No, you don't. That won't make you feel any—"

"It's not about me. I won't let her die alone again."

THIRTY-NINE

Ronan finally agreed though with obvious reluctance. He kept hold of her arm, as if to steady her, but she knew it was to restrain her, should she have any urge to rush in and save Guin.

Of course she had the urge. But as she'd lain there crying, the tears had washed away the panic, and she realized he was right. Now, as they moved around the side of the cart, she could see it, too. Guin was chained, surrounded by Alvar's men, with more ringing the crowd. Perhaps earlier, if Ashyn had acted when the crowd rose up, in that initial surge of horror and rage . . .

Perhaps she could have turned the crowd against the false warriors.

Or perhaps she'd have gotten them all killed along with Guin.

While the others fought and wept as the blade came down

the line, Guin only stood there. Perhaps it was shock, but it seemed like resolve. She'd been dead before. So she would be again. It was not what she wanted—so desperately not what she wanted—but from everything Ashyn knew of Guin's mortal life, she'd not been a girl accustomed to getting what she wanted. And so it was again.

Ashyn tried to ignore the executions, but that was as futile as ignoring a raging fire if you were caught in the middle. She heard the sobbing of the prisoners and their relatives and friends in the crowd. She heard the thwack of the blade, then the chortles of Alvar's men. She smelled blood and urine and vomit.

She kept her gaze on Guin and kept moving forward. When she was only a few paces away, the young woman noticed her. Her eyes rounded, and her gaze shot to Ronan, head shaking as she motioned for him to keep back, to take Ashyn away.

Ashyn shook her head and motioned that she'd not try anything, but she was staying where she was. She would not leave. Even Ronan seemed to realize that and finally released her.

I'm sorry, Ashyn mouthed as fresh tears streamed down her face.

Guin gave a wry smile. "Don't be."

The leader finished executing the man beside Guin. The girl tensed, fear finally crossing her face. He took a step toward her.

"No!" a voice called from deep in the crowd. "Not the women. Please, my lords. Spare the women."

I know that voice.

She turned to find that Ronan was no longer beside her. It was him shouting from the middle of the throng. A few people moved away from him, distancing themselves, but he stayed where he was, his blades hidden under his cloak, his gaze downcast, his posture servile.

"Please, my lords. Show mercy on the women. Take them if you must. Put them in service of the empire. But spare them."

There was little hope of that. Alvar's men wanted to portray imperial warriors as monsters, so they *would* kill the women, and Ronan's words could neither sway them nor goad them on. But there was still a chance of spurring the crowd to action. If they rose up, Ashyn and Ronan might be able to rescue Guin. That's what he was trying to do. Provide a distraction.

While others took up his cry, their voices were low, their tone submissive, begging for mercy toward the two women. And that was all they did. They stayed in their places and they begged.

The leader motioned for one of his men to grab Guin's hair. Ashyn squeezed her eyes shut and spoke new words then. New pleas. To the ancestors and to Guin's spirit itself. *Leap free, if you can. Let go.*

Take her out of there. She does not belong in that body. Spare her this final moment.

Guin gasped. Ashyn's eyes flew open. The false warrior was wrenching Guin's head up as the leader's sword swung down.

Please, please, please. Release her. That's all I ask. Release her.

Before the sword struck, Guin's body went limp. Ashyn felt her spirit pass in a soft breeze and heard a whisper in her ear. "Thank you." Then Guin was gone and her body lay in the square.

"Come," Ronan whispered, appearing beside her, his hand on her arm. "We ought to get inside."

She turned and stared at him, and when she did, she felt as if it were *her* body on that stage, empty and cold. She looked at him, and all she could think of were the times they'd fought about Guin, all the times he'd cursed the inconvenience of her. Had she not done the same? Quietly and to herself?

We're finally rid of her, she thought, and began to sob.

They were in their room now, waiting for a chance to flee. She'd wanted to leave right away, but Ronan had said it wasn't safe. The false warriors would be watching for anyone running away from the "lesson" too fast. Indeed, in the short time that followed, Ashyn heard several screams, including a horse's, presumably killed carrying a traveler swiftly from the scene of the carnage.

As they waited, she spoke for the dead, easing their passage and offering one last heartfelt apology to Guin and a prayer that the ancestors would help her find her place in the second world.

Once Alvar's men were gone, the burbling rage of the crowd hit full boil. People began shouting, snarling, fighting. Grieving relatives blamed onlookers for not helping. Onlookers blamed the grieving relatives for raising sons and daughters who'd betray the empire. The anger and the confusion seemed almost a living thing, a dragon lashing through the crowd.

Twice, when she'd heard a scream, she'd marched to the

door to tell them what had truly happened. But Ronan dragged her back and blocked the exit.

Otherwise, he sat on the sleeping pallet and stared at the wall. Tova moved between them, offering comfort. Ashyn took it, with hugs and pats. Ronan simply kept staring.

"I couldn't wait to be rid of her," he said, echoing her earlier thought.

"Not like that."

He turned dull eyes toward her. "Does it matter?"

"Yes, it does."

"No, Ash. I called her useless. Too useless to look after my brother and sister. She was proving me wrong. When she came in, she overheard me talking about volunteering, so she did it. To prove herself."

"You didn't—"

"I ought to have been more careful with my words. Like you were. Shown her how to be useful, not harangued her when she wasn't. I was thoughtless, and I was careless." He paused. "I've learned nothing. Nothing at all."

She knelt to sit beside him. "Learned nothing about what?"

He shook his head. "It doesn't matter." He went quiet, then said, "Do you think I sealed her fate by begging for mercy for the women?"

"No, they were going to kill her. You hoped to rouse the crowd and cause a distraction. I understood that. Even if your pleas had no effect, Guin heard them. The final words she heard from you were kind ones. That meant something."

He nodded, his gaze to the side, then said, "The noise seems to be dying down. We'll leave as soon as we can and head to Lord Okami's lands to meet Tyrus."

"What? But we have to go to the city. More than ever. The emperor must be told—"

"It won't help. Those men fulfilled every disgruntled commoner's fears about the empire and its warriors, and this story will spread a day's ride by sundown. In fact, I'll wager it'll go even faster. Surely we didn't just happen to make rest in the one settlement they targeted."

"You think there were others."

"I'm certain of it. There's nothing Emperor Tatsu can do to stop the lies." He finally reached out and patted Tova as the hound lay his head on Ronan's knee. "This is the sort of thing I grew up with, Ash. To trick people, you prey on their worst fears by weaving a scenario just realistic enough to convince them. No matter what the emperor says, those who wish to see him guilty of this will."

Ashyn's insides folded on themselves, hope suffocating. "And there's nothing we can do to help?"

"Nothing except take this story to the only person who might know what to do with it."

"Tyrus."

FORTY

B y the time Ronan and Ashyn felt it safe to leave the inn, the moon was well past its zenith. Then they were faced with a quandary: what to do with Guin's pack.

"Leave it," Ashyn said.

Ronan hesitated. "I know you will not wish to wear her clothing, but she was carrying some of our food and money and—"

Ronan's head snapped up, and he began patting his pockets. "She bought something tonight. She gave it to me." He pulled out a small cosmetic pot and handed it to her. "Henna cream. She said she remembered women using it to darken their complexion. She thought it might help you pass more easily."

Ashyn took and opened the pot. She dipped a tentative finger into the reddish-brown cream.

"She was so pleased that she'd found it," he said. "I never even thanked her."

She was trying, Ashyn thought. *She truly was.*

She didn't say that, of course. His guilt was heavy enough.

"I'll use it," she said. "I have no looking glass, so you'll need to tell me how it works."

Up close, the cream made for a rather obvious disguise, but from a distance, it would help, as long as she kept her hair covered and her face downcast.

As they stepped from their room, Tova went ahead to wait near the road. Ashyn looked at the square. The bodies were gone, thankfully. When she and Ronan rounded the building to the stables, though, they saw the heads on pikes near the roadway.

"They forbade us to remove them," the stable boy said as he got their horses. "The innkeeper is sick about it. It's a terrible tragedy, of course, but it'll be even worse for business. He's saying we might as well shut down."

Ronan hesitated, then glanced at Ashyn before saying, "I'll wager they won't be left up past the first imperial warrior or courtier riding by."

The boy tensed, one hand gripping Ashyn's reins. "Why's that?"

"Because I don't believe those men were imperial warriors. I've lived in the city all my life. I've seen plenty of guards. Oftentimes as I was running from the point of their blades."

The boy laughed and relaxed. From the cut of his clothes, he was low caste himself.

"I bear the imperial army no goodwill," Ronan said. "But they're proud men. They don't dress in mended uniforms and laugh at commoners. They consider themselves too good for that, the arrogant sons of whores."

The boy nodded. "When they stable their horses here, I won't even get a copper if their steeds don't leave as curried and combed as a court lady's mare."

"And I've never seen warriors led by one without ink." Ronan shrugged. "I could be wrong. I'm not staying to see if I am. But I don't think you'll need to keep those heads up more than a day or two. Now, we should be off . . ."

"Didn't you come with three horses?"

"Yes," Ronan said. "And we leave with two."

The boy hesitated, then his eyes went round. "I—I'm sorry."

Ronan nodded and they mounted their horses.

"About the third . . ." the boy said.

"Keep her. I suspect you'll have a few more horses today than you did yesterday. Perhaps that will be some compensation to the innkeeper."

Ashyn thanked the boy and paid him a few coppers. Before they left, Ronan paused, then he turned back and gave the boy five coppers more.

"If there's any chance of taking one of those heads down, could you make sure it's the girl with the longer hair. Don't get yourself in any trouble for it, and I understand if you cannot, but if the opportunity presents itself . . . Perhaps the innkeeper can be persuaded that it's best to remove both the girls' heads . . ."

"I'll do what I can."

"That's all one can ask." Ronan bowed to the boy, and they rode into the night.

FORTY-ONE

The cushion caught Gavril in the side of the head, sending him stumbling backward with an oath.

"I suppose I should be thankful there's nothing harder for you to throw. Or sharper."

She yanked a long, jeweled pin from her hair and whipped it. She'd been aiming for his eye, but sadly, he turned at the last moment and caught it in the cheek instead. It still scratched, and he let out a hiss, not loud enough to bring the guards, who'd retreated with Rametta.

"Moria . . . I know you're angry—"

"Do you? Truly? Give me your dagger, and I'll show you how angry I am."

"Do you think I asked for this? Do you think I've not argued since the moment he mentioned it? It isn't a real betrothal. You don't have to marry me."

"I don't? Ancestors, have mercy. Because otherwise, I'd

have gone through with it." She strode over and glowered up at him. "Going through with it is not in question, Kitsune. If your father dragged me to the marriage shrine, I'd commit ritual suicide before I got there. With a hairpin if needed. After I killed you with it."

Her gaze moved to the floor. He stepped back, his foot coming down to cover the hairpin.

"My father has assured me there is no question of an actual marriage. It's a betrothal for political posturing. A sign that even the goddess favors his ascension to the imperial throne, having given her child to his in marriage."

"Is he mad? A Keeper cannot marry. It's an *insult* to the goddess—"

"There's a precedent."

She stared at him.

"There's a precedent, and my father is using it to bolster his claim on the imperial throne by saying it's a portent."

"No, it's insanity."

"I am not disagreeing. But as I said, there will be no marriage. Simply a betrothal. The wedding will be postponed until he takes the throne, when it can be properly celebrated."

"Then you are correct. I have nothing to worry about, because he's never going to take that throne."

"The point, Moria, is that we are stuck with this performance. We need to play our parts, and if we do not, we will be punished."

He resumed pacing the floor. She'd noticed he hadn't even argued when she said his father wouldn't become emperor.

"My father wishes . . ." More pacing. "He requires . . ."

Gavril cleared his throat. "He insists that it must appear as more than a political alliance."

"More . . . ? What—"

"It must appear to be a love match," he said, spitting the words. "You must act as if you are . . ."

"In love with you?" She stared at him. "Then you might as well escort me to the dungeon now, Kitsune, because there is not enough performing skill in the world for that."

"It is not the dungeon he threatens you with."

His words were almost too quiet to hear, but there was no way she could miss them. She stared at him.

"He . . . He threatens me with . . . ? He threatens a *Keeper* with death?"

"You know that I never would have brought you here. Yes, I tricked you. I betrayed you. I regret none of it. But I do not wish to see you dead, Moria."

"Then help me escape."

With a short laugh, he shook his head, pacing away again.

"What?" she said. "That is the solution, is it not? To both our problems? You aren't telling me anything I haven't already realized. I know you don't care for me but—"

"And you are correct. I do not. I never did. When I say I don't wish you dead, I accord you the courtesy of your position and the basic humanity I would feel for any other innocent party."

"The basic humanity you would feel for any other innocent party . . ."

He fixed her with a cold look, his gaze shuttered. "Yes, Moria. I know you don't like to hear that—"

"Why? Because I still hold out hope that you're not a treacherous son of a whore? Do I flinch when you insult me? When you tell me I mean nothing to you? I do not. What I marvel at is any notion that you possess basic humanity. Was my father not an innocent party?"

He'd been pacing again as she spoke. He had his back to her now, and it stiffened as he stopped. Then he stood there, facing the wall.

"Do you want my help in pulling off this performance?" she said. "This is my price. Admit what you did. The role you played in the massacre of Edgewood. In my father's death."

"I have already—"

"You have not. I want to hear it from your lips. Exactly the role you played."

He stayed there, his back to her. "As I said, I have done whatever you believe."

"That's not what I'm asking for."

She strode in front of him and stood there, looking up. His gaze was fixed straight ahead, his jaw tight.

"Tell me exactly what you did," she said.

"I have done whatever you believe."

She grabbed for his dagger, but he caught her by the wrist, squeezing as he bent over her. Now his gaze did meet hers as he said exactly what he had on the night she confronted him.

"I have done whatever you believe. I have deceived you. I have betrayed you."

Remember that, he'd added that night. *Whatever happens, remember that.*

She tried to shake off his hand, but he kept his grip tight as he leaned over her, so close his braids brushed her face.

"This is not a matter for negotiation, Keeper. I do not expect you to walk into that reception and pretend you are in love with me. But you will not act as if you wish to put a dagger between my ribs. You will behave as though you are pleased with the engagement. If you can manage that, we will both escape this trap unscathed." He straightened. "Now, I will ask Rametta to return and help you freshen up. Your face powder is smeared. You must be quick, though. My father will not be kept waiting."

If Gavril was in such a hurry, he ought to have told Rametta. By the time the old woman returned, Moria had stopped pacing and was sitting cross-legged on her sleeping pallet. Rametta shuffled into the room bearing touch-up powder and a folded towel with warm water. She fixed Moria's makeup and brushed her hair again. Then she motioned to the towel and water.

"I'm to bathe now, after I'm dressed and groomed?" Moria said.

Rametta made a show of washing under her arms, then sniffed, making a face.

"If you're saying I stink of sweat, then I'd suggest you bring sweet pine perfume to cover it, because in this gown, I'll be sweating all evening."

Rametta laid the towel in Moria's hands, then walked out. Moria tossed the towel to the floor. It hit with an odd clunk. She bent and unwrapped the towel to find . . .

Her dagger.

She lifted it carefully, as if it were a mirage that might

evaporate the moment she touched it. It didn't. She lifted it and turned it over in her hands. Her blade. It was truly her blade.

Was it a trap? Perhaps Gavril had told the old woman to give it to Moria. He wanted her to try escaping so he could capture her. Prove to his father that this betrothal business was dangerous, that Moria was dangerous. Get her thrown back into the dungeon until he could negotiate terms for her release and be rid of her.

I don't care. If that's his plan, I'll upend it on him. I'll escape, and he can deal with the consequences of that.

She secured the blade deep within the sleeves of her voluminous gown. There, now she was properly dressed.

FORTY-TWO

Moria had never attended a grand reception, but she'd often read of them in books, particularly the type Ashyn liked to secret under her pillow while pretending to be enraptured by a tome on the social history of nomadic desert tribes. Receptions and balls featured prominently in many a romantic tale. This particular scenario seemed straight out of one. The awkward girl, transformed by silk and rice powder, walking into the party on the arm of a dashing warrior, as the gaping crowds part to let them through.

In books, Moria always skipped that part. And so she did tonight, at least mentally. She walked in on Gavril's arm, and the assembled guests could have pulled faces and stuck out their tongues for all she noticed. She was too busy looking about for escape routes.

If she did attract attention, it could be attributed to the fact that she was one of very few women at the reception. It mattered little anyway. When admiring glances lingered for more than a moment, they were scattered by a glower from Gavril. That was perhaps the most unfair part of all. She had to smile and twitter and act as if he was the most wonderful boy she'd ever met. He could be his usual cold and surly self, and if anything, it enhanced the performance, giving the appearance of a possessive and attentive fiancé.

She did have one source of petty pleasure, and it came from the fact that he seemed as uncomfortable in his dress attire as she felt in her gown. He'd been wearing it earlier. She'd not noticed, any more than he'd noticed her dress. It was only when she caught him pulling and tugging at it now that she took note. It was, like hers, formal wear. His trousers were loose and pleated. Over his tunic he wore a robe nearly as intricately embroidered and bejeweled as the top layer of her dress.

As for how he looked in it, she did not allow that assessment to cross her mind. She knew him for what he truly was—a liar, a traitor, the young man who'd have let her rot in a dungeon— and that was all she saw when she looked at him. Which made it all the more difficult to feign those admiring glances.

Fortunately, Moria had too much else on her mind to simmer over the outrage of this charade. Each time they passed an exit—there were three—she noted how well it was guarded. She mentally configured this room within the outside of the building, based on her walks about the grounds, determining which exit led to which door and which would provide the best escape route. The answer seemed simple—the northern exit, which would take her to the less guarded northern end of the compound. And tonight, the goddess truly did shine on her, because that exit also led to the toilet pits.

Moria made sure to drink too much water and tea, ensuring she'd need to make several trips to the toilets. When the need first arose, not long after they'd been in the reception, Gavril seemed happy for the excuse to leave the party. So happy that he didn't even insist on escorting her all the way, waiting instead in the first hall. That gave her time to explore.

In between trips, Moria took careful note of who she met. The main guests were the two warlords. They were debating whether to join Alvar's forces, which Emperor Tatsu would be very interested in knowing. There were others, too—men of varying positions who either hadn't declared themselves for the Kitsunes yet or hadn't done so officially, acting as spies in the imperial court. All useful information.

Moria and Gavril made their rounds of the guests. They ate and watched a poetry recital. Moria managed not to fall asleep during the recital, which would have pleased Ashyn. Gavril barely even feigned interest in it, looking about, paying her and the poet little heed.

"I'll need to use the toilets again soon," she whispered as the primary poet left the stage, to be replaced by the secondary one.

"It's the middle of a performance," Gavril said, shooting her a look of annoyance.

"Which is why I said *soon*. After it's over."

When it finished, he was the one to remind her, saying this would be a good time, before the acrobatic performance began.

He was escorting her toward the exit when they were stopped by Lord Kuro Tanuki and his son. They'd met both earlier—a short and formal conversation. That was when the two men were sober, which they no longer were. In fact, they were clearly, exceedingly, not sober.

Lord Tanuki stumbled into their path and thumped a meaty hand on Gavril's shoulder.

"You've grown up well," Tanuki said. "Very well indeed. The last time we met, you were just a skinny boy, running around court with the emperor's bastard. A useful friendship, as it turned out."

He winked at Gavril, then did the same to Moria. He seemed to expect some response from her, but she was struggling to think of a way to word her own question. *You speak of Tyrus. Does he live? Tell me he lives.*

There was no way to ask without betraying herself, so she held her tongue and prayed he'd give some sign that he did not speak of the prince in the past tense.

"Yes, you've grown up well," Tanuki said. "Strong and sturdy, like your father. But you take after your mother in looks, which is particularly fortuitous." He laughed at his own joke, then thumped his son for comment, but his son was too busy staring at Moria to notice.

"They do make a striking couple, don't they?" Tanuki said. "They'll have very handsome children."

"I've never bedded a Northern girl," his son blurted.

Even his father sputtered at that. The son seemed too drunk to realize his impropriety and kept staring at Moria.

"Her hair is like golden fire," the son said. "Is it the same color down—?"

His father cut him off with a thump to the back of the head hard enough for the son to stumble. Lord Tanuki laughed, too

321

loudly, as if he could drown out any more indiscreet comments. "We'll need to find you a Northern girl to check for yourself. *Another* Northern girl. This one is taken, and from the looks young Gavril is giving you, if you continue speculating in that fashion, we'll all be witnessing a sword fight instead of an acrobatic performance."

"My apologies, Lord Tanuki," Gavril said stiffly, sounding not apologetic at all. "I am unaccustomed to being betrothed."

"And my son is unaccustomed to your father's rice wine. It is good to see you so taken with your bride. As a man who has been married nearly three decades, I can assure you that it helps a great deal. You will be very happy together. Not that there was any doubt of your mutual affection, given what the young Keeper did for you."

Before he could continue, one of his men came to tell him that Alvar wished to speak to him. Lord Tanuki said he'd be right there and then turned to Moria. "That was quite a feat, my lady. A difficult one, I'm sure, leaving your sister and your wildcat behind. The empire may not hold you in very high regard now, but once Alvar Kitsune triumphs, people will understand the sacrifice you made."

"Sacrifice?" Moria said, but Tanuki was already walking away, following his man to Alvar. Moria turned to Gavril. "What is he talking about?"

For a moment, Gavril seemed not to hear her. He stared after Tanuki and there was an odd look in his eyes, as if a horrible thought had just dawned on him.

"Kitsune," she hissed, tugging his arm. "What is he talking about?"

"I—I don't know." He turned to face her, but his gaze didn't meet hers. He appeared genuinely confused, and more than a little concerned. "Wait here. I must have a word with my father."

"But—"

He strode off. As he did, Moria glanced around. She was at the party, alone. *Completely* alone, as people returned to watch the acrobatic performance.

She peered toward the hall leading to the toilet pits. A few guests still streamed out, rushing back to the main room as the performance began.

Moria gave one last look around. Her gaze settled on Gavril, now across the reception hall, speaking to his father and completely preoccupied.

She hurried for the hall.

Moria knew exactly where she needed to go. Getting there was somewhat more complicated. Not least because she was stuck wearing the blasted dress for as long as she could reasonably expect to bump into someone. And until then, she was as inconspicuous as a peacock.

She took the circuitous route she'd noticed earlier and managed to avoid two guards. Then, as she was creeping down the final corridor, a voice whispered by her ear, *Wait.* She paused.

Not yet, child, the spirit whispered.

Moria tilted her head, and as she did, she caught the grunt and sigh of a bored guard at his post ahead. She zipped around the corner.

"You deign to help me now?" she muttered. "About time."

A second spirit answered, *Impatient child.*

Impertinent, a third spirit sniffed.

Moria glowered. What good did it do to hear the dead if they would not even help when you were trapped in the enemy camp? Ashyn would point out that there hadn't been a way to help until now, but Moria was in no mood to be charitable.

Shhh, child. It was the first spirit again. *Heed me.*

Heed *only* me—that's what it meant. Moria focused on the first spirit and ignored the mutterings and mumblings of the other two.

This way.

Moria followed the first spirit's whispers back down the hall, then along another one. She ended up near where she'd been heading, but approaching from the opposite side. When she peeked around the corner, she could see a single warrior guard, shuffling and grunting with boredom. Wide-awake and alert, though. Looking for trouble. Hoping for it, to break the monotony.

Blast it.

The exit door was right there. Once through it, she'd be outside, on the north end of the compound. All she had to do was get past one guard.

She fingered her dagger and peered out again. She could throw it from here and catch him in the neck.

And raise a commotion that would bring every other guard running.

Was that truly what stayed her hand? A fortnight ago, she'd never have considered hurting an innocent man, possibly killing him. Now . . . ? There was still hesitation, but how much of it was reluctance and how much was simple concern that the ploy would fail?

It was only three paces to the door. If she could distract the guard . . .

She reached under her gown. All she carried with her were the dagger and the wildcat figurine. There was little question of which she should use, but still she hesitated. She clutched the figurine. To lose it felt like losing Daigo himself again, and her chest seized at the thought.

Yes, child, the spirit whispered. *You must.*

She braced herself, then she took aim and pitched the figurine as far as she could down the hall, letting it bounce off the distant wall.

The guard jumped. He looked around. Then he started toward the object on the floor, pulled by his boredom and curiosity. Moria slipped from her hiding place, crossed the three paces to the door, eased it open, and escaped.

FORTY-THREE

Moria made her way across the north end of the compound. It was not protected, but she'd been out here often enough to know that the guards had their routes and their favored stopping places. Avoid those and she was fine. Or she would be after she shucked the dress. She didn't strip all the way down to her shift. That was white, meaning she'd streak across the night like a comet. She went to the third last layer—a dark green silk. Then she took one of the dark, discarded layers and tore it into a long strip to wrap over her bright hair.

Dagger in hand, she made her way toward the north wall. Scaling it wouldn't be an issue. According to Brom, the compound itself was an abandoned military training camp. They'd cleaned it up, but what it lacked was a proper fence. So far they'd encircled it with a makeshift barrier of wood, no taller than a man's head.

She headed toward that wall, taking a circuitous route to avoid the guards. The ancestors continued to favor her, perhaps deciding she'd suffered quite enough punishment for any past offenses. Finally, she was close enough to see the wall. Then she heard a noise. Footsteps. Running. She froze and swung around, her back pressing against the nearest building. She'd barely gone still when a figure stepped between the buildings. A figure with dark braids and tattoos on his forearms.

Gavril had his back to her as he moved from one building to the next. He did glance her way, but only briefly, as if he expected to see someone running in her dress, light hair flowing behind her, an easy target to spot. When he looked away again, she gripped her dagger and lifted it.

She could throw it at his back. He wore no armor. She could injure him, badly. She might even be able to kill him.

Instead, she pressed herself against the building and waited for him to pass. He stopped on the other side of the passage. Moria held her breath. He took one more careful look around before putting out his hand and saying something, and as he spoke, his fingers began to glow with an unearthly light.

His fingers lit the passage as well as any lantern, and as he turned her way again, the light turned with him, and she knew it didn't matter how dark her dress was or how deep the shadows. His gaze lit upon her, and she clenched her dagger, ready for him to pull his blade and run at her.

Instead, he exhaled, the sound sliding through the silence.

"I've found you," he said.

"And you will un-find me," Moria said, raising her dagger. "You will walk away or I will throw this. You know I will."

"I—"

"Did you not tell me once that daggers were an inferior weapon? In close combat, yes. But from ten paces? You will be dead before you reach me, Kitsune."

"I'm not trying . . ." He extinguished his fingers with a wave, but not before she saw his face, tight and glittering with sweat. "I'm going to come closer, so no one overhears us. I will keep some distance."

She let him get two arm lengths away, then stopped him with a flourish of her dagger.

"I won't attack you, Keeper. But you cannot escape. You absolutely cannot."

"No? I suppose you'll tell me your father has the forest filled with monsters and—"

"I misspoke. I do not mean you are unable to escape. I mean you must not." He took a step toward her. "I talked to my father after Lord Tanuki made those remarks. You cannot return to the imperial city or they'll exile you as a traitor. Perhaps worse, as there is no forest to exile you to."

"Traitor?" She laughed. "You'll have to do better—"

"They say you betrayed Tyrus. That you seduced and counseled him to lead his men to slaughter and turn his back on a town under siege. They blame you for the massacre at Fairview and the death of Tyrus's men. They say you are my lover and you betrayed the empire for me."

"Do they truly? My, that is a terrible story, and I thank you, Lord Gavril, for warning me before I escaped. Please take me back to my cell. Or perhaps, to be safe, return me to the dungeons."

Even through the darkness she could see his mouth tighten. "You aren't taking me seriously, Keeper."

"Because you've made it clear exactly how low an opinion you have of my intelligence, Kitsune."

"I only said that because—" He bit the sentence off. "You don't need to return to your cell. We'll make other arrangements. I can insist that because we are betrothed, you must be given quarters. Your own quarters. My father cannot ask you to share mine before the wedding, which will never—"

"You're stalling until someone hears us. I'm leaving, and if you try to stop me . . ." As she let the threat hang, she caught a glimpse of a low-slung, dark shape on the rooftop. It almost looked like . . . No, it was gone now. A trick of the moonlight.

"Blast it, Keeper. Listen to me—"

"I will not. You always were a terrible teller of stories. Your skill has not improved. I have the advantage here, and you are resorting to lies to convince me to stay and save yourself from any punishment. Hopefully your father will realize my escape wasn't your fault—"

"Of course it was my fault," he snapped. "Who do you think secreted that blade into your cell? Who let you go out on walks, accompanied by an idiot and a smitten young warrior? Who let you hear him complain about poor security in the north end of the compound? I *orchestrated* your escape, Moria."

She hesitated. He relaxed, but she was only thinking it through, and after a moment, she said, "You orchestrated it to be rid of me. You resented the obligation and responsibility. But now you've had second thoughts. Perhaps your father said he suspects something and—"

"By the ancestors," he said through clenched teeth. "You give me no quarter, Keeper. No matter what I say—"

"I think it a lie. Why ever would I do that? Oh, yes, because you have done nothing but lie and betray me. You pretended to be my ally, after you had murdered my entire—"

"I murdered no one."

"Does that absolve you of guilt, then? If you only assisted your father in unleashing shadow stalkers—"

"I did not, Moria," he said, taking a step toward her. "I killed no one. I had no idea what my father planned. When you told me the village had been massacred, I refused to believe you. Why would I argue if I knew it to be true? You were there when I saw it. You saw my reaction. I did not know."

"You admitted to it."

"I admitted to doing whatever you thought I'd done, because it was safer for both of us. But I will deny that I ever said I played a role in the massacre of your village or the death of your father. I cannot explain now—"

"You cannot explain at all."

He ground his teeth, green eyes burning as he took another step her way. "You believe not a word I tell you? After all we've been through?"

"Correct. After all we've been through, I will not believe a word you tell me. After you betrayed me. Threatened me. Left me in a dungeon. Showed not one iota of kindness or sympathy. You refused to even tell me if Daigo lived."

"Not in front of my father," he said, moving forward. "But I *did* tell you, Keeper. I gave you—"

"Stop," she said, lifting her dagger. "If you take another step toward me—"

He raised his hand, and in it she saw his sword. She pulled back her dagger, but he was too close for her to throw it. Then his blade was at her throat.

Fury and rage surged, so hot and sudden that for a moment, she thought he'd driven that blade into her throat.

"You tricked me."

"I'm only trying—"

"You would do and say anything to keep me from escaping."

"No, Moria. I would do and say anything to keep you from running back to the imperial city and being branded a traitor. But what I said *is* true and—"

A black shape dropped from above, knocking Gavril away, his sword swinging on the new target, only to see what he was aiming at and stop short. Daigo stood between them, his yellow eyes fixed on Gavril, his fur on end as he snarled. Moria stared.

Was she asleep? First, she'd escaped with ease. Then Gavril had told her he didn't help massacre her village. Now Daigo was here, improbably and impossibly. She was dreaming. She must be.

"Daigo . . ." Gavril said, his voice low. "I wasn't trying to hurt her."

"No, you only had a blade at my throat."

"Because it's the only blasted way to stop you from racing off to your death. Daigo—"

"He's a beast. He doesn't understand you."

"He understands me as well as you do, and listens as well, too, which is somewhere between a little and none at all. I'm no threat to her, Daigo. I never was. But she cannot leave—"

Moria ran for the barrier. Behind her, Gavril let out a soft shout and Daigo answered with a snarl, and she glanced back, dagger raised, ready to throw it if he had his blade drawn on her wildcat, but they only faced off, Daigo blocking his way, Gavril gripping his sword at his side and snarling something back at the wildcat.

Moria reached the barrier. She leaped onto it easily, swinging herself up until she was on the top. Then she turned.

"Daigo!" she called as loudly as she dared.

The wildcat wheeled and ran toward her. Gavril did, too, sword still in hand, falling steadily behind as Daigo raced full-out.

"Don't do this, Keeper," Gavril called.

"I'll remember what you said, and I'll not present myself at court until I know the truth."

"It doesn't matter. You're still in danger. If you're out there, they'll find—"

She jumped down as Daigo sailed clear over the barrier.

"Keeper!" Gavril said from the other side, still running, footsteps pounding. "Moria! Do not do this."

She looked out at the forest. Then she ran toward it with Daigo at her side, Gavril calling behind her until she was too far away to hear him.

FORTY-FOUR

Moria ran through the forest following Daigo, leaping over logs and skirting fallen trees until she ran right into him as he stood there, peering into the darkness. He stayed stock-still, only his tufted ears moving, pivoting until he heard what he was searching for—the sound of pursuit, she presumed. Then he took off again. She managed to keep pace until she heard the sound of running footfalls and stopped short. They were heading *toward* the footfalls.

"Daigo . . ."

He stopped.

"I hope you know who that is," she said.

He huffed, as if offended she'd question him. Moria still lifted her dagger, poised, watching in the direction of the footfalls until a cloaked figure appeared. It peered into the darkness.

"Moria?"

She heard that voice, and she raced forward, Daigo barely getting out of her way in time. Even before the figure pulled down his hood, she knew who it was. She tucked away her dagger as she ran, and when she finally reached him, she threw her arms around his neck. He caught her up in a hug, swinging her off the ground and embracing her so hard she gasped for breath, gasping and laughing, tears prickling as relief washed through her.

"You're all right?" Tyrus hugged her so tight she couldn't back up to look at him, and had to settle for nodding into his shoulder. She tried to say yes, but the word caught in her throat.

He released his grip, and as she pulled back to look at him, those threatening tears filled her eyes and his face wobbled in front of her.

"I didn't know," she said. "They wouldn't tell me . . . No one would tell me if you were . . ."

She couldn't get the rest out. So she kissed him, which seemed a perfectly reasonable alternative to speaking.

He kissed her back, deep and hard, his arms tightening around her again, and it was the kiss she'd barely dared to remember, lying in her cell, not knowing if he lived. It was the same . . . yet not the same.

The first time, if someone had suggested she'd been holding back, she'd have drawn her dagger at the insult. No matter what Tyrus said, she'd been certain no part of her had not been fully engaged, not fully committed to being with him.

But he'd been right. There had been a ghost between them, a little part of her still hurt and bewildered by Gavril's betrayal, still thinking he had some excuse, and even though she had hotly denied any romantic feelings for him, there'd been some confusion there, that part that hadn't quite figured out what she *did* feel. Now it was gone.

Gavril had done what she suspected and, worse, had been willing to lie about it to lure her back into captivity. He was nothing more now than a reminder of how easy it was for some to deceive and how easy it was to be deceived.

Everything she'd felt during her imprisonment—fear, shame, rage, helplessness—evaporated in Tyrus's kiss and his embrace. He was here. He was alive. She was free. Perhaps that did not mean the world was right again, but it was right enough.

Unfortunately, one member of their party did not share her conviction. It was a gentle nudge at first. Then a growl. Then a knock, hard enough to make them both stumble, their kiss breaking.

"Enough, Daigo," Tyrus said with a growl of his own. He reached one hand into Moria's hair, pulling her to him, his lips coming back to hers. "We'll leave in a few—"

Daigo grabbed Tyrus's cloak and yanked him so hard he landed on his rear. Tyrus twisted up, growling in earnest now, and Moria had to laugh at the two of them, scowling at each other.

"He's jealous," Tyrus said as he got to his feet, brushing himself off.

Daigo snorted and rolled his eyes.

"Are, too," Tyrus said. "I'll wager your greeting wasn't nearly so effusive."

"Because I already knew he lived," Moria said. "And because he doesn't kiss half as well as you."

Tyrus laughed. "He is right, though, as much as I hate to

335

admit it. We ought to get moving."

"Is Ashyn nearby?" Moria asked as she took out her own blade.

Tyrus shook his head. "She left with Ronan to check on his brother and sister. They'll meet us near the compound of Lord Goro Okami. It's . . . It's a long story."

"But she's safe?"

He nodded. "She's with Ronan. I was at Lord Okami's the day before last to speak to him. His men will be watching for her. With any luck, she's already there."

Moria peered into the forest. "So you're alone?"

Daigo growled.

"I meant the two of you, of course," she said, giving the wildcat a look. Then she turned to Tyrus. "Thank you for taking care of him."

Another growl from Daigo.

Moria rolled her eyes. "Thank you for taking care of each other."

Tyrus grinned and leaned in for a quick kiss. "And thank you for getting yourself out of there. The ancestors were smiling on us today, because I had no idea how I was going to manage the actual rescue part of my rescue plan. I'm sure Daigo didn't either, however much he might like to claim otherwise. Now, let's get out of this forest before someone sounds the alarm."

"Did anyone see you leave?" Tyrus asked as they walked.

"Gavril."

Tyrus's face tightened. He tried to hide the reaction, but Moria caught a glimpse of it before he said, carefully, "So he helped you escape, then."

"Hardly. He was trying to stop me."

A flutter of relief, followed by a flash of guilt and then worry and finally something like disappointment. As a romantic rival, he would want Gavril kicked from Moria's mind. But Gavril was more than that. He was a boyhood friend, and Tyrus still hoped for some sign that the Gavril he remembered lived, that he'd not lost his honor, not betrayed them and held Moria captive.

"We'll speak of that later," she said, taking Tyrus's hand and entwining her fingers with his. "For now, I'm not surprised we haven't heard him raise the alarm. He'll not want his father to think he let me escape. He'll pretend he was occupied and did not see what happened."

"Does he fear his father?" Tyrus asked. "Perhaps that's why—" He cut himself off. "I'm sorry."

She tightened her grip on his hand. "I know. It would be easier to think he's held there, as much a prisoner as I was. But he's not, Tyrus. I'm sorry. We'll talk more later, but Gavril isn't cowering in his father's shadow. He's free to come and go, and he chooses to stay and play his role—as heir—in his father's plan."

Tyrus nodded. "As he must." And that, Moria knew, was how he would make sense of this. Gavril was doing his filial duty. It did not make him a good person or mean that he was not now Tyrus's enemy, nor that he was less culpable of the evil he might do. It was simply the only way to accept that his old friend could do these things and not be a monster. Which was what Tyrus needed. What they both needed.

FORTY-FIVE

As they walked through the shadowy forest, Moria tilted her head to listen and heard only the rustle of wind in the leaves. "It's quiet here."

"Very. You're in the western provinces. Beyond the trees, you'd see the Katakana Mountains."

"Where the Kitsunes are from."

"Exactly. Also not far from Lord Okami's compound, which is almost a day's ride in that direction. In this direction"—he hooked his thumb toward the camp—"you'd be in the ocean by sunrise. Go that way"—he pointed left—"and you'd land in Lake Shiko. The other way? An ocean inlet."

"Which means the Kitsunes have chosen an isolated location with one way in or out. This forest."

He nodded. "That's why it was a good location for a camp. But after a decade of peace, it was abandoned, and it's been empty almost ten summers. Lord Okami had already figured out that this was the most likely spot for Alvar Kitsune to be holed up. When I reached him, he was preparing to send men to investigate, so he could notify my father."

"Are his men nearby, then?"

"A few. Beyond the forest. That's where Alvar's guards were. Okami's men helped me deal with them. Now they are out there keeping watch. The forest itself, as you see, is empty. As long as you are correct, and Gavril doesn't raise the alarm, it's likely to stay that way."

"He won't."

"If he does, we'll hear it. I've caught the bells signaling every meal. It's so quiet out here that it's impossible not to hear them."

So quiet . . .

Like the Forest of the Dead. Which was not the way a forest should be at all, as she'd learned from her travels.

"Have you heard or seen *anything*?" she whispered.

He shook his head. "I suspect Alvar's been here long enough to empty the forest of prey. That's one disadvantage to his situation. He can't simply travel to the nearest town and purchase enough supplies for an army."

When they stepped into a clearing, she looked up to see the dark shape of a bat flitting past. Not empty, then. Just very, very quiet.

Tyrus adjusted his grip on her hand and cleared his throat. "A lot has happened since you were taken. I'm not sure how much of it you know."

"None. I wasn't exactly an honored guest, privy to rumors and news."

He looked at her sharply. "You ought to have been. Not privy to news, I mean. But an honored guest. I presumed . . . You are a Keeper and surely Gavril . . ."

"I was not a Keeper within those walls. I was a prisoner and Gavril's responsibility, one he—" She shook her head. "I just want to be out of this forest, and as far from this place as I can get."

He took her other hand, tugged the dagger from it, and tucked it into his own belt as he pulled her to a stop in front of him.

"I'm sorry," he said.

She looked up at him. "For what?"

"We did not . . ." He inhaled sharply. "No, I'll accept responsibility for this. Full responsibility. I did not come after you immediately, Moria. I presumed Gavril . . . I was certain he would care for you."

Moria saw the guilt in his eyes and hurried on with a lie. "It was not a pleasant experience, but I was not mistreated. Gavril saw to that. I—"

Daigo cut her off with a growl.

"Yes, I know," Tyrus said to the wildcat. "You're right. This isn't the time for—"

He stopped again as Daigo peered suddenly into the dark forest, his long tail puffing as it swished.

"He hears something," Moria whispered.

Tyrus handed Moria her dagger and took out his sword. But when they went still, all they could pick up was Daigo's growling.

Shadow stalkers.

The thought had flitted through her mind earlier, and she hadn't entertained it because her gut had told her she was mistaken. While it was possible that Alvar would keep his shadow stalkers here, she detected none of the negative spiritual energy she'd felt in the Forest of the Dead. The strum of spirit life was weak but present.

Yet something must be out there or Daigo wouldn't keep growling. Some predator afoot. One that frightened every living thing into hiding.

She looked up, thinking of the thunder hawk, but this dense forest would be a poor place for a bird the size of a house. It needed open ground.

Speaking of ground . . . She glanced down, but again, it was the wrong terrain. No death worms could live beneath these thick roots.

"Moria?" Tyrus whispered. "Talk to me."

Tell me what you're thinking.

She didn't know what to say. She feared if she put her thoughts into words, he'd think her foolish. Like Gavril. Mocking her for her stories and her imagination.

"Moria . . ."

Tyrus leaned against her, his hand on her waist, his breath warm against the side of her head, both the touch and the whisper of breath reassuring. *You can talk to me. I'm not Gavril. I don't mock.*

"I don't hear anything," she whispered. "That's not natural, and I fear . . ."

"That whatever's out there isn't natural either."

She nodded, and he said nothing. She expected to see that

recoil of disbelief, of not wanting to insult her but thinking she was indeed being foolish. Instead, she saw him peering into the shadowy forest, his dark eyes bright, his lips slightly pursed. Looking and thinking, equally hard.

"Not thunder hawks or death worms," he mused. "Wrong landscape for either. Not shadow stalkers either."

She could have laughed as he voiced exactly what she'd been thinking.

"It could be someone with a tracking hound," she said.

"A very quiet hound. Having spent time in Tova's company, I'm not sure that's possible. A hunting cat, perhaps."

Daigo harrumphed, looking pleased.

Tyrus continued. "But if it was a hunting cat, I would hope Daigo would know. In fact, I should hope he'd know what it was regardless."

The wildcat's eyes narrowed.

"Daigo," he said. "Why don't you go see what's out there?"

The wildcat backed up, bumping into Moria's legs and sitting on his haunches at her feet. He stretched out a giant paw, claws extending.

"No, you don't need to watch over Moria. I can do that."

Daigo motioned with his nose to the forest, as if to say, *I'll stand guard. You go investigate.*

"He listens about as well as you do," Tyrus said to Moria. "And argues as much, too."

"Which is why I don't try to give him orders."

She lowered her hand to Daigo's head, rubbing behind his neck. He let out a rumbling purr, looked at Tyrus, and sniffed.

"We don't see anything and neither does he," Moria said. "I'd suggest, instead of standing here debating our next step, we simply move. This way?"

She motioned, and Tyrus nodded. "The forest thins after a while. I was able to ride partway in, and I brought a horse for you. They're camped over there."

"Good. If there is something in this forest, we'll do better escaping it on horseback."

As they set out, the moon passed behind cloud cover, stealing the little bit of light that guided them. Tyrus pulled a torch from his cloak and handed it to Moria, leaving both his hands free for his sword. The torch was small, barely enough to light their way. Larger, though, and it would have been a beacon for anyone who came after them.

Daigo's head swiveled as they walked. With every few steps, he'd pause, gaze whipping in one direction or the other. He'd peer into the pitch-black forest, then chuff, telling Moria he could see or hear nothing, and they'd continue on.

Something was out there. But perhaps it wasn't a threat. Not every fantastical creature was inherently dangerous.

"It can't be dragons either," Tyrus said as they walked. "They'd be larger. Noisier."

He was smiling wryly, as if he knew she was doing the same thing, running through the list of possibilities.

"Definitely not dragons," she agreed. "Nor—"

She caught a glimpse of red in the forest and stopped short. Red eyes. She'd seen red eyes.

"Did you . . . ?" she whispered.

Daigo grunted, and Tyrus shook his head. Neither had

noticed. She resumed walking.

"Not water horses either," she said, "given the complete lack of water."

Tyrus chuckled. "I've seen a stream or two. Perhaps they are much smaller than in the stories."

"Sadly, so far, nothing is smaller than in the stories. But I would be quite happy with tiny water horses or dragons the size of dragonflies or . . ."

She trailed off.

"Moria?"

I think I know what it is. That's what she wanted to say, but she stopped herself. There was an entire bestiary of magical and lost creatures that Alvar Kitsune could have resurrected, and while they were joking about narrowing the possibilities, the truth was that it would be nearly impossible to guess. If she thought she knew, that was only because her mind was leaping to the worst possible conclusion.

Or the most likely conclusion?

If something fantastical lived in these woods, it was because Alvar Kitsune put it there to keep out those who slipped past the guards at the forest's edge. And if one had to resurrect a creature to quietly guard a forest, it would not be a death worm or a thunder hawk or even a dragon, but a monstrous spirit of myth, like shadow stalkers . . . only worse.

She peered into the forest again and caught another flash of crimson.

"I saw that," Tyrus whispered. "Red eyes."

She nodded.

"That's all I saw. No shape."

That's all you will see, if I'm correct.

"How much farther?" she asked.

"We're almost there."

"Can we go faster?"

He nodded.

"Just don't run," she said. "Whatever you do, don't run."

"You think it's—" He cut himself off with a curse. "Of course."

"I could be wrong." *I hope to the ancestors I am.* "Just keep moving. Don't try to see them."

"Believe me, I don't want to see them."

She made a noise of agreement under her breath. Daigo had fallen back beside her now, guarding her on one side, Tyrus at the other.

"It's a grove of white birch," he whispered. "I see it ahead."

She detected the faint glow of the trees, visible even in the darkness.

"Are the horses tied?" she whispered.

"Well tied."

"Good. We'll have to be fast. Jump on, slash the ropes, and go." And hope the steeds could outrun the beasts that followed. If anything could outrun the beasts that followed.

"The gelding is on the left," Tyrus whispered. "He's a bay. The gray mare is yours."

She nodded. They both clutched their blades, slowing their steps, peering toward the glade, ready to rush forward the moment they saw—

Daigo let out a snort and tried to leap in front of Moria, but she was already stumbling over whatever he'd noticed in her path. It looked like a fallen branch and she was righting herself, cursing, when Tyrus inhaled sharply.

Bone protruded from the end of the "branch." Bloody bone and shredded flesh and, on the other end, a hoof.

"The horses," he whispered. "They've killed . . ."

He didn't need to finish. He and Moria raced forward, both calling a warning to the other to stop as they realized, simultaneously, what they'd done. They'd run, and it was only for a few steps, but it was enough. All around them the forest erupted in growls. Red eyes flashed in the darkness.

They stumbled into the clearing. Tyrus tripped this time, and Moria looked down to see him stagger away from the head of the gray mare. The remains of the horses were everywhere, whole pieces and sometimes no more than bone, the flesh stripped as cleanly as if vultures had feasted for days. There was blood, too, and she slid on a rope of entrails.

Tyrus grabbed her arm to steady her. Then he swung her around behind him, his blade out, the two of them back-to-back. The forest had gone silent now, but Moria could sense the beasts circling. Daigo hissed and spat. When those red eyes flashed in the darkness, he lunged, only to slide on the blood-slick grass and dance away, snarling, his fur on end, ears laid flat. When Daigo looked up, Moria whispered, "Trees. We need to climb a tree."

"The birch are too small."

"I know."

Moria lifted her torch and squinted into the semidarkness.

"There," she whispered, pointing to an oak outside the grove.

Tyrus shifted, as if flexing his knees while he contemplated the distance.

"Twenty paces," she said.

"I have the bigger blade. You'll go first."

"No, you ought—"

Daigo cut off her argument with a growl. *Just go.*

Moria inhaled and they turned as one, putting her in direct line with the tree.

"You'll be right behind me?" she whispered.

"You have my word," he said.

Which meant yes—without question, yes. She exhaled, adjusted her dagger and the torch, crouched, and counted to three under her breath so Tyrus could hear. Then she ran.

FORTY-SIX

Moria held the torch as high as she could to light the way for Tyrus. She could hear him right behind her, so close the sound of his breathing seemed to drown out the pounding of his boots. When she strained, she caught the swish of grass as Daigo ran off to Tyrus's side. What she could *not* hear was the sound of pursuit. It didn't matter. The beasts were there, right there, on Tyrus's heels, and she didn't need to look back to confirm that.

When Moria reached the tree, she whipped around. There they were—a seething mass of red eyes and dark shadows. She pitched the torch at them, wheeled again, and jammed her dagger into the tree trunk. She used it as a climbing spike, yanked herself up, and grabbed the lowest branch. She swung onto the limb, leaving the dagger behind. She leaped up onto the branch and took the next one. Soon, Daigo was beside her and Tyrus was on the limb she'd just vacated. She kept going until she was as high as the branches would hold her weight. Then she stretched out on her stomach.

Tyrus reached the branch below hers and handed up her dagger. They both lay with their arms wrapped around the tree, staring down into the night.

The thrown torch had ignited the dry grass, but it only smoldered and smoked, obscuring more than it revealed. Then, as they regained their breath, the clouds overhead drifted past the moon, not clearing it but stretching thin enough for the beams to penetrate.

At first, Moria still saw only red eyes. But as she watched, she could make out shadowy shapes, writhing in the darkness below. When she squinted, one of the shapes seemed to take form into—

"Don't look." Tyrus reached up to grip her arm.

"I know but—"

"Don't look. Please. I don't care if the stories are true or not. Don't take that chance, however curious you are. Please. For me."

She tugged her gaze from the shapes below.

"Think of something else," Tyrus said. "Tell me about them."

"You already know—"

"A little." He managed a wry smile. "Share your expertise and perhaps we can figure a way out of this."

We can't. It doesn't matter if we've seen them or not. There's no escape from—

"Fiend dogs," she blurted, feeling a mix of relief and fear naming them. "They're fiend dogs. You'll see only shadows and eyes. But if you look long enough, they'll take the form of

349

giant black dogs. They're both a warning of death and death itself. If you see one, it'll chase you until it catches you, and then it'll kill you." She hesitated. "There's no escape."

"Ignore that part. I don't believe it. Keep going."

She opened her mouth, but her heart hammered too hard for words. Thunder hawks, death worms, even shadow stalkers . . . they could be stopped, if not killed outright. Fiend dogs caught scent of their prey and chased it right into the second world.

"Moria . . ."

She swallowed hard. Even without looking down, she knew the fiend dogs were there. Growling now, snarling and snapping invisible jaws. Snorting and grunting. The tree vibrated as one jumped against it.

"They can't climb," Tyrus said. "Keep talking. You'll find something useful. I know you will."

She nodded. "Fiend dogs aren't like death worms or thunder hawks or dragons. Those are beasts of legend. True beasts, like a hound or a cat. They live and feed and breathe and bleed. They're said to have once roamed the earth and died out. Fiend dogs are like shadow stalkers. They aren't alive, not truly. Legend says they're the souls of warriors who betrayed their lords, forced to forever roam the earth in service of their new lord: death. They're—"

"Spirits."

"Yes, which means they're incorporeal and can take the form of shadow or dog."

"No, I mean they're spirits. Like shadow stalkers. You can fight shadow stalkers."

"In corporeal form, yes, you can—"

"No, Moria." He met her gaze. "*You* can fight shadow stalkers. You have fought them. Banished them. You're the Keeper."

It was a testament to her terror that she had to process his words, slowly realizing the truth of them. The obvious truth. If these were like the shadow stalkers, she could banish the spirits.

"There's no guarantee," she said slowly. "It was not easy with the shadow—"

"You can do it. I know you can." He grinned, and when he did, that smile seemed to snatch her fear and pitch it as far as her dagger might fly. It wasn't a grin that said, *You'll save me.* It said, *I believe in you, and whether you can banish them or not, I know you'll try, and if you can't do it, then no one could.*

The tree shook as one of the fiend dogs threw itself against the trunk. Then another did the same, and she had to grip the limb with both arms as the spirits battered the tree from below.

"Just hold on," Tyrus said. "I won't let you fall."

Again, this wasn't anything he could promise. He meant that if she dropped, he'd grab her, and if it pulled them both down, then he would fall with her. Die with her. She looked into his eyes and thought, *So this is what all the fuss is about.* This was what the bards sang about. What Ashyn swooned about. And it wasn't nearly as silly and pointless as she thought.

"I can do this," she said.

That grin blazed again. "Of course you can."

"And the sooner I start, the better, right?"

He chuckled. "I wouldn't say that."

"Even if you'd secretly and heartily agree." She smiled back at him and the last of her fear evaporated.

I'm the Keeper. I don't fear spirits; they fear me.

351

Moria closed her eyes and focused her energy, as she had with the shadow stalkers.

Begone. You don't belong here. By the power of the ancestors . . .

And on it went. Not the most exciting of rituals. In fact, its only saving grace was that she could say the words in her head. Otherwise, she'd have felt like an idiot, spouting them aloud like the mad prophets who wandered through the Wastes.

She called on the ancestors and all their power, and if, perhaps, there was an occasional deviation from the script, one that reminded the ancestors of all that Moria had been through, and all the times the ancestors seemed to have forsaken her, with the very impious suggestion that, perhaps, she deserved a little extra help now, well—as Ashyn would say, that only proved Moria was feeling more herself.

Below, the fiend dogs continued leaping at the tree, shaking it more each time, as if they'd realized that their combined efforts had more effect.

Were Moria's own efforts doing anything at all? Truly? They were spirits, blast it. She ought to be able—

"There!" Tyrus said.

Her eyes flew open.

"Sorry," he said quickly. "I didn't mean to interrupt, but it's working. You banished one. I saw it leaping at the tree, and then it—"

Another bash, this one hard enough to knock his chin against the limb he was lying on, and he must have bit his tongue, cursing as he did.

"You ought not to be looking down," she said.

"I'm *glancing* down. Now keep at it."

She did, harder now, spurred by her success. She kept her

eyes squeezed shut and listened as Tyrus said, "There's another gone. And another."

Daigo had leaped onto the branch over her head, and his tail dangled, flicking against her shoulder as if patting her on the back. Below, though, the fiend dogs grew frenzied, fighting her efforts by throwing themselves ever harder at the tree trunk. When a particularly hard knock pitched her forward, she grabbed the limb, her eyes flicking open as she stared down to see a huge black shape leaping at her.

She saw the beast. Saw its fangs and its form, coming straight at her, high in the tree. Tyrus let out a gasp and went for his sword.

"No!" she shouted.

He realized his mistake in time and grabbed for the tree branch instead. The fiend dog hit the trunk just below Tyrus and fell, but another was already leaping.

"Higher!" she said. "We need to go higher!"

And what good would that do? It didn't matter how high they went. It was like running from them—they could not escape.

"Begone!" she snarled, throwing all her power into the word. "I command you, begone!"

The beast evaporated in a puff of black smoke. Another was already coming up, not leaping but climbing, scrabbling up the tree as if it were merely a steep incline.

"Begone!" she shouted.

It kept coming. She kept shouting, louder now, until her ears rang, but the beast continued climbing. She gripped her dagger.

What good will that do?

Probably none, but she had to try. The fiend dog was almost an arm's length from Tyrus now, and she wasn't letting it get any closer. She pulled back her dagger—

The fiend dogs below hit the trunk all at once. The tree jolted so hard it knocked the climbing beast to the ground. She went to grab the limb, but it was too late. Her dagger fell and she followed, one arm still wrapped around the branch, holding on as tight as she could as her legs dropped. Then hands grabbed her around the waist.

"I've got you," Tyrus said. "Just find your balance. I've got—"

The fiend dogs hit again. Tyrus's eyes widened, and she realized he wasn't holding onto anything except her. She scrambled to grab him, but as soon as he started to drop, he released her.

"No!" she shouted.

He fell, dropping into the leaves and the darkness below. To the fiend dogs below. A snarl sounded overhead. Then a dark shape leaped past her. Daigo jumping down, branch by branch. The fiend dogs snarled and snapped. Tyrus let out a stifled cry. Moria was already climbing down, right behind Daigo, but that way was slow, too blasted slow. She remembered the horses in the grove, ripped to pieces, and she let go, hurtling like a rock toward the ground. Toward Tyrus. Toward the fiend dogs.

FORTY-SEVEN

When they stopped for the night, Ronan figured they were still nearly a day from Okami's compound. They made camp by a stream.

"Do you think Tyrus will be there yet?" Ashyn asked as they ate dried fish and fruit.

Ronan shrugged. "Equally likely either way."

Which was the only answer he could give, and the one she expected. She'd asked in hopes of starting conversation, but he lapsed into a silence that forbade small talk. She waited until he rose to wash his hands and then followed him.

"He said to wait at the inn until he arrives," she said. "Which sounded simple, but now that we're getting close . . . Should we stay at the inn or make camp nearby?"

"We'll figure that out."

They bent to wash their hands in the stream and refill their water skins.

"Are you angry with me?" she asked.

"Of course not, Ash. I'm just tired."

"Perhaps we ought to have made a quick stop in the city. Quickly. I know you truly wanted to check on—"

"They're fine."

"But you—"

"I'll be there soon enough."

They began walking back to the campsite.

"Once I'm with Tyrus, you'll go back to the city," she said. "You ought to stay there a few days to be sure everything is all right. You'll feel much better when you return, knowing that they are safe at home."

He nodded and seemed ready to let silence fall again, but as they reached camp, he cleared his throat and said, "I ought to tell you now, Ash. I'm not returning."

"What? You said . . ."

He crouched by the campfire. She stayed standing. She wanted to say, *You are angry with me*, but that was arrogant, to think he would change his plans so drastically because of her.

"I understand," she said carefully as she lowered herself cross-legged to the ground. "You're worried about Aidra and Jorn. That your aunt will make them steal for their keep. You've done enough, and you should go home to them. I don't know if Tyrus can presume upon Lord Okami to borrow money to repay you—"

"I don't care about that."

"Well, *he* will, obviously. As soon as he's able, he'll pay. I know it won't compensate for—"

"It was never about the money, Ash. I wanted—"

356

He swallowed the rest and rose to poke at the fire.

"What did you want?" she asked.

It seemed as if he wasn't going to answer. Then he said, "Caste. I wanted caste."

She hesitated as she remembered he'd been trying to talk to her about caste outside the stables, before they heard the accusations against the prince. "A higher one, you mean?"

"What caste am I, Ash?"

"I don't know. Your family were warriors, and I'm not sure what the demotion is when that's stripped. It seems to vary, so I haven't wanted to ask."

"You wouldn't want to be rude." He crouched beside her. "You're correct, it varies. Warriors can be demoted to artisans or to farmers or merchants. It depends on the crime. If it's serious enough . . . My family backed the wrong heir to the imperial throne. Before Emperor Tatsu's reign. It was considered high treason."

"So you're merchant class then." She managed a smile. "Like me."

He shook his head. "You're not merchant class, Ash. You're—"

"My father was, so I am, too. That's what Moria always says. The empire can raise us up, but we owe it to our ancestors to recognize where we come from."

"Which is very pious. At least, in your case. With Moria, I suspect she's just being contrary." Ronan settled in, sitting, his legs extended to the fire as he stretched out beside Tova. "High treason is the worst crime. There is one punishment worse than being exiled to the forest. Your family can have their caste stripped altogether."

It took her a moment to realize what he was saying. "You mean you . . . you have no caste."

He smiled wryly. "You were about to say I was casteless, and decided there must be a better way of phrasing it. There isn't. When I said I wanted caste, I meant exactly that. A caste, not a higher one. I am casteless. Like the girl you met on the way to the city. The one taken by the slavers."

Ashyn remembered the girl. Belaset. They'd been captives together and helped each other escape. Then Belaset had demanded Ashyn's mother's ring in payment. Ashyn hadn't given it, of course, and she had been shocked and hurt by the demand. At the time, Ronan had tried to help her understand. The girl was casteless, rejected by her family because of a deforming skin condition. Belaset would do what she could to survive, and her demand was neither an insult to Ashyn nor a failure to recognize that Ashyn had assisted her.

When Ashyn had told Ronan that the girl was casteless, she'd admitted she didn't know quite what that meant. She'd heard of it, in books, of course. The casteless were the lowest of the low, shunned by the goddess, the ancestors, and ordinary people alike. They were beggars and slaves, and in books they had always done something terrible to deserve their fate. But Belaset had not. Nor had Ronan.

"I . . . I want to say I'm sorry, but I'm not sure I ought to or . . ."

"You can. I know you mean well, as always. But there it is. My big secret. I'm casteless."

"And it was a secret because you feared how I'd judge you?"

He shook his head. "Not after I knew you. But there are strict rules for the casteless. I should not even be permitted in your company, let alone be with you unaccompanied and share a room with you. Of course, the fact that the casteless aren't branded means you can't tell by looking at me, no more than you could tell a farmer from a merchant, if they dressed alike."

"Because it's considered the responsibility of each citizen to embrace and communicate their proper caste."

"Which only a fool does if they don't have one. So, yes, those who know my family know our situation. We're registered as casteless, and that registry is checked each time we might try to take employment, purchase a home, or apply for a trading license. The penalty for falsely representing oneself is exile. With you, though . . . I didn't hide it because I wasn't concerned you'd report me."

"Does Tyrus know?"

"I'm sure he suspects. If I'd told him, though, he wouldn't have been able to hire me." He shifted and patted Tova. "My hope was that if I proved myself, he would plead my case with his father and allow me merchant caste. That is looking increasingly unlikely."

"So you're leaving. I can understand that."

His head whipped up. "No— I mean, yes, I'm leaving, but only because I don't believe I can be of any further service to either of you."

They sat in silence before Ashyn said, "I could strenuously argue that we still need you, but if I do, then I pull you away from your family again. There is only one duty higher than one's duty to the empire, and that is one's duty to family."

"I'm not concerned with duty, Ash."

"The point remains. We could use your protection, but your brother and sister need—and deserve—it more."

"My protection?" Now the smile turned bitter. "Ask Guin how she fared under my protection. Ask my—" He cut himself off with a sharp shake of his head and got to his feet.

Ashyn scrambled up with him. "If you blame yourself for Guin—"

"I blame myself for a lack of care," he said. "A lack of attention. True, it's not as if I told her to volunteer herself. Nor would I have allowed it if I'd known. But the fact remains. I was careless. As I always am."

"You are never—"

He cut her off with a kiss on the cheek. "Go to bed, Ash. It'll be a hard ride tomorrow, and I want to make it to the inn before sundown."

She watched him walk away. She glanced at Tova, who was watching him, too. The hound looked up at her, as if in question.

"Ronan?" She jogged after him and caught his sleeve. "Tell me what you mean, that you are *always* careless."

He looked at her, and there was such sadness there that she moved forward, wanting to kiss his cheek, to embrace him, to offer some comfort for whatever put that sadness in his eyes. But she didn't move. Didn't dare.

"You can talk to me," she said. "About anything."

"I know." He touched her face, one finger tracing a line down her jaw, and he leaned forward, as if to kiss her, but stopped short, turning away, his hand dropping.

"I'm too tired to talk, Ash," he said, his voice soft, gentle. "Another time."

"I—"

He squeezed her hand. "Truly, we will talk. Just not now. I'll scout the perimeter while you prepare for bed." He kissed her again, a mere brush of his lips on her cheek. Then he walked away, and she could not bring herself to give chase.

FORTY-EIGHT

Ronan hadn't been exaggerating when he'd said it would be a hard ride. They were heading west, toward the mountains. Soon Ashyn was wishing for the empty desolation of the Wastes. At least the lava fields were flat. Toward the imperial city, the land was mixed plain and wilderness, but the woods there were usually sparse, confined to pockets where farmers and settlers hadn't chopped them down. Here, as the population dwindled, there were places where the road seemed barely a scar in the wilderness.

She could see the mountains in the distance. They reminded her of Gavril. His family had been imperials since before his birth, but they would still have relatives there and allies, too. Did that include allies like the Okami clan, whose compound they were nearing even now?

Ronan didn't dismiss her fears, but he didn't change his

plans either, probably because he had no intention of entering the compound itself until Tyrus escorted them there. They found the inn, made camp in the forest, and then went in for dinner.

The inns they'd visited on the road may have been rough, but they were still intended to host travelers—often noble ones—heading to the imperial city. This particular road ended at Lord Okami's compound. The inn was for tradesmen, but also, Ashyn suspected, for those who might have cause to make such inhospitable land their home: poachers, mercenaries, and brigands.

The man at the table beside theirs bore the tattoo of a convict from the imperial city. It was two unconnected marks now, but if he committed a third crime, lines would be added to complete the symbol for "swine." The former convict sat at the table with an elderly woman who looked as if she'd stepped from the imperial court fifty summers ago, with white hair reaching to the floor and teeth yellowed from a lifetime of blackening. This was, in short, not the sort of place Ashyn had ever expected to visit, which made it all the more fascinating.

Ronan had helped her reapply the henna. They'd learned it worked best with a light touch, one that made her look like Moria after a long summer exploring the Wastes with Daigo. Once inside the inn, though, Ashyn wondered if they'd needed to bother. It was colder in this region, with the thick forest and higher elevation, and inadequate ventilation from the blazing fire left the room so smoke filled that she swore she could pull down her hood and no one would even note the color of her hair.

There were few women in the inn, but the men there—rough as they were—seemed inclined to take as little notice of her as possible, as if to do so might suggest an interest that wasn't safe so close to the warlord's compound.

Ronan confirmed that. "Lord Okami is known as a harsh man. He tolerates this rabble on his doorstep—even encourages them—because they're valuable allies for a man living in such a wild place. In return, though, they must keep their activities far enough from his lands that merchants and artisans won't fear to travel here."

Ronan motioned to the serving girl and ordered rice wine. After a long day's ride, Ashyn could see the attraction, but she was better warmed—and calmed—by a pot of tea. The girl brought it with a date-stuffed sweet roll.

"I'm looking for news from the lord's compound," Ronan said as he handed the girl a generous tip. "The empire is an unstable place these days, and we hoped it would be calmer out here."

"It is," she said. "The trouble hasn't reached this far."

He added two more coppers to her palm. "So nothing at all?"

"Something did happen inside two nights ago. Rumor says men from the imperial city slipped past through the forest. We've seen more activity inside his lord's compound since then. They say his warriors are preparing."

This was not good. Either the emperor was simply alerting all his warlords . . . or someone in the imperial city had figured out this was where Tyrus would run.

"Is there news from the city?" Ashyn asked. "The last we

heard, they still hunted the traitor prince."

The girl stiffened. "If you mean Prince Tyrus, then I've heard no news, but I'll warn you to watch your tongue when you speak of him."

"And why is that?" said a man at the neighboring table. "He *is* a traitor, girl, and a coward to boot. If the goddess is just, he's rotting in a field somewhere."

A man from across the tavern strode over. "Prince Tyrus apprenticed under Lord Okami and many here know him. The girl is right. Hold your tongue. He's not had the chance to defend himself. I'll wager his story is vastly different."

"I'll wager it is, too, because a bastard isn't above lying—"

The second man hit the first, knocking him almost into Ashyn's lap. Ronan sprang to his feet, grabbed her arm, and pulled her toward the exit as others joined in the brawl.

"Apparently, I ought not to have mentioned Tyrus," she said as they hurried outside.

"Apparently."

When they'd first stepped out, Ronan had warned Ashyn not to rush off. They didn't wish to look as if they'd incited a riot and fled. Nor did they want to lead anyone back to their camp.

Others had left the inn, too—those not wanting to be caught in the melee. Fortunately, they simply hurried past.

"Let's go," Ronan said. "Quickly."

"I thought—"

"There are two warriors at the inn doors watching us."

When she made a move, he grabbed her arm. "Don't look over."

"Presuming they are behind me, I believe I was turning in the other direction, toward the forest, which is where we are headed, is it not?"

He nodded.

"I'd suggest you let me storm off, as if we've argued. Then you give chase. That provides us with an innocent excuse for speed." Before he could reply, she took a step back. "Truly? Truly, you blame me for that? I asked an innocent question—"

"I did not mean—"

"Did you even hear what I asked? I'll wager you didn't. You were too busy ogling the serving girl and giving her our hard-earned coppers. I've had enough. Find your own sleeping blanket tonight."

She wheeled and broke into a run.

FORTY-NINE

Tova shot from his hiding place, caught up, and raced along beside Ashyn when he could, behind her when the forest grew too dense. Ronan took over the lead. They'd barely gone a hundred paces before he stopped her.

"Enough. We'll not hear them pursuing if we're crashing through the woods."

She stayed behind him as he cut a silent path through the forest. In truth, she wasn't even certain which direction to go. It all looked the same in here. Ronan seemed to know, though, stepping surefootedly through the dense undergrowth.

Then he stopped, his arms out to halt her, as if she might barrel past. He tilted his head and peered into the woods. Tova's nose worked madly, as if he too had picked up something but was equally uncertain if it posed a threat. When Ashyn herself listened, she heard only the sound of a small animal scurrying.

After a moment, Tova grunted, as though agreeing that's all it was. Ronan didn't look quite so certain, but they started forward again.

When Ashyn heard the snorting of their horses, Tova went still. Then he started to growl.

"Mind your hound please, Seeker," said a man's voice. "We wish you no harm."

Ronan glanced over his shoulder.

"And do not bolt, please," the man continued. "We can see you better than you can see us. There are more of us. We're better armed, too, I'll wager. Now, come into the clearing so we can speak."

Ronan tried to stop Ashyn, but she moved past him with Tova at her side. Four mounted riders waited in their campsite. The one in front swung off his steed. He looked to be on the cusp of his second decade. Bronze-skinned and gray-eyed, with wild hair in desperate need of a comb. His clothing was simple, but she recognized the high quality of the fabrics. He wore a fur-trimmed cloak with a sleeveless tunic under it, the cloak pushed back to reveal his arms, tattooed from wrist to shoulder in wolves with yellow eyes.

"I am Dalain," he said. "Son of Lord Goro Okami. I believe you were traveling to my father's compound, Seeker?"

"You are mistaken, my lord. I'm not a Seeker."

He glanced down at Tova, his brows lifting as if to say, *Truly?* He smiled. "Your hound might be explained away, my lady, but I suspect if I ask you to lower your hood, your hair will betray you, as do those blue eyes. You are Ashyn, Seeker of Edgewood. You traveled with Prince Tyrus, and you are here to meet with him. So I am here to escort you."

"And Prince Tyrus?" she asked.

"He's in my father's compound. I was out on patrol when my father's men found me to say you'd been spotted at the inn."

"I do not wish to doubt your word, my lord, but as you know, the situation is difficult. I trust the prince and few others. I'll ask that you bring him here before we'll enter the compound walls."

The young Okami hesitated. As he did, Ashyn motioned behind her back to Ronan.

Dalain cleared his throat. "I fear I was untruthful, my lady. Tyrus is not at my father's compound—"

Ashyn turned and ran. Behind her, she heard the clink of Ronan's swords as he leaped to defend her retreat.

"Wait!" Dalain said. "I can explain. Tyrus was here. He told—"

Ronan must have lunged in attack. Dalain stopped short. Thumps sounded as the warriors leaped from their horses. A clash of metal. Then footsteps pounded. She turned to see Ronan racing after her. Dalain stood behind him, his blade drawn, as he ordered his father's men to run them down.

"Go!" Ronan said. "Don't look back. Just go!"

Ashyn obeyed. Tova did not. He circled back behind Ronan, snarling and snapping, startling Dalain and his men and slowing them.

"Seeker!" Dalain shouted. "Ashyn! I won't harm your hound. Call him off and listen . . ."

The young man's voice faded as they ran. A crashing

sounded behind them, and Ashyn did look back then to see Tova tearing after them.

"Why didn't they attack?" Ashyn panted as they ran.

"Because they are pious men. And because we're in their forest. They think they can run us to ground easily."

"Can they?"

"Probably. Just keep going. Once we can no longer hear them, we'll find a place to hole up and think."

He took the lead again, his eyes better in the darkness. He ran, short blade in hand now, slicing through vines and branches. Ashyn had her dagger out, too, ready for attack, but it wasn't long before the sounds of pursuit faded.

"They'll get hounds," Ronan said. "The Okamis are renowned hunters. They'll give us time to escape, and then send the hounds after us."

"Then it won't help to hide, will it?"

"It will if we do it right." He kept going, pausing between words now as his breath grew short. "We need to find a stream or a river. The dogs can't track us—"

Ashyn heard a whistle of air. Tova let out a snarl, racing forward as Ronan halted in his tracks and stumbled. Another whistle. Ashyn saw the arrow this time as it struck him hard in the shoulder, knocking him down. That's when she noticed the first—lodged in his throat. He gasped and wheezed, eyes bulging as he yanked at it.

"No!" she said, racing forward. "Do not pull—"

Something hit her from behind. She went down, her dagger falling uselessly from her hand. She fought whatever had her. She heard Tova yelp, as if injured. A hand clamped a noxious-smelling cloth over her mouth and nose, and her legs slid out from under her as everything went dark.

Ashyn had been drugged once before. It was not enough to qualify her as an expert, but this time, when she woke, the period of "where am I?" confusion did not last nearly as long. Her eyes cracked open, and she felt a familiar tightness in her throat and looseness in her brain. It all rushed back. She bolted upright in the darkness.

"Tova!"

He licked her face, and she threw her arms around him, then went still.

"Ronan," she whispered. "He was . . ."

Shot. In the throat. With an arrow.

She scrambled to her feet. The room, she realized, was not pitch-black. Thin light filtered in through a hole in the ceiling. Her eyes were still adjusting, though, and all she could see were that hole and Tova's pale fur.

"Ronan," she whispered to the hound. "Where's Ronan?"

Tova made a noise in his throat. A whimpering whine that said he didn't know and was wondering, too. Ashyn stumbled about, as if she might find Ronan, though she knew he wasn't there—Tova would smell him if he was.

An arrow in the throat.

He'd been pulling it out. She'd tried to tell him not to. If it had hit a vein that was the worst thing he could do. *Had* he pulled it out? Was he . . . ?

She swallowed hard and lowered herself to the floor. Her hands came down on rock. For a few moments, she just sat there, knees drawn up, thinking of Ronan, running over what had happened, hoping to recall some proof that he'd survived, trying to visualize him falling and see exactly where the arrow had gone in. It did no good. She couldn't remember.

She blinked against the numbing sedative. Fretting and worrying weren't going to fix anything or answer any questions.

She pressed her fingertips against the rock and ran them over the surface, feeling bumps and crevices and tiny sharp pebbles.

Why was there a rock floor in a room?

She blinked again, harder now, and then looked up at the strangely shaped hole. She rose. It was indeed a hole . . . in rock. A rough, natural hole that wound its way up to sunlight. She looked at the wall.

It was all rock.

I'm not in a room. I'm in a cave.

Then there had to be an exit. It was still nearly impossible to see more than that distant light and Tova, but as she squinted and turned, she made out another pale shape at least ten paces away. As she started toward it, the light seemed to catch something on the wall, making it gleam, and she jumped, startled.

A picture had been drawn on the wall. When she stood close, she saw lines. Once she backed up for the full view, though, the lines vanished into the shadows.

What had caught the light looked like the lacquered wood tiles used for armor, but it was twice the size of her hand. When she stood on her tiptoes, she realized it wasn't brown wood. It was . . . every color. Iridescent, like a fish scale. She touched it and that was exactly what it felt like. The biggest fish scale she'd ever seen.

Tova whined, telling her this was no time to solve a mystery. That pale shape across the cave might be the exit. While she suspected she'd find it guarded, at least she could find out who held her here. The Okami clan, presumably. She only hoped they'd tell her what had happened to Ronan.

As she walked toward the pale object, it did indeed seem like a door. An oddly shaped one, with light coming in around the edges. The closer she drew, the less like a door it appeared, but her mind was still fixed on that image, and she couldn't figure out what exactly she was seeing. It sat on the cave floor and reached to her head. Something white, with a dark hole in the middle. A dark, jagged hole with . . . teeth. She was looking at teeth, each as big as her forearm.

It's . . .

She stopped short.

It was a massive skull, twice as big as Tova's entire body.

What creature grew that large?

Moria had said the thunder hawk had huge, jagged teeth and horns, and Ashyn could see horns, long and curving. But this skull had a snout, not a beak.

Tova crept toward the skull, cautiously, as if the skull was still affixed to a living beast. He sniffed it. Then he crouched, whining.

"What is it?" she whispered.

He looked back at her and stayed where he was, hunkering down in front of the skull. She took the last few steps toward it.

What is it?

"I don't know," she whispered.

Yes, you do.

She swallowed and reached out to touch the skull. It felt ice-cold, but instead of pulling her hand back, she pressed it against the bone, and the chill of it made her shiver, her eyes squeezing shut. As soon as they closed, she smelled ice, sharp and cold, and she heard the flap of massive wings and a deafening roar.

"A dragon," she whispered. "It's—"

"My lady," a voice said behind her.

She jumped and whirled. Tova leaped up, too, and raced in front of her, growling. Light flooded the room. Torches, carried by three figures in long, white fur cloaks, the hoods pulled up over their heads, their faces lost within.

"You know what that is then, my child?" the first figure said.

She nodded.

He paused, as if waiting for her to say the words aloud.

"A snow dragon," she said.

He pulled down his hood, and she saw a man, pale-skinned and white-haired, with tribal tattoos on his cheeks. Tattoos of dragons, done not in the imperial style, but in the intricate art of the North. And his eyes . . . He had golden eyes with slitted pupils.

Like a dragon . . .

He dropped to one knee, the other two doing the same behind him.

"My lady Ashyn," he said. "Seeker of Edgewood. Blessed

of the empire and the North alike. Child of my child." He rose. "I am Edwyn of Coldwall."

"Of Coldwall? My parents were from . . ." She slowed, remembering what else he'd called her. "Child of . . . ?"

He smiled. "Of my child. Daughter of my daughter. Your family welcomes you. Your true family."

MORIA

FIFTY

Moria fell from the tree, branches lashing her legs. When she passed Daigo, he let out a yowling cry and snapped at her, as if he could grab her tunic and haul her back up.

She hit the ground, one foot squarely down, the other twisting as she dropped to her knee. Pain shot through her. Something touched her hand, startling her, and she jumped, only to feel a warm hand wrap around her wrist.

"Don't move," Tyrus whispered.

She turned to see him. He lay behind her on his back. Blood soaked one sleeve. One leg of his trousers was shredded, more blood below. When the cloud cover thinned, she could see half his face wore a red mask of blood. She bit back a gasp and reached for him, but he tightened his grip on her wrist.

"Don't move."

He was propped up on his elbow, one hand gripping her,

the other slowly pulling his sword. Red eyes and shadows circled them, some so close she could reach out and grab them.

Grab what? A shadow?

That was all they were now. Shadows and eyes. Watching and waiting.

There were so many. Had she truly banished any?

She had. She must have. That's why the rest were staying back.

"Reach down with your free hand," he said. "Carefully. Toward me."

She did, and he directed her until she felt the cool handle of her dagger. She pulled it to her. At a chirp overhead, she looked up to see Daigo on the lowest branch, his tail twitching as his gaze swung from her to the fiend dogs.

"You'll use your powers to hold them back," Tyrus said. "And we'll get out of the forest. Lord Okami's warriors will be there."

And what will they do? We can't fight these things. My powers can barely—

"You're going to hold them back." He met her gaze and held it, his voice low and strong. "Just keep them at bay."

It might work; it might not. But it was the only chance they had, so that was what they'd do, and she must believe it would work, because if she didn't, they had no chance at all.

She nodded. Tyrus pushed to his feet. One of the fiend dogs charged him. Moria slashed out with her dagger, knowing even as she did that steel couldn't cut shadow. But the beast still fell back, snarling. When it did, she saw fangs and a snout, the shadow taking form, and she started to look away—

No. She'd already seen them. If she was doomed, she was doomed, but if she cowered and looked away, then she'd have no chance. Fear would kill her.

Moria took a deep breath and met the beast's red eyes. It stared back at her, growling, lips curling, and slowly it took the form of a giant dog. A giant hound. A black Tova.

Except you aren't Tova. He was a great warrior. You were a coward. He is honored. You are damned.

The fiend dog snarled, as if she'd spoken aloud.

I don't fear you. You are but a spirit. I'll send you back from where you came.

She focused her power and the beast began to fade. Before it vanished, though, another one lunged and broke her concentration. She let out a snarl of her own.

"Don't try to banish them," Tyrus said. "It puts your focus on one. Just hold them back. Daigo?"

The wildcat leaped down beside them. The fiend dogs grumbled and paced, but none moved forward.

"This way," Tyrus said, nudging her.

She started walking with the young warrior and the wildcat flanking her. She focused on keeping the fiend dogs back, but as soon as she began moving, the beasts did, too, as if freed from a spell. They snapped and lunged, getting ever closer despite her efforts, until Tyrus hissed in pain as one caught his leg, biting him and then jumping back when his sword flashed.

"Keep moving," Tyrus said. "We'll be fine."

Another jumped, this time at Daigo. The wildcat snarled. The beast grabbed him by the back of the neck. Moria swung her blade, but it passed through the shadowy figure as the fiend dog ripped at Daigo, blood flying, the wildcat yowling.

"Begone!" she shouted. "By the ancestors, begone!"

The fiend dog fell back, growling, fangs flashing. Daigo puffed himself up and faced off with the beast.

Moria kept retreating. Behind them, the fiend dogs parted, but only enough to let the group pass. One leaped at Daigo. Moria spun on it, another slashed at Tyrus.

"We can't do this," she said. "It's too slow, and they're growing bolder. We must run."

"We—"

"Run or creep, it doesn't matter now. They have our scent. I'll hold them back while you go on ahead."

"Absolutely not."

She turned to meet his eyes as he lifted his sword.

"I'll not—" he began.

"You will."

"No, I—"

"Then we die. I can't keep them from you. I can only give you a head start. If you don't take it, then we continue going like this."

Another fiend dog jumped at Tyrus, snagging his leg before he kicked it off with a stifled cry of pain. He glowered at Moria, and she knew that while her point had been made, nothing in Tyrus would let him flee from battle, flee from her side.

"Daigo?" she said.

The wildcat spun and charged Tyrus. The prince stood his ground, his feet planted.

"Don't you dare—" Tyrus began.

Daigo hit him, knocking him away from Moria. The fiend dogs saw their chance and rushed at him. Daigo spun, hissing and spitting while moving backward, bumping into Tyrus, forcing him to retreat.

"Leave them!" Moria shouted at the shadows. "They are no threat. I'm the one who can banish you."

She wheeled on the one closest to her and boomed, "Begone, spirit!" so loud the forest rang with her words. To her surprise, the shadow exploded, black shards flying up and dissipating. The rest of the pack hesitated.

"Run," Moria said to Tyrus. "You can't get past Daigo."

He scowled, sword rising as if he'd like to use it on the wildcat.

"I can't hold them for long," Moria said. "I'll be right behind you."

"If you are not—"

"You'll stop. I know. So I will be."

Still he hesitated, rocking, unable to break whatever barrier told him, *Thou shalt not*. Not run. Not turn his back on danger. Not abandon her. Finally, Daigo had to charge him again, forcing him to turn and then battering him until he ran. The fiend dogs tore after them.

"No!" Moria bellowed. "If you touch him again, I swear I will send every last one of you curs to eternal damnation."

They turned toward her, eyes glowing as their growls rippled through the night.

"Yes, you hear me, *curs*. That's what you are. It's what you were in life, and now you're condemned to your true forms. Slinking curs. Traitors and cowards."

The fiend dogs growled louder, pacing around her now.

"You dare attack them?" she said, jabbing a finger at Tyrus and Daigo as they fled. "An imperial prince and a Wildcat of the Immortals? True warriors? Honorable warriors? And me? I'm the Keeper. A mere girl who can grind your worthless spirits beneath her boot—"

They charged at her, but she was expecting it and had been gathering her power as she taunted them. As they came at her, she shouted, "No!" with everything in her, with the power of the goddess herself running through her like bolts of pure energy. The beasts fell back as if hit by a giant wave of force, turning to shadows and red eyes and enraged snarls.

Moria spun on her heel and ran as fast as she could, the ground flying under her feet. There'd been a time when she would no more have fled than Tyrus. When she'd have stood firm, confident in her powers, expecting to see every last fiend dog disappear in a puff of smoke. Now she knew better. Her powers were strong; her powers were not invincible.

Sure enough, she hadn't gotten far before the beasts recovered and tore after her, howling and baying, hounds on a scent. Ahead, Tyrus looked back for her.

"Keep going!" she shouted.

He did, and as she ran, the clouds thinned again, and she could see Daigo dropping back, running midway between them, close enough to the prince to keep driving him forward but close enough to Moria to return to her if needed. She waved for him to continue on.

Though the fiend dogs' paws made no sound as they ran, their howls and snarls told her they were gaining ground. When

381

she saw a shape flash out of the corner of her eye, she twisted, and as she did, she hit something in her path and stumbled.

I cannot fall. If I do, I'll never get up again. They'll swarm over me as they did Tyrus, and I'll be lost.

She skidded and grabbed for whatever was nearest—a spindly sapling. Ahead, Tyrus wheeled. The fiend dogs sensed victory. One leaped at her. Fangs slashed her arm, blood spraying.

She wrenched the sapling to propel herself upright, then flung off it, running again, her ankle throbbing, blood flicking from her arm. Another fiend dog lunged and knocked into her, and she pitched forward, both hands out to brace her fall—

No! I will not fall. I will not.

Again, she managed to stagger into a run. Daigo was there now, snarling and hissing at the fiend dogs as he raced alongside her. Tyrus had circled back, and she shouted for him to keep going, but he wouldn't. He came as close as he dared, then led the way, running barely five paces ahead of her.

"There's something up there," he said. "I see light."

All she saw was dark and treacherous forest. Then shards of moonlight flooded what looked like open plain. The edge of the forest. Where Lord Okami's men waited.

Did that help?

Yes, it must. Something kept the fiend dogs in the forest, or they'd wander out into the world in search of prey. Magics bound them there.

And if not, then the men would have horses. Fast horses.

Daigo let out a grunt of surprise, and she looked at him quickly, thinking one of the fiend dogs had grabbed him, but they were falling behind, as if they knew their boundary approached. Daigo's ears twisted as he ran, his nose moving, too. His eyes went wide, and he started skidding to a halt just as two of the fiend dogs found one last burst of determination and barreled forward.

"Go!" Moria shouted.

Daigo looked from the creatures to the clearing ahead, but he didn't move. Moria grabbed him by the scruff of the neck and heaved him forward, muttering, "Blast you" as he let out a yelp of surprise. Moria saw what was wrong. Tyrus stopped, his arms flying out to hold her back as he stood on the edge of the forest. No . . . on the edge of the world, which seemed to end here. Simply end. There was land, and then there was sky, dark, night sky as far as the eye could see.

Old stories told of breaks between this world and the next, where you could fall through, lost forever as a mortal in the second world.

Behind them, the fiend dogs had stopped, too, as if they also sensed what lay ahead and dared not approach. Tyrus was creeping toward the edge, and she wanted to snatch him back, but feared if she startled him, he'd lose his balance and topple over. He continued on, feeling his way, and she followed, doing the same, until he stood at the very edge, his arm out to block her again, and she looked down and saw . . .

Water. Endless black water. They'd run the wrong way and come out at the sea.

"We can . . ." Tyrus began, then trailed off, as if wasn't certain how to finish the thought.

"Could we climb down?" she said.

383

He leaned, and she struggled against the urge to pull him back.

"The cliff bank recedes from the edge," he said. "We'll have to walk along it."

She glanced at the fiend dogs. They'd taken form now, that swirling, shadow-like canine form, and they'd started to pace, seeing their prey so close and trapped.

She nodded. "Quickly. While they're still—"

One charged.

"Back!" she shouted, and it stumbled, then regained its balance, shaking itself, its head low as it growled.

A second started forward, cautious, but emboldened by its pack mate. When nothing happened to hold it, the beast kept coming. Then another stepped toward them.

"Can you swim?" Tyrus said.

"What?"

"We have to jump. There's no other way." He sheathed his sword. "Can you swim?"

She took a deep breath, pushed her dagger into her belt, grabbed his hand, said, "No," and jumped.

FIFTY-ONE

As they hurtled through the darkness, Moria reflected that this was not much different from falling from the tree. Except for Daigo's yowling. At least there were no branches to strike on the way down. Just—

They hit the water, and it was like plunging through ice. She'd done that once at a fishing hole, having underestimated the thickness of the ice. It was not an experience she'd ever wished to repeat. First there was the incredible cold that actually seemed to burn, searing the air from her lungs and threatening to stop her heart in her chest. Then, pain took over. Excruciating pain, which at least had the effect of slapping her out of her shock.

As the icy water enveloped her, her mind shed that last veil of shock and she thought, *The sea. I've leaped into the sea.* Also, *I can't swim.* She recalled grabbing Tyrus's hand, but the moment

385

they'd hit the water, the force of the blow had knocked them apart.

She had to go up.

A wise idea, except as she flailed, she realized she had no idea which way that was. She'd been tumbling through the water and—

Whichever way you're falling? That's not up.

Which made perfect sense. As she turned her body, she could see the dim glow of moonlight overhead. So she started climbing—or what passed for climbing when one was submerged in water—pulling and kicking toward a surface that seemed to get no closer.

Because you're kicking and pushing through water. All you're doing is stopping yourself from falling farther.

She shushed that doubting voice, but the panic that came in its wake propelled her to fight harder. The water was so cold, so unbelievably cold, encasing her body like ice, heavy as lead, pulling her down. She'd been eating barely enough to stay alive, exercising barely enough to keep her muscles from atrophy. Then she'd run through the forest, climbed trees, raced from fiend dogs . . . She was exhausted, and she could not breathe. Most of all, she could not breathe.

So it's too much. You'll just give up. Sink to the bottom and die after escaping Alvar Kitsune and his fiend dogs. No one escapes fiend dogs, and you did.

But she hadn't, had she? Perhaps it truly was fated. She'd seen them and now—

Didn't I tell you not to leave, Keeper?

That voice sounded like Gavril's, whispered as if he stood behind her, bending to her ear. Her imagination, not sorcery.

I warned you, Keeper. You won't escape. You aren't strong enough. You aren't clever enough. You fancy yourself a warrior, but you're a foolish little girl.

She pushed her hands over her head, propelling herself up.

You jumped into the sea, Keeper. Knowing you cannot swim.

Because I had no choice. You didn't warn me of the fiend dogs.

I didn't see the point. It wasn't as if you were likely to escape anyway. And if you did? Well, you did not get far, did you?

She squeezed her eyes shut and kept going, past the pain and the exhaustion, pushing up through the water until she was certain—yes, certain—that the moon overhead was growing brighter. Then, suddenly, a black shape passed over it.

No! I need the light . . .

The shape dove lower and her panic sparked until a form grabbed her arm and started hauling her up, and when the moonlight pierced the water again, she could see dragon bands on the arm that pulled her and noticed another dark shape overhead—Daigo treading water.

Tyrus dragged her to the surface, and she broke through, sputtering and gasping. She struggled to fill her lungs, not noticing that he was still pulling her until her feet touched the bottom and the two of them stumbled from the sea onto the beach, and she collapsed there, heaving and shaking. Daigo huddled, soaked, beside her as Tyrus thumped her back, knocking water from her lungs and saying, "Can you speak? Moria?"

"I think . . ." she wheezed. "I think I need you to give me swimming lessons, too."

He whooped a laugh, coughing at the end of it. Then he gathered her up in a crushing hug, and she collapsed against him, thinking she'd never felt anything so wonderful. And warm. Especially warm. He was as soaking wet as she was, but all she felt was the heat of his body.

"You're all right?" he said.

She nodded against him and he brought her into a kiss, and if his embrace had been a warm blanket, this was a lick of fire, his mouth and his breath so incredibly hot that she wanted the kiss to last forever. And she would have let it, too, if she wasn't so short of breath that she had to break off, coughing slightly before kissing him again.

"So you're fine with this now, it seems," she said as they parted.

"Gavril had his chance to explain, and he did not. Even if he had . . ." He pulled back, holding her hands. "I decided there was a line between being honorable and being foolish. If you want to be with me, then that's your choice. *Our* choice. No one else's."

"Ah, so you've finally come to your senses."

He laughed and embraced her. "Yes. Now, since we don't dare start a fire still so close to Alvar's compound, we need to find a way back to Lord Okami's men, who will have dry clothing, before you freeze solid."

"You were doing a fine job of keeping me warm a moment ago."

"And I would love to continue that, but I fear it won't be enough. So I'll promise more later, if you want it."

"I might. You're rather good at it."

A laugh. "Thank you. Now, if we continue down this beach, we're bound to find a way back up the cliff . . ."

They did find a way up . . . or "up" found a way to them, as the cliff dwindled into a hill leading from the beach to the field beyond the forest. As they climbed the hill, Tyrus said, "I need to tell you a few things before we reach the men."

He told her what had happened at the battle, how Lord Jorojumo's men had turned on them, which she already knew. The aftermath, she did not. It seemed Gavril hadn't lied about that after all. Tyrus was in exile, and she was branded a traitor.

But whatever Gavril's claims, she was certain that he had known this all along. Which made another part of Tyrus's tale all the more horrifying.

"They think I was Gavril's . . . lover?" she said.

"They say you fell under his spell on your escape from Edgewood. Or perhaps in Edgewood itself."

She sputtered a laugh. "Fell under his spell? Clearly who-ever tells these tales does not know Gavril Kitsune very well. But that's what they think. That I betrayed my empire and abandoned my sister and my bond-beast for my lover."

"Yes, to anyone who has known you even for a moment, the story is preposterous."

"Almost as preposterous as saying you'd fall under *my* spell, betray your empire, and run from battle. Your father will know that isn't true."

"My mother will, and I take comfort in that."

"No," she said, meeting his gaze. "Your father will."

"I would like to share your confidence, but I don't want to

seem a fool for presuming. The truth is that it doesn't honestly matter what my father thinks. Not as much as it should. My half brothers will spread this story as far as they can, as will their mothers. Those within the court know it is politically wise to side with them. They will rule one day; I will not. If my father defends me, it makes him seem a sentimental old man at a time when he can least afford that." Tyrus lifted his bare arm, flashing his banded tattoos. "My father is truly of the dragon clan. He is strong-willed and brutal, but he's also crafty and cautious. He knows when to defend his treasure with fire and fang, and when to lie low and outwit his opponents."

"And your brothers are his opponents."

"Yes, oddly, as much as they are mine. As long as he lives, he keeps them from the imperial throne. Succession is an ugly thing."

"Which is one reason he favors you. Because you want nothing from him, least of all his death."

He shrugged. "I won't presume he favors me but, again, it wouldn't matter if he did. Whether he thinks I could have done this thing or not, I can't run to him for safe harbor. Which is why I went to Lord Okami."

They crested the hill, then walked in silence before he cleared his throat.

"All of this is to say that your prince is no longer a prince. Taking an exiled traitor for a lover might not have the same appeal."

"Do you truly think I care? Even a little?"

"No. I'm just pointing it out. To be fair."

She rolled her eyes. "You are unreasonably fair sometimes,

Tyrus. If I was to think anything at all of a potential loss of title, it would be only the very selfish reflection that at least I don't have to worry about running my blade through some dainty princess who fancies you . . . or running it through *you* if she catches your eye."

He let out a laugh, cutting himself short as he looked around, then lowered his voice when he spoke. "That would be of no concern even if I remained a prince. Yes, I know you've heard the stories. A young prince—even a bastard—does present a temptation to visiting princesses and ladies, and I will admit that I've taken advantage of that."

"As well you should."

He glanced over to see if she was joking.

"I mean it," she said. "If girls make themselves available, and you do not dishonor them, then there is no harm in dallying. If the situation were mine, I'd certainly take advantage."

He laughed again. "Thank you, and I can assure you that whatever you heard, it was exaggerated, but the truth . . ." He sobered and looked over at her. "The truth, Moria, is that as entertaining as those dalliances were, there was not a girl whose memory lingered moments after she left the city gates. Only once has one stayed in my mind as if branded there. A girl I could not wait to see again, would seize on any excuse to see again, offering anything from garden tours to swordsmanship lessons. After I recovered from battle, all I wanted was to find you. I told myself Gavril would care for you, that my duty was to inform my father of Jorojumo's betrayal, and that my best hope of rescuing you was with a contingent of his finest warriors at my back."

"You were using your head."

He slowed to a stop. "I didn't want to use my head. If Ashyn hadn't been there to keep me on track, I think I'd not have managed it. The moment I learned what had happened—that there was no use in returning to the city—I almost felt relieved. I could shuck duty and follow my heart. Find you. Save you." He paused and gave a tiny smile. "Even if you did not need saving."

"I appreciate the effort."

She leaned in to kiss him, but he stopped her, his hands on her shoulders. "You saved yourself, Moria. More than that, you saved me. I'd have died in the forest, with those fiend dogs."

"But you'd not have been there if you hadn't come for me."

"You still did it, and you truly did save me on that battlefield. If you had not called my name when the warlord struck—"

"I'd rather not think on that."

"Nor would I. But I just want to say . . ." He kissed her. ". . . that *you*. . ." Another kiss. ". . . are incredible . . ." A third. "And *I* . . ." A fourth. ". . . am incredibly lucky." He looked into her eyes. "I'll not forget that. Ever."

She leaned forward and kissed him, and the simple press of the lips became more, deliciously more, until Daigo's surprisingly gentle growl reminded them that they needed to be on their way again.

FIFTY-TWO

To their relief, Okami's men were where Tyrus had left them. While neither dared voice it, Moria knew they'd both feared Alvar's men would come or the fiend dogs would lure Okami's warriors into the forest.

All Okami's men needed to do now was give up a couple of warm cloaks. Of course Tyrus insisted he didn't require one; of course Moria made him take it, threatening at blade-point when needed, which greatly amused Okami's warriors.

After Moria and Tyrus found a private spot, removed their wet overgarments, and fastened on the warm cloaks, there was a checking and cataloging of injuries. Each reassured the other that his or her own injuries were not so bad as they might have seemed in the forest. Certainly not so bad as they'd seemed before the plunge into deep water cleaned away the blood. Moria's arm required a cloth binding. Tyrus's injuries were more numerous, but none severe, though Moria examined each bite and scratch before agreeing further care could wait.

They returned to Okami's men, hung the wet garments from their saddles, and set out. Tyrus had not asked why she'd been wearing only under-dresses. Moria suspected he'd mistaken the layers for a simple gown. Her footwear was covered with enough mud and darkness that it wouldn't be obvious they were finely made sandals. She did not wish to explain the party and the fake betrothal. Even more, though, she did not wish to mention the dungeon cell. Tyrus had been correct to head for the city after the battle, but his guilt over that was heavy enough. Let him think Gavril had been a serviceable host.

They rode through the night and into dawn, heading toward the mountains, with Okami's compound at their base. The party took rutted forest paths whenever possible. At dawn, they reached a roadside public house—not an inn, but someone's home, the owners offering food and beds to the rare traveler who came that way. While Tyrus and Moria stayed with Daigo and a blazing fire, Okami's men commandeered the place, turning out a group of fellow travelers and taking their breakfast for themselves. They were on the edges of Lord Okami's land now, and his men could expect such service.

Their host brought out food and drink, a veritable feast after Moria's captivity, and she dove in like a ravenous beast, to the others' amusement—and encouragement. They were rough men, these warriors of the Gray Wolf, as Goro Okami was known. Not the sort of warriors she was accustomed to, but the sort that seemed more accustomed to women like her—men who found it not the least bit odd that a girl knew how to use a dagger and how to pack away a man's breakfast, a girl who was treated as equal by a prince.

As for Tyrus, they did not treat him as a prince either, yet there was no disrespect in their easy talk and teasing. They were clearly fond of him and comfortable in his company, which settled any fears on the situation. Tyrus had said earlier that his father truly reflected his clan totem, and Moria suspected that this was often true of the men who bore them. Alvar Kitsune was as crafty and duplicitous as the nine-tailed fox. Jorojumo was a sneaky web spinner, like the spider. And Goro Okami seemed, like his wolf totem, independent yet loyal to his friends.

The land here was as wild as the men, and while one might think Moria had had enough of forests to last a lifetime, the one they rode through that morning was different. Lush and green, it shimmered and crackled with life, and she found herself regretting each time they had to leave for a stretch on the road.

It was nearly midday when Daigo informed her they were being followed. He started by casting looks to his side, repeatedly, as if spotting something. Then he slowed to sniff the air, his ears rotating.

"Would Lord Okami send other men to escort us?" she whispered to Tyrus. "Men who'd keep to the shadows?"

"Lord Okami does not keep to shadows very well," Tyrus said with a slight smile. "Nor do his men, as you may have noticed. If you see someone, it's likely local bandits."

When she tensed, he let out a soft laugh. "You've little to fear. Lord Okami's relationship with the bandits is . . . atypical. They'd sooner die by their own swords than attack his men. If they follow, it's curiosity." He sobered. "Which may be more dangerous than robbery, under the circumstances. They can be trusted not to waylay us, but I'm not as certain they can be trusted to keep our presence a secret if the bounty is high enough. You saw someone?"

"Daigo has. He and I will fall back and look."

"I'll join you."

She shook her head. "That will be too obvious. Let the girl lag behind with her wildcat. If you get too far ahead, you can circle back, as if checking on me."

He agreed, and Moria stopped, ostensibly to examine Daigo's paw, as if he'd stepped on something sharp. They both scanned the forest as she fussed with his forepaw.

Daigo's ears swiveled west a moment before she caught a crackle in the forest. She snuck a look that way just in time to see a slight figure slipping through the trees.

"I see only one," she whispered. "If it's a bandit, I don't think he's very old. He's not much bigger than me."

Daigo grunted, as if confirming. The figure snuck closer. His cloak was a mottled brown that blended with his surroundings, and his footsteps made no sound after that one unfortunate crackle.

"Will you take him down for me?" she whispered to Daigo.

The wildcat charged before she could finish. The boy saw Daigo and yanked a sling from under his cloak. Moria loosed her dagger. It caught the boy's cloak just as he let his stone fly, and the missile launched harmlessly to the side as Daigo leaped on him. Moria ran over.

"Well," said a lilting, high voice. "Aren't you the prettiest kitten ever. Those fangs are truly impressive, though I'd prefer they weren't quite so close to my throat."

"They won't be if you promise to rise without running."

"Agreed," the girl said. "You've caught me fair and square, and I'll cede victory to you, young Keeper."

"Tell her to set aside her sling first," Tyrus's voice called behind them.

"Ah, the little prince," the girl said as she rose. "I thought that was you. Not quite so little these days."

"Lay down your sling, Sabre," Tyrus said, moving up beside them. "I know better than to be distracted by your chatter."

The girl only laughed, and set aside her sling. As she stood, she pushed back her hood. She had called Moria "young" but she couldn't be more than a couple of summers older. She had the regional look of the warlord's men—wild black hair, high cheekbones, bronze skin, and eyes that seemed somewhere between blue and gray.

"You know each other, I presume," Moria said.

"I met the little prince when he was training under Lord Okami," Sabre said. "And when he was half a head shorter than me."

"Which I no longer am," Tyrus said. "So you can stop calling me that."

"At least I still call you prince, which is more than most would." When he opened his mouth, she said, "You don't need to defend yourself to me. I know you wouldn't run from battle. You trained too long under Dalain, and you're as stupidly honor bound as he. You'd both stand in the face of a charging army rather than give ground." She rolled her eyes at Moria. "Warriors."

"Despite your insult," Tyrus said, "I appreciate that you didn't doubt my bravery."

"More stupidity than bravery. I will admit I was somewhat swayed by the rumor that you'd been tricked by a girl. But I see now I was mistaken, and I congratulate you on how much your taste has improved. I'll wager this one doesn't call you to slay mice in her quarters."

Sabre looked at Moria. "Some distant relative of Lord Okami brought his daughter once—the most vacant-headed, timid child you could imagine, though she knew how to catch a boy's attention. She'd run from her quarters shrieking of mice and insist the valiant prince slay them for her. Which Tyrus fell for. Repeatedly. But she was terribly pretty."

"Did your father send you to interrupt our travels, Sabre?" one of Lord Okami's men called as they arrived.

"Her father is the local bandit leader," Tyrus said to Moria.

Sabre bristled. "My father is a nomadic tribal chieftain—"

"—who accepts generous offerings from travelers for safe passage through these treacherous hills." Tyrus leaned toward Moria. "He's a bandit. A powerful one, though."

"I believe I've heard the exact same said about *your* father."

"Sabre . . ." a voice called as a rider rode up. "Waylaying my guests on the roadside?"

The newcomer was a young man, perhaps twenty summers

of age. Tall and well-formed, with gray eyes and unruly black hair. On his arms, Moria could see the tattoos of the Okami clan: dark wolves with yellow eyes.

"Tyrus." He slid from his horse and thumped the prince on the back. "It is good to see you safe." He bowed to Moria. "Dalain Okami, my lady. Son of Lord Okami."

"*Youngest* son," Sabre cut in, with a tone that said that barely qualified him for kinship at all.

He shook his head. "As soon as I heard the sounds of trouble, I knew who it was. Now, off with you, Sabre. You've delayed my guests quite enough."

The young woman's eyes flashed. "I was not bothering your guests, Dalain. I was helping them." She turned her attention and her words to Moria. "I spotted your party when you rode through the valley. Then I realized that I wasn't the only one who had noticed you."

"Bandits, I presume?" Dalain said.

She gave him a withering look. "Go hunt something, Dalain. The pursuit suits you much better than thinking."

"Actually, I *was* hunting something. Or someone. And it's rather urgent, so if you could be quicker with this story, that would be appreciated."

She scowled at him, then turned to Moria again. "There were three riders following you. They were dressed as simple travelers, but I could see blades under their cloaks, and while their steeds were not fine, the men rode exceedingly well. I tried to get closer, but when you paused at a stream, they went on ahead. That's when I noticed that Tyrus was with you, which meant this was no hostage situation. I was getting closer to warn him when you caught me."

"She caught you?" Dalain said. "Truly?"

"I admitted it, didn't I? The Keeper of Edgewood is very skilled with her blade and her wildcat, and I am not so arrogant that I can't admit defeat."

"I wouldn't say it's lack of arrogance so much as vast experience with defeat."

Dalain was teasing Sabre, but the young woman only seemed to grow more irritated. Moria heard Ashyn's voice whispering in her ear: *Because he's treating her as a child, and she does not wish him to see her as a child.*

Perhaps. It was none of Moria's concern right now. Her sister's voice, however, was a concern—a reminder.

"The three riders," she said. "Were they clearly men? My sister is supposed to come this way. She'll be accompanied by a young man and a young woman. They may have been following us trying to determine if we were in your men's custody or not before they approached."

"It is . . . possible," Dalain said.

"He'll not answer straight," Sabre said. "So I will. That's who he was hunting: your sister. She was here, and Dalain frightened her off, and now she's lost."

"Lost?" Moria said, her voice sharp with alarm.

Dalain shot a glare at Sabre, then turned to Moria. "I'm sorry, my lady. Some of our locals are more plainspoken—and less considerate—than they ought to be. Yes, I did speak to your sister. While I will not say that I 'frightened her off,' she was understandably cautious, given the circumstances, and I may have underestimated the degree of her caution."

Sabre snorted. *"May have?* You can pull on pretty manners for the Keeper, Dalain, but I'm not the only local given to plain and ill-considered speeches."

"Ashyn didn't trust you so she ran," Tyrus said. "Which is why I told you not to approach her until I returned." He held up a hand against Dalain's protest. "Yes, I know you meant well. But it's not the Seeker you needed worry about as much as her escort. Ronan would never have let her go with you until I was there to say all was well. What happened then?"

"She ran with the boy and her hound. They disappeared into the woods, and it seemed wise to bring our own hounds to track them."

"Which would have put them perfectly at ease," Sabre murmured.

Dalain ignored her. "One of my men spotted her outside the inn last evening. There was a . . . commotion. I feared she would not fare well in these woods, and I thought I could convince her to come with me. I was mistaken. But I will find her. My men are out there now, with the best hunting hounds in the empire."

"Then I'll go with them," Moria said.

She turned toward her horse. Dalain stepped in her path, but Tyrus cleared his throat and steered Moria aside.

"You'll not stop me from finding my sister," she said.

"I wouldn't dare. But may I suggest we get you to the compound for a change of clothing? We'll pack food and water and set out for a proper search."

"While I appreciate the Keeper's concern," Dalain began,

401

"I think this is best handled by hounds and men who know the terrain—"

"I know the terrain," Tyrus cut in. "And Moria knows her sister, as does Daigo. I appreciate your concern, Dalain, but once we've partaken of your father's hospitality, we will hunt for Ashyn and her escort. If you wish to join us, you are most welcome, but I would prefer you did not search on your own, as it is likely to drive them deeper into the wilderness."

Tyrus's words came softly, but his tone left no room for debate. It reminded Dalain that, while Tyrus was still several summers younger, he was no longer a boy under the Okamis' tutelage. He was an imperial prince.

Sabre smirked and opened her mouth to say something, almost certainly an insult. Before she could speak, Tyrus cut her off.

"Sabre? I don't know what the situation is—how many realize that the Seeker is in these woods. I hope the answer is 'very few,' and that it remains that way, but I know your father is loyal to Lord Okami, so I trust he will let us know if he spots Ashyn or her escort, and that no attempt will be made to communicate with them directly."

"Yes, your highness." There was a lilt to the title—more teasing than mockery—and she said, "You've grown into that ink on your arms, little dragon. There will be many here who'll be pleased to see it. My father, for one. He has hopes for you, despite your insistence on ducking attention."

"Which has not changed at all," Tyrus said. "I'll be quite happy if I can return to pursuing the life of a warrior, not a prince in exile."

"Rebel prince. That has a better ring, don't you think?"

"No, thank you. Now, if you can speak to your father, I need to get to Lord Okami's compound. Moria is eyeing her horse and wondering how badly she needs my help with the search. I'll take my leave before I'm abandoned by the roadside."

FIFTY-THREE

"She's out there and she's safe," Tyrus whispered as they rode. "Ashyn is smart, Tova is loyal, and Ronan is capable. I'm sorry this happened—"

"It had nothing to do with you." Moria shot a look at Dalain, riding at the front of the group.

"Don't be too hard on him," Tyrus said, lowering his voice further. "He truly thought he was helping. But he was correct when he said that the people of this land are forthright. They do not always pause to consider their actions, and they are ill accustomed to subtlety and subterfuge." He smiled her way. "Perhaps you can sympathize a little?"

He was right, of course, but she was in no mood to acknowledge it. Since meeting Sabre, she felt unsettled and out of her depth, an outsider here, as if she were back in court. Now, discovering Ashyn had been here only increased both her worry and her sense of alienation.

I want my family. I want my home. I want a place that's familiar and mine. And I'll never have them again.

Daigo growled softly, sensing her change of mood. He rubbed against her foot, and she longed to climb off the horse and walk beside him, to have at least that comfort.

Everything has changed, and it'll never be the same again.

"Moria?"

Tyrus moved his horse closer, until their legs brushed, and she could feel his gaze on her, troubled.

"We'll find Ashyn," he said.

"I know."

They continued riding. When she kept her gaze forward, he whispered, "Is it something more?"

She shook her head.

"Let me rephrase that," he said. "I can tell there's something more. Is it Dalain? Sabre?" He paused. "No, it's everything. This place, these people . . . Normally, you'd barrel in and make yourself at home, but you've spent nearly a fortnight in captivity, had a harrowing escape, and now you find yourself in another strange place, surrounded by other strange people, and your sister is not waiting. You want to tell me to go on ahead, partake of the lord's hospitality, and leave you to hunt for Ashyn with Daigo."

When she glanced over, he said, "Am I close?"

"If you were any closer, I'd accuse you of being able to read minds."

He smiled. "No, I'm just good at reading *you*." He glanced forward at Dalain, then back to her. "If that is what you truly want, Moria, I'll only ask that you take a couple of his men until I can join you. Sabre's talk of someone following us concerns me. I'd set out with you now and send others to fetch clothing and supplies—"

"But that would be rude. You must pay your respects to Lord Okami before presuming on his hospitality and tramping through his lands. My manners may need polish, but I understand what I do not practice."

"I know you do. So is that what you'd like? Take two of the lord's men and set out?"

It was exactly what she wanted. But it also was impulsive and immature. More important, Tyrus had an imperial bounty on his head and Okami was an imperial warlord. After spending almost a fortnight thinking Tyrus was dead, she was not letting him set foot past those compound walls alone.

"I want to search for Ashyn as soon as we can," she said. "But I'll not leave your side to do it."

His smile seemed almost shy, certainly pleased. "Thank you. I'll keep the hospitalities brief, and we'll find Ashyn before sundown."

They took a path to the compound through the forested foothills, avoiding the road and the inn. Dalain led them around to a secondary entrance. As Moria's mood lifted, the young lord fell back to ride with them. His people might be rough, but Dalain seemed to sense that she'd not wanted his company earlier and had left her alone. Now, as they rode together, he avoided talk of the situation, instead regaling Moria with humorous and affectionate tales of Tyrus's time with them.

"How long ago did you last see each other?" she asked as

the compound walls came into view.

"Too long," Dalain said. "Almost two summers now. He seemed happy enough in these hills, but apparently, the court holds more attractions."

"More pretty girls?" she said with a sly smile.

Dalain laughed. "Oh, I suspect so, though he'd hardly dare admit it in front of you, my lady."

"Actually, I would," Tyrus said. "Moria finds my past dalliances very amusing."

"Not amusing so much as understandable," Moria said. "Even desirable, given that it implies practice, and practice improves skill."

Dalain laughed louder now. "Very true, my lady. I like the way you think."

"Just don't like it too well," Tyrus said.

"I won't. I can tell that would land me on the wrong end of your blade, and I've heard you've much improved since you trained under me. Of course, it would have been difficult to do worse."

"True, which is the real reason I stay in court. It's the only place I can find adequate trainers. Out here in the wilds . . ." Tyrus shrugged. "I'll admit you're quite skilled . . . when your opponent has tusks and bristles."

"I'll wager our boars are tougher than any of your court warriors."

"You wouldn't know, since you've never actually been to court. Despite several personal invitations from your former apprentice."

Dalain nodded. "We're both to blame for the length of the

separation. It won't happen again. Which is not a promise that you'll ever see me in court, but perhaps I can send some of Sabre's father's men to abduct you and bring you here more often. Now, the rear gates beckon, and I'll suggest we slip in quietly, speak to my father quickly, and be on our way, before my mother discovers you've arrived and insists you take tea."

FIFTY-FOUR

Awarlord's compound was not dissimilar to Alvar Kitsune's camp. It was like a small village, comprised of homes for the lord and his extended family, plus barracks for his warriors and various other buildings for storage and service—armory, kitchens, blacksmith, stables, and so forth.

The fence that surrounded it was meant to act more as a boundary than a barrier. There would be a main gate with towers and warrior guards, but in a region like this, that was mostly for show. No one waged war on the Gray Wolf. His reputation was too fearsome and—equally important—his lands were both strategically and productively worthless, unless the empire suffered a sudden shortage of wood and boar meat.

The rear gate was manned only by a single guard, who didn't even have a tower to stand watch on. There was little need. The gate faced the forest, and the only people who used it were Okami's men, coming back from the hunt and not inclined to ride all the way around to the front.

The gate itself was simply a double door. The men had ridden around to the front, leaving only Dalain, Tyrus, and Moria to slip through this way. Dalain unfastened the gate as the other two climbed off their steeds. One didn't ride into a warlord's compound. That would be as rude as walking into his home wearing shoes.

As they led the horses through, Tyrus and Dalain told Moria what to expect—how many men they had, what services were offered in the compound, which members of the lord's family were at home. Her nerves were eased best with information rather than empty reassurances. Tyrus understood that, and Dalain was astute enough to follow his lead.

"You will eventually have to meet my mother," Dalain said. "I apologize in advance."

"He's joking," Tyrus said.

"Not entirely," Dalain murmured.

"Lady Okami is court-born," Tyrus explained. "She has devoted herself to bringing a touch of civility to these hills, but she is . . . not exactly a timid court lady."

"Tyrus is being civil himself. Possibly because my mother is of his clan. First cousin to the emperor. Even my father ducks when she starts breathing fire."

"They adore her," Tyrus said.

"We have to. She'd devour us otherwise. My mother—"

"My lord!" The warrior guarding the gate had, apparently, not been guarding it too closely. The young man hurried over from wherever he'd been. "Wh-what are you doing here?"

410

"I live here," Dalain said. "We're only stopping in briefly to let my father know Tyrus and the Keeper have arrived, then we'll head out again. I trust you'll hold our steeds?"

"Th-they said you were coming in the front. The scouts saw your search party."

"We are not with the search party because we are in a hurry and avoiding my mother. Now, hold these—"

"You ought to go around the front, my lord. Your father awaits you there."

Dalain's gray eyes narrowed. "You interrupt me to say I'm not allowed in this gate? I know we are not quite as rule bound as other clans, but I would suggest a little more respect, boy, at least in the company of guests."

As the young guard stammered, Moria glanced at Tyrus and saw that his hand was already on the pommel of his sword. Daigo backed into Moria's legs and peered about, his tail swishing.

"While the boy's tone was disrespectful," Tyrus said slowly, "perhaps we ought to retreat and go around the front, Dalain."

"Certainly not. Whatever foolishness—"

"Dalain!" a voice boomed. "Bringing our guests in the back door? Hasn't your mother taught you better than that?"

A figure rounded one of the buildings. It was a big man, tall and broad-shouldered, wearing a fur cloak that Moria recognized as a wolf hide. His long hair was completely gray, though he couldn't be out of his fourth decade. His hair had been turning that color since he was little more than a boy—hence the name the Gray Wolf. As for why it started graying early, there were many stories, and Moria knew them all. Most

411

were tales of encounters with horrific monsters that Okami had miraculously survived, the experience so terrifying his hair turned even as his blade stayed true and strong. Ashyn said it was simply because his family always grayed early, Goro Okami just more than most. Ashyn had no imagination.

As Moria watched the big warlord approach, she could believe the tales more than she could any scientific explanation. She'd sooner take her chances with another fiend dog than face Goro Okami in combat. He was grinning now, his arms open in welcome, which only made him look more like a wolf, fangs bared as he swooped down for the slaughter.

"Tyrus, good to see you back. You're staying more than a few moments this time, I hope. And you rescued your maiden, I see. Moria of Edgewood. And that"—he pointed at Daigo—"that is a grand hunting cat. No wonder our hounds are whining."

Despite the effusive welcome—or perhaps because of it—Moria stood her ground and glanced anxiously at Tyrus. His hand still brushed his sword as he watched Lord Okami's approach. His expression was guarded, but Moria saw traces of apprehension mixed with something worse—grief and pain as waves of unease emanated off the one person in the empire he had truly trusted.

"My lord," Tyrus said stiffly. "I fear we only stopped in to tell you we were on your lands. As you have doubtless heard, Moria's sister is at large, and we'll take our leave now to search—"

"She's only been gone since last night, and these hills are as safe as a mother's embrace. I'm told she has an armed guard and, of course, her hound. We'll get you out there as soon as we can, with my best hunters and hounds. In fact, I plan to join the search myself. First, though, food and drink, baths and fresh clothing. Come with me, and we'll get you ready to head off into the wilds again."

Moria noticed the figures of warriors, appearing behind their lord, seeming to come from all directions, slinking up like a pack of wolves, fanning out behind their leader. She struggled not to reach for her dagger as Daigo choked back a snarl.

"I beg your indulgence, Lord Okami," Tyrus said. "And I apologize deeply for any rudeness, but the Keeper is most anxious to find her sister. She's spent almost a fortnight captive—"

"Which is why she needs a brief respite, even if she thinks otherwise." He met the prince's gaze. "I'm afraid I truly must insist, Tyrus. As your host."

"Father . . . ?" That was Dalain, his voice barely audible, and Moria looked over to see confusion on his face. Whatever was happening here, the young man knew nothing of it. "This doesn't seem the time to insist on hospitality. Why don't I gather clothing and food for—"

"No," Okami said with a low growl. "They'll come in."

Moria turned sharply. She wasn't fleeing. Not yet. She had turned to see what lay behind them, but the moment she moved, one of Okami's men lunged—blade drawn—in Tyrus's direction. Daigo charged the man and Moria pulled her dagger. Lord Okami yelled something—she didn't catch what he said, because all she saw was another warrior pulling his sword on her. Then Tyrus was on him, knocking the blade from his hand.

That time, when Okami spoke, she heard him—barking at his men to pull back, threatening to skewer the next idiot who so much as touched his sword. Tyrus was already in front of her, blade at the ready, with Daigo beside him. Dalain was shouting for everyone to stop, just stop, and then—

"Enough," a voice said. It was not a booming voice or even a particularly loud one, but it seemed to cut through the chaos like a blade through soft butter. "Truly, Goro? I don't know why I bothered asking you to handle this diplomatically. One might as well ask a cudgel to strike softly."

Tyrus's gaze swung to the newcomer. A man stepped past Lord Okami. He had a cloak drawn up, his face hooded, but even Moria went still upon hearing that voice.

Emperor Tatsu tugged down his hood. "Tyrus . . ."

Tyrus took a step back. Both Daigo and Moria swung in front of him. The emperor smiled. "You and my son work well together, Keeper. I'm glad to see you reunited."

"After I betrayed him and ran off with Gavril Kitsune?"

"Anyone who has spent time in your company would laugh at the thought. Clearly I'm not here to drag my son back to face charges of treason."

"*Is* that clear?" Tyrus said as Moria backed beside him. "Forgive me, Father, but I'm not certain it is."

"Tyrus . . ." Lord Okami said, a touch of growl in his tone. "This is your father. Watch yourself."

"He is," the emperor said. "He's watching himself very carefully, and I'm pleased. I'll admit I've worried that he'd hear the rumor and hurry back to the city regardless. They say filial duty has no bounds, no exceptions, but I'm sure you'd agree that's not true, Goro. I'd not want either of our sons to bow his head meekly to the executioner's sword if he thought his father believed him guilty of a false charge."

"I beg your forgiveness anyway, Father," Tyrus said. "Given the circumstances, though, you will understand if I'm wary."

A look passed from Tyrus to the emperor, one that said, however much he loved his father, he knew him, too, and he knew what came first in his life. The empire. As it should be.

"I do understand, son. You should be wary. But as you can see, I did not come with an army to drag you back. It's just me and Lysias . . ." He motioned to the head of the guards, whom Moria now saw standing to the side. "We've come quietly and in disguise to find and speak to you."

"And the third man?" Moria said.

Tyrus stiffened at the blunt question, his court manners returning, but then he nodded and stepped closer, brushing his hand against hers, telling her to go on. She glanced at Okami and his men, but not a single one gave any indication that they thought her interruption disrespectful.

Moria cleared her throat. "We were told there were three figures following us on horseback. Since it would seem that you only just arrived before us—given the dust on your boots— that suggests you were one of the three. You said you came with only Lysias, though, so who was the third?" A momentary pause before she added, "Your imperial highness," and Lord Okami's lips twitched in a smile.

Emperor Tatsu nodded. "Yes, that was us. As for the third party, I would suggest we go speak to him now." When Tyrus tensed, he said, "No, I'm not leading you into the compound,

Tyrus. I can see your gaze moving, however subtly, to that rear gate, judging the distance should you need to flee. This meeting will be held out there, in the forest, where he waits. If you'll come with me, we'll share what we both know on the ride."

Tyrus and Moria looked at each other. Not a word passed between them, but she knew he was thinking the same thing she was. Did they truly have a choice? The emperor might have men waiting outside to ambush them, but they'd rather be out there, with a chance of escape, than trapped inside these walls.

"Only Lysias will escort you?" Tyrus asked.

His father nodded.

Dalain stepped forward. "I ought to come, too, your imperial highness. The, um, land here is treacherous and, uh, it would be wise to have an escort who can help you navigate it."

Emperor Tatsu smiled, shook his head, and turned to Lord Okami. "Sometimes I think letting you marry my cousin was a very poor idea. She has managed to teach her family the need for pretty lies, but not the art for telling them." He turned back to Dalain. "You wish to add your sword to Tyrus's, should this meeting prove less friendly than it seems."

Dalain's eyes widened. "Of course not, your—"

"Your loyalty to my son is appreciated more than your loyalty to your emperor. You know Tyrus. You do not know me. Yes, you may come. Now, we'll take our leave. The day grows short, and there is much to be done."

FIFTY-FIVE

They rode from the compound. Five of them, plus Daigo, who stayed so close to Moria that he made her horse uneasy.

"Tell me what happened," the emperor said as soon as the gate closed behind them. "Start with Fairview."

Tyrus did. He explained what they'd found there, and the decisions they made after that. He let his father know that his choices had been supported by the counselors, without impressing the point so deeply he seemed defensive. He told him about the merchant by the roadside, whose story had seemed to support Tyrus's decision. He told him about Jorojumo and the plan to attack the camp. He took full responsibility for any poor choices, and when Moria leaped in to defend him, he quieted her with a look.

"It's all right," Emperor Tatsu said to Moria. "I do trust that he made informed choices that my men supported. I will also be the first to admit that he should not have been placed in a position where he had to make them. It was a mission that a seasoned veteran would have struggled with." He looked at Tyrus. "You did well."

"I'd have done better if I'd won the battle."

"There was no chance of that. You'd have done better if you'd realized Jorojumo planned to betray you, but that is a skill you were never taught, and it isn't one that comes naturally to you. You have your mother's good heart and trusting nature. I would not ever say that I'm glad of this experience, for teaching you mistrust, but I am glad that it was a lesson you learned with more speed than I would have expected."

He paused at a fork in the path, then led them east before he continued, "When I left the imperial city three nights ago, I told Marshal Mujina that I wished to meet quietly with some of my warlords to discuss the impending war. The truth is that I was looking for you. Lord Okami was not the first I visited. I thought you might have taken refuge with one of my relations or even your mother's people. I am pleased to see that you were more cautious than that. You made the best possible choice. The Okami clan are loyal to their own above the empire, much like a wolf with its pack."

Dalain made a noise in his throat.

"I take no insult in your choice," the emperor said, glancing at the young man. "Every clan has its way, and the trick to leading them is to know what those ways are and work within those boundaries."

"And what clan is this person you're taking us to meet, your highness?" Moria asked.

The emperor laughed. "You could be an Okami yourself,

child. You struggle with the niceties as much as they do. Yes, I know you're anxious to learn who it is, but it's best to wait. This meeting was not my purpose in coming here. I left the city with only Lysias and met our third party just this morning, when our paths crossed by fortuitous happenstance. In coming after Tyrus, though, my purpose was to ensure he was safe and to tell him to stay that way."

"Keep lying low," Tyrus said. "Hiding."

"Which you will hate, as I can tell by your tone. But you're a more gifted politician than you care to admit, Tyrus. You know full well that I do not dare plead your case under the current circumstances. That doesn't mean, however, that I'm not trying to clear your name. The first step is to break Simeon, which won't be easy when he's now considered a hero. I can hardly throw him into my dungeons and interrogate him."

"So where is he?"

"He was in the court. As an honored guest . . . under very close guard, supposedly for his own protection. He's now joined an expedition heading to the eastern provinces. Sadly, he'll vanish in the night. Perhaps he already has. It's difficult to schedule these things."

"I'm not sure you'll get more from him than the admission that he lied," Tyrus said. "While it's possible someone was directing his betrayal, I fear he may have acted on his own, after Ashyn rejected his advances."

"Rejected his . . . ?" The emperor shook his head. "I would certainly hope he would have a better reason than that for accusing an imperial prince of treason, but with young men, one never knows."

They crossed a streambed riding single file. Daigo took a

running leap and jumped from shore to shore.

"Now, Moria," the emperor said. "We've heard Tyrus's tale. I'd like to hear yours."

"First, if I may ask, your imperial highness, has there been any word of the children?"

"No, child. My scouts and spies search, but there is no sign of them. I can only trust Alvar realizes their value and would not harm them."

She nodded and told him her story, starting with the events on the battlefield and ending with a simple, "I was captured and held hostage until I managed to escape."

"May I ask about the nature of your captivity? You were cared for, I presume?"

Moria tried not to hesitate. She could feel Tyrus's gaze on her, and she was determined not to let him know about the dungeon.

"I was adequately cared for, your highness. My needs were met, though I was clearly a captive."

"And who was in charge of your keeping?"

Now she did hesitate. When the silence stretched too long, he glanced at her. "Rumor says it was Gavril Kitsune. Well, that is, the rumor that confirms you were a captive, which is harder to come by than the one that says you were his . . ." His gaze slid Tyrus's way and he cleared his throat. "That you were Gavril's ally. My sources are, fortunately, more widespread than that, and one within the Kitsune camp says Alvar put his son in charge of your care. Is that true?"

"Yes."

"And he *did* care for you. You were not abused?"

"I . . . was not."

He didn't seem to notice the catch in her voice. "As I should expect. Beyond the lack of abuse, though, did he care for you well?"

Moria swore she smelled the faint stink of sweat waft up. This was like treading across a field laced with traps. To admit she'd been mistreated would cause Tyrus further guilt. To say she'd been treated well was a lie that spoke kindly of someone who'd done nothing to deserve her kindness.

"Gavril ensured I had what I needed. Food, water, clean clothing. . . . He eventually allowed me to take walks, under guard. His father keeps him very busy, so days would pass without my seeing him, making it difficult to judge his level of involvement with my care."

The emperor nodded. He seemed not to pay undue attention to her words, as if he'd already drawn conclusions and asked only to be polite.

"Now, speaking of rumors, Moria, I hear that on the night of your escape, Alvar hosted a party."

"Yes . . ."

"And that party was to celebrate your betrothal to Gavril Kitsune."

"What?" Tyrus said, pulling his horse up short.

"No," Moria said. "I mean, yes, it was, but there was no— It was— It had nothing to do with me."

"I wasn't questioning that," Tyrus said, his voice softening. "I mean, is this some scheme of Gavril's? If he tried to force you into a betrothal—"

"No, he was as upset over it as I was. It was his father's

scheme. And even he knew well enough to promise Gavril there would be no wedding. The ruse was intended to—"

"—spiritually validate his claim to the imperial throne." The emperor turned to Tyrus. "What Moria says is exactly what I heard. While we do not allow our Keepers and Seekers to marry, there is precedent from the Age of Fire. The clans were at war, and the goddess supposedly bestowed a Seeker on one of the chieftains as his wife. He began winning his battles, which solidified his claim to hold the goddess's favor. He became king—a ruthless one—and his successor passed the law against marrying Keepers and Seekers. Now, suddenly, people are whispering the name of that forgotten king and embellishing his deeds. Alvar was always a master at the art of spreading stories."

"So he says his son has won the love of a Keeper," Tyrus said. "Proving him a young warrior truly blessed by the goddess."

Emperor Tatsu nodded. "While that makes a good story, he has more prosaic reasons for the union. The tale of Moria's betrayal is prevalent, yet there are whispers of the truth—of her captivity."

"If she is betrothed to Gavril, it squashes those rumors."

"Yes. I'm sure there are more reasons, too. Where a normal man has a single purpose for any given action, Alvar has nine."

"But . . ." It was Dalain now, and they all turned to look at him. "While this is interesting, the Keeper is now free. Are you telling us we must be careful? That he'll come for her?"

"No." Emperor Tatsu turned to Moria. "I'm telling you, child, that you must go back."

Silence. Stunned silence.

Tyrus broke it, saying carefully, "You could not have said what I think you did, Father."

"I fear I did." The emperor swung off his horse. "Dalain? Could you mind the steeds for us? I need to walk with my son and the Keeper."

"No," Tyrus said. "I don't believe you do. If you are suggesting that Moria ought to return—"

"I'm saying she *must* return. To help us win this war."

Moria scrambled off her horse. "Go back? To Alvar Kitsune? As what? A spy?"

"Exactly. I mentioned that I do have a contact in the camp, but it's an imperfect one. A warrior who is simply an old man uncertain where his devotions lie and hoping war can be averted. He has no rank and cannot get me anything of use. I need a true spy in that camp. One who will, because of her new position, be free to slip about, assessing the situation, overhearing strategy, and reporting back to me. I need you, Moria. Back in Alvar's camp."

"How exactly would I do that?" she said. "Run to the gates and tell them I made a terrible mistake? If you suggest that I return and pretend I'm secretly in love with Gavril Kitsune and came back to be with him . . ." She choked on the words. "If I even attempted it, I'd give myself away so badly that Alvar would execute me as a spy before I finished my declaration."

"I know," the emperor said. "You're no performer. I'd not ask you to do that. You will instead return as you originally arrived. As a hostage. Captured by someone who has been pursuing you since you escaped last night."

"Who?"

"Me."

The voice came from the forest, and with it her heart stopped.

No, it cannot be. I cannot recognize a voice from one word.

Everyone turned toward that voice as a figure stepped from the forest. A tall figure. Cloaked and hooded. He reached up to pull the hood down, and even as he did, Moria saw those fingers—long, dark fingers, the nails trimmed to the quick, and she knew she was right.

I cannot recognize a man by his fingers. I cannot.

Yes, she could.

Gavril pushed his hood back and stepped into the clearing. "You'll be coming back with me, Keeper."

The captivating
AGE OF LEGENDS TRILOGY
blends fantasy and horror with
pulse-pounding action and romance.

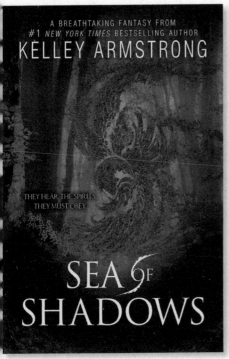

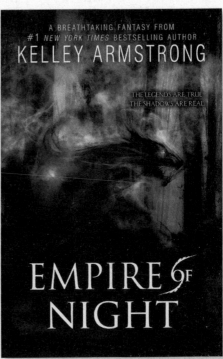

HARPER
An Imprint of HarperCollinsPublishers

www.epicreads.com